Dreaming of Xeres

Orion T. Hunter and
Kyros Amphiptere

Orion would like to dedicate this book to the Snohomish Kickstart Writers Meetup Group for three years of relentless prompts and encouragement and to Kyros, for teaching me many things, including applying butt to chair six hours a day, five days a week to bring this novel to life.

Kyros would like to dedicate this book to David and Scott, who believed in me when I wasn't even sure I believed in myself. Thank you so much for giving me this opportunity and for your unconditional support. And to Orion, thank you for teaching me long ago that stories can't be kept inside, they must be let out to shine. I love you all.

The authors would like to thank Laura LaRoche of LLPix Designs, www.llpix.com for her amazing cover artwork. We would also like to thank our fantastic beta readers, Kori K., Jeromy J., Leslee F., Toni K., and David W., who gave us exceptional feedback that made this a much better book.

Chapter 1

"Three...two...one."

Tessa cracked open her eyes, dark lashes veiling her expression from Riley. Sitting up slowly, she took a deep breath and stretched.

"How do you feel?" he asked, struggling to keep his voice calm. With any of his other clients, this would be easy. This client, and what she'd revealed, made his insides roil with questions. He forced himself to stay professional, at least until his subject was back in the here-and-now, not the there-and-then.

"Wonderful!" his subject said. "Like I've just had a nap."

"And do you remember any dreams you might have had during your nap?" he probed.

She frowned, her eyes unfocusing. After a moment, she shook her head.

"No, nothing." She looked up at him from the worn sofa they'd found and brought home to their third floor walk-up. It had taken several friends to horse it up the two flights of stairs, almost flattening Alex at the second bend. "That's good, right?"

Riley smiled down at her. "Yes, that's good," he assured her. Then he frowned. "I do have some questions, though, if you don't mind."

"About what?"

He tried to act nonchalant. "Oh, just some background. That's all."

"Background, huh?" She raised a lone eyebrow at him and swung her legs over the side of the couch. Stretching one arm along the back cushions, she cocked her head at him. "Go for it, Doc Mezmer."

He smiled. She'd given him that name when they'd first met in college. *Maybe this won't be so bad*, he thought.

1

"Okay. First, have you been playing any new online games? One set on an alien planet, perhaps?"

She considered for a moment, then shook her head. "Nope. There *is* a new one I'd like to get my hands on, but it won't be out for a couple of weeks yet."

Riley sighed. *So much for that idea.*

"Uh, have you ever written a story about an alien planet?"

"Hmmm." He could see her consulting her inner filing cabinet. "I did make up a world of sparkly unicorns in the fourth grade. They could make cookies out of leaves and change water into lemonade. Does that count?"

He snorted a laugh. "No, but thanks for the visual." Turning serious, he continued, "Did that world have silver grass and trees with orange bark and blue leaves?"

Tessa's eyes widened and she went still. After a moment, she asked, her voice laced with tension, "Where did you come up with that image? I dreamt of that place a lot when I was little. It had turquoise waterfalls and the clouds were somewhere between gold and pink. The sun seemed smaller than normal, too." She paused, shaking her head. "I hadn't thought of it in years. Until recently. Those dreams started up again a few weeks ago." Her brow furrowed and she looked at him suspiciously. "How could you know about that? Am I talking in my sleep? Or have you been rummaging around in my brain during regressions?"

Riley reared back. "Who, me? That's not ethical and you know it!"

"Then where did you get it from?"

Riley inhaled deeply, steadying himself for whatever happened next. Taking her hand, he plunged ahead.

"I got it from your regression. Not just this one, but several of the previous ones too." He paused, letting her absorb that. He'd regressed her several times since he'd finished his hypnotherapy internship. He needed the practice and she was a willing and handy subject. It wasn't until he tried to delve into past lives that this unfamiliar world had begun to manifest. He'd tried to make sense of it, turning the information around and around, examining it like a gemstone cut in a novel way. No matter how he looked at it though, he couldn't find any explanation that made sense.

"And just now, you gave me more information that I hadn't gotten through the regressions." He paused, thinking about his next move. "Are there other details you can remember from that world? Scenery, people, anything?"

Tessa looked down at their joined hands. "Details? Hmmm."

She looked up, meeting his gaze. Her face reddened slightly before she continued. "You're going to think I'm crazy."

Riley smiled at her. "Honey, I love you. I don't think you're crazy. But I *would* like to know more about this world you've dreamed of."

"Well, if you're sure. Let's see. The people there are shorter and more muscular, for a start."

Riley nodded. "Okay, so the gravity is heavier than ours. Good, good. Go on."

With a sigh, she dropped his hand and squirmed into a more comfortable position. She curled her legs under her and leaned her dark head against the heavy fabric of the sofa. Riley watched as her face lost its frown and took on a rather dreamy expression.

"I dreamt I had a kurvan named Jesler. I remember a small warm orange sun in a blue-green sky with fluffy honey-pink clouds. The trees are orange with blue leaves."

"Wait a minute, what's a kurvan?"

Tessa smiled, "You'd call it a pony."

He glanced down at his session recorder. *Good, it's still on.* At least he'd have something concrete to show his mentor, Dr. Jake Adams, when he saw him at the hypnotherapy convention in Seattle next weekend.

Tessa blinked and sat up straight. "Now, where did all that come from? Growing up, I soooo wanted a pony."

"Like you don't want a pony now," he scoffed. "If I have to watch another rerun of The Black Stallion, I'm gonna scream."

She smirked at him. "I only watch that when I'm really stressed. It's only been—"

"Let's see, six times this year? And it's only March!"

"It hasn't been that many."

"Trust me. I've counted."

She grinned sheepishly. "Well, business *has* been a little hectic lately. Diana and I finished our last project just under the wire. Okay, the client was extremely impressed and we *did* get a bonus, but stress is stress.

"And speaking of Diana, while you and Alex are away at the convention, we're having a spa day. If, that is, she can get away from her husband. I swear, if Bryce weren't so darn good looking, I'd tell her to

3

ditch him."

"He's possessive?"

"Oh, yeah. She told me they got into fight after BayCon. Remember that picture of her getting hugged by some costumed Klingon? When Bryce saw that picture, evidently he flipped out. Demanded to know who she was having an affair with at the convention." Tessa laughed. "She told him, 'What? You think I'm having an affair? The only person I've ever slept with besides you is Tessa. And before you ask, we *just slept.*' As you can imagine, that didn't go over very well. She said it took a week before he stopped grilling her about it."

Looking Riley in the eye, she asked, "What if it'd been me in that picture? Huh?"

Riley wrinkled his brow and shrugged. "I'd have figured he was from the Klingon Embassy and had had too many prune juices. You know how they are. Mostly harmless, despite their looks."

"See? No big deal." She sighed and stood up, stretching her arms over her head and rolling her shoulders. She paused. "Well, to give the guy the benefit of the doubt, he's never been to a science fiction convention, ever. Maybe he'd mellow out if he could tear himself away for a weekend in Never Never Land."

Riley had to agree. *Most people don't understand the sci-fi convention subculture. People seen in normal society as nerdy, flourish when surrounded by 'their people.'*

"I suppose," Riley said, shutting off the recorder. He stood and threw his arms about Tessa, impulsively kissing her on the nose.

"Gotta run, Tess. Still have some packing to do for *my* convention."

She laughed. "Well, it wouldn't do if the eminent Dr. Riley MacPherson, Clinical Hypnotherapist and Doctor of Psychology," She made air quotes around his name and titles. "was late for anything, now, would it?"

He sighed. *I never have to worry about getting an overinflated ego with her around. She'll always be there to pop my bubble if it gets too big.*

He shot her an affronted look, but that only caused her to giggle. Pulling her closer, he kissed her properly. After a few breathless moments, he stepped back and cocked his head. "Gonna miss me while I'm gone?"

"Not a bit," she said with an impish look in her eye. "After the spa, I might just laze about the house watching horse movies and eating bonbons."

He smirked. "Bonbons?"

* * *

Mezmer Notes - Update 12:

Subject Alpha still has no memory of the strange environment described during our regression sessions.

Information related in the most recent session:
- *Trees with orange bark and blue leaves*
- *Silver grass*
- *People are short and muscular (higher gravity perhaps?)*
- *Small orange sun*
- *Blue-green sky*
- *Fluffy pinkish-gold clouds*
- *Subject had a kurvan, a "pony-like" pet, named Jesler*

Information from previous sessions:
- *Turquoise water*
- *Pale orange ground*
- *Orange squirrel-like creatures*
- *Blue fruit that tastes like a mix of strawberry and mango (that the Subject didn't like and was being forced to eat)*
- *Bright red clothing (Subject could not explain what the clothing looked like)*

The level of detail that the Subject provides in our regression sessions amazes me. It's obvious they feel they are physically there in that place. But these details must be some made-up fantasy that the Subject is creating in their own mind. Other than the few questions after this regression, I have not discussed this with the Subject for fear of creating false memories or causing the Subject to make up details simply to please me.

I plan to discuss this case with Jake at the conference this weekend. Hopefully he can provide some insight into this strange 'world,' for lack of a better term. Maybe he's encountered something like this before and can advise me how to proceed. I haven't seen any other indications that the Subject possesses mental issues as might be indicated by the fabrication of an entire world like this.

Saving…

Chapter 2

Alex slid into the vacant seat next to Riley. Opening ceremonies were well underway in the ballroom. There were so many men and women in dark suits, Alex had the fleeting suspicion that he'd gotten the wrong conference, one for *Men in Black*.

"About time you got here," Riley hissed.

"Sorry. My plane was late and the bus from the airport was standing room only." Tapping Riley's arm, Alex asked, "How'd the workshop go?"

Riley replied, keeping his voice low, "Not sure. We'll talk later."

Alex settled back in the cushioned chair, trying to pay attention as prominent hypnotherapists were introduced, said a few words, then sat down. He grimaced. *Ye gods, this is enough to put anyone to sleep.* Fidgeting, he noticed several annoyed glances from both Riley and the man sitting on his other side.

A presence on stage caught his eye. Sitting up straighter, Alex focused as a Dr. Matthew Cadwallader was introduced. Though not particularly tall, the man exuded an aura that intrigued Alex. From his charcoal grey pin-stripe suit and black tie to his silvery hair and piercing blue eyes, the man radiated self-confidence and trust-worthiness. And he was fit, really fit.

"Who's he?" Alex whispered.

Riley turned, frowning. "That's the presenter who ran the workshop I took before the conference. We'll be seeing a lot of him this weekend. "

"Huh. He seems...intriguing."

"Well," Riley said sourly, "you'll certainly get a chance to meet him. Besides having a table in the vendors room to promote his new book, he's also all over the program schedule. I doubt he'll have time to sleep."

The emcee wrapped things up and dismissed them. Around the room, people gathered up their belongings and filed out.

"Come on, Alex. I've got two panels before lunch. Then you and I are meeting Jake Adams for lunch."

The younger man nodded. "I've been looking forward to meeting him. From what you've said, he really knows his stuff." Smiling devilishly, he said, "I'd like to run some of my pet theories past him too."

Riley rolled his eyes. "No, not that. I have no idea *where* you get half your ideas."

"On the internet, of course," he replied. "Even something like my government hypnosis theory is worth considering, if only for a laugh."

"Right. We'll see whether Jake'll laugh at that one. I'm heading to my panel." He pulled out his schedule. "Life Between Lives: Filling Out the Forms." He looked up and grinned at Alex. "Sounds like fun, huh?"

Consulting his own pocket schedule, Alex countered with, "I have Interactive Sleep Hypnosis. I wonder if they'll provide pillows?"

Riley huffed a laugh and waved as he moved off. "Meet you at the hotel cafe at noon."

After his panels, Alex hurried to meet Riley. Spotting him from the cafe door, he quickly threaded his way through the crowded tables. He noticed Dr. Cadwallader holding court in a corner booth. The whole group seemed to be hanging on his every word. Alex pursed his lips and thought, *Man, that Cadwallader guy's charismatic, but there's just something…oily about the man. He's treating those people like they should be honored to worship at his feet.*

Coming up behind Riley, Alex saw he was in deep discussion with an older man. *So this is Riley's mentor, Jake. Damn. He's like a teddy bear done in silver and smiles. I bet his clients feel really comfortable talking to him.*

Riley looked up when Alex got to the table. Introductions were made while the waitress took their orders.

When she'd gone, Riley resumed his conversation with Jake. "I don't quite know what to think about the workshop I took from Cadwallader," he said, casting an eye at the crowd around the man. "His theories sound good, but…." He covered his face with his hand, then lowered his voice. "He raises the hairs on the back of my neck, Jake."

"Oh," said the big man, "so he gets to you, too."

Riley started. "You mean—"

Jake huffed. "Yeah. I've seen him around, sat in on a couple of his panels, read some of his theories online. I get the feeling there's something behind the façade, something I might not like. I can't quite put a finger on it though."

"Also, there was something odd that happened in that workshop." Riley paused, staring down at the white tablecloth for a moment. Looking up, he continued, "One of the therapists said, 'Next thing you know, everyone will be telling us about a world with orange-colored trees with blue leaves.' Weird, huh?"

Alex saw Riley holding his breath, waiting for…what? Alex didn't know.

Jake's eyebrows rose. "Orange trees and blue leaves?" the man sputtered. "Someone *else* mentioned that in a regression?"

Riley's eyes widened. He let out his breath in a rush. "You… you've heard that too?"

The man nodded, reaching for his water glass and taking a sip. "Twice. A thirteen-year-old abuse victim and a sixty-eight-year-old PTSD patient with chronic nightmares." He turned a querying look upon his protege. "You?"

"Once, so far. A twenty-eight-year-old woman."

Alex sat up straighter in his chair at the mention of Riley's client. *Wait, Riley doesn't have any clients that age. But isn't that how old Tessa is? I know she's asked Riley for a past life regression before. Still, what do orange trees and blue leaves have to do with her?*

"Four cases? That sounds like some kind of conspiracy to me," Alex said with a grin.

Riley threw him a sour look, then returned his attention to the older man. "Anyway, Jake, I wondered if you would ask around at the conference. See if any other therapists are getting these same odd descriptions. I have a few meetings set up for this weekend, I'll ask them too."

Jake gave Riley a sharp look. "What are you thinking?"

"Right now, I really don't know. I need more evidence, more cases to work with." Riley caught first Alex's, then Jake's eyes. "Don't let anyone else know about our four cases, okay? I don't want to start a rumor or give anyone ideas or…or anything. Or," he said, glancing sharply at Alex, "start any wild ass conspiracy theories."

9

Alex gave Riley a 'Who, me?' look as both men nodded.

Their meals arrived, tabling further conversation on the subject.

* * *

Alex sat on the edge of his bed watching Riley crawl around on the floor trying to plug in his laptop.

Backing out from under the desk, Riley banged his head, grousing, "Is this room intentionally badly lit?" Twisting around, he ended in a cross-legged position on the beige carpet, looking up at Alex's knees.

Alex rose. "Need a hand up?" he asked, smiling.

"Sure."

Alex hauled him upright and suddenly found himself nose to nose with his friend. For some reason, the man seemed a little out of breath.

"Wow, Alex, I didn't know you were that strong."

Alex contemplated the linked arms between their chests.

"There are a lot of things you don't know about me, Riley."

Staring into Alex's eyes, Riley asked, "Like what?"

Alex didn't speak for a moment, pondering his answer. *Is now the right time? I've been hoping for a chance. Maybe now is the right time.* Taking a deep breath, he plunged ahead.

"I'm bisexual."

The words hung in the air between them and the silence became almost tangible before Riley replied, "So?"

"I've been attracted to you ever since you saved me from getting crushed by that monster couch. I wondered…."

Alex left his words hanging. *He's not saying anything. He's disgusted. He's never going to speak to me again. Oh shit, why did I have to open my big mouth.*

Riley's eyes widened as the implications sank in. "You mean…you and me?" He gestured, indicating the two of them.

Alex could only nod. His tongue refused to participate.

Riley's lips quirked up in a wry twist. "I don't think that would be such a good idea, Alex. I'm supposed to be your mentor, your teacher. I'd feel like I was taking advantage of you." A lopsided grin broke over his face. "Not that I'm not flattered, mind you. If circumstances were different? Well, who knows."

Abruptly self-conscious about their linked hands, Alex pulled away. Riley, suddenly lacking Alex's support, stumbled, and plopped down heavily on the desk chair.

Alex gasped. "Are you okay?" He could feel the heat in his cheeks and his ears seemed to be on fire. Reaching out, he laid a hand on Riley's shoulder.

Riley looked up at him and nodded. "I'm fine." He turned to plug the power cord into his laptop, causing Alex's hand to slide from his shoulder.

Did he do that on purpose? I hope he doesn't feel uncomfortable around me now. Maybe I should ask….

Riley glanced over his shoulder. "I have to get these notes downloaded before I can get some sleep. My first panel tomorrow starts at nine. If I don't get some breakfast before that, I'll be nodding off all day."

Seeing Riley busy with his computer, Alex grabbed his toiletries bag and fled to the bathroom. Closing the door, he put his back to it and slid down to the aqua-tiled floor. Lacing his fingers behind his head, he brought his elbows in around his bowed head.

Crap! Well, at least that went better than I thought it would. Maybe after this mentoring thing is over.

* * *

Mezmer Notes - Update 15
National Hypnotherapy Conference in Seattle:

The pre-con workshop was interesting, but the facilitator, Dr. Cadwallader, seemed more interested in pushing his new book than he was in actually teaching anything or answering any questions. However, I had some good conversations with the other participants, which made up for the lack of information in the actual workshop. The most surprising thing was something mentioned by a Dr. Thompson. He has a client who described trees with orange bark and blue leaves, exactly like Subject Alpha. When I questioned him further, I found other similarities between his patient's descriptions and those of Subject Alpha. He even offered to help with my research. I gave him one of my cards, and he promised to send me excerpts from his notes, minus any personal information, of course.

Over lunch with Jake and Alex, I mentioned my conversation with Dr. Thompson. I was surprised that Jake had also encountered this before, in two separate cases: a thirteen-year-old abuse victim and a sixty-eight-year-old PTSD patient with chronic nightmares . That makes four unrelated cases of orange trees with blue leaves that I

11

have discovered. I was curious when Subject Alpha described this strange landscape, but now I am eager to find if there are even more cases. How can these widely divergent people all be describing the exact same thing? Especially about something that doesn't exist.

On a personal note, I'm a little flabbergasted that Alex told me he's attracted to me. I had no clue. I am a little concerned about how this might affect our working relationship. I rely on his assistance and really like him, but don't want to send the wrong message. If he wasn't my intern and I wasn't with Tessa, I might have taken him up on his offer. He's really sexy and handsome, but I love Tessa. Still, it's tempting.

Saving…

Chapter 3

When Alex and Riley entered the vendors room, they found it buzzing like a subdued beehive. Tables ran around the walls and clustered in a square in the middle, all draped with linen in the hotel colors. Most vendors were promoting something, from devices to software to books. Lots of books.

Riley swept a glance across the room, then he and Alex joined the line moving to the right.

After they'd rounded the first corner, Alex jogged Riley's elbow. "Look, it's that Cadwallader guy."

"Yeah. He's pushing his new book. He seems to have something new for every conference."

As the two men drew near the display, they could hear Cadwallader's cool, confident voice oozing from hidden speakers. The man himself was walking a tan-suited woman with long blond hair through the expensive-looking, M-shaped exhibit. Holding her small hand, he led her past a seven-foot panel filled with his smiling face. The next two walls featured flowing silver, white and blue swirls, making the books, CDs and DVDs on their acrylic bookshelves seem to float in space.

Alex rolled his eyes. "Gee, it's so rare to see someone as famous as Cadwallader who isn't narcissistic or anything." Sarcasm rolled off his friend in waves.

Riley chuckled. "I know, right?"

As the two men watched, the author pulled down a DVD and placed it into the woman's hands, ushering her into the next bay of the exhibit. There, waiting patiently, stood a stout man of average height holding a smartphone with the ever-present white square affixed, ready to process the woman's purchase.

Handing his customer over without so much as a nod, Cadwallader spun neatly and stepped back to the beginning of his booth, donning the same plastic smile as his giant portrait.

"Ah," he said, approaching Riley and Alex. "Weren't you in my workshop on Thursday? Robert—"

"Riley. Yes, yes, I was." He felt obligated to accept the hand Cadwallader extended. He turned to his friend. "And this is Alex."

Cadwallader's focus shifted to his new target, Alex. Appropriating the young man's hand, Cadwallader gave him the full wattage of his smile. "Pleased to meet you. Are you a hypnotherapist also?"

"Uh, pleased to meet you. I…I'm new to the field."

Poor Alex. The look on his face is priceless. I bet he's having second thoughts about Cadwallader now.

The man turned up the brightness on his smile a few degrees. "Well, then, perhaps you'd like to read some of my books. Get some grounding in hypnotherapy before you set up a practice of your own." Keeping a secure hold of Alex's hand, Cadwallader smoothly moved him toward his displayed products.

Alex shook his head, withdrawing his hand with difficulty from the man's grip. "Uh, no thanks. I just completed my internship with Riley. I'm not ready to set up a practice of my own just yet." He put both hands behind his back, out of harm's way.

"And maybe he just doesn't need your brand of bullshit, Caddy, old boy."

All three of the men turned toward the voice.

Across the aisle from Cadwallader's calm, soothing display stood a six-foot combination of red and gold drapery and jazzy banners proclaiming 'So You Want to be a Hypnotherapist, A New Book by Evelyn Sloan'. The strains of a newer Michael Bublé song played softly behind her. The petite woman was stunning, her softly-draped bright red dress contrasting beautifully with her dark skin. Riley caught a gleam in her dark eyes that was almost devilish.

Glancing at Cadwallader, he saw the man's face redden and his expression turn sour. *This should be interesting,* Riley thought.

"What's Caddy trying to peddle off on you boys? *How You Can Kick Any Bad Habit Overnight?* From what I saw at the bar last night, the only habit he's ever kicked was on a nun. And that was for turning him down when he made a pass at her."

"I don't believe anyone yanked your chain, Evil-lyn" Cadwallader huffed.

Waving a hand in the man's direction, she told Alex and Riley, "Ignore him. I do." She extended a hand to them. "Hello, gentlemen, I'm Evelyn Sloan. I've known Caddy here," she jerked a thumb to indicate Cadwallader, "since he first started coming to these things ten years ago. Even then, he was insufferably convinced of his own greatness."

"Jealousy is *such* an ugly emotion, Evil-lyn. You really should learn to let it go." He turned and grabbed a book off of one of the nearly invisible shelves. "As a matter of fact, my new book *Emotional First Aid, Hypnosis for Overcoming Jealousy and Insecurity* would be perfect for you."

"The only one that's gonna need first aid is *you*, Caddy," she said, poking his chest with one finger, "if you don't stop trying to push that off on me. I've already told you a hundred times that I'm not interested in your crap."

"The only crap around here is your pathetic *So You Want to be a Hypnotherapist* book. You know the old saying, those who can, do, and those who can't, teach. Says something about your practice, doesn't it, old girl?"

"Funny," she said snidely, "you didn't have that attitude when I was giving *you* pointers when you first started out."

"You're so-called 'pointers' were less than useful, Evelyn. I taught myself everything that I *really* needed to know about being a hypnotherapist."

Turning to head back to her own booth, she fired off one last zinger. "That's Cad for you. A self-made man who worships his creator."

Cadwallader's back straightened, eyes widening at her riposte. Riley hid a grin behind his hand while Alex coughed, turning his head away.

As they moved to leave, Cadwallader pressed a card into Riley's hand. "Please, let me make amends for that…woman. Come to my book release party this evening, after the banquet. I promise you," he said, watching Evelyn's back as she marched over to her own booth, "*she* won't be there!"

Riley nodded his thanks. Maybe he and Alex would drop by, for a minute or two at least. "Come on, Alex," he said. "We have a panel in five minutes. We won't get seats if we don't get moving."

Alex looked surprised. As far as he knew, the next panel was "Using Hypnotherapy in Medical Situations," something he doubted would be standing room only.

He shrugged. "Gee, you're right."

When they were safely several booths away, Alex paused. "Room party? Seriously?"

Riley shook his head. "I don't know why, but that guy sets my teeth on edge. I've never had that kind of reaction to anyone before...." He lifted his shoulders, pressing his lips into a thin line. "Although he might be useful in figuring out this weird trees-and-leaves thing. He's something of an expert in the regression field, after all."

"Well, in his own mind, anyway," Alex muttered. "Okay, I guess stopping by his release party does make sense." He brightened. "Maybe that Sloan lady *will* be there. I've always loved a good fireworks display."

Riley snorted. "I doubt very much she'd get in. I don't think Cadwallader enjoys having his balloon burst at regular intervals. She sure got him going, though," he said, shaking his head in admiration.

Glancing at his pocket program, Alex said, "We'd better get a move on or we'll miss that important, crowded panel you mentioned."

Riley laughed, launching the two of them back into the travel stream that would take them toward the open doors.

* * *

That evening Alex had the dubious pleasure of listening to presenter after presenter congratulate themselves on their accomplishments during the banquet. Afterwards, he and Riley stopped to say goodnight to Jake.

"Where are you boys off to now? Turning in for the night?" Jake inquired.

Riley glanced at Alex before he spoke. "I think we'll check out Cadwallader's book release party."

"You got tickets for that?" Jake asked, raising both eyebrows. "I heard those were hard to get. Lots of big wigs, champagne, reporters."

"Really?" said Riley. "He almost forced the tickets on us, down in the vendors room today. I think he was trying to counteract the impression he made on us while trading barbs with Evelyn Sloan. You know her, Jake?"

"Oh, for years," he said waving a hand. "Knew her when she first set up her practice. That was after her husband died and before she adopted her son." Jake looked around vaguely. "The boy's always around the conference somewhere, making food runs for his mom and other vendors. Bright lad."

He glanced at his watch. "Well, I'm off to find some real food." He got a crafty look on his face. "Since my husband isn't around, I can eat whatever I want to for a change. And, the night air'll help clear my head of all the dull speeches we were treated to this evening. Bye now." He walked off, giving a wave over one shoulder and disappearing into the crowd.

"Shall we?" Riley asked Alex.

"Let's," he replied. Grinning, Alex took Riley's elbow and turned them both into the moving crowd, humming loudly, "We're off to see the wizard, the wonderful wizard of Oz."

After a startled moment, Riley laughed and joined in.

Several people gave them curious looks as they passed, but that had no noticeable effect on the two men.

When they entered Cadwallader's suite, Alex gave a low whistle.

"I'm impressed," he whispered behind his hand to Riley.

The top floor suite was swankier than their modest room. Floor-to-ceiling drapes flanked large windows displaying a panoramic view of twinkling city lights. Tables loaded with hors d'oeuvres and small desserts occupied one corner, next to a small bar with its own uniformed bartender. Fake tea lights in glass cups were scattered about, lending an air of mystery to the gathering. Several well-lit displays of the author's books were strategically placed about the large room. The author himself, in a brilliantly white suit, glided from one display to another, holding a martini in one hand while shaking hands with the other.

"How do you think he affords all this?" Riley wondered aloud. "I've been in business for a few years and I'd be hard pressed to afford one of his displays, let alone three. Plus the bar and the food, not to mention this suite." He shook his head. "I can't believe he makes this kind of money on his books. They aren't exactly page turners and the subject matter is kinda specialized."

"The gossip is," Alex said, "he charges a lot for his public speeches and workshops. How much did yours cost?"

"Two hundred bucks, for two days. There were only fifteen of us in the workshop, though."

Alex did some quick mental calculations. "That's still over three thousand bucks."

Riley shook his head. "That wouldn't even cover tonight's book signing."

"Ah, I see you made it." Cadwallader reached to shake the two men's hands like they were valued colleagues. "You don't have a drink yet. Come, let me get you something."

He shepherded them towards the bar like a nanny herding children on the playground.

Riley looked uncertainly at the bartender. "Uh, can I have a caffeine-free soda, please?" Cadwallader frowned at him.

"Tomato juice for me," Alex said, drawing another frown from their host.

The bartender, his dark coloring, black hair and beard probably placing him from somewhere in the Middle East, poured their drinks into short, ice-filled glasses, adding a spear of celery to Alex's.

As the two men thanked the bartender and reached for their drinks, Cadwallader set his own glass down.

"Another one." The bartender made Cadwallader a new drink, which the man took without thanks or comment.

Waving his free hand around the room, Cadwallader said, "Feel free to browse my books. The newest one is over there." He pointed to one of the shelves over by the door. "Oh, I see a reporter from the IJCEH. Excuse me…." His voice trailed off as he hurried to intercept the man who'd just passed his ticket to the attendant at the door.

Alex and Riley made their way to the buffet table, collecting a few of the tiny sandwiches. Alex pointed his plate toward the door.

"Say, isn't that the clerk from Cad's booth this afternoon?"

Riley peered at the new man stationed by the door. "You know, I think it is. Wonder if he helps him dress in the morning, too?"

Alex was grabbing a piece of cheesecake from the desserts spread across the table when a commotion drew his attention back to Cadwallader's clerk. He seemed to be shoving someone back through the door. After a moment he recognized Evelyn Sloan.

"You don't have a ticket, ma'am, so you can't come in," the clerk said.

The woman was not deterred. "It's a book-signing. I'm an author, too, you know. Why should I be excluded?"

"You don't have a ticket," the clerk repeated.

Cadwallader appeared as if by magic. "You are not welcome here, Ms. Sloan. This gathering is by invitation only. Have to keep the riff-raff out, you know.". His tone had taken on the air of a nobleman offended by having to deal with peasants.

Damn, Alex thought. *All he's missing is a monocle and a walking stick.*

"Riff-raff? Who are you calling riff-raff, you pompous, overbearing jackass?" She reached for him.

The doorman intervened, wrapping his arms around the small woman and lifting her off the ground, shiny black heels and all. Turning in place, he clumsily deposited her in the hall, facing away from the door.

"Go away, ma'am," he said in an almost-pleading voice. "You mustn't disturb Mr. Cadwallader's party."

"Of all the nerve. Come on, Kier." Her voice trailed behind her until it was cut off by the closing door.

Cadwallader turned, straightening his already perfect suit jacket. "I apologize for that intrusion," he said to the room in general. "Some people just don't know when they're not wanted." He left the doorway without another word, easing through the crowd.

From their vantage point near the bar, Alex and Riley had seen it all. As the ambient noise level rose again, Alex mused, "Gee, and I thought we were going to have some entertainment."

Riley snickered. "We would have, if Evelyn had gotten inside. She really doesn't like Cad, does she? I wonder why?"

"Competition, maybe? They're both authors, selling to the same audience."

"I don't think that's it. There are a lot of other authors. Why pick on him?"

"A falling out, perhaps?" Alex ventured. "Could you see them as friends?"

Riley shook his head sharply. "Nope, they're too different. Come on, let's circulate and see what everyone else's up to."

Alex shrugged. "Aside from those three reporters by the bar getting drunk on free booze, everyone else seems to be hanging on Cad's every word. He's a real schmoozer, that's for sure."

Alex didn't see how it started, but the smell of the burning draperies suddenly demanded everyone's attention. They turned to find

19

the bartender tossing water on the drapery behind the food table. Alarms blared and lights began flashing. Then a torrent of water spewed from the sprinklers on the ceiling.

Women, holding paper brochures over their heads, made for the door while a hotel employee with a fire extinguisher shoved his way in.

Spotting the flames burning merrily despite the sprinklers, the man raced over and doused the whole corner in foamy spray, finally putting out the fire.

Over the noise, Cadwallader yelled, "Can't someone turn off that water? It's ruining my books!"

Alex and Riley, too amused by the spectacle unfolding in front of them to even notice the rain, gaped as Cadwallader clutched the shoulder of the man with the fire extinguisher and spun him around. The spewing nozzle swung with him. Cadwallader's already soggy white suit blossomed with foam, covering him from knees to chin before the other man could react.

Sputtering in outrage, Cadwallader grew red, then purple as his rage built.

Oh, oh, he thought. *He's about to burst.*

"Thar he blows," Riley warned, smiling.

Sure enough, Cadwallader grabbed the hotel employee, screaming into the man's face. "This is an outrage! I'll have your job for this!"

Cadwallader's clerk touched his arm. "He's only doing his job, sir."

Turning on the short man, Cadwallader snarled, "You keep out of this, if you know what's good for you!"

The clerk shrank in on himself and backed away, keeping his eyes pinned on the larger man.

Several suited-up firemen rushed in the door. They began ushering people toward the door. Alex saw one of the drunk reporters holding Cad's latest book over his head, presumably to save his hairdo.

He and Riley were among the last ones into the hall.

"Guess I was wrong about nothing happening in there." Alex grinned as he wiped his face on his shirt.

Riley shook his head. "You get pleasure out of the oddest things. I think I'm ready to crash for the night. You?"

"Yeah. Enough excitement for one evening."

From down the hall, a voice chimed, "You boys okay?"

Both men turned at the soft inquiry, finding Evelyn Sloan leaning in a doorway, clad in a leopard-spotted robe. Peeking around her was a teenage boy with almond-shaped eyes and golden skin who looked nothing like her.

Alex thought he caught a flash of fear in the boy's eyes. *What's he afraid of?*

Moving toward her, they accepted her beckoning wave to come into her small suite.

"This is my son, Kier," she said to them. "Kier, these are the two men I told you about, from the vendors room today."

"Hey," said the young man, raising a hand.

Alex nodded at the boy. *He's what? Fifteen, maybe? But he's already almost as tall as she is.*

"Pleased to meet you," Riley said, extending his hand. The boy looked at Riley's hand a moment before reaching out his own.

"What was that all about?" Evelyn asked as the two men found seats. "We were evacuating when a hotel employee said we could go back to our room." She hovered near the door, while Kier threw himself down sideways on an over-stuffed chair.

Riley answered her. "Somehow, the drapes by the food table caught fire. Maybe something electrical? Cad didn't take it so well, especially when the sprinklers went off and a hotel employee hosed him down with the fire extinguisher."

Evelyn snorted a laugh. "I'll bet he didn't! Wish I could have seen that. I'd have taken pictures. Wait, did either of you get a picture?" She looked hopefully at them.

Alex smiled and pulled his phone from his jacket pocket. "I did. Want to see?"

"Oh, you bet!" Evelyn said, crossing the room. Kier came to peer over the sofa-back with his mother. "Priceless! Just priceless! Send me a copy, please?"

Kier touched Evelyn's arm tentatively. "Mom, do you think anyone got hurt?"

She glanced up at his concerned eyes in surprise. "I don't think so, honey. Why?"

Alex looked up from the pictures on his phone. "Nah, kid, the only thing that was hurt was Cad's merchandise and dignity."

Kier shrugged his shoulders. Crossing to one of the beds, he plopped down and took out his phone. The sounds of Alex's favorite mobile game soon issued from the device.

Following the boy with his eyes, Alex wondered, *Why was Kier so worried that someone might have been hurt? It's not like he's the one who caused the fire. He wasn't even in the room.*

Alex turned his attention back to Evelyn, who was sitting beside him with laughing, puppy-dog eyes. Smiling, he picked up their earlier conversation. "Give me your email address."

Riley cleared his throat. "If you two are done, I feel a need for dry clothes."

Alex huffed. "Yeah, guess you're right. We have to check out early tomorrow morning and I'm still hungry."

Evelyn's laughter was joined by her son's. "You mean you didn't get enough rubber chicken at the banquet?"

They all laughed as Alex and Riley rose to leave.

"We'll see you tomorrow maybe, before the vendors room closes." Riley said. "Thanks for inviting us in."

"It was good meeting you, Kier," Alex said, bringing the boy into the conversation.

Shyly, Kier nodded. "You too."

* * *

Mezmer Notes - Update 16
National Hypnotherapy Conference:

Asking around, I found three more cases of clients mentioning orange trees with blue leaves or pink clouds. One was a thirty-five-year-old gay man who wanted to know if he was connected to his current lover in another lifetime, a sixty-six-year-old school bus driver, and a twenty-five-year-old admin assistant who thought she had been Cleopatra in a past life. If I had a dollar for every person who thinks they were King Arthur, Guinevere, or Cleopatra in a past life, I'd be rich. I guess no one was ever a peasant in a past life.

In the vendors room, I again had the 'pleasure' of meeting Matthew Cadwallader. I don't know why, but the guy rubs me the wrong way. Thankfully, we were saved from his overbearing salesmanship by a fascinating woman named Evelyn Sloan. She seemed to take great delight in deflating his ego. It was like watching a stand-up comedian skewer a heckler. Apparently, they have history, and based on the comments flying back and forth, it isn't a good one. He called her Evil-lyn, but her nicknaming him Cad almost caused Alex and I to bust out laughing there right in front of him. Thanks to her, he'll forever be Cad to both of us.

Alex and I went to Cad's room party. I have to admit, the man knows how to throw a party. How the hell he can afford to have an open bar and catering is beyond me. Those people were drinking alcohol like they had just found an oasis after weeks in the middle of the desert. I make decent money, but I could never afford to pay for something like that. What the hell am I doing wrong?

At the end of the evening, something very strange happened. The curtains in Cad's suite caught fire. On our way out, Alex and I ran into Evelyn and her son Kier. When we told them what had happened in Cad's suite, I noticed Kier seemed more upset that he should have been about the fire. But Kier wasn't even in Cad's suite, so what was he upset about?

Note for next conference: Make sure I bring plenty to eat. The banquet food is inedible. Also, thank Tessa for insisting that I bring snacks this year. I hope she's not too lonely with me being gone.

Saving…

Chapter 4

"How's your soup, Diana?" Tessa asked. She brushed aside a dark strand of hair the early afternoon breeze had dislodged.

"Yummy! This is the best French onion soup in the area. I haven't had this since...." Diana searched her memory. "Oh, for a long time now." Tessa's business partner, Diana Lundee, sat across from her at one of the outside tables at Steve & Mike's, a trendy restaurant in Oakland.

"How come it's been so long?" Tessa asked. "You and Bryce eat out fairly often, don't you?"

She made a face. "My *husband* insists that I watch my diet. When I gained five pounds on our vacation to Mexico last year, he had a major meltdown. He said it reflected badly on him that I was letting myself go like that. Said he married a slender girl and he expected her, that is, me, to stay that way."

Tessa's eyebrows lifted. *Wow. I knew Bryce was a little controlling, but having a meltdown over gaining five pounds on vacation? She's such a tiny thing to start with. I wish I had her figure.*

"Isn't that a little out of line? I mean, if Mac quibbled about my weight, I'd tell him to piss off." She giggled at the image that sprang into her mind. "Politely, of course."

Diana laughed with her. "Mac's so easygoing. I really envy that." She sighed. "Bryce has definite ideas of how I should look and behave. Sometimes I feel like I'm a Barbie doll he plays dress-up with."

Seeing her friend's mood darkening, Tessa put on a bright smile. "Well, let's get the business part of our morning out of the way. How is the design for Ingram's Firebird Suites coming along? He's already laid the foundations."

"Well, he liked our sketches and the color swatches I sent him last week. Now he wants us to expand on our ideas and to create a sample suite. We have a month to get it to him."

"A month! Can we do it in that little time? The swatches, the furniture—"

"Calm down, Tessa. We have plenty of time. It'll take awhile to find the right furniture and build the 3D-rendered models, but we can do it, partner." Diana patted Tessa's arm. "Speaking of clients, where are things with the Deveraux account?"

"I emailed them three options for their new corporate logo last night. Once they decide, I'll order the final proof and send over the bill." Tessa chuckled. "It's a good thing we're having our spa day today. I really need this."

The waiter appeared with their food. It tasted so delicious that it was a few minutes before either came up for air.

"So, Tessa, what package did you book for us at the spa?"

Tessa held up a finger, holding her answer until she finished chewing the last bite of her sandwich. "Okay. First there's the Water Ritual, which is a whirlpool bath with a panoramic view of San Francisco. Next, we spend some time in the steam room getting cleansed. Whatever that means." She shrugged. "According to the brochure, it's supposed to clear our sinuses, detox our skin, and prepare us for the next treatment. After that, we have a shower. Ten jets, so it's like getting a massage standing up. Then we each get an herbal facial and a deep tissue massage. Finally, we get back together for a mani-pedi. We'll be able to chat more then," she chuckled quietly. "Or maybe just fall asleep."

"I'll say. We'll be limp noodles by then."

"And the best part is, it's just across the street." Tessa pointed to the white-washed façade rising from the trees, so close it appeared to loom over them.

"At the Fairemont?" Diana exclaimed. "I've never been to their spa." She shivered in anticipation. "Now I'm really looking forward to it."

* * *

Tessa adjusted her robe before climbing into the chair for her pedicure. "These things are always too big on me."

"Wait, you have a tattoo?" Diana squeeked, peering at Tessa's chest. "I never noticed that before. What is it?"

Tessa pulled the material aside, exposing the area just under her right clavicle. "It's a symbol I dreamed about when I was a kid. I doodled it on everything: books, notepads, jeans, you name it. It always seemed to comfort me, so after high school I got the tattoo as a graduation gift for myself."

"Kinda...industrial, don't you think? I mean, a gear?" Diana shook her head and laughed. "Your Art Deco roots are showing."

"To me, the gear teeth represent science and technology. The spaces created by the spokes are for the four elements, earth, air, fire, and water. And the hole in the center represents my spirit which binds everything together."

Why am I telling her all this? I've only ever told Riley, and he was kind enough to humor me at least. Diana's going to think I'm crazy after that explanation.

"That's cool," Diana said sadly. "I wish I had something comforting like that."

Tessa nodded. "Work's been so busy lately, that I've started looking forward to when Riley regresses me. It seems like the only time I get to unwind."

"How's that going? Did you find out you were Guinevere or someone famous? Maybe something closer to your actual heritage, like an Aztec princess?"

Tessa could barely produce a mild chuckle at Diana's proposal. The quiet of the room enfolded her like a warm blanket, sending her mind into that pleasant place just before you fall asleep. *Like the last time Riley regressed me,* she thought. One thought led to another, then another.

"I see pink clouds in a turquoise sky," Tessa whispered. "The silver grass is tickling my ears. I can hear my kurvan Jesler chomping nearby. Our tigla is curled up on my lap, making that rasping sound that means she's happy."

Diana's voice floated lazily from the next chair. "I know what you mean. I love to lie on my back and pick out shapes in the pink clouds. I never had a kurvan, but I did have a pet jorgat." Her voice dropped into a darker tone. "My brother's hunting tigla ate it while I was away one day. My father got me another one, but it was never the same. One time, I had to collect all the different blue leaves I could find, press them dry, and mount them for a school project. I got first in my class. My father was pleased. Said he was proud of my display. Not of me, but my product. That hurt, but I loved him so, and wanted him to love me back."

Blinking her eyes and grasping for alertness, Tessa raised her head from the padded chair.

"Diana?" When her friend didn't reply, she raised her voice, injecting a sharpness that drew startled looks from both pedicurists.

"Diana! Answer me."

Opening her dark brown eyes, Diana said, "Huh? What? I think I fell asleep."

When Tessa sank back, the two women attending to their feet went back to their work.

"Wait, pink clouds? Diana, what did you say something about pink clouds?"

"Um, pink clouds?"

"Yes, you were talking about pink clouds and a jorgat that your brother's tigla killed."

"I don't have a brother. You know that. But…" her voice trailed off. "I did have an imaginary world with pink clouds and blue trees when I was a child. I peopled it with loads of brothers and sisters, because I was lonely, being an only child."

"Are you sure? You were talking like it was real. Like it was a memory."

"Oh, I must have been remembering things I made up as a child. Only, I've been dreaming about that stuff again lately. I hadn't dreamt about it in years. The only person I've ever told about those dreams is Bryce and that was when we were in high school. I've always wondered if that was why he asked me out, because I had such a vivid imagination."

Tessa filed the episode away. Maybe they'd both loved the same children's show or something.

Changing the subject, Tessa said, "Apparently the Fairemont Hotel has a monthly Wine and Dine evening twice a month and tonight is one of them. It would be the perfect ending for our girls' day out, don't you think?"

When Diana didn't reply, Tessa opened one eye and swiveled her head enough to see her friend. "What? Not up for wine tasting? We'd planned to go to dinner afterward anyway."

Diana gave a small shake of the head. Tessa could see she was worrying her lower lip. "I know we were supposed to get supper after, but I think I'd better beg off."

"Too worn out, Di?"

"Oh, no. That's not it. It's just…I'd better go home."

Tessa shifted in her seat, earning her a warning look from her pedicurist. "We can get down to work on the Ingram account tomorrow. We've earned a day off."

With a quirk of her lips, Diana shook her head. "I know. It's not that, it's Bryce. I had a devil of a time getting even this much time away from him on the weekend. I think it's best if I go home earlier than he expected. Maybe he'll be more amenable tomorrow if I do, instead of keeping me standing around hand-holding the entire day."

"Hand-holding? Literally?" Tessa wrinkled her forehead, trying to mesh the concept of her friend, the husband, and holding hands.

Diana chuckled briefly. "Not actual holding hands, Tessa. More like being at his beck and call all day. Like a kid needing his parents to hold his hand and pay attention to him constantly."

She processed that for a moment. "So you mean he demands, no, *expects* your undivided attention all weekend?"

"No. Well, not exactly. He expects me to drop whatever I'm doing to come and see something, hear something, confirm his judgment or just bring him a drink. Heaven forbid I should be doing anything more important than he is."

"It sounds like your child analogy is pretty apt. And he does this every weekend?"

"When he's not out of town, anyway. Even then, he calls me, asks what I'm doing, who I'm with, and tells me what he wants to do when he gets back. I used to think of my phone as a tether. He's turned it into a leash!"

Reaching across the space between their chairs and pointedly ignoring the dirty look from the woman working on her feet, Tessa patted her friend's hand. "That doesn't sound healthy, Diana. Has he always been like this?"

Diana laughed, though it was more of a huff. "Oh, no. He and I… we'd been friends since, oh, junior high. In high school, we started going together in…what? Freshman year, I think." She made a face. "I do regret losing my best friend Jimmy. Bryce…didn't like him hanging around me." Her face was so sad Tessa wanted to put her arms around the woman.

Diana shook her head and essayed a smile. "And that was it. I never dated anyone else. We got married right after we graduated college.

"I'm not sure how or when it started, but lately I've been feeling— I don't know—fenced in." She got a pensive look on her face. "At first I told myself Bryce was just being manly, wanting to take care of me. But it's gotten progressively worse. Now, I feel like I'd be better off as a stuffed head on his office wall, with a little plaque underneath that tells when and where he bagged me." Diana swiped the sleeve of her robe across her face.

"Oh, honey, I had no idea. What you're describing is abuse in my book."

Diana leaned forward, burying her face in her hands. Her long, luxurious auburn hair cascaded down around her legs and into her pedicurist's face. The woman reared back, eyes wide and concerned.

Tessa sat upright in her chair, desperately wanting to wrap her arms around Diana, but knowing she shouldn't move from the chair. She settled for patting her friend's arm.

"Diana, you know I'm here for you. Whatever, whenever. Just call me." She paused. "Or Skype me. Or Facetime me." A longer pause. "Hell, you can even send me a carrier pigeon if you have to."

That got the response she'd hoped for. Diana straightened, lifting her hair away from her face and revealing a weak smile and watery eyes.

Diana hiccupped once. Then again. When the hiccups persisted, her pedicurist sprang to her feet and brought a small bottle of water for her client.

After sipping at the water, Diana's hiccups subsided. Handing back the empty bottle, she smiled a thank-you to the woman, then turned to Tessa.

"I'm sorry I broke down that way. It's just—"

Tessa broke in. "No, no, that's all right. It was probably the relaxation that brought it out." After a moment, she went on. "Just remember I care for you and you're not alone. You don't have to take this from Bryce, understand?"

At Diana's nod, Tessa continued. "I don't know exactly what Riley would recommend, him being the professional and all, but I'd bet he'd suggest you both get some counseling. If Bryce won't agree, at least get some for yourself."

"That's probably a good idea. I'll look into it on Monday." Diana looked more composed now, and maybe there was a glint of determination in her eyes.

"Good. Now let's get back to enjoying our pedicures, huh?"

The two friends laughed and lay back, their ladies no doubt breathing a sigh of relief that the storm had passed, allowing them to get back to business.

Chapter 5

"I demand to see the manager!"

Riley and Alex, chatting with Jake in the checkout line, turned at the voice raised in anger.

All three clerks behind the desk had paused, staring at an irate Matthew Cadwallader who loomed over a slight man on the far end of the customer service desk.

"Here we go again," Alex muttered, rolling his eyes.

Jake asked, "Again? What's he been up to now?"

"Last night's fire alarm?" Riley began. "That was his suite. I heard someone say they thought it was caused by some lights he plugged in that weren't grounded properly. They shorted out and caught the curtains on fire."

Jake raised his eyebrows. "Really? Ole Caddy? Was anybody hurt?"

"The only thing hurt was his pride. And probably a bunch of his books."

Alex sniggered. "And Cad got doused with a fire extinguisher."

"No way." Jake said, laughing. "Wish I could have seen that!"

"Here, let me show you," Alex said, pulling out his phone.

While the two men browsed Alex's pics, Riley watched the scene playing out with Cadwallader.

"I'm sorry, sir. The cost of the damages to your room has exceeded this credit card. Would you like us to try a different card?" The customer service man was oh-so-polite, but that didn't even slow Cadwallader down.

"Maxed out? Impossible! You put extra fees on it behind my back!"

"No, sir, just the damages we already listed for you."

"I demand to see your manager! I won't put up with thieving underlings." Cadwallader was gripping the lip of the desk, knuckles white. He leaned into the young man's space, forcing him to back up.

"I…I…I'll get the manager for you, sir," he said, fleeing the desk through a door behind him.

"You'd better!" Cadwallader threw after him. Turning, he braced himself against the counter, crossing his arms.

He's so worked up, Riley thought, *you can practically see steam coming from his ears. Maybe he should practice what he preaches in his books and deal with those anger issues.*

Alex touched Riley's arm to get his attention.

"I said, let's ask Jake if he has time to join us for supper before we all catch our planes."

"Uh, sure. We can check our schedules and see if we all have enough time."

They put their heads together as the line inched forward, comparing flight times.

"Well, not this time, I guess," Jake said, pocketing his tickets. "We'll have to get together sometime back home, to discuss the…uh, topic we started at lunch yesterday."

Riley smiled and nodded. It was nice of Jake to keep their research under wraps. "You could also email me, you know. People *do* use that new-fangled thing for conversing."

Jake laughed good-naturedly, waving a hand at Riley. "Yeah, yeah. I know I'm behind the times on computers. You don't need to remind me."

Alex and Riley laughed at their friend's sour look.

"May I help you, sir?" asked the hotel clerk.

Riley turned to her, noting that Cadwallader was now grousing at a different hotel employee. All business, Riley pointed at Alex, saying, "We need to split our room bill…."

* * *

It was significantly noisier in the vendors room when Riley and Alex stopped in to say goodbye to Evelyn and Kier.

Several of the vendors had already torn down their booths. Cadwallader had blocked the aisle with a hotel cart and his clerk was hurriedly tossing boxes and pieces of the display onto it. When Alex heard them exchanging heated words, he judiciously steered them the other way around the square toward Evelyn's booth.

As they approached, they overheard Evelyn ask, "Did you get Mr. Johnson's stuff loaded out okay?"

"Yeah. His van was way the heck in the back of the parking lot, though. Sorry I took so long," a youthful voice replied.

"That's okay. We're not in any hurry. We just have to be out of here by six." They heard a pause. "Kier, honey, pull down that end of the banner first."

From around the corner, they saw Kier hop up on the table. "I can't wait to get to Portland! I love stopping at Powell's Books. Do we still get to ride the Great Wheel before we leave town?"

"You bet. I haven't been on it yet, either," she said. "It opened after the last time I was in Seattle."

"You'll love it," Alex said as he rounded the end of the booth, careful to stay out of Cadwallader's sight. He raised an eyebrow, though, when the clerk from yesterday set yet another bundle of the backdrop atop an already unstable load. *So, the man is Caddy's caddy now?* Alex chuckled to himself. *I've got to tell that joke to Riley later. He'll get a kick out of it.*

"When did you get time to see it?" Riley asked, turning to look at him.

"I came through here on my way to a conspiracy conference in Vancouver last year. I had a long layover in Seattle so a couple friends picked me up and took me to see the sights and of course they had to take me there. Besides being a spectacular way to see Seattle, it's a lot cheaper than the elevator to the top of the Space Needle."

"Hey, boys. All done with your panels?" Evelyn asked.

"Just finished," Riley said. "We came to see if we could help with anything. We still have a couple of hours to kill before we have to catch our plane."

Alex sidled into the booth past a stack of boxes, taking the banner from Kier as he detached it from the poles. "How was your weekend, Evelyn? Good sales?" he said over his shoulder.

"Yeah," she said, sounding surprised. "I hadn't expected as good of sales as I had. I think I sold more after Caddy ran out of unsoggy books." She grabbed a stack of her books off the shelf. "Riley, could you put that empty bin on top of the others?"

Riley put the bin where she indicated. "He ran out?"

"I heard he had most of his books in the suite when the sprinklers went off. Dead loss. You should have heard him slamming around here this morning. But as soon as the doors opened, his plastic smile came out in full force. Just like magic."

Kier finished disconnecting the other end of the banner. The material sagged between him and Alex.

"Wait, Alex," Kier said. "We need to stretch it out before we fold it or it'll have wrinkles the next time mom uses it." Kier backed up into the aisle between Evelyn and Cadwallader's booths to tighten the banner. Before Alex could warn him, Kier backed into one of Cad's cases, bringing it down with a crash.

"You stupid boy!" Cadwallader yelled, coming around the luggage cart. "That's an expensive piece of equipment!" He stormed up to Kier and cuffed the boy on the side of the head.

Like a protective mother hen, Evelyn flew out of the booth in an instant. Coming nose to chest with a startled Cadwallader, she shook her finger in his face.

"Don't you lay a hand on my son, you jackass. If your stuff wasn't taking up the entire aisle, there would have been plenty of room. I've half a mind to knock you senseless, but obviously someone beat me to it."

Kier scurried back into the safety of his mother's booth, standing shoulder to shoulder with Alex, the banner's folds pooling at their feet.

"This is going to get ugly," Riley whispered from Alex's other side.

Alex could only nod as he watched the scene unfold.

"I know your cheap knock-off booth was made in China, but did you have to import one of them to operate it too?" Cadwallader sneered. "I imagine a woman like you needs all the help she can get."

Her voice dropped to a dangerous growl. "How *dare* you talk like that about my son? And what do you mean, a woman like me?"

Yikes! Alex thought. *Most men would back-peddle at that tone, but apparently Cadwallader isn't that smart.*

As the man opened his mouth to dig himself a deeper hole, Alex felt a strong, hot breeze blast him in the face.

Where did that come from? Did the heaters kick on? If they're that powerful, I wonder how these booths made it through the weekend without being blown over.

As if to illustrate the point, the top-most piece of Cadwallader's booth toppled into him, closely followed by the rest of the cases, bins, and boxes. He flailed about, trying to catch everything, but only succeeded in ramming a stack of boxes off the other side. One rather large item landed on his shiny shoes. The resulting cusswords made Alex want to take notes. Glancing at Kier, he found the boy grinning from ear to ear as though he'd been responsible for the calamity, not just an observer.

Riley and Evelyn, meanwhile, were doubled over in laughter they didn't bother trying to hide.

Gasping for breath, Riley said, "For once, karma got here on time!"

Evelyn, her tension broken, moved back into her booth, shooing Alex and Kier into the far aisle to fold up the banner, while she and Riley finished packing up the books.

Across the aisle, Cadwallader turned his full wrath upon the clerk. *I feel sorry for that poor guy,* Alex thought, as the thoroughly cowed clerk reloaded the cart piece by piece, stacking each item as though he were playing Jenga in reverse.

* * *

Mezmer Notes - Update 17
National Hypnotherapy Convention - Wrap up:

Overall, the convention was a success. It's definitely worth going again next year. Several panels gave me good resources to use in my practice.

What I didn't count on was finding more cases matching Subject Alpha's. Why are these disparate people suddenly remembering the same past life? On the plane home, I asked Alex to do some online research for any other references to orange trees with blue leaves or pink clouds. Thankfully, if it exist online, he'll find it.

Alex suggested that it might be some form of government mind control where fake memories are implanted to control people. His conspiracy theories get weirder every day. Maybe these 'memories' are from a book or a movie or something that people are subconsciously remembering when they are under hypnosis. I simply can't believe that these odd details are a shared 'past life.' With all the information I've gathered, it would have to be another planet. That's impossible!

I've emailed several people that I spoke with at the convention who had clients who've mentioned orange trees with blue leaves. I've asked them for excerpts from their cases.

Hopefully, one of their clients gave this place a name. I should also email Evelyn and see if she has encountered anything like this.

I need to ask Jake's advice about how to continue Subject Alpha's sessions. If I am going to research this, maybe I shouldn't be the one performing their regressions. If I'm not careful, I might end up accidentally biasing the results by asking leading questions.

One last note: After seeing Cad lose his temper at the checkout desk and some comments from Evelyn, it appears he's not as well off as he pretends. Maybe I'm not doing as badly as I thought. And the way he treated Kier and Evelyn in the vendors room. I was ready to pound him myself. The man is an ass. I should really learn to trust my gut instincts more.

Saving…

* * *

"Thank you for calling LeRoux Worldwide. How may I direct your call?"

"This is Matthew Cadwallader. I must speak with Thierry LeRoux on an urgent business matter."

"I'm sorry, sir. As I'm sure you can imagine, someone of Mr LeRoux's stature is a very busy man. May I take a message?"

"I don't have time for that, damn you," Cadwallader muttered, rummaging through the litter of paper on his desk. Finally, beneath a stack of bills, he found what he was looking for: a narrow, handwritten grid of numbers and words. Reading from it, he told the receptionist, "Sheitan Protocol: Code Alpha Four, Bravo One, Charlie Three."

The woman's voice changed tone immediately. "Thank you, sir. One moment please."

When elevator music began playing in the background, Cadwallader almost threw the phone across the room. With difficulty, he refrained, instead laying it down very gently in the center of his desk. *The nerve of that woman, putting me on hold,* he fumed. *Doesn't she know who I am? I'm the Area Captain. I will not be ignored!*

It was several minutes later when the woman's voice came again. "I can put you through now."

"About damn time," Cadwallader swore while waiting for the connection.

"Matthew? Explain to me why you need money. Again." Thierry LeRoux sounded pissed, even in his usual soft French-Canadian accent.

Suddenly Cadwallader felt like hiding under a rock, but his need was urgent, so he squared his shoulders and spoke, trying to keep his voice calm and respectful.

"Uh, hello, sir. How are—"

Thierry cut him off. "Cut the pleasantries. I don't have time for that. You've interrupted me during an important discussion. Get to the point."

He cringed, infinitely grateful they weren't talking face to face. "Um, yes. I had an unfortunate incident this past weekend. Therefore, I am extremely low on funds. I'll need to withdraw some of my—"

"No. You have already used up almost all of your liquid assets." Cadwallader felt his stomach sink to the floor. "I could, however, make you a loan. With interest, of course."

Cadwallader collapsed into his deluxe office chair. Exhaling a long sigh. He considered his dilemma: *I can't replace my display and my stock with what I have on hand. Not and pay the rent on both my condo and my office this month. Damn Denny for destroying my display. I don't see any alternative. I'm going to have to accept Thierry's terms and be even more obligated to him than I already am. Double damn!*

"I need the money, so, yes, I'll take the loan." He heard his voice shake, but hoped Thierry wouldn't notice.

"I need—" Cadwallader started.

"Yes, yes." Thierry said dismissively. "I'll have my new aide, Latham, call you. He'll arrange the details."

Yeah, Cadwallader thought, *details like the interest rate. Damn the man. He makes it sound like this is an insignificant transaction, but to me, it's everything.*

"Thank you, sir," he said through gritted teeth. *Kowtowing to him is hell. I feel like a beggar with a tin cup.*

Cadwallader heard a smooth voice in the background ask, "Shall I arrange for your dinner with Miss Renata Abielle, sir?"

The line went dead.

Chapter 6

From: Hypnocrat@***.com
To: DocMezmer@gmail.com

Hey Riley,

I've attached my excerpts on the subject we talked about at the conference. Look them over and let me know if you have any questions. Regarding your worries about being impartial, my personal belief is that if you are in a relationship with your subject, it might be best to have another therapist regress them. You've got Alex working with you, right? This might be a good time to let him get more practice. Under your supervision, of course.

Just my two cents worth.

Jake

* * *

"You sure you're all right with this, Tessa? Having Alex do your regression this time?"

Alex was already in the living room of their small walk-up, looking as relaxed as Riley felt tense.

"Of course," she said, rolling her eyes. "We've gone over this a thousand times. I can see it's a professional thing and I trust Alex. He is *your* student, after all." She raised her face to look him in the eye. "I trust you. If you think this is needed, then it's okay with me."

Even as Riley breathed a quiet sigh that Tessa was on board with the idea, he still had qualms. *Could Alex somehow harm Tessa? Does he have enough skill, or the right skills, to handle the regression? Maybe I should—*

Alex spoke up, cutting off Riley's line of thought. Moving to the chair next to the sofa, Alex asked, "Okay, Tessa. Ready?"

She nodded, lying down on the worn sofa. "Whenever you are." She closed her eyes. Riley watched as her body seemed to melt into the lumpy cushions. Alex walked her through the relaxation steps and began to regress her.

"Where are you, Tessa?"

"Out in the meadow. I love how the grass feels on my toes. The stream is my favorite place to cool off on a hot day." She giggled like a little girl. "Jesler's caught up with me. If I don't give him a treat, he'll rip off my pocket again."

Alex chewed on his lower lip, then asked, "Are there any other animals around you?" A strange look came over his face, before he continued. "A tigla or a patoo, perhaps?"

Tessa grinned. "How did you know my tigla'd followed me? She doesn't usually come with me into the pasture. I think she's afraid our steantles might step on her. Besides, my parents won't let me have a patoo." The last was said with a little girl's pout.

Riley nodded, watching Alex. *Wait? Where did he get that name? Patoo?* Riley started as realization struck. *Tessa recognized it, whatever it is.*

"Which breed is she? Common house tigla or one of the big hunting ones?" Alex leaned forward. It seemed to Riley as if he was eager for the answer.

"Oh, just a common one. My friend's father has one of the hunting ones. Corlan is his name. He comes up to my shoulder and he scares me a little. He's black with white points."

"Ohhhh, one of the black ones. I always love seeing them in the sun. There's darker spots within the black of their coats."

Riley sat up straighter. *Where is Alex coming up with this stuff?* It was all Riley could do to keep from interrupting the dialog. He glanced at the recorder laying on the table. *Thank goodness this is all being taped. I need proof that I'm not imagining all of this.*

"Yes! I know what you mean! Isn't it beautiful?"

"What is your tigla's name and what color is she?" Alex asked next.

"Maygon's white with turquoise, like water but darker. She's a good hunter. She keeps bringing me little headless zelts, wanting me to make a big deal over her kill. I have to play along until she gets tired and wanders off before I can get rid of it."

There was that girlish giggle again. *I've never heard Tessa sound so young and carefree.*

"Do your parents let her sleep with you? Mine wouldn't. Said he was dirty and might have bugs or something."

Tessa giggled. "Guess I'm lucky. My parents have one, Lanta, that sleeps with them every night."

Riley couldn't stand it any longer. He reached across the end table and laid a gentle hand on Alex's shoulder. In a quiet voice, he said, "Alex, come back to me. Come back to my living room here in Oakland."

Curiously, he watched Alex process his request. The younger man's eyes blinked rapidly a few times, then he straightened up in his chair, looking around the room as if seeing it for the first time.

If possible, Alex's eyes opened wider when they landed on Riley. Riley tried to look non-threatening, smiling widely and remaining still. Slowly the alarm left his student's eyes, replaced by recognition.

"What happened?" Alex said softly.

"Go on. Bring Tessa out of her regression. We'll talk later."

Alex nodded, turning back to Tessa's silent form. Speaking with professional calm, he initiated the routine that would bring Tessa out of her regressed state and back to reality.

Alex asked her, "How do you feel?"

"I feel like I just had a nap." She sat up, her face glowing with health and energy. "I feel so good. In fact, I think I'll bake some cookies. Any requests?" She looked at them with one raised brow.

"Chocolate chip peanut butter!" Riley proposed.

"Snickerdoodles!" Alex said.

Tessa squinted suspiciously at the two men. "Hey, did one of you plant a suggestion in my head that I should bake cookies for you?" She huffed a laugh. "Whatever. You're in luck, boys. I think I'll make both kinds." With that promise, she was gone.

The two men sat, silence stretching out between them. Finally, Alex broke it.

"What happened? I remember putting Tessa under and getting to her regressed world, then things go fuzzy and I can't remember anything until I was staring at you."

Riley sighed. *This should be interesting. I hope he doesn't freak out on me.*

"Well, I think you slipped into a light trance yourself. I suppose, since you are more used to being the subject rather than the therapist, your mind followed your instructions to Tessa and just...floated along with her."

"I knew something happened, because I remember being frightened when saw you. Why would I be frightened?"

"Um, I think you became part of Tessa's world somehow. You and she were talking about tigla's and—"

"Tigla's?" Alex's eyebrows shot up. "I've never mentioned them to anyone, not since I was a little kid. They were an animal that I made up for a game with my brother."

"Well, it seems you and Tessa had the same imaginary world, then," he said dryly, letting the idea settle in. "What color was the water, in your imaginary world?"

Alex's furrowed his brow, thinking back across the years. "Greenish blue, like Native American turquoise, I think. Why?"

"Bear with me. Were there any other animals that you remember?"

"Now that you mention it, there were these creatures that were almost like squirrels."

"And what color were they?" Riley could feel a headache building in the back of his head.

"Squirrels? You want to know about squirrels?"

"Yes, what color were they, in that world of yours."

"Um, rusty orange, if I remember rightly."

Riley drew a deep breath. *Things are getting complicated. If Alex was part of this shared world, of at least...what? A dozen people, now? Then there must be others out there, maybe a lot of others. So much for having Alex regress Tessa. That's out the window now.*

"I'll let you listen to the tape later, but for now, let's just say that you appear to be part of the world Tessa's describing. Somehow. I probably shouldn't have you regress her again."

"Drat! Then how are we going to find out more about this shared world?"

"Well, the only way I can see is for me to regress you instead."

* * *

Mezmer Notes - Update 19

After looking over the excerpts forwarded to me by Jake and Dr. Thompson, I am starting to put together a better picture of this shared world that our subjects are describing. The details seem to exactly match the descriptions provided by both Subject Alpha and Subject Beta.

On Jake's suggestion, I had my intern lead Subject Alpha through the regression today. I wasn't prepared for my intern joining Subject Alpha in the regression 'world'. There were new details that my intern (aka Subject Beta) brought up that sparked recognition in Subject Alpha. I felt as if I was watching two old friends comparing childhood memories. Subject Beta would mention a fact and then Subject Alpha would elaborate on it. Subject Beta was so far under that I had to rouse him like I would if he were the one being regressed. When he first looked at me, he didn't appear to recognize me. He was with Subject Alpha, wherever that was.

Later, I regressed Subject Beta separately. I can't believe I am writing this, but under hypnosis, he not only supplied information I had not shared with him that came from Jake and Dr. Thompson, but he actually gave me a name for the world: Xeres.

I have to face facts. This is not some shared delusion. All of these people lived on another world sometime in the past. This is exciting, but I need to gather more information before I let anyone else in on this. If I shared it now, my peers would laugh me out of the business.

I desperately need to discuss this with Jake, but I need to gather all the available information together first. I still haven't gotten Evelyn's excerpts. I can't believe that she doesn't have digital copies of her notes. Maybe I should send Alex by her office in Berkeley to pick them up.

Saving…

* * *

 The spring sun felt good on Alex's back, and the air was so fresh he wanted to cut off a slice and eat it. BART had been unusually crowded for a Monday afternoon, but thankfully he'd still had plenty of room for his bike. The AC had been flaky, as usual. The first car he'd tried had been stiflingly hot, but when he changed cars at the next station, he'd ended up in an arctic hell. Thankfully, he didn't have far to go to the Downtown Berkeley station and Evelyn's office.

Rolling up to Evelyn's building, Alex couldn't help but admire the architecture. There was a wall of living grasses above the entrance and, craning his neck, he could see branches from trees on the roof overhanging the side of the building. *Eco-friendly. Nice. I wonder if the building is solar powered as well?*

He found Evelyn's office on the third floor. As he entered the waiting room, a motherly woman with salt-and-pepper hair looked up.

"Are you Alex? From Dr. MacPherson's office?"

Alex nodded. "Yes, ma'am."

The woman chuckled. It's low, rich sound immediately put Alex at ease. "I seldom get ma'amed these days. Good to know some people still have manners. I'll let Dr. Sloan know you're here." She reached out with a well-manicured finger tip and pressed a button. "Your messenger is here, dear."

A slightly tinny version of the voice Alex remembered from the conference responded from the speaker. "Send him in, Maeve."

The woman nodded toward a dark wood door on her right, framed by lush plants and a potted tree. "Go right in, son."

As Alex headed toward the door, Maeve, the receptionist, handed him a large, stuffed envelope. "Would you give her these copies, please."

"Yes, ma'am."

The woman smiled, shaking her head. "I'll never get enough of that."

Alex opened the door and entered a veritable jungle. Plants in pots, cups, terrariums and boxes took up much of the office space. Bookshelves lined the walls, with more plants cascading down from any place that wasn't filled with books. A bank of windows let in the afternoon sun, briefly blinding Alex. He shaded his eyes with one hand, making out a petite desk and a figure behind it.

"Alex? Is something wrong?" He knew it was Evelyn Sloan's voice but it seemed to include the scratch of nails on a blackboard. *Her voice didn't sound like that at the conference, did it?*

He stepped to the side into shadow.

Evelyn rounded the desk, holding out her hand.

He looked down at it. *I would rather put my hand in a crocodile's mouth than shake that hand!* he thought. *Wait! Where the hell did that come from? She was so nice to us at the conference. I enjoyed talking to her, but now I…I don't know why, but I feel threatened by her. Like I just know she's going to try to kill me if I don't kill her first.*

He just couldn't bring himself to shake hands with her, so he thrust the large envelope into her hand. "I…I…Your receptionist sent this in for you."

She looked down at it, a puzzled frown on her face. "Uh, thanks, but those are the excerpts Riley wanted. Maeve does my copying." She snickered. "I just can't seem to get electronics to work reliably for me."

Looking up at Alex, she said, "Can you sit and chat a moment before you run off? Kier and I had such a wonderful time driving back from Seattle. Especially the Big Wheel. Oh, the view!"

Alex shook his head emphatically. "Can't. Sorry." *I have to get out of here!* He rushed to make an excuse, any excuse. "If I don't get back to the BART ASAP, I'll hit rush hour and there won't be room on the train for my bike. Then I'll have to wait for a mostly empty car and stand all the way back to the office."

Turning, Alex felt blindly for the door handle, opened it, and fled.

As the door closed behind him, he heard Evelyn say, "What's gotten into that young man? He was so friendly at the conference. Was it something I said?"

Once Alex was outside, he looked down at his hands. They were shaking. He called Riley.

"Hey, Alex, did you pick up Evelyn's excerpts yet?"

Alex shuddered in the warm sunlight. "Umm, yeah, I did. But something weird happened at her office. I don't know how to explain it. Did I give you any indication that I didn't like her at the conference?"

"What? No. You guys got along fine. Did something happen?"

"No. I think she was just as nice as when we first saw her, but for some reason I was so angry with her today that I'm still shaking. I felt like…Riley, I wanted to hurt her. What's going on?"

"You what?" Riley said sharply. "Please tell me this is another one of your pranks." Concern colored his voice. "You really wanted to hurt her? That's…that's messed up."

He ran his hand through his hair. "The only thing that's changed since then is I've been regressed back to Xeres. Could this be some latent bias from a past life? You gotta believe me. I'm really freaked out right now."

"I've never heard of anything like that happening, but I'll run it past Jake when we meet on Tuesday. Maybe he can make something of this. You liked her just fine before, so why would you dislike her now?"

"It's not dislike, I…I *h-h-hated* her. I wanted to hurt her." Alex stuttered.

"Calm down. Why don't you come by the office and we can talk. If you feel up to it, you can digitize Evelyn's notes. I know that doing anything involving computers seems to relax you."

Alex let out a heavy sigh. "You're right. If I don't keep busy, I'll obsess about this. I'll be there as soon as I can. Bye."

Alex put his phone away and hopped on his bike. *What's going on? First it was Tessa, now I'm evidently wrapped up in this Xeres stuff too. And how does Evelyn fit in?*

Chapter 7

"Let's find a peaceful corner out on the patio," Jake suggested as he and Riley moved through the lunch crowd at Jake's favorite spot, a little English pub in San Jose. "Should be quiet enough outside for us to talk while we have lunch." He spotted an empty table and headed for it.

When the waitperson tried to give them menus, Jake waved them away. "I'll have the Oriental Chicken Salad with vinaigrette." He raised an eyebrow at Riley, who nodded. "He'll have the BBQ Pulled Pork. We'll both have bottled water."

After the young man had left, Jake said, "The husband's got me on a diet."

"Ah," said Riley, nodding. "So Sully says no more bangers and mash, huh?"

Jake grimaced. "Not in the foreseeable future. He quizzes me when I get home about what I ate during the day. When he doesn't like my report, I get two leaves of lettuce and a cube of tofu for supper."

The man's mournful expression caused Riley to laugh out loud. "You poor thing. I know how much you love the bangers here."

"So, what's up today, Riley?" He grinned. "More orange-colored trees?"

Riley sucked in his lower lip before answering. "Yeah, something like that. I took your advice and had Alex regress Tessa. That backfired, though." He grimaced.

"I should have known better than to have Alex do the regression. He hasn't had a lot of practice working with other people, and no experience with past life regressions." He closed his eyes and shook his head. "When he put Tessa under, he apparently followed right along with her. That wouldn't have been a bad thing, except he and Tessa began interacting in her orange-tree world. Something about some kind of pet cat."

Jake chuckled. "Well, it can't be all bad if they have cats wherever this place is."

"When I touched him, he fell out of the trance and clearly didn't know me or where he was. He oriented himself quickly enough, but it was plain to me he'd been with Tessa in that other place. Neither of them remembered the regression afterward, which is probably a good thing."

Jake leaned toward Riley. "And what about Tessa?"

"She had energy to burn. But she used it to bake us some cookies, so that was a definite plus." Riley smiled broadly at the memory.

He sobered, then continued. "Alex, however, was kinda freaked out. He demanded to be regressed. While he was under, he confirmed information I'd gotten from Tessa and from several other sources about this shared world. Then he revealed a new piece of information, the name of this 'world'. Xeres."

"It has a name?" Jake asked, sitting forward and bracing his elbows on the table.

"Apparently so. Something even stranger happened the next day. Evelyn Sloan had a few relevant cases too. "I sent Alex over to Berkeley to pick up her excerpts. Can you believe that woman doesn't keep her notes digitally?" He shook his head.

Jake huffed. "I can believe it. She's a bit of a Luddite, that way. Like me, I guess."

"Anyway, Alex was still tense when he got back to my office. He got along fine with Evelyn at the conference, but at her office he reported having an almost-psychotic reaction to even touching her hand. Said he'd never felt that way before."

"Did this happen before or after his regression?" Jake asked.

"After," Riley said tersely.

"So, you think the two incidents are connected?"

"Yeah, I do." Riley ran a hand through his short hair. "I don't see *how* they can be connected, but before I jump to any conclusions, I'd like to get Evelyn's perspective on the incident."

Jake nodded, then sat back as their food arrived.

Riley, still tense, barely contained himself until the waiter left.

"About Evelyn's notes," he continued. "Did you get a chance to read through the digitized copies I sent?"

"No," Jake said, dousing his salad with vinaigrette and making a face at it. "I've had back-to-back clients all week. I scanned through a few of them, but not all. What's so special about her notes?"

"Well, she had three clients who mentioned orange trees with blue leaves. And one of them also named the world Xeres."

Abruptly, Jake sat back in his chair, a forkful of salad hanging forgotten in his fingers. When it clattered to the table-top, he gave it an annoyed glance. "That means...." He let his words trail off, waiting for Riley to offer his conclusion.

"It means that we now have a handful of widely scattered people with no obvious connection to each other, who, when regressed, remember an impossible world, Xeres." Riley went silent. He met his mentor's eyes, hoping to find some answer there. Instead, he saw Jake's face take on a hardness Riley had never seen.

Jake broke eye contact. Running a big hand over his face, he breathed a long sigh. "Riley," he began slowly, "I don't know what to tell you. This is way beyond my experience. I dismissed my two clients as a coincidence. And, now that I think about it, there is something else I observed." He folded his hands across his stomach, ignoring his meal.

"I'd just finished a session with the man. When I went out to greet my next client, the little girl. The abuse victim? Normally, she avoids all contact with men, it's one of her defense mechanisms. But that day? She was chatting with the old man like they'd known each other all her life. She was laughing and even touching his arm. I looked around for her mother. She was standing away from the pair, jaw open in amazement. The mother told me he was the first man her daughter had ever willingly touched and she hadn't a clue why he was different."

Jake raised his eyes to Riley's. "And neither do I. This is too weird. I honestly don't know what the next step is." Jake shook his head. "This whole thing is so far outside my experience. Much as I hate to say it, I think you're on your own now. I don't think I can be of any help to you from here on out, no matter what direction you go."

"You mean I can't come to you for ideas or...or anything?" Riley couldn't believe his ears. "You won't help me?"

The big man took a moment to ponder Riley's words, then shook his head. "I'm not saying you can't share your concerns with me. But this is your baby. I can't tell you how to proceed. I wouldn't know where to start."

Riley took a deep breath, then nodded. "Fair enough. I guess I *am* the one leading this investigation. Alex may be my student, but he's involved too, so I should probably discuss all of this with him now. Maybe Tessa, too, although I'm nervous about bringing her in on the whole thing until I absolutely have to."

The older man nodded. "I think that's a wise move. She's still your primary source, even though you now have several other confirmed cases."

The two men sat in silence for a few moments. Finally, as if by some prearranged signal, they resumed eating their lunch. When they spoke next, it was of mundane matters, just two friends enjoying a bite to eat.

* * *

Mezmer Notes - Update 26

My meeting with Jake didn't turn out like I'd hoped. One, he hadn't had time to look over the notes I sent him, but what little he had read obviously disturbed him. And two, he told me that he couldn't help me with this project because it bothers him too much. Until now, I've always relied on Jake to help me understand things or to sort out problems with my clients. To hear him say that he couldn't, no, wouldn't help me. I don't know how to take that. It appears I'm on my own with this.

One thing that I wish I could have talked to him about more was an interaction between his two Xeres-connected clients. The young girl, previously unwilling to interact with any men, to the surprise of both Jake and the girl's mother, began chatting with the other client, an elderly gentleman, 'like they'd known each other all her life.'

I can't help but wonder if that pair's sudden 'attraction' and the 'repulsion' that Subject Beta felt when he encountered Evelyn are connected. Why would these people, after being regressed, suddenly have vastly different reactions to certain people? It just doesn't make sense. I need to regress both Subject Alpha and Subject Beta...

I can't do this. I can't keep referring to them as Subject Alpha and Subject Beta. I can't keep a clinical distance when I'm talking about my girlfriend and my assistant. Assistant? Who am I kidding? He's my best friend after Tessa. I need to regress both Tessa and Alex again and see if I can get them to explain why they have these strong emotional responses to specific people.

Should I bring them both into the loop about what I've found out about this Xeres place? I didn't want to contaminate their subconscious with the information I've collected, but after what happened when Alex regressed Tessa, maybe sharing what little I've put together will help me connect the dots.

Saving…

* * *

"This is your office?" Evelyn Sloan turned slowly, surveying Riley's office. She sniffed. "I mean, I've seen bigger closets. I'll give you the plants though, nice touch. And those two windows are probably at a premium."

"The plants were Tessa's idea. When one of them dies, she replaces it with something she thinks is hardier and can withstand my neglect better." *I know she's just teasing me. I mean, she's right, it is tiny, but it's all I can afford at the moment. It may be small, but it's homey. And it's mine. My clients never complain about it.*

She moved to the couch and perched on the edge, remaining silent.

Why is she here? he thought suspiciously. *She seems tense. I'm not sure I buy that she was 'just in the neighborhood.' This isn't a very nice neighborhood, and there's no reason I can see for her to be here. She came specifically to see me. Why?*

He explored his feelings for Evelyn. *Do I feel any differently about her? Nope. I still like her. So whatever put Alex off hasn't affected me. This must have something to do with his regression.*

"How's your practice?" Riley ventured, not so much curious as to break the silence.

She waved an elegant, dismissive hand. "Same, same."

"And Kier?"

That earned him a smile and a slight relaxation of her shoulders. "He's fine. Busy, though. He's working on a costume for a little convention he and his friends are attending this weekend. He's going as some anime character he's into right now." Another wave of that small hand. "His favorite changes week to week, I think."

Riley grinned, raising his eyebrows. "He goes to sci-fi cons?"

"Wait. You're into sci-fi, too?"

"You better believe it. Tessa and I are looking forward to the next Westercon we can reach. Tessa's in charge of the costuming. She sews a mean cape. Alex likes cons too, but he goes mostly for the gaming."

"I never would have taken you for the sci-fi con type." She paused for a moment, then asked, "How *is* Alex these days." Riley recognized the carefully-schooled expression that therapists wore when dealing with a client.

So that's why she's here, to find out why Alex was so upset. Riley answered neutrally, "He's okay, I guess. Why do you ask?"

She sucked in her lower lip before she answered. *Trying to assemble the facts or to obfuscate?* Riley wondered.

"Well, last time I saw him, he behaved…I don't know. Weird? Wouldn't shake my hand, wouldn't talk to me, acted like…like I was a bug-eyed monster or something," she finished. Her shoulders slumped, breaking their padded horizontal line. Looking into Riley's eyes, she demanded, "Did I do something to offend him? I can't think of anything I might have said or done, but there has to be something."

Riley rushed to reassure her. "Oh, no, you haven't done anything wrong. At least, as far as I can tell."

"You mean he told you what happened?"

"Oh, yeah. He was still upset about it when he got back here with your excerpts."

"Then, why—"

"I have my theories, but I'm not ready to share them. At least not yet."

Evelyn leaned forward, elbows on knees. "But you're sure I'm not the cause?"

Riley shook his head. "I don't think so. Well, not directly, anyway."

She breathed a sigh of relief. "Phew, that's a load off my mind."

Riley leaned back in his chair, staring at the wall for a moment before he spoke again. "Trust me, there are a lot of strange things going on right now, not just this thing between you and Alex. That's why I asked for your excerpts."

Her lips thinned to a line and one elegant eyebrow rose. "You don't want me involved in whatever this is?"

He rushed to reassure her. "It's not that. It's just that I'm still collecting information, putting the puzzle together. I don't want to share it with anyone until I have a better handle on the whole picture."

She gave him a sharp nod, then stood stiffly, heading for the door. "Well, let me know if you have anything you want to share." A cold, hard edge crept into her voice. She fired off one last parting shot. "Whenever you get around to it."

Riley rose and gripped her arm. "Don't be like that, Evelyn, please. I do want your input, but right now, if I tried to explain it to you, you'd probably have me locked up. Hell, even *I* wonder if I might be going off the deep end." He rubbed a hand across the back of his neck.

Pausing, Evelyn turned toward him with a sigh. "Okay. I'll wait. Just remember, I'm here for you. When you're ready." She patted his cheek, turned and left.

He stared after her, lost in thought.

From the stairs came a clatter of books.

Rushing to the door, Riley found Evelyn going down his narrow staircase, with Alex flattened against the outer railing. He was as far as he could get from her petite figure, his knuckles white where they gripped the handrail. Alex's messenger bag lay upended at his feet.

Hearing Riley behind her, Evelyn turned, a panicked look splashed across her face. She mouthed, "What should I do?"

Riley stepped onto the small landing, calling softly, "Alex?" When that didn't get the young man's attention, he tried again, louder. "*Alex?* Look at me."

In slow motion, Alex turned his head, eyes finally focusing on Riley.

"Huh?"

"Let Evelyn pass and come on up here. *Now*, please."

Still in a daze, Alex kept eye contact with Riley and sidled along the railing, mounting the last three steps to the landing. He passed Evelyn, not even daring a single look.

Frowning, Evelyn shrugged and stalked down the stairway. At the bend, she cast a we'll-talk-later glance over her shoulder at Riley.

* * *

Mezmer Notes - Update 29

Evelyn Sloan dropped by to see me today. I knew she was digging for something, but I wasn't sure what until she asked about Alex. I think she was as shaken by his reaction as he was. I tried to reassure her that she hadn't done anything wrong. As she was leaving, she ran into Alex on the stairs. It wasn't pretty.

Alex told me about his reaction to Evelyn, but I have to admit, actually seeing it was a shock. He seemed completely caught up in whatever he was experiencing. I had to raise my voice just to get his attention. He seemed…at war with himself, part of him repulsed, part trying to figure out why. Once Evelyn left, he came out of whatever it was he had fallen into. Curiouser and curiouser.

Alex had stopped in to go over the results of his research. He found a few websites referencing the information I've cobbled together so far about Xeres. Most of what he found were blog posts from people talking about dreams that contained details I've already gathered, but one or two actually provided some new information.

After talking for a bit, he confessed that the real reason he didn't just email me the information. He 'wants—no, needs' to be regressed again. I have to admit, seeing his reaction to Evelyn, I want to know what's going on as well. We've set up a time tomorrow so I can regress him and dig deeper into this whole Xeres business.

Saving…

Chapter 8

Riley rubbed his hands across his face. *I'm glad this day is finally over.* As if on cue, a very distinctive knock came from his office door. *No rest for the wicked.*

"Come on in, Alex" Riley called. He typed one last note into his client's file, then closed his laptop.

Turning, he found Alex intently perusing his bookcase. As he watched, his friend clasped his hands tightly behind his back and moved over to the comfy couch, all the while studiously *not* looking at him.

Wow. He's really wound up, Riley thought with dismay. *Is it about the regression? Or what we might find? Hmmm.*

Alex finally looked up. Riley watched him paste on a fake smile. "Oh, sorry."

"You seem…not yourself." *This is weird,* he thought. *We're usually so comfortable around each other, but all of a sudden I feel like I'm just his therapist rather than his friend.* After a moment, he asked, "You ready for this?"

Alex nodded jerkily. "I'm ready for whatever you've got. You want me on the couch?" At Riley's bemused nod, Alex laughed at the double entendre, which eased the tension a bit. He flopped down on the couch.

"Be gentle, Doc, it's my first time."

"I find that hard to believe. Now shut up and get comfortable," Riley teased back.

"How comfortable should I get?" he joked with a leer and an arched eyebrow. "I'm already not wearing that much."

Riley laughed in spite of himself. "Enough out of you. Get serious."

Alex muttered, "Like that's gonna happen."

Riley shot Alex an exasperated look. "What's with you today? You only get like this when something's worrying you. Out with it."

"Sorry." He wiggled his shoulders and twisted his neck to find a better position. "It's just…I've always believed that aliens are out there in the universe. I just never imagined that I *was* one."

Riley let out a long sigh. "You're *not* an alien. You're as human as I am."

"My body is human, but what about my soul. It's alien. Look at what happened between me and Evelyn. That had to be because of the regression. What if this time it's you and Tessa that I can't stand to be around. I don't think I could take that." Alex looked like he was on the verge of tears.

"You don't have to worry about me," Riley said, trying to ease his friend's fears. "I'm not involved in this whole Xeres thing. And if you were going to have a problem with Tessa like you did with Evelyn, you would have noticed it by now, right?"

Alex shrugged. "Okay, you have a point." He slid down into a more comfortable position on the couch. "Let's get this over with then. I need answers."

As Riley walked him through the relaxation phase, Alex gradually calmed down, like a spring unwinding. His clasped hands loosened, falling limply to his sides. *Time to start digging.*

"Alex, I want you to go back to Xeres."

"Okay."

"What do you see around you?"

"It's a beautiful day. There's a few clouds skittering across the sky." Alex smiled. The memory seemed to please him.

"Are you in the country or in a city?"

"I'm in the capital today."

"Are there any other people around you?"

"Oh, yes. It's quite busy."

"How do you feel about the people around you?"

"Everyone here is agreeable."

"Is there anyone there you don't like?"

"No, why would there be? We're all from the same guild."

"Guild?"

"The science guild."

"Is there anyone you don't like?"

"The others." His voice was tinged with disgust. "The magical guild."

Well, Riley thought, *that's interesting. I wonder....*

"Do these guilds have names?"

"Of *course* they do. I'm Bylantian, I'm a scientist."

"And the others? What do they call themselves?"

"Klymurians." He spit out the word. "They use magic instead of science. We're not compatible. That's why we separated in the first place." Alex spoke to Riley as though to a child, like the information was so basic anyone would know it.

"Do you know who Evelyn Sloan is?"

"She's one of *them!*" He snorted. "A Klymurian."

"Is that why you don't get along? Because she's Klymurian? There isn't any other reason?"

"Isn't that enough? We barely speak the same language anymore. We don't have *anything* in common."

Riley could hear the disgust in Alex's voice. The man he was speaking to really didn't like Evelyn.

"You used to get along with her. What changed?" Riley asked.

"I remembered who I truly am, not this human shell I'm wearing in this life."

What? Riley thought. *Who he truly is? Human shell? Crap! What kind of Pandora's Box have I opened here?*

Cautiously, Riley asked, "Remembered who you truly are?"

"I woke up to my true self when you asked me about Xeres. You made me remember that I'm not this Alexander person that I appear to be on Earth. My true Xerian self, Ponacowa, has been asleep for a very long time."

"Oh." In near panic, Riley thought, *Now where do I go?* After a moment, he asked, "Do you mean you reincarnated into Alex?"

"Of course. That's how it's done. Are you dim-witted?"

Right, thought Riley. *Of course.* Realizations cascaded over him like a waterfall, relentlessly pounding into his brain. *This...entity is fully aware of both its life on Xeres and its current life here as Alex. What else does it know? What about Tessa?*

"Do you know who Tessa Connors is?"

"She must be Bylantian. I didn't feel threatened by her when we were talking about her tigla before. She's just beginning to remember her true self. You started that."

"Me? How did I do that?" Riley said, straightening from his elbows-on-knees position.

"You asked her questions that made her remember Xeres. She's starting to put the pieces together."

Riley groaned. *That's precisely what I didn't want to do.*

After a moment's thought, he asked Alex, "Are there any other Xerians around?"

"The only other Bylantian, besides Tessa, is her business partner... what's her name? Ah, Diana."

"Diana? Hmmm. Are there any...what's the other guild again?"

"Klymurians. Besides the one known as Evelyn, there's her son Kier, too. And...."

The sleeper's voice trailed off, like he was searching for something.

"There are other Xerians that I've recognized, but for some reason, I can't figure out which guild they belong to."

"Who would that be, *Alex?*" Riley asked. *Dammit, I want to talk to my friend, not that guy Ponacowa. He scares me.*

"For one, that obnoxious Cadwallader person. For another, Diana's husband. What's his name?" He thought for a moment. "Oh. Bryce. Those two are connected to Xeres. It's odd though, I can't tell which guild they belong to."

Riley leaned back in his chair, appraising his friend's condition. Alex's breathing had grown shallow and he'd started to sweat.

I think I'd better end this. If I keep probing for more information right now, I might hurt Alex. He's obviously in distress. Besides, he huffed to himself, *I've got enough to think about already.*

Leaning forward, he began bringing Alex out of the trance.

As soon as he recovered, Alex demanded to know what Riley learned during the regression.

"No, Alex," Riley said firmly, shaking his head. "I can't give you an answer right now. I have to connect the dots before I discuss this with you."

"But it was *my* regression," Alex protested. "At least let me listen to the recording."

Riley felt the hair on the back of his neck rising at the very thought of letting Alex hear the session. *He was already worried about being an alien. What would hearing the recording do to him?*

Although he does have a right to know....

"No. Not now. Just let me figure out a few things first, then I'll tell you the whole story. Right now, I couldn't even give you a coherent answer." Riley rubbed his neck, his eyes going unfocused. "Please, Alex," he pleaded. "Just give me some time to process this, then I'll tell you everything. I promise."

Alex stared at Riley for a moment, then finally nodded. "All right. I trust you. Just don't leave me hanging too long, okay?"

Riley sighed. *Well, at least I bought myself a little breathing room.* Taking Alex's arm, he moved him toward the door.

"Not much longer, I promise."

* * *

Mezmer Notes - Update 30

Alex's regression was different than any I've ever seen or heard. This person, Ponacowa, was fully aware of Alex as an individual who was and yet wasn't himself. He said that I had made him remember his 'true self' from a past life. Like I had awakened him from a long sleep.

According to Ponacowa, there are two guilds who do not get along with each other to the point where they 'barely speak the same language.' His group, the Bylantians, are a science guild, while the other group, the Klymurians, are a magical guild. (Magic, really?) He indicated that Tessa and her business partner, Diana, belong to his guild, while Evelyn and her son Kier are from the magical one. Also, he pegged Diana's husband, Bryce, and, of all people, Cadwallader as being from Xeres, but he couldn't place them in either guild.

Here's what I know about Xeres:
- *The trees have orange bark and blue leaves.*
- *The grass appears silvery.*
- *The water looks turquoise.*
- *The sky looks aquamarine.*
- *The clouds are a pinkish-gold.*
- *The dirt is orange.*
- *The gravity is greater than on Earth.*
- *The sun appears smaller than it does on Earth.*

There are:

- *Orange squirrel-like creatures called lunts living in the trees.*
- *Two types of cat-like creatures called tiglas, a smaller house variety and a larger hunting one.*
- *Domesticated dog-sized reptiles called patoos.*
- *Large domesticated horse-type creatures called steantles. Smaller ones are called kurvans.*
- *Bird-like creatures called jorgats.*
- *Dove-sized creatures that fly like a hummingbird.*
- *Plants that can move. They're a pest, somewhat like our mosquitoes, that people on Xeres wear some kind of repellent to keep them away.*
- *Tubular fish that taste like avocadoes.*
- *Clothes made from some synthetic fiber that adapts to the ambient temperature to either hold in heat or disperse it, as needed.*
- *Round fruits that taste like a combination of strawberry and mango.*

Alex is demanding I share my notes and the recordings of his sessions with him, but I am uncomfortable doing so right now. I desperately wish I could talk to Jake about this, but he's chosen to take himself out of the picture. Maybe Evelyn? She could give me a fresh eye on all of this. After all, Alex and Tessa are still my main subjects. Also, as much as I hate to admit it, the personality that talked to me through Alex… frightened me a little.

Saving…

Chapter 9

Opening their apartment door was like being drowned in cookies. *She's baking!* he thought, his mouth already salivating. *She's been so busy on that new project that she hasn't made cookies for weeks.*

Dropping his backpack and keys on the end table by the door, he tiptoed across the living room to the kitchen.

Tessa stood, hands on hips, facing a rack of cooling cookies on the counter. In the softest voice he'd ever heard, she said, "What's taking so long? It should happen instantly."

She's talking to herself, but what an odd thing to say. He kept his place, curious to see what she'd say next.

When she didn't go on, he questioned softly, "What should happen instantly?"

Tessa spun around, one hand flying to her chest. "Riley! You about gave me a heart attack!"

He stepped into the room, putting his arms around her. Suddenly he felt like he needed to protect her, though he didn't know why or from whom. He dropped a soft kiss on her cheek. "Sorry, didn't mean to."

She huffed and gave him a pouty face. "Well, you did. And you'll have to pay!" Abruptly she changed from a little girl into a raging lioness who wanted nothing so much as to tickle his sides.

Riley dodged away but he was no match for her. In no time he was on his back on the kitchen floor, his body drawn into a fetal position, laughing so hard tears were running down his cheeks.

Tessa, giggling herself, collapsed beside him.

When their laughter tapered off to hiccups, Riley said, "What did you mean before? What should happen instantly?"

She wrinkled her nose at him. "Huh? Did I say that?"

He nodded. "Uh-huh."

She bit her lip a moment before replying. "I don't know. Until you showed up and scared me, I'd been having a lovely afternoon baking cookies. I don't remember saying anything like that."

"Taking time off from working with Diana?"

She closed her eyes and pinched the bridge of her nose. "We both decided we deserved it, since we just finished the Grimes' account." Theatrically, she brought the back of her hand to her forehead. "Eight weeks of nitpicking about exactly where to place their logo on the letterhead and what Pantone color to make it! Enough already!"

Riley rose and helped Tessa up off the floor. He gestured toward their tiny table. They sat down for their nightly ritual, catching each other up on their day.

"How did Alex's regression go?" she asked. "I figured that was why you were so tense this morning."

He thought for a moment, wondering how to tell her and not taint her as his subject. Finally, he shook his head.

"I'm sorry, but I'm not ready to talk about it just yet. I need to get some things straightened out first." He reached out and took her hand. "Is that okay?"

I hate that I'm keeping things from her. She's more worried about upsetting me than she is about what I'm not telling her. Gods, I don't deserve her.

She wiped the worry from her face and smiled. "Of course it's okay, silly." She rose, looking down at him.

"Besides, I've got baking to do. I promised Darla next door that I'd make eight dozen cookies for the elementary school's bake sale."

Riley grabbed her arm as she turned.

"You mean these aren't for me?" he said plaintively, giving her puppy dog eyes.

She smacked his arm, reached across to the cooling rack. Grabbing two warm cookies, she stuffed them both in his mouth.

Licking chocolate goo from his fingers and lips, Riley walked down the short hall, past their bedroom, and into their shared office. It was a small room, probably meant to be a kid's bedroom or storage area.

He edged around their conjoined desks and into his chair. They'd set their desks facing each other along the narrow window opening onto the same fire-escape ledge as the kitchen door.

His desk faced Tessa's and the closet where her snakes lived in a luxurious high-rise of plexiglass, sand, branches, and heat lamps. He glanced over to check on the boa constrictors, Meg and Calvin, named after characters in *A Wrinkle in Time*. The book had been Tessa's favorite from childhood, and had also been the source of her nickname, Tesseract. Both snakes were asleep at the moment, one curled up under a log, the other doing a decent imitation of a Gordian knot around a tree branch.

Brushing away the loose papers leftover from his last project, he reached for a yellow pad, pulled his phone out of his pocket, and dialed a number.

"Evelyn? Hi, this is Riley MacPherson."

The voice that came across the line sounded harried. "Hi. Hold on for a minute, I've got a pizza in the oven." Riley heard a voice in the background. "I said I have a *pizza* in the oven, not a bun. I'm not giving birth to it, I'm attempting to cook it." She raised her voice. "My son, the comedian, everybody. He's here all week." Her voice took on the same mocking tone she'd used on Cadwallader. "Grounded, if he isn't careful." Riley could hear what he now knew was Kier, protesting in the background.

Riley laughed at their good natured banter. *So she has more uses for that rapier wit than just battling Caddy. She has to keep up with her teenage son.*

Riley used the wait time to order his thoughts. *I need someone to talk to. I hope she's willing. I'd like to have someone who knows as much as I do so they can help me make sense of this…. What the hell do I call this Xeres thing, anyway? A conspiracy? Mass hysteria? Collective memories? I doubt anyone has ever encountered something like this before, so there probably isn't a name for it.* He laughed to himself. *Or if they have, they've been locked up in a looney bin somewhere.* He ran a hand across his face. *Maybe that's where I belong. It's all so confusing.*

When Evelyn came back on the line, she seemed out of breath. "I'm back. Sorry. Finally settled. I almost burnt the frozen pizza. Again! Kier is still shaking his head at me, but at least he's eating."

"Now, how can I help you?"

"I was wondering…." he began, abruptly unsure of himself.

Breathing a calming sigh, he dove in.

"I've run into some…oddities that I could use a second opinion on. I was wondering if you have any interest in assisting me?"

"Oddities, huh? Does this have anything to do with the excerpts you requested?"

"Them and a lot more. Could I drop by your office and discuss the problem? I'm warning you, it'll take awhile."

"Hold on a minute, I need to look at my calendar. How about day after tomorrow, around four? Would that work for you?"

Riley checked his own calendar. "Yeah, that's good. Do you have any appointments after that?"

"Nope. Just Kier's empty stomach dictating dinner time."

He heard Kier in the background. "Feeeed me! Feeeed me!"

Riley laughed at the *Little Shop of Horrors* reference. *That kid's growing on me*, he thought.

"Okay, I'll be there. I didn't want to interrupt your schedule if you had clients afterwards. Explaining everything could take a while."

"No worries," she said, laughing. "We'll have plenty of time. If we *must* feed Kier, we can continue our discussion while I feed the beast."

"Hey, who you calling a beast?" Kier growled from the other end of the call.

"You, you bottomless pit. Get back to your pizza and let me talk with a grown up for a change."

Riley chuckled. "Is that what it's like, being a parent?"

"That and more, much more. So, day after tomorrow at four then?"

"Yeah. See you then. I'll let you get back to your pizza."

Evelyn laughed. "Pizza, here I come. Bye."

"Bye, now." He hung up.

Sitting back, he pondered the conversation. *I envy how close she and Kier are. And I love her wit and humorous outlook on life. Am I making a mistake bringing her in on Xeres? Do I have the right to complicate her world?*

He shook his head. *Well, I'm committed now, aren't I? Can't back out at this point.*

His stomach chose that moment to remind him that he hadn't had dinner yet. As he stood to remedy that oversight, Tessa called from the kitchen, "Dinner's ready." *Her timing is perfect, as usual*, he thought as the heavenly smells beckoned him toward the kitchen.

* * *

Riley whistled. "Wow. Classy." He moved about Evelyn's office, taking in the ambiance. *Well, what I can see of it around all the plants taking over the room.*

"Thank you," Evelyn said, smiling and gesturing for him to sit on the caramel-colored leather couch. She perched on the matching chair across from him. "It was pretty much a dump when I acquired the building."

Riley couldn't keep the shock out of his voice. "You *own* this place?" *Wow, she must be doing very well if she owns the whole building. Property costs are astronomical in the Bay Area. Tessa and I've been saving for a while now and we don't even have a decent down payment yet.*

"Yes. I bought it for a song. It was practically falling down, but I fixed it up a little at a time. It's worth a whole lot more now. I couldn't imagine trying to buy a place like this at today's prices." Evelyn sat back and crossed her knees, displaying her slender legs. "After my husband died, I sank a lot of his insurance money into the renovations. Then, when I adopted Kier, I began thinking of the building as a legacy for him."

"I'm impressed," Riley said, glancing around. "This is the perfect office for a hypnotherapist." Her desk, bare of anything personal, was mahogany and graced only by her laptop. The desk chair looked so comfortable and cushy that his own office chair seemed comparable to a park bench. Overhead, a white-bladed fan stirred the air just enough for comfort without causing undue noise to distract a client.

"Is that original molding?" he asked.

She smiled with pleasure. "You noticed. Yes. The building dates from the thirties. I liked the contrast of the creamy walls with the white molding."

"I'm going to be stuck in that tiny little office for the rest of my career. My girlfriend, Tessa, and I have been saving up for a house, and that has to come first. Hell, I couldn't even afford to *rent* a nice place like this."

"Oh, you might be surprised," she said coyly. "All of my tenants are therapists, too, so we share the waiting room and Maeve as our receptionist. Plus there's wi-fi and ample parking. We're even close to BART, which makes life easier for my tenants *and* their clients. I make most of my mortgage renting out the shops on the first floor."

"You have other tenants? I thought it was just you up here. How many more offices are there?"

"A total of five. There are two more on this floor and three on the third floor. We share a break room in the back, near the elevator."

"Elevator?"

"I had it installed in 2004 to make the building ADA compliant. I had an uncle who was in a wheelchair, so I would have done it anyway. I think we have the area's largest client base of people with disabilities. That investment certainly paid off."

"I'll say. I have to admit, I am more than a little jealous. You saw how small and crowded my office is."

"I hadn't noticed," she said dryly, then laughed. "I don't know how you work in such a small space and without any help. Don't you get claustrophobic?"

He shrugged. "It's what I can afford."

She sat forward in her chair, one elegant finger tapping her lips. "Just out of curiosity, what are you paying for that hole in the wall?"

He named a figure.

Evelyn's eyebrows shot up. "Isn't that a little high for a closet? Sorry," she added hastily, waving her hands. "That sounded better in my head. I didn't mean to be offensive."

Pursing her lips, she sat back, eyes on the ceiling. "You know, I currently have an office that's vacant, and the rent wouldn't be a lot higher than what you currently pay." She leaned forward again, meeting his eyes. "Would you like to see the space?"

He blinked at the offer. "Now?" he asked with growing excitement. "You bet."

Twenty minutes and some intense negotiations later, Riley sank back down onto the leather sofa.

"Well, now that you've taken me on as a tenant, shall we get into what I originally came to see you about?"

Evelyn nodded. "You were very mysterious about that on the phone." She looked expectantly at Riley.

"Well, it all started with Tessa. She was one of my first past life regressions. She was hoping to find a past life involving her current obsession with everything Celtic."

"What? She didn't think she was Cleopatra? Or maybe Guinevere?"

He chuckled, breaking up some of the tension that had been building inside him. *Besides Jake, I haven't talked about this to anyone yet. Honestly,* he told himself, *I'm afraid I'll see the same look in her eyes I saw in Jake's, like I'm crazy. Maybe I'd be better off just committing myself.*

"No, but she did start talking about a life she'd lived on another planet."

Evelyn's eyebrows flew up. After a few moments' silence, she sat forward, placing her elbows on the armrests and steepling her fingers in front of her face. "Let me get this straight. Tessa claims to have lived on another planet?"

"No, I got that information from her regression. Consciously, she only remembers it as a place she used to dream about as a child. "

"Okay. Go on."

"I didn't think too much about it until I overheard a conversation at the conference. They were talking about orange-barked trees with blue leaves and pinkish gold clouds, exactly like she'd mentioned. I started asking around and several other therapists had similar stories. The same oddly-colored clouds and trees."

She nodded. "Well, that explains your curiosity about my two clients. How many cases have you found so far?"

"Let's see, about two dozen." He smiled. "I've even compiled a list of attributes and animals shared by these people. Like," he paused to select a detail, "the tigla Tessa says she had as a pet."

The woman bolted up from her chair. "Tigla? You're sure she said tigla?"

Blinking in surprise, Riley said, "It's come up in several regressions. Why?"

Sitting back down, she pursed her lips in thought. "I've run across a tigla, too."

"Really? Where?" Riley asked. *Why wasn't that in her excerpts?*

She sighed. "From Kier, when he was little. I'd taken him to the zoo for the day. When we entered the Lion House and turned to the first cage, the one with Siberian tigers, Kier stopped dead, then panicked. Like he thought the tigers would attack him." She laughed a little and shrugged. "I mean, both of them were sleeping. I couldn't figure out what had triggered his panic attack. We had to leave the zoo and it took hours to calm him down. Even then, he couldn't tell me what had made him so upset. He just kept repeating, 'The tiglas will get me! They'll eat me, too.'" She laughed shortly. "As you can imagine, the name stuck with me."

"So you regressed him?"

"Yes. He didn't mention your pink clouds or trees, though. His scenario had a tigla killing his...what was the name? Patoo, that's it. The tigla killed his patoo. Best I can figure, it's some kind of dog."

"I believe you're right about the patoo being a dog. From what Tessa described, it must have been a hunting tigla that killed his patoo. "

She stabbed a finger at him. "Yes, that's exactly what he called it, a hunting tigla. That doesn't sound like a cat to me."

"I think it's more along the lines of a cheetah."

"Oh, that would certainly scare a little boy."

"Putting Kier's episode aside, there's also Alex."

"You mean, why he doesn't like me anymore?" she said, arching a delicate eyebrow at him.

She's not going to let this go, is she? She knows everything was fine at the convention, but not when he came to her office and definitely not when they met outside mine.

"I think I know why now. I had Alex regress Tessa. When he did, he slipped into a light trance. He and Tessa had a whole discussion about their tiglas and whether the tiglas were allowed to sleep inside. Afterward, he didn't remember anything, so he asked me to regress him, to see if there was more to it."

"I take it there was."

Riley huffed. "Oh, yeah. He gave the planet a name, Xeres. In his second regression, I learned there were two guilds. Alex claims he and Tessa were from the same guild, one he called Bylantians. Apparently, you and Kier are from the one he called Klymurian."

"Hold on, I'm supposedly from this place too?"

"Yeah, and there's some sort of friction between your guilds. Then there are others that Alex remembers from Xeres, but can't figure out which guild they belong to. Just another mystery to tack onto this whole mess." He smiled and gave a half-hearted shrug of one shoulder. "I imagine you think I'm crazy for even suggesting reincarnation from another planet. Hell," he said, rubbing at the back of his neck, "*I* think I'm crazy. When I told Jake, the look in his eyes...."

"He didn't believe you, did he?"

"Ha! He didn't want anything to do with it."

"I can imagine. I've always found him a bit...well, no offense, but a bit of a stick in the mud. If it weren't for what I saw with Kier, I might wonder if you're were crazy, too. He was utterly terrified when he saw that tiger, and your explanation fits, for all it's out of this world."

They both laughed at her inadvertent joke.

"So," she asked, "what's the next step?"

Even though he suspected she wouldn't like his answer, he said, "I think I need to regress Kier."

She shook her head sharply once. "Nope, no way. Not going to happen."

"Then what do you propose?"

"Since I seem to be part of that world too, I should have pieces of the same memories. Regress me."

* * *

Mezmer Notes - Update 35

I did it. I told Evelyn Sloan everything, all my suspicions and theories about this Xeres place. Well, almost everything. Thankfully, she didn't immediately have me committed. Turns out her son, Kier, mentioned tiglas when he was little, so she wasn't taken completely by surprise like Jake was. She actually seemed receptive to my theories, wild as they are.

When I asked her to let me regress Kier to get more information on the other guild that Alex mentioned, she was adamant that she didn't want Kier involved. She wants me to regress her instead, since she and Kier were from the same guild. It makes sense, but I have some serious misgivings about regressing her. After what happened with Alex, it seems that once someone starts to remember Xeres, the animosity that existed there starts showing up here. What if she starts having the same reaction to Alex that he has to her now? It's bad enough having to deal with him *being hostile. I don't know if I can handle both of them acting like that.*

Maybe Evelyn will know what guild Bryce and Cadwallader belong to. Could there be more than just the two guilds that Alex mentioned? I'm missing something vital, but what?

Saving…

Chapter 10

Alex pounded on Riley's office door. *I can't believe he didn't tell me first. How could he? I thought we were friends.* When there was no immediate response, he imagined himself as an invading army, beginning to rain blows upon the gates of the city.

The gates flew open. A bear of a man stood in the opening, scowling out at him.

"*What!?*"

The army advanced into the city, marching past it's defender at the door and seeking something to destroy.

After two circuits of the room, the invading army ground to a halt by Riley's desk. Alex turned and fired, his voice like a cannon.

"You! Don't! Trust! Me!" he blasted out.

The impact of his words rocked Riley. "Huh? What brought this on? I'm confused."

"It's been over a week!" Alex spit out. "You said 'I'll tell you everything when I get it sorted out.' What part of 'not much longer' equals a week?"

"Um, I'm just now putting everything into a cohesive narrative."

"Just now? You seem to have had plenty of time to tell *that woman!*"

Alex watched several emotions play across Riley's face.

In an unnervingly quiet voice, Riley said, "So you took it upon yourself to hack into my personal notes?"

Alex felt himself teetering on the edge of a vast gulf. *Whatever I say next could drastically change my relationship with Riley. I don't want to lose him as a friend. Why couldn't he have just told me instead of that Sloan woman. He forced me to hack his computer to find out.*

"What other choice did I have? You weren't talking to me. I've barely heard from you lately. It's like you've cut me off or something. All because of this Xeres thing? How did you think I'd react, anyway? Try to have you committed? Hell, man, it was *my* regression that gave you the information. *I'd* be the one that would be committed, not you."

Riley sat down in his interview chair, gesturing Alex toward the couch.

Riley placed his head in his hands. Looking up, he nodded. "I can see your point. But couldn't you have just called me on it? Instead of invading my—"

"I emailed you. Didn't you see it?"

Riley lowered his eyes, looking anywhere but at Alex. "I've been so busy, I haven't really checked my personal email account. Hell, I've barely checked my work email."

"Sheesh, Doc, get with the times," Alex said with exasperation. "Nobody just calls anyone anymore. And I knew how much you hate texting, so I didn't even consider doing that."

"So you hacked my files. Just like that."

Alex smiled craftily. "It wasn't that hard, Riley. You really need to come up with a stronger password if you don't want everyone reading your stuff. Heck, I bet even Tessa could hack your password."

Riley slammed his fist on the arm of the chair.

"That still doesn't make what you did right, dammit."

"I was desperate. Okay?" Alex shrugged his shoulders, trying for a smile, hoping it would disarm his friend.

Riley shook his head. "I sort of understand. You were worried and I wasn't available, so naturally, you felt your only recourse was to hack into my personal files. Knowing you, that logic kind of makes sense. Make no mistake," Riley said, shaking his finger at Alex, "it was wrong, but I understand you well enough to get why you did it."

"I knew it was wrong at the time, I was just so worried. You always share your theories with me, so it freaked me out that you didn't this time. What could be so horrible, in my own regression no less, to make you not trust me?"

"Okay, you've got a point." He pulled a hand down his face, then looked up at Alex. "I'll give you a pass on this one. Just ask me face to face next time you're worried, huh?"

Alex knew he was grinning like a school boy. The relief he felt was akin to what he'd experienced after Riley had turned down his advances at the convention. They were still friends, no matter what.

"So," Riley began. "What do you think now that you know everything? Past lives, an alien planet, warring guilds? At least we found an explanation for why you feel so enraged by Evelyn."

"There's a lot to take in," Alex said truthfully. "I mean, it's kind of cool, but it's also scary. It's one thing to say 'I believe in aliens,' but it's a whole different matter to hear my own voice saying I *am* an alien."

Riley laughed outright. "Now you know why I didn't want to come to you with this right away. How do you tell someone that they've admitted to being an alien? 'Excuse me, did you know that while under hypnosis you confessed to being a little green man?' You'd have thought I'd lost my marbles."

Alex nodded. "Point taken."

"That's why I needed to talk to someone else first, and since Evelyn is a fellow therapist and you said she was from Xeres too, I thought she would be a good person to talk it over with. It's easier to tell a stranger something than it is your best friend."

Alex caught his breath. *Best friend?? Riley thinks of me as his best friend, not just his intern anymore?*

Alex was so deep in his own thoughts, he missed the next thing Riley said. Surfacing, he heard Riley say, "I know you don't like her, but her office is so much nicer than this one, and the price is comparable, so I couldn't pass it up. That's why I'm moving my practice into her building."

"Wait, *whatttt!?*"

"I thought you knew that already. It was in my notes. That's part of why you were so upset, wasn't it?" Riley covered his face with his hands for a moment. "Oh, crap. I've been so busy I haven't put it in there yet." Riley spread his fingers, looking out through the hands still covering his face. "Dunce!"

"Who, me? What did I do?" asked Alex.

"No, me," Riley replied irritably, dropping his hands. "I planned to tell you I was moving, but not like that."

Alex glared at Riley. "Another thing I'm out of the loop on, eh, Doc?"

Riley sucked in his lip. "Not exactly out of the loop. I haven't told anyone else yet, not even Tessa. I wanted to make sure I could get out of my lease here before I said anything. I just found out this morning that the landlord will let me go without a penalty. Says he's got another renter ready to move in."

"B. . .but. . .you're moving into HER building? I can't stand to even be in the same room with that woman. How am I going to continue working with you if you're there?"

"You won't have to interact with her on a regular basis. You won't even see her much. Mostly, you'll be dealing with her receptionist, well, our receptionist, Maeve. You probably met her, when you picked up Evelyn's excerpts." He grinned and rubbed the back of his head. "From what I've seen of her, you'd better like her. She's the kind of motherly person that doesn't take no for an answer."

Alex remembered Maeve. *She seemed like a nice older lady. And at least I won't have to interact with Evelyn. I can't resolve the difference between how well we got along at the convention with how I feel about her now. It's like night and day. Even knowing that the feelings I have toward her are from a past life, I can't get beyond them. Logically, I know that this is still the woman that I enjoyed talking with at the convention, but every instinct I have now screams* 'Get away from her! This woman is your enemy.'

Alex let out a sigh. "Okay, Doc. We'll do it your way and see what happens."

"I think it's time I came clean with Tessa, too." Riley grimaced. "It doesn't feel right, having her be the only one still in the dark about all of this." Riley sucked in his lips. "That's a discussion I am *definitely* not looking forward to."

* * *

Riley glanced up from his chair when Tessa walked in.

"How's Meg feeling today?"

Tessa sat down on the sofa, the small boa constrictor weaving through the hands and up one arm.

"Not as lethargic as she's been the past week. Maybe she's just missing being out with people."

Riley moved to the sofa, reaching a hand out to the cream and russet snake. Meg flicked her tongue at him a few times, identifying him as a friend, then extended herself to wrap around his arm.

His girlfriend laughed with pleasure. "You're really coming along, Doc. The first time I introduced you to Calvin, you teleported to the other side of the room!"

"That was before I knew what snakes were like. Calvin is just a puppy dog in scales. Megan here? She's a real lady." By now, the boa had wrapped herself around Riley's neck and was drooping across his chest, all four feet of her. He stroked her scales with one finger, enjoying the smooth and silky feel of her.

His finger traced a bulge in Meg's silhouette. "I see she's eating again."

Tessa leaned over, running her hand down the snake's body. "Finally. She took the mouse yesterday."

Riley inhaled, then sighed it out. *I'd better get it out of the way. Gods know, I've rehearsed it enough.*

"Tessa, I need to tell you.... Well, let me play you part of one of your regressions."

"Really?" she said, raising her eyebrows. "I finally get to hear what I've been saying to you that has you so spooked?"

He raised an eyebrow. "Spooked? You think I've been spooked?"

"You have," she said, nodding. "I'd catch you looking at me like I was some kind of alien you couldn't classify yet."

Riley chuckled to himself. *If you only knew....* "Sorry about that. This whole thing has me going around in circles. Here. Listen. I'll answer all your questions after that."

Riley wrestled to get his mini-recorder out of his coat pocket. He grinned sheepishly at Tessa. "This would be much easier if Meg wasn't helping." Finally freeing the recorder from the combined grips of pocket and snake, he clicked it on, watching Tessa's face intently as it played out.

Alex: "Where are you, Tessa?"
Tessa: "Out in the meadow...

When the recording ended, Tessa sat unmoving for several minutes. Coming to herself, she reached out, gathering Meg to her. *Snake as security blanket,* Riley guessed. When she looked up at him again, there was something in her eyes he hadn't expected.

Anger.

"You kept this from me? All this time?" Her voice rose. "How could you?"

Riley stammered, "I...I...had to process it myself before I could tell you or Alex. Besides," he offered with a lopsided smile, "I was afraid you'd think I was crazy. There is so much more to this story. It only started with you." He rushed to explain. "When I was at the convention, I found other hypnotherapists with similar cases. And that part where Alex and you talk about the tiglas? Well, when I regressed Alex, he remembered even more of that world. It's called Xeres, by the way."

He stopped to take a breath.

Tessa stared at him for a moment, then stood up.

"I'm going to put Meg back in her terrarium. I'm afraid she's getting cold. And I think some peppermint tea is in order."

Turning her back on Riley, she went down the hall.

Oh, crap. What have I done? She only puts on peppermint tea when she needs to relax. Great. She's pissed at me. I don't know how else I could have told her, though. His hand went to the back of his neck and began massaging the stiff muscles there.

He was up pacing the room when Tessa returned.

She set the tray on the coffee table, then took the chair with the crocheted afghan on the back. After pouring the tea, she handed one to Riley. He took the proffered mug and perched on the corner of the sofa.

"Riley, relax," she said with a tiny lift of one corner of her lips. "I'm not going to have you committed." The smile came fully into existence. "Yet."

Breathing a sigh of relief, Riley sat back on the couch, sipping the hot tea. Some of the knots in his stomach began to unravel.

"The tea was a good idea, Tessa." He ran a hand over his face. "This whole thing is so far outside the realm of reality, it's almost like I'm living on a holodeck."

That earned him a genuine laugh.

"You're right! We haven't gone so far as to step into the Twilight Zone, just into Star Trek."

As long as she can laugh about this, he thought, *I'm safe.*

Plunging in, Riley asked, "Now, do you want to hear about Xeres or about the people who are from there, besides you and Alex?"

"I want to hear it all, Doc. Every little detail."

"Then we're gonna need some snacks."

* * *

Dipping a chocolate chip cookie into her bowl of ice cream, Tessa exclaimed, "There's magic too? Cool! I've always wanted to live in a world that had magic." She gave him a pouty look. "But why do I have to be from the science guild? I can't believe Diana and Bryce are part of it too."

"Well, according to Alex, Diana is from your guild. Bryce we don't know for sure yet."

She sat up straight on the sofa, dropping her folded legs to the hardwood floor and pulling out of Riley's arms. The blue and tan afghan fell away from her shoulders, sending an empty chips bag flying.

"What?" Riley asked, alarmed.

She turned toward him. "Remember I told you how Diana and I were going to that spa while you were away? We were really relaxed after our massages when we started talking about Bryce." She pursed her lips and wrinkled her nose. "The man's a real jerk. So controlling. And I think she's afraid of him."

Riley tensed. "Do you think he's hurting her?"

That's always been a hot button with him, she thought. *Ever since his best friend Paula was beat up by her drunk boyfriend when they were in high school. Riley broke his hand with a hockey stick, telling him to never raise his hand to a woman again.* She shivered. *I remember the venom in his voice when he told me what happened. Thankfully, his therapist training taught him better ways to deal with his anger.*

"No," she said slowly. "At least not physically. Yet." She screwed up her face and shrugged her shoulders. "Anyway, she told me they'd been friends since middle school. In high school, she told him about a dream she'd had, a place full of pink clouds and orange trees and blue leaves. Even told him about a jorgat she had that her brother's tigla ate." Tessa raised an eyebrow at him. "Do you know what a jorgat is?"

Riley shivered as something icy streaked up his spine. "Some kind of bird, I think. She must have been in a light trance from the massage. What else did she say?"

"Let me think." She tapped a finger on her lips. "A science project?" She brightened. "Oh, I remember. It was a leaf collection for school. Said her father was proud of the award she got, not proud of her. She sounded so hurt, poor thing. When I interrupted her to ask a question, she didn't remember anything she'd said to me. And she mentioned she's been having dreams of that place again lately." She jerked back in surprise. "Just like I have. What do you think it means?"

"I don't know exactly. It seems everyone who's dreaming of Xeres reports the same thing. They remember dreaming about it as children but then forgot all about it until the dreams resurfaced recently. It's as though the memories were locked away but something happened to let them out. Maybe…."

Tessa watched Riley, almost able to see the gears in his mind turning as he sorted through these new ideas. *Doc Mezmer always comes up with the answers, doesn't he?*

Riley shrugged. "My best guess is that hypnotherapy is becoming more mainstream now. After all, that's why I took the course in the first place. I wanted to add another tool to my regular therapy practice."

Tessa interrupted. "So since more people are having past life regressions, more people are discovering…what, a connection? To this world…Series? That's a really odd name for a planet."

"No," Riley protested. "Not like the World Series. With an X but pronounced like a Z."

"Xeres. Okay. But that still doesn't tell me why so many people would have dreams of the same place, a place that's not even here on Earth."

"I don't know yet." To Tessa, he was beginning to sound grumpy. "This all came from past life regressions, so I have to assume that they, and you, believe you are remembering a life on another planet." He sagged, like a huge weight had landed across his shoulders. "How that could be, I haven't a clue."

Taking pity on him, she leaned over and kissed him on the tip of the nose. When he blinked at her in surprise, she said, "I know you'll figure it out, Doc. Alex and I will help. And that other hypnotherapist. What's her name?"

"Evelyn. And if Alex's reaction is any indication, you'll probably take an instant dislike to her. Alex and I really hit it off with her at the conference. Her son Kier, too. But after Alex had his regression, he couldn't stand to be in the same room with her."

Tessa tilted her head. "I hope that won't be a problem. But she's involved in this, so she'll help too. Especially now that you're moving into her building."

She started gathering up the debris from their tea and snacks. Tray in hand, she turned to Riley and smiled wickedly.

Riley's eyes widened. "What? You're planning something. I can tell."

"When do I get to see your new office space? I need to see it before I decide on the furniture for it."

"Wait. Before *you* decide on the furniture?" He narrowed his eyes at her.

She turned, heading into the kitchen. Over her shoulder she called, "Well, you didn't think I was going to leave that in your hands, did you?"

Chapter 11

"You didn't tell me it was so nice," Tessa said, spinning in the middle of the empty room, taking in the whole space. "It's bigger and brighter, for one thing. I'll have to find a lot more plants for you to kill."

"Nope. No more plant killing for me. Maeve, our receptionist, takes care of all the plants."

"Really? I've got to meet her then. Find out what works best here, before I go looking for plants."

"You will. We'll talk to her as soon as you're done ogling my new office." Riley smiled. *It's good to see Tessa in such an upbeat mood, and about my new office, too. I was a little worried about making the deal for it without talking to her first.*

"Any preferences for furniture? The stuff that came with your old office was definitely sub-par."

"Well, I would like a desk with drawers this time. I was forever having to dig pens out of my briefcase. The desk monstrosity in the old office may have been modern, but it just wasn't for me."

"Drawers, got it," she said, moving to measure the walls and windows.

After several minutes, Riley asked, "Had enough fussing over my new space?"

"Let me finish my notes first," she said, typing measurements into her tablet computer. It didn't matter where Riley took her, she'd see something interesting and worth noting for later: an architectural detail, a font on a handbill, the way the light looked on a puddle of water. She was forever making notes or taking pictures of things.

A few minutes later, they entered the waiting room. Maeve was on the phone. She waved them in and held up a finger, then returned to her conversation.

"I'll be ready at five like usual, hon," she said. "Yes, yes, I'm looking forward to the weekend…. Are you kidding? Two days of biking and wine tasting in Napa Valley is my idea of a great weekend…. Listen, Corky, I gotta go. Our new tenant is here with his wife—" Riley and Tessa both began waving their hands at her. "Um, girlfriend, then," she amended. "Anyway, talk to you later, okay, hon?" She was smiling broadly at the person on the other end of the phone. "Love you, too," she said, hanging up.

"That was my significant other, Corky," she explained. "He doesn't like being called my boyfriend, says he too old for that."

"That's okay. Tessa and I don't feel marriage is necessary at this point in our lives. So, Corky…?" He left the question hanging.

"Oh, he drives for BART, when he isn't lusting after a full-sized locomotive. He's batty over all things railroad." She laughed. Pointing at Tessa, she rolled her eyes. "You know how men are, they refuse to grow up. You gotta love them."

She offered Tessa her hand. "Hi, I'm Maeve O'Malley, receptionist, stock clerk, gardener, and all-around handywoman around here."

Smiling, Tessa shook the woman's hand. "I'm Tessa Connors. I think we'll get along just fine, Maeve. So, you take care of all the plants?"

Maeve rolled her eyes. "I had to do it. Couldn't watch another beautiful plant die at the hands of folks that should know better."

Tessa laughed lightly. "Oh, so you've met Riley?"

"He's just the newest one, honey." Maeve arched an elegant white eyebrow at Riley. "Kill plants, do you?"

"Oh, yes, he does. And I'm tired of continually trying to find a hardier plant that he won't end up killing."

Maeve laughed. "I know. I had the same problem with Evelyn. I swear, that woman has a black thumb." She waved a hand at her inadvertent double entendre. "Sorry about that. Anyway, now I take care of everyone's plants."

"Did I hear voices?" Evelyn came out of her office. "Ah, Riley. And this is…?"

"Evelyn Sloan, I'd like you to meet Tessa Connors."

Tessa hesitated, then held out her hand. "Pleased to meet you. I've been hearing a lot about you lately."

Evelyn barked a laugh. "At least some of it good, I hope."

"Actually, all of it."

"Shall we go into my office and sit down?" She bent down and ran a finger around the inside of a stylishly high heel. "These shoes are killing me." She made a face. "I don't know what I was thinking, wearing new shoes to work today."

Riley and Tessa followed her through the doors.

"Oh, I love this color scheme," Tessa said. "It's close to the one I was thinking about for Riley's office." She wandered around, pausing here and there to admire one of the many different plants. "Still, maybe this is too feminine for his space. Maybe...."

Riley laughed. "Watch out, Evelyn, she'll have you redecorated too if you're not careful."

"No," Tessa said, ignoring Riley's comment. "For your space, I'll add red and black accents. Much more masculine, but still great with the cream and white."

"Oh, that'll be nice," Evelyn said, taking her interview chair, and motioning them to the client's sofa.

"What do you think of...." And they were off, talking decorating and materials.

Riley watched them chatting animatedly. In his head, questions and observations bounced around like ping pong balls. *According to Alex, Tessa's in the same guild as he is. Bylantian, I think? I'm sure that's what Alex called them. But when she met Evelyn, she didn't even blink. She should have been put off by her, at least. But that didn't happen. There they are, chatting like old friends. Evelyn is definitely from the other guild, the Klymurians. What does that make Tessa?*

"Riley? Earth to Riley."

Breaking out of his thoughts, he was startled to find the two women standing over him staring. *What did I miss? Did they ask me something?* "Huh? What?"

The women burst out laughing.

"Are you in there?" Tessa reached over to knock on his skull.

"Have a nice trip, Riley?" Evelyn asked, raising one dark eyebrow. "How are things in the Twilight Zone? Did our conversation about decor put you to sleep?" Turning to Tessa she said, "Oh dear, we've hypnotized the poor boy. I wonder if I should charge him for that. I make good money hypnotizing people in this office." She raised both eyebrows. "Which comes in handy when Kier wants to take off for a science fiction convention. That boy sure can spend money when he gets in the dealers room. Though I have got to admit, for his age, he's good at saving up for special items."

"Kier's your son, right?" Tessa asked.

"Adopted son. I lost my husband a few years before I adopted Kier." Her smile was beatific. "Somehow, I think we were fated to be together."

Evelyn laid a hand on Riley's arm. "By the way, if you tell me what day you'll be moving in, I'll make myself scarce. That way, Alex won't have to keep looking over his shoulder, worried I'll ambush him when he least expects it. "

Riley shook his head. "He's got to get over this…whatever it is with you."

"I know, but let's cut him some slack while you get settled, shall we?"

"Thanks, Evelyn. That'll help." Riley rubbed his goatee. "He blew a gasket when I told him I was moving in here."

"Maybe you should plant a post-hypnotic suggestion that we're best friends," Evelyn said.

They all laughed.

* * *

"This feels flat weird," Evelyn said as she reclined on her own therapy couch.

"No complaints from the peanut gallery," Riley admonished. "It was your idea to work in your office and not mine."

"It was either my comfortable salon or your rinky-dink office." She shuddered dramatically.

Riley laughed. "You could have just waited till I moved in down the hall. After all, I couldn't just up and move without informing my clients. It'll only be two more weeks before my practice gets moved."

"Yeah, yeah, I know all that. It's just that this's the first time I've ever used my own couch this way. I didn't even test it out before I bought it." She twisted her shoulders and scrunched her neck trying to get comfortable. "Well, this's acceptable, I guess. At least for a smaller person like me. I'd hate to be a tall, wide-shouldered man, though." She glanced up at Riley, occupying the chair she usually sat in. "Remind me to get Maeve to order a wider, longer version, huh?"

Riley nodded. "You bet. Now, can we get down to business?"

"I suppose. Okay, Dr. MacPherson, lay it on me. Gimme your best technique."

Riley gestured, wiggling his fingers at Evelyn. Dropping his voice into a theatrical monotone, he chanted, "You're getting sleepy, verrrry sleepy—"

"Riley!" Evelyn said sharply, smacking her hand on the leather couch. "Be serious!"

He held both hands up in surrender. "Okay, okay, you win."

It took a bit longer than usual for Riley to put Evelyn under. *She's subconsciously resisting me,* he thought. *I suppose I would too, though the occasion's never come up.*

Regressing her backwards in stages, he finally got to the earliest memories she had of being a child.

"Who am I talking to?"

A small, young voice, said, "I'm Elippa."

"And where do you live, Elippa? What planet?"

"Planet? Where everyone else is, Xeres." She scoffed at his ignorance.

"Do you have any playmates, Elippa?"

"Only Sailie. She lives next door." Her voice brightened. "She has a tigla. And I have a one, too. Mulav. She's gray."

"I bet you and Sallie did everything together growing up."

"No," she said, her voice turning dark, "we didn't get the chance."

"What happened to Sailie?"

"She died."

Riley was taken aback. He tried to keep his voice gentle and even, but it was difficult. Now the voice was older than the small child with a cat named Mulav.

"Elippa, where are you now?"

"I've started school now. I'm supposed to be a big girl." Her voice was hard for a child. Her words portrayed a disillusioned person much older than one just starting school.

"Why are you supposed to be a big girl, Elippa?"

"I can't cry about Sailie. I'm not allowed to even mention her name."

"Why's that?"

"She's gone and I miss her so much." Riley could hear the edge of tears in her voice.

Riley thought a moment, trying to decide how to get the information he needed without further upsetting this hurt and bitter child.

"Elippa, it's all right to talk about her with me. I won't punish you for it. I'd like to hear about your friend. Will you tell me about her?"

Evelyn's face scrunched up, as if the child was trying to decide whether Riley was telling the truth or not.

"You sure it's okay?" she asked suspiciously.

"Yes, Elippa. It's okay."

Evelyn was quiet for a few moments, then breathed out a sigh, her whole body relaxing.

"Sailie was my age. Before we could start school, we had to take a test. It was a silly test. All about science and computers and weird stuff like that."

"What happened after the test?"

Evelyn was breathing in shallow gasps now. "They took Sailie away! Right after we were done with the test." Tears streamed down Evelyn's cheeks, soaking into the small pillow.

"It's okay, Elippa," Riley hastened to reassure the child. "You're fine. This happened a long time ago. You're looking at it from an adult's viewpoint now."

He watched as Evelyn squirmed on the couch. The tears dried up. Her face took on a harder look and her lips pursed tightly.

"It was a long time ago." The voice was now adult. Sharp, crisp, no-nonsense. And hard.

"Can you tell me why Sailie was taken away?" Riley hoped his question wouldn't upset this new adult as much as it had the child.

"Oh, I know exactly why. She didn't pass the test. Her answers indicated she had a proclivity for science. She was a hidden Bylantian." Now there was distaste in her voice.

"Bylantian?"

"You really are stupid, aren't you? She was one of those Bylantians. Like that misbegotten associate of yours, Alex."

"And that makes you…"

"I'm Klymurian, of course. Like your girlfriend Tessa and that boy. Kier." Her voice took on a boasting quality. "We are magicians. Unlike those filthy Bylantian scientists ."

I need to redirect her. Reliving the conflict between the guilds is stressing her out too much. He nodded to himself. *I know. Maybe* she *can place Cadwallader.*

"What about Matthew Cadwallader? What guild does he belong to?"

"Caddy?" She tilted her head a bit. "I really don't know. Isn't that odd? I know he's from Xeres, but…."

"Are there other…groups on Xeres?" he asked carefully.

"Well, there used to be." She frowned, like she was searching for a long lost memory. "The Tesham." She spat out the last word with such vehemence that Riley thought she must be even more disgusted with these people than with the Bylantians.

"What happened to them? Why aren't they around anymore?"

Her voice rose. "We killed them! Every last one of them! *That's* why they aren't around anymore. They're all *dead*!"

Riley drew in a breath and let it out slowly. *Another group? Tesham? This puzzle gets more complicated by the minute. Every time I think I have it figured out, a new piece appears.*

"Why did you kill them?" he asked carefully.

"Well, we had to protect ourselves, didn't we? The accursed Tesham started causing wars, after we'd had millennia of peace." She huffed with disdain. "They thought they were better than everyone else because they had mastered both science and magic, not just one or the other like normal people."

"So, let me get this straight. Some people are good at science, while others are good with magic, but these Tesham were good at both science and magic? Wouldn't that make them a resource for the common good?" Riley's head had started spinning.

Evelyn's voice rose, obviously furious. "They were, once. Before they turned on us and began causing trouble and starting wars. That's when we knew that they had to be eliminated for everyone's safety."

Riley knew he had to bring this session to a close. Not only did he have a lot of new information to process, but Evelyn was getting progressively more agitated.

"Evelyn, it's time for you to return to the present," he said, as calmly as he was able. "You will awaken feeling refreshed, like you've just had a nice nap, unburdened by the memories you've just experienced. You'll wake up in three…two…one."

Evelyn opened her eyes, yawned, and sat up from the couch. She pierced Riley with a look and said, "Okay, MacPherson, talk. What did I miss?"

Riley ran a hand down his face. "Ummm, this could take a while. How about we grab dinner and I'll tell you everything?"

* * *

Mezmer Notes - Update 42

I've been listening to the tapes of Evelyn's regression and I just heard something I couldn't believe. I don't know how I missed it before. Evelyn clearly states that Tessa belongs to her guild. What the hell? How can both Alex and Evelyn claim Tessa as part of their guild? How's that possible? So far, everything indicates that these two guilds despise each other and have a very visceral reaction to one another. I need to go over everything from scratch. I must have missed something.

Evelyn says her name was Elippa on Xeres. She told me that every child undergoes a test at a very young age. Apparently, the authorities are looking for science aptitude, and if they find a child who does, that child is summarily killed. That's barbaric! It takes some serious hatred to kill a child who hasn't done anything other than show a competency for something.

Evelyn mentioned that they'd once been a peaceful society for 'millennia,' until a third guild, the Tesham, upset the balance, causing fighting and provoking wars. Evidently this led the other guilds to completely wipe out these Tesham, who were supposedly masters of both science and magic.

Since neither Alex nor Evelyn could identify which faction Caddy was from, I wonder if he might be one of these Tesham. That could explain why neither of them can place him. But they both claim Tessa too. Maybe she's the Tesham. This doesn't make any sense. How can they both claim Tessa, but neither of them can figure out where Cadwallader belongs? Come to think about it, Alex said the same thing about Diana's husband Bryce.

So what do I know so far?
1. *Alex is a Bylantian, a guild of scientists.*
2. *Evelyn and her son Keir are Klymurians, a guild of magicians.*
3. *Evelyn said that there used to be a third guild, the Tesham, who mastered both magic and science.*

4.   *Evelyn reported that the Tesham were all killed off by the other guilds for inciting war.*

5.   *Evelyn said that all children are tested at a very young age to see if they have scientific aptitude. Any child who does is killed.*

6.   *There are at least three separate guilds on Xeres, the scientific Bylantians, the magical Klymurians, and the Tesham, who use science and magic.*

7.   *Both Alex and Evelyn claim Tessa is in their guild.*

8.   *Neither Alex nor Evelyn can tell which guild Cadwallader belongs to. Alex also said the same thing about Bryce.*

Why do both Alex and Evelyn think that Tessa is in their guild? The only way I'm going to figure that out is if I regress Tessa and ask her directly which guild she belongs to.

Why does that thought frighten me?

And why can't anyone identify Bryce and Cadwallader?

Maybe I should reach out to Cadwallader to see if he is going to be at the hypnotherapy conference next month. He might be willing to let me regress him. Knowing the man's ego, I could probably talk him into it if I tell him that it would be an honor to regress someone like him. Perhaps I'll tell him that one of my clients told me he was King Tut or Julius Caesar in a past life. Yeah, that might actually work.

Saving…

* * *

"Oh, you're here!" Maeve said as Alex, Riley, and Tessa pushed through the doors into the waiting room. "Your furniture arrived a few minutes ago. I gave the deliveryman the key. Hope you don't mind."

"Of course not," Riley said "Anything to get this whole moving process finished as quickly as possible."

Alex chimed in, "At least I don't have to lug a couch up two flights of stairs this time."

Tessa laughed. "As I remember it, the sofa almost did you in."

The younger man groaned. "No, not the sofa." He turned, including Maeve in his explanation. "I helped a bunch of Riley's friends move a scavenged couch into their apartment. It was Red Tom who almost did me in. Just as I got to the bottom of the second flight of stairs, he dropped it. Damned sofa slid back down the stairs and nearly smooshed me into the wall like a bug."

This time, everyone chuckled at the image he'd painted.

Riley recovered first. "Maeve, this is Alex Wilson. He started off my intern. Now he helps me with special projects. He'll be in and out at odd times. He has his own key."

Maeve stood and came around the desk. When Alex offered his hand, she looked down at it curiously, then up into his eyes, arching an eyebrow at him.

"You're family now, young man. I only shake hands with clients. We hug family." She invaded his space, catching the young man in an unequal hug. Her arms ended up around his waist and his, after a moment's startlement, carefully landed around her shoulders.

"Uh, thank you, Maeve. Pleased to meet you, too." He pulled away gently.

Riley grinned. *I bet being hugged by a small white-haired woman is not something he's used to. Most little old ladies probably pinch his cheeks.*

Tessa spoke up. "Come on, boys. I need to show those delivery men where to put the furniture. No way they'll get it right."

"Okay, okay," Riley said, raising his hands, "you don't have to get pushy. We're coming."

"Oh, Riley?"

"Yes, Maeve?"

"Evelyn wanted to say welcome to the family too. She won't be in today. Kier has something or other going on that she had to attend."

"Thanks, Maeve. Tell her thanks too if she calls, will you?"

Riley hastened down the hall to his new office, where he could already hear Tessa ordering the delivery men around like a drill sergeant.

The delivery men don't stand a chance.

Chapter 12

Tessa sat down at the small table, putting her over-priced coffee next to her laptop. Following Diana's gaze, she realized the woman was practically drooling over the hot Nordic barista.

"Ah, yes, that's right. Eric is behind the counter today."

Coming out of her daze, Diana blinked. "Huh?"

"Eric. Behind the counter," Tessa prompted.

In a dreamy voice, Diana replied, "He always draws cute things for me with the foam."

"He does? I never noticed."

"You never noticed? How could you not? He's the cutest guy working here."

"Maybe because we're here to work. On the Williams account? Ding ding. Ring a bell?"

Diana sat back with a laugh. "Yeah. But there's no harm in admiring the scenery, is there?"

Tessa sighed and nodded. *Good to know I can still count on Diana to notice all the yummy men around. I like to ogle occasionally too, but she's making it into an Olympic sport. Is she so unhappy with Bryce that she's looking for someone less...possessive. Someone she feels will treat her like an equal rather than as a piece of property?*

"Okay," Tessa said, pulling out of her thoughts, "back to work. Now, about these carpet swatches—"

Diana's phone began to vibrate, dancing it's way across the table. "Wait, wait." Catching her phone just before it fell off the table, Diana checked the caller ID and froze. "Oh, dear. It's Bryce." She stared at the pink thing in her hand, as though it would bite her.

Tessa eyed her partner. Usually Diana was so upbeat and full of energy. Lately she'd become dull and lifeless, like a beautiful corpse.

"Are you going to answer that?" she asked gently.

"Oh. Yes. I...." Tessa watched Diana come to a decision and punch the accept button. "Hello—" she began. What little color remained on her face evaporated. "I...I'm working with— Home? Now?"

Tessa watched her friend. Diana didn't say another word.

Ending the call, Diana began gathering up her things and closing her laptop. "I have to go now," she muttered without even glancing in Tessa's direction.

Diana grabbed her hoodie from the back of her chair and turned toward the door before Tessa could object.

"But...." Tessa protested. "Now?"

Diana turned a tear-stained face toward her partner. "I...I forgot to leave Bryce a note telling him where I was going. He's awfully mad. I don't know what he'll do if I don't come home right now."

I can't let her go now. Not alone, anyway.

Decision made, Tessa quickly closed her laptop and stuffed it in her bag. She stood up and hurried to join her friend. Putting a gentle hand on Diana's arm, Tessa said adamantly, "I'm going with you, Di."

Diana straightened, a look of horror on her face. "No, you can't —"

"Just watch me."

It didn't take long to reach the Lundee's condo. Diana dropped her access card twice before she managed to open the street entrance. Hurrying through the lobby, they took the elevator to the second floor. Diana darted down the hall to Number Four where she had to dig into her capacious handbag to find her key. Before she could find it, the door swung open, crashing into the wall behind it.

"It's about time you got here!"

Bryce Lundee stood framed in the doorway. To Tessa, he looked like some ancient warrior, angry with one of his lesser subjects.

Her partner actually cringed backward, stepping on Tessa's toes. *Poor Diana...OW!*

"I...I...came as soon—"

"Get in here! I came home from the office and the place was a wreck!"

Diana sidled by him and fled down the book-lined hall. That's when the man noticed Tessa.

"And what are *you* doing here? You're always taking up her time when she should be home. This is where she belongs."

Tessa was taken aback. *What the hell? This is not the same Bryce I've met before. Normally he's the life of the party. Well, the center of attention, at least. Now he's acting like a drill sergeant. Why haven't I seen this side of him before?*

"We were working on a project when you called. Diana seemed worried," Tessa said, carefully choosing the word in an attempt to divert the man's anger. "I came along to see if she needed any help."

"Well, she doesn't," he spat out, a nasty sneer marring his handsome face. "She's just shirking her duties. Leaving me in the lurch."

Tessa had had enough of this overbearing bastard. She advanced on him, forcing him to move aside or be stepped on.

"Diana?" she called.

She found her friend in the middle of a spotless living room. The woman was looking around frantically. From what Tessa could see, everything was clean and organized. Nothing was out of place.

Diana looked up at Tessa. "I don't know…."

"Are you blind, woman? Just look at those magazines!"

Both of them looked down at the glass coffee table. Yes, indeed. One of them was twisted, misaligned with the rest.

While Diana stooped to right the problem, Tessa wheeled around on Bryce.

"That? That's what was bugging you? A magazine? Seriously?"

"We have company coming over for dinner tonight. She needs to have everything ready before they get here," Bryce said a note of anger creeping back into his voice.

"When are they coming?" Tessa asked. "I can help Diana get everything ready."

"They'll be here at eight," the man growled.

"Eight? It's only one-thirty in the afternoon. What are you having, a seven-course meal? Made from scratch?"

"She was wasting her time playing designer with you." He threw the words at her like darts. His face darkened like an impending storm. *I guess he's not used to anyone talking back to him. Ha! Too bad for him. Irresistible force, meet immovable object,* she thought grimly.

Bryce strode over to Diana and grabbed her arm. Spinning her around, he shoved her toward the kitchen. Diana stumbled, catching herself on the marble counter.

Diana rubbed her upper arm, briefly flashing a series of bruises that Tessa hadn't noticed before.

Elbowing Bryce aside, Tessa rushed to her friend. Pulling up the sleeve of Diana's shirt, Tessa could see the mass of bruises that told all too well that what she'd just witnessed was not an isolated incident.

Tessa glared over her shoulder at Bryce, standing unconcerned behind them. "How long has this been going on?"

"What? She's clumsy and bruises easily. " The coldness in the man's tone infuriated Tessa even more than the actual violence.

Turning back to Diana, Tessa said, "Come on." She helped Diana to the couch.

"She needs to get in there and start dinner. My clients will be here before you know it."

Tessa turned to face the man, feeling herself go cold to her very core. "You should be comforting your wife, not making demands, Tessa half-shouted. "That's it, we're leaving!"

"What? No, she has work to do." Bryce's face shifted from anger to shock as his breath plumed in the suddenly frigid air.

"Not anymore," Tessa gritted out. Glancing at Diana, she saw equal measures of surprise, fear, and possibly, hope on the woman's face. "We're going to my house," she told her friend. "You can't stay here."

"Go? With you? But I have to—" Diana glanced around, waving her hands helplessly.

"You don't have to do anything, Diana. Come on." Wrapping an arm around her friend's shoulders, Tessa helped Diana up, then shepherded her toward the hall and the still-open door. Along the way, she grabbed Diana's purse and laptop, lying abandoned near the door.

Behind her, Bryce shouted, "Diana, come back here! You have work to do. And guests are coming! I'll look foolish if they arrive and nothing's ready! You can't—,"

Tessa closed the door on the man's ranting. In the sudden quiet of the hallway, she felt Diana's shoulders relax ever so slightly.

"It'll be all right, Diana," she said, patting the woman's arm "We'll go to my apartment. Bryce can take care of cleaning the house and making dinner himself."

That elicited a weak chuckle from Diana. "He's never had to do anything for himself. He's always had either me or his mother to take care of every little detail." She sniffed back some tears, trying to compose herself.

"Thank you, Tessa. You're a real lifesaver.

* * *

"You what!?" Cadwallader's baritone voice made Bryce cringe inside. He hated that about himself. *Why should I grovel to him anyway? It's not like I couldn't run the West Coast operations just as well as he does. And I have! Even after all the time we've known each other, he still treats me like an inferior. He's such a crass blowhard.*

"I lost her. She's gone."

"How could you let that happen? You know how important she is to our long term plan. She can lead us to others of her kind." Cadwallader went quiet for a moment. When he continued, he sounded exasperated. "What happened?"

"Um, well, it just got out of hand. Diana had been spending way too much time with that Tessa Connors person. When I encouraged Diana to work with her, I didn't know how well the two would get along. It's like Diana would rather spend time with her than with me!" He ran a hand through his short jet-black hair, leaving it in disordered spikes.

"You've met this Connors woman? Is she one of them, too?" the voice on the phone demanded.

"Um, I've only just met her," he lied smoothly. *Connors is my ace in the hole. You don't need to know about her just yet. And you really don't need to know that she's Klymurian. What else could she be, after magically dropping the temperature in here like that?* "I didn't get a chance to really look at her to see. Everything happened so fast."

"Tell me *exactly* what happened."

Bryce shrugged. "Nothing out of the ordinary. Diana left to work with Tessa and didn't leave me a note. When I got home, I was worried, so I called her cell. Asked her to come home, because we were expecting guests for dinner. When she got home, Tessa was with her. She started cleaning up the great room and stumbled into the counter. Tessa barged in and took Diana away before I could help her."

"Uh-huh. Just like that. You didn't do anything to exacerbate the situation?"

"No, of course not! It was all that woman's doing. She took Diana away from me."

"So where is Diana now?"

"I assume she's at Tessa's. What should I do?" Bryce was pacing the floor, from kitchen to landing and back to the kitchen. He'd already kicked aside a throw rug and an ottoman that had gotten in his way.

Bryce could hear Cadwallader sneering at him through the phone. "Well, you have to get her back again, don't you. Get her to come home of her own accord. Make her see things from your point of view, not this Tessa person's."

"But how? Tessa's put ideas in her head. She seems afraid of me now." Bryce sounded desperate, even to his own ears. He fought to control himself, trying to calm his roiling mind. *Great! As if I don't have enough problems, Cadwallader's going to think I'm weak if I can't do this one simple thing. Why is this bothering me so much? Why can't I just be happy she's gone? I've been saddled with her since high school.*

"Are you a dunce, Bryce? How does any man appeal to a woman?"

He's talking to me like I'm a child now. Bryce bit his lip in frustration.

"Do I have to spell it out for you? Make yourself presentable. Take her flowers. Candy even. Anything you think she might like. Apologize. Abjectly. Get down on your knees, if you have to. Court her. Lie to her. Anything to get her to come back to you." He paused for dramatic effect. "Get the woman back. Whatever it takes. Understood?"

"Yes, sir. I understand."

"Let me know when you've got her back under control. You wouldn't want me to report this failure to Mr. LeRoux, would you?"

Bryce shook his head, then realized he was on the phone and Cadwallader couldn't see him.

"No, sir! I'll make it happen, sir."

He heard the line go dead as he grabbed his keys and bolted for the door.

* * *

"Will you get the door?" Tessa called from the kitchen where she and Diana were ensconced, talking over a pot of chamomile tea and cookies, the chewy oatmeal ones Riley loved. He'd had his share last night, so he couldn't begrudge the plate that Diana and Tessa were sharing.

"Okay," Riley said over his shoulder as he opened the apartment door. Turning his head, he saw a smartly-dressed man, flowers in hand, waiting patiently to be acknowledged.

"Bryce. What are you doing here," he said coldly.

"Um, is my wife here? I'd like to see her, please."

Come to make amends, it appears. Riley thought grimly. *As well he should.* He'd come home from the office to find Diana crying in their bedroom. Tessa had pulled him aside to fill him in on the afternoon's events.

Riley's face hardened and his lips thinned. He had absolutely no respect for any man who'd abuse a woman. *Control your temper, MacPherson. Resist the urge to punch his lights out. Breathe!*

"Is she here?" He raised his voice, calling into their apartment. "Diana?"

By now, Riley could feel Tessa's presence behind him. Turning his head, he arched an eyebrow in silent query. She took a single breath, then shook her head. Her face told him everything he needed to know. She hated the man.

Turning back to Bryce, he said, "She is, but she's not ready to talk to you." *Right now, all I want to do is slam the door in his damn face. Hopefully, it'd break the man's nose, saving me the trouble.*

A thin voice spoke up from behind them. "Let him in."

Riley turned toward the voice, catching sight of Diana, puffy-eyed and red-faced, standing in the kitchen doorway.

"Diana? Please," the man pleaded. "I just want to apologize. What I did was wrong." He shook his head. "I was just stressed about the business dinner I was supposed to have tonight." He waved a hand. "I canceled it. You're more important to me than any client. Please, let me make things up to you?"

Stepping around Riley and Tessa, Bryce hurried across the living room. He stopped uncertainly a few feet from her, holding out the flowers.

"I bought these for you. I know you like lilies." The man waited, not saying another word.

Diana eyed him warily. As Riley watched, emotions flickered across her face, from timidity to hurt, fear to hope, determination to… what? Riley couldn't tell.

Tessa stepped around Bryce, taking up a position next to her friend. Diana, comforted by Tessa's presence, squared her shoulders and straightened.

"Well...." Diana began, raising her hand to take the flowers.

Tessa gently touched Diana's arm.

Diana looked down at Tessa's hand. Her expression changed, became harder. She cocked her head.

"Flowers? You think flowers will make up for what you did?"

Bryce's arm fell away, the flowers dangling forgotten. "I'd hoped you could forgive me." He put on a penitent expression, like a puppy caught wetting the carpet.

Riley, looming behind Bryce, was glad to see that Diana wasn't fooled. *Talking with Tessa must've helped her see the way Bryce manipulated her in the past. Right now, probably for the first time in their relationship, she has the upper hand. You go, girl!*

Riley felt like a spectator at a cage fight. *Is she strong enough to face him down? Or will she cave and let him win? From what Tessa's told me, that's her normal pattern. Come on, Diana, stand up to him.*

"I'm so, so sorry, Di. I never meant to hurt you. You know that. It was an accident. Nothing more. Please. You're the best thing that's ever happened to me. I love you."

Riley caught the hard look on Tessa's face. *She's not buying it and neither am I.*

Diana though was wavering.

"I love you too. But how can I trust you, Bryce?" Diana said.

Riley saw the man's shoulders relax. *Dammit, he's got her. Hook, line, and sinker.*

"Come home, darling," he cajoled "Let me cook you dinner and we can talk about us. I promise, things will be different now. I didn't realize how much I've taken you for granted. I want to be a better husband."

Diana smiled. "You? Cook dinner? Are you trying to kill me now?"

Tessa protested. "You can't believe him, Diana! He's—"

Diana cut her off. "What he's doing is trying to change. For me."

Tessa snorted, shaking her head. "Change? I seriously doubt it."

Her friend rounded on her. "What do you have against him, Tessa? He's my husband. He'll change. He loves me. You don't know him like I do. You'll see."

Tessa shook her head. "So now what? You go home with him?"

Diana was tearing up again. "You just saw him on a bad day. I need to be home with him so we can work through this."

Riley saw Tessa's shoulders droop. *She's conceding defeat.*

Tessa pulled Diana into a hug.

"If that's the way you want it, then go ahead. Just remember, I'm here for you."

Straightening, Tessa glared at Bryce. "And you, know this. If you hurt her again, there's no power on this Earth that will save you. I have friends, friends with large, sharp, pointy swords and they know how to use them."

Bryce paled.

Riley couldn't help but smile, thinking of all the the medieval faires they'd been to and the large, extremely-fit fighters that adored Tessa. She wasn't kidding about being able to have Bryce hurt. While part of him wanted to see just what those men could do to Bryce, that would mean Bryce had hurt Diana again, and that was the last thing he wanted.

Recovering his dignity, Bryce took Diana's arm. "Shall we go, darling?"

Diana nodded, letting him lead her to the door.

Tessa hurried up behind them. "Here, don't forget your hoodie."

Bryce turned and took the hoodie from her hand. As he did, their hands briefly touched. He blinked in surprise.

He looks like he just got a shock. It's been raining the last few days. The air's not dry enough for there to be static. What shocked him then?

Tessa looked up at Bryce. Riley saw an anger like he'd never seen before before on her face. *She's usually so cool-headed, but I swear, right now, she'd kill him herself. No need for friends with sharp swords.*

Wait a minute. He's supposedly from Xeres, but her reaction doesn't fit the facts. Alex said he hated Evelyn the first time he saw her after his regression, but this? This reaction seems way beyond that. Why? And is it because he's something else or because she is?

The door closed behind Bryce and Diana. Riley held out his arms and Tessa moved into his embrace.

After several moments, Tessa raised her face to his. "I couldn't stop her, Riley. She just doesn't want to see the truth about him. And Riley? I...I wanted to kill him." A look of keen distress crossed her face. "I literally wanted to kill him! I've never felt such hatred toward *anyone* in my entire life. Why?"

"I don't have an answer to that." Riley sighed, confusion fogging his thoughts. "It's just another piece of the puzzle we'll have to figure out."

Chapter 13

Alex scanned his laptop screen. *I never realized there was an entire subreddit devoted to reincarnation. Hunh. Some of these ideas are too far out even for me. Why did I let Riley talk me into doing this for him? It's mind-numbing. He's really going to owe me for this. I mean seriously, who writes these things?*

—Tesla, Energy and Reincarnation. *What do these even have to do with each other?*

—Immortality Notes. *Sure, you can just take notes on immortality. Write today for your free guide.*

—Belief in Reincarnation can solve all your current problems! *Because you've been a loser in every incarnation. Just accept that and your life will be so much easier.*

—JFK was the Reincarnation of Lincoln. *Well, duh! Who doesn't know that?*

—Can a soul be reincarnated into the soul of a living person? *Sounds like that New Age concept of Walk-Ins.*

—Reincarnation occurs backward in time. *Then, wouldn't we be dreaming of the future? Like, who wins the World Series next year?*

—My cat is the reincarnation of my lost dog. *So, what? The cat eats dog food and chases cars? Or does it hump your leg?*

Wow, there's even some threads on here from that pompous jerk Cadwallader.

—Reincarnation: Emotional First Aid
—Find Eternal Love With Your Past Life Soul Mate
—Were You King Tut or Cleopatra? Find Out Through Past Life Regression.

Trolling for sales. He's like a used car salesman who just doesn't quit.

OMG! A thread, no, lots of threads that sound like they're about Xeres!

—Anyone out there have memories of orange trees with blue leaves?
—I dreamed I had a pet called a Tigla.
—I had a past life regression and I remembered looking up at pink clouds.
—I recently started dreaming about a weird place where I could do magic. There were scientists who could do magic there too.
—I remember fighting in a war between people using magic and people using science. The landscape was covered in fallen trees, but they were orange, not brown.

Wait till Riley hears about this!

* * *

"Can I give you a hand with the dishes?" Alex asked, pushing his chair back from the tiny table in the kitchen.

Riley laughed. "You can not! She cooks, I clean. You seriously don't want it the other way around." He grabbed Alex's plate, added it to his own and Tessa's, then headed for the sink. "Besides, the dishwasher does most of the work anyway. You two head for the living room and get comfy. I'll be along in a minute."

Alex glanced at Tessa and shrugged. "Fine, be that way."

Riley and Tessa both laughed.

Who would have thought when I took Riley's hypnotherapy training course that I would be sitting here a year later, hanging out with him and Tessa all the time. I was just a starving student when they took me in. Riley even gave me a second job as his intern. I love the freedom of being a bike messenger, but it barely pays my bills. Now I've got enough money to live, great friends, and, he chuckled to himself, *all the cookies I can eat.*

The two were exchanging jokes when Riley joined them, sliding onto the sofa beside Tessa.

"So," Riley said. "What's on the agenda tonight?"

Alex, perching on one of the arm chairs, leaned forward, elbows on his knees.

"You wouldn't believe what I found online. I was digging through reddit last night when I discovered some posts that looked like there are

99

even more people out there having dreams and regressions that involve Xeres."

"Really?" Tessa said. "A lot of people?"

"Wait. Let me get your laptop and I'll show you." Alex hurried to their office, grabbed it, and returned before either could say a word. Opening the browser, he showed Riley and Tessa his saved search for all references tied to Xeres.

"Wow." Riley sat back, a dazed look in his eyes. "There are so many."

"And you've only seen the first page. There were seven pages when I was on last night." Alex checked Riley's screen. "And now it's up to nine pages."

"Nine pages!" Tessa said, leaning over Riley's shoulder. "That's fantastic. Let me see...."

"Don't expect all of them to be rational," Alex put in. "Some of the posters here are...um, flakes is a polite term. I mean, I'm a fan of crackpot conspiracy theories, but some of these people really go above and beyond."

"Ohhh, I see what you mean, Alex," Tessa said, then read aloud, "My cat comes from another planet." She tilted her head at Riley. "We already knew that cats come from outer space. Where has he been?"

Alex furrowed his brow. *What the hell are they talking about? Cats from outer space? They've been watching too many reruns of Thundercats.*

Riley laughed. "It was a joke from our D&D group in college that cats were alien information gatherers who reported to someone off-planet. It explained why cats were always watching us."

"You're right, it does." Alex laughed, "Hey, maybe we all came here in the UFO that crashed in Roswell in the 50's."

Riley and Tessa glared at Alex.

They both look like they want to slap me. My work here is done.

Suppressing a grin, he leaned over and clicked the next-page key several times. "And look here, Cadwallader's posting in these subreddits too."

The others bent toward the screen.

"Oh, my stars," Riley said. "That man is everywhere. Always promoting himself. He's like an infomercial salesman on steroids."

Tessa chuckled and nodded. "Yep, that's it exactly."

Infomercial? Hmm, Alex mused. *Not exactly, but I do know what would help us find more people who remember Xeres. Some place for people to share their memories and dreams.* Alex straightened quickly.

"That's what we need!"

Riley blinked. "Huh? An infomercial?"

"No, an online forum. For Xeres."

"On reddit?"

Alex rolled his eyes. *How did Riley manage before I came along. The man is absolutely clueless about what's out on the internet.*

"An online forum of our own, where people can talk about their memories of Xeres. We would be the moderators. Then we'd be able to interact with anyone posting to the forum."

A stunned silence followed. Alex looked at Tessa, then Riley. "What? I think it's a good idea."

Riley recovered first.

"It is. A fantastic idea. But how do we go about it? I haven't a clue." He turned to Tessa. "You?" She shook her head.

"Well, of course you don't!" Alex said. "But I do. I helped a friend set one up for his doggie daycare site. I'll register a domain and get it set up for you. What domain should we use?"

"How about xeres.com?" Tessa proposed.

"No," Alex said. "It needs to be something that anyone can remember if we want people to find it. Something broader than just the name of the planet. What if someone just remembers the tigla or just that the trees are orange colored?"

"I know! How about reincarnate.com?" Riley said.

Alex opened a new tab and surfed to a domain registry site. His fingers blurred across the keyboard as he entered Riley's suggestion into the site's search engine. "According to this, that name isn't available, but the .net version is. Want me to go ahead and grab that?"

Riley shivered. "Reincarnate.net? Yes, that will work. I actually like that better. It's like we are casting a net for all the people who have been reincarnated." Alex could hear the chuckle in his voice.

"Do you need help, Alex?" Tessa asked. "I have some time on my hands, since Diana and I are only working together online right now."

Riley turned to her. "Why's that? I thought you two enjoyed getting together."

"She and Bryce are 'trying to work things out' and we both agreed it would be easier if he wasn't upset that he doesn't know where we're meeting on any given day."

"Humph," Riley said. "Sounds to me like Bryce finally has his way. Diana stays at home, awaiting her lord and master's orders."

She shook her head and sighed. "Yeah, sounds like that to me too, but it's what Diana wants. For now, at least. I'm betting she gets tired of being his slave 24/7."

Alex could tell they were both getting upset, so he broke in. "If you've got the time, sure. I'd be glad to have some help. Especially on the design stuff."

Tessa smiled broadly. "Oh, you mean you'd like a high-priced consultant on your team for free?"

Alex shot her a sour look. "Hey, you offered. And sure. Having a high class designer like you on the team would be a plus." He chuckled. "And it would really set our website apart from all those amateur ones."

"Great! Then it's a deal. Bring your laptop over tomorrow afternoon and we'll get started."

"You got it. And then, once we get the forum up and running, I can post a link to it on the various subreddits where people are already talking about extra-planetary lives or reincarnation." Alex said. *This is going to be so cool. I have so many ideas already. And I get to work with Tessa. It'll be a good chance to brush up on my web design skills.*

"That's a great idea," Riley said.

Riley has no clue what we're talking about, but he's caught up in the excitement anyway. This could be huge. I just know we're going to find a lot more Xerians this way.

"And I can also post links on some of my other more, shall we say, esoteric sites to get the word out," he said, grinning.

Alex flipped Riley's laptop closed with one finger. "Now that we have that business taken care of, can we try out the board game I brought?"

"What's it called again?" Tessa asked.

"The Birds and the Bees."

* * *

"NO!" Thierry's voice was adamant.

"But if I can't afford to go the Las Vegas Hypnotherapy Conference, I'll lose my business. I depend on the sales from that conference to help me get through the rest of the year. If I don't go, it'll take me longer to pay you back the money you already loaned me."

The man was trying to sound reasonable, but Thierry heard the wheedling undertone. He sighed, leaning back in the lounge chair. *The heat here in Hong Kong feels good after the chill of Buenos Aires. Now if only I didn't have to deal with this incompetent fool.*

"What happened to the last loan I gave you?"

"I needed that just to restock my books and media. After the fire and water ruined everything, my workshop and conference appearances had me back-ordered for three months."

More excuses, Thierry thought.

"Why? Are you unable to support yourself with your sales and your practice?" Thierry didn't bother keeping the irritation out of his voice. *The man is supposed to be overseeing the whole North American West Coast, but he cannot even manage his money!*

"You don't understand. Besides all my normal expenses, I have to fly all over, consulting with our other operatives on the West Coast. Plus going to conferences. Airfare, membership, table space, room, meals. It all adds up. Airfare is expensive when you have to fly commercial planes. And I have to pay for my assistant, too, you know."

"Is your cellular phone broken?" he asked archly. "I handle hundreds of operatives around the world and I never need to actually see them in person." *Thankfully*, he thought. "And your conference expenses are part of your normal overhead, no?"

A dulcet voice pulled him away from his phone conversation. "My dear, must you do business right now? You are ignoring me."

Thierry turned to his lovely companion. *I invited her to Hong Kong for a vacation. I do not need this imbecile interrupting my seduction. Renata Abielle is one of the most powerful CEO's in all of Europe. Netting her will vastly increase my influence.*

He pressed the mute button. "I won't be a minute, darling." She sat back and pulled her wide-brimmed hat down. *I will remove that sulking pout from those lovely lips. With a lavish dinner and champagne. Perhaps even a dinner show.*

As soon as he got rid of Matthew Cadwallader.

Unmuting his phone, Thierry growled, "I don't want anymore of your excuses! Latham will send you the money. But, be warned. This is the *last* time I want to hear from you on this matter. Do you understand?"

His threat hung in the air for several seconds before Cadwallader answered. Thierry could hear the man's gulp and almost smell his fear over the phone.

"Yes, sir."

He hung up. Taking a moment to bring his mind back, Thierry turned to his companion and summoned up a smile. "Shall we take a dip in the pool? It would be a shame to waste such a beautiful day."

"As long as that person doesn't demand your attention again," she said haughtily.

Thierry gritted his teeth. "Do not worry, my dear. He shall not get much more of my attention before I have him removed.

"Permanently."

Chapter 14

Cadwallader stared at his phone for several moments before he slammed it down on his desk.

Just who does Thierry think he is anyway, treating me like that? It's not my fault that I'm in a financial bind. It was Danny's fault. Well, the fire's too, but that wasn't my fault either. The cost involved in printing my books and other media go up every time I order! Plus there's going to conferences, putting on workshops, hosting reviewer parties. It all adds up much too fast.

The whole world is conspiring against me, stealing every dollar I make. He pulled a hand down his face. *And the next conference is only a few weeks away.*

Cadwallader settled further into his leather wingback desk chair. For a few moments, he allowed himself to luxuriate in its embrace. *Nubuck leather. Mmmmmm. I love this chair. It may have cost a small fortune, but it fits me perfectly. And it was worth it. It made me look devilishly handsome in my author photo. That one picture has tripled my book and DVD sales.*

He pulled up the expense file for the conference. Looking at the potential cost, he made a decision and reached for his phone again.

When the call connected, he said, "Danny?"

"Ummm, Dr. Cadwallader? It's Denny, not Danny."

"What? Oh right. Denny." *Do you think I really care what your name is, you silly little man? Ugghh, why must I be surrounded by idiots.* "Anyway, how are you? Business good?"

"Why, yes. My sister and I opened a second office in a much more upscale part of town—" he began.

"Fine, fine," Cadwallader said, cutting him off. He sat forward in his expensive chair. "The national conference is coming up soon. It's in Las Vegas this year. I assume you already have it on your calendar?"

"Yes, I do, but with the new office, I'm too busy—"

Continuing on as if the man hadn't spoken, Cadwallader said, "Good, good. And you have your airline tickets and room reservation, right?"

"Sir, as I was trying to say, I'm too busy at the moment to go to the conference. Even if I wanted to, I couldn't go. I don't have airline tickets or a room reservation." The man whined out one last excuse. "I haven't even registered for the conference.

I've had to put up with his toady behavior for years. I graciously allowed him to assist me when he first showed up. Anything to get him to stop pestering me for my opinion on his dumb theories about using hypnotherapy in his dental practice. Dental hypnotherapy? Who does that? Just give the poor sap some painkillers and extract your fee from his wallet like every other dentist.

"What? You don't have them already? You do realize it's going to cost you more at this late date, don't you?"

The man sputtered out, "Cost *me*? I can't afford that right now. If you could pay for my—"

"Me pay for them? Not this time. Finances, you know."

Denny's voice on the other end of the line began to sound desperate.

"I understand that you lost a lot of money on the last conference, but it's not my fault. I have financial obligations too. I just opened a new office and—"

"Well, to tell the truth," Cadwallader cut in, "my financial ills *are* all your fault."

He waited while Denny sputtered incoherently.

"Maybe the fire wasn't entirely your fault, but there wouldn't have been as much damage if you had gotten the fire out before the sprinklers kicked in. Plus you *were* the one who destroyed my expensive display."

"I didn't—"

"Now, now. Because of our long association, I didn't pursue having you pay to replace my display. But is it too much to ask for you to pay your own way to the conference and assist me in recouping my losses?"

He heard man's long sigh through their connection. Cadwallader smiled to himself. *Got him!*

"I'll text you my itinerary. Be sure to get there early or I'll have to pay a porter to lug all those boxes around the airport and hotel."

Without another word, Cadwallader hung up.

* * *

Tessa poked her head around the door jam of Riley's office. "Are you done for the day? I was in the area and thought we could have dinner together."

Riley looked up from his desk. "Hey there. That's a good idea. Let me finish these notes. It'll only take a few moments."

"While you finish, I'm going to visit with Evelyn and Maeve."

"Okay." He waved, turning back to his notes.

She waved back at him, knowing his mind had already dismissed her. Within moments she was opening the door that led to the joint waiting room.

"Tessa! What a surprise!" Maeve rose and came around her desk to give Tessa a big hug. "Haven't seen you around here much since Riley moved in."

"Hi, Mrs. MacPherson," came a soft voice from the corner.

She glanced over and found a teenager sprawled on the floor in the kiddies' area, open textbooks and a laptop spread around him.

Smiling, she said, "You must be Kier. Pleased to finally meet you. And I'm not Mrs. MacPherson. My last name is Connors. Tessa Connors." Walking over to the boy, she asked, "What are you studying?"

"Math. It's always math." He sounded so put-upon, both Tessa and Maeve laughed.

"Well, I won't tell you it gets easier, 'cause it never did for me, but keep at it."

The boy rolled his eyes. "Like I have a choice."

"Tessa! Long time, no see." Evelyn appeared around her office door. "You just couldn't resist, could you? Now that you're done with Riley's office, you're going to redecorate our waiting room next, aren't you?"

She chuckled. "No, I'm just taking Riley to dinner."

"Oh?" Evelyn said. "Special occasion?"

"Nope. I was just in the neighborhood, collecting swatches and paint samples for my current project."

"Sounds fascinating. *Not.*"

Laughing, Tessa said, "No, not so much. I'm hoping Riley can perk me up. It's just too nice a day to go back to the apartment and cook."

107

"Hummm. Would mind if Kier and I tagged along? I haven't had any time to catch up with Riley lately."

Tessa nodded. "Yes, I'd like that. It'll give me the opportunity to get to know Kier, too."

The young man in question popped up off the floor. "Yay! Supper out!" He quickly gathered up his stuff and shoved it all into his backpack. "Can we get pizza?"

His hopeful puppy-dog look made them all laugh.

Evelyn said, "Him and pizza. I swear, he'd eat that every night, if I'd let him."

Kier corrected her. "No, only every other night. In between, we usually have Chinese take-out."

She turned to him and pointed a finger. "Don't you get cheeky with me, young man. Anyway, it all depends on what Tessa and Riley have planned, doesn't it?"

"Oh, we haven't thought that far ahead. Although I have to admit, it's been awhile since we had pizza that didn't ring the doorbell first."

"Pizza it is, then. Let me get my jacket and briefcase." Then Evelyn had a thought. "Maeve, would you like to join us or is this your evening to cook at Corky's place?"

"The cooking comes later," said Maeve. "First, we have a five-mile bicycling route. Can't miss our workouts, if we're going to cross the finish line of our marathon in a few weeks. Thanks for the invite, though."

Riley strode in and looked around curiously at the four.

Furrowing his brow, he asked, "Did somebody call a meeting and I missed the memo?"

Tessa hooked an arm through his. "No, we've all decided to go out for pizza."

"Pizza!" Kier echoed from the corner.

"Pizza, huh? You mean, one that doesn't come to the door?"

The others all laughed.

"Yes, dear, with a table and forks and desserts, too. That okay?"

"Yup. Hey, Kier, how's the math?"

The boy groaned. "No better. Maybe you could help me some more?" he said hopefully.

"Is tomorrow all right?" Riley asked. Kier nodded.

Putting his arm around Tessa's shoulders, Riley announced, "Let's get out of here then. I'm starving."

* * *

The aroma of pizzas hit Tessa long before they arrived at the white-framed doors.

"Man, am I hungry," Kier pronounced.

Evelyn waved a dismissive hand at the boy. "You're always ready to eat your way through a grocery store, never mind a restaurant."

He threw her a look. "But at least I always clean my plate. Can't forget those starving kids in Africa."

"For a fact, you do," she conceded. "Helps with the dishwashing, too."

Tessa glanced at Riley. They'd been discussing having kids for awhile now. Their current argument was about how big of a family to have, once they'd saved up enough for a house. Right now, every penny they didn't need to live on went straight to their savings account, the one labeled Home At Last.

Pushing through the door, Kier headed straight for the counter, reading the specials from the nearby chalkboard. "Can I get one all to myself?" Eyes pleading, he turned to look at his mother. He even gave out a fake whimper in a bid for sympathy.

Evelyn glared at her son. "Yes, yes. That's the only way the rest of us will get a piece to ourselves."

"YES!" Kier pumped the air and did a little dance step.

"I'm ready to order," said Evelyn. "You two?"

Glancing at Tessa, Riley asked, "Our usual?"

"Well, as long as we can get it deep dish. I'm tired of thin crusts. This'll be a real treat."

"That's my girl, the carb-ivore."

"Me? You're just as bad. Pasta, my cookies, cakes."

"What? Your baking is out of this world."

They all laughed at his inadvertent joke.

"Besides," he continued, "I have to do *something* to keep this bearish figure, don't I?"

Tessa mockingly hit him on the arm and turned back to the counter to place their order.

After paying the cashier, the group found two tiny unoccupied tables to pull together. Kier immediately dove into a game on his phone, to 'distract his hunger,' he said, until the pizza arrived.

"So," Riley began. "What's new with you, Evelyn?"

"I just got an email telling me that a panel I'm supposed to be on at the Las Vegas conference was canceled. The person who was presenting the information for the panel had a death in the family and isn't able to attend, so they asked if I wanted to put on a panel on a topic of my choice instead."

"Really? What topic did you choose?" Riley asked.

"I didn't. I don't have time to prepare a panel. The convention is only a couple of weeks away. Plus, I don't feel comfortable leaving Kier to deal with the table alone for longer than necessary."

"I can't go anyway, Mom," Kier said, pausing his game. "Remember? I have a science project due the Monday after the conference. Corky said he'd help me with it."

Evelyn sighed and sat back wearily. "That's great. I forgot about that. Yes, yes, I know it's on the calendar, but I didn't think to look at your school calendar when I planned the trip." She shook her head. "And I've already planned a bunch of sightseeing stuff on the way, too."

Riley sat up straight. "I have an idea."

Evelyn perked up a bit. "About what?"

"I'll contact the con and offer to host a panel."

"About what? How are you going to get people to be on the panel on such short notice?"

Riley was silent for a few moments. "What do you think of 'Orange Trees with Blue Leaves: shared past lives or mass delusion?' Has a nice ring to it, don't you think?"

Evelyn's eyebrows rose. "And where did that come from?"

"Well, in all the cases Alex and I have found so far, those two things keep showing up. This is a national conference. It's the perfect chance to gather information on other cases. Hopefully, we'll catch anyone who has run across them in their regressions. It'll give me a chance to network and get even more information for our research. It's perfect."

Pursing her lips, Evelyn nodded. "That's not a half-bad idea. It just might work. I'll send you their contact information."

"Great. Thanks." Riley was practically bouncing with energy. "And you'll be on the panel too, of course. You can represent the shared past life hypothesis and I'll convince Jake to make a case for mass delusions."

"You really think he'll agree to be on this panel?" Tessa asked. "From what you said, he doesn't want anything to do with the subject."

Riley shook his head. "I think he's the perfect person to argue against it being real. I know his style. He'll research the hell out of it and have some elegant psychological theories to present."

"Then I can shoot them down." Evelyn smiled. "I'm already looking forward to this." Her face fell. "But I can't do a conference alone, especially if I'm on a panel. I tried that once. I nearly killed myself trying to do everything." She placed a finger on her lips. "Maybe I could ask one of the other therapists in our office to go with me. I don't have an intern like you do to help out with details like that." She fixed Riley with a pointed stare. "And I don't think asking Alex to help me would be a good idea, not with the way he reacts to me right now."

"Yeah, after what happened on the stairs, I can't imagine what having him help you would look like."

"I could come along, help with the booth," Tessa offered.

Both Riley and Evelyn turned to stare at her.

"B...but," Riley stuttered, "you've never even been to a hypnotherapy conference with me."

Oh, ye of little faith, Tessa thought. "But I *have* gone to plenty of sci-fi cons. Besides, I've always wondered what really goes on at your hypnotherapy cons." She wiggled her eyebrows at him. "Wild parties and strippers, I'll bet."

"Not that I've ever seen," Evelyn said drily. "Maybe I just don't get invited to the good parties. But," she said, redirecting the conversation back to the subject at hand, "if you really want to come and help me, I'd be more than happy to pay for your membership and expenses."

Riley slumped in his chair, groaning. "I already had a double room reserved for me and Alex. I can't very well expect him to room with Evelyn. He'd jump out a window first," he said, making a face.

"It'll be okay," Evelyn said, waving him off. "Tessa can room with me. That way, you boys won't have to get up early to open the vendors room with us."

Riley nodded. "That would solve our problems." He cocked his head at Tessa. "You sure you want to do this? You know I'd rather have you stay with me, but...."

Tessa laughed. "I know. It'll be fine." She grabbed his arm, pulling him in for a hug. "You'll see."

Clapping her hands together, Evelyn crowed, "Oh, I am so looking forward to this. We'll have such a good time driving there. And I'll finally have an adult to talk to."

"Hey! I'm fun, too," Kier protested.

She patted the boy's arm. "Of course you are, dear. It's just a different kind of fun. Don't worry, I'll miss you, Kier. And I'll tell you all about the drive and the con when I get home."

Mollified, the boy gave her a little smile. "I'll be staying with Maeve, then?"

Evelyn pulled out her phone and punched a number. After chatting with Maeve for a few moments, she hung up.

"Yep, she's fine with you staying there. Says Corky will love butting in, I mean, helping on your project."

They all laughed.

"I need to meet this Corky person sometime," Riley said. "He sounds interesting."

Evelyn rolled her eyes. "You have no idea. He's currently an engineer for BART, but he's retired from the Marines."

"Really?" Tessa looked at Evelyn. "So's my dad. He's retired too. After my grandparents passed away a few years ago, he and my mom took over the family business. They run a huge bed and breakfast in Portland."

Kier brightened up. "We drove through there on the way home from the conference in Seattle. Mom and I love going to Powell's bookstore there."

Tessa laughed. "Wrong coast, kid. They are in Portland, Maine."

Kier's face fell. "Oh. I've never been there." Suddenly smiling, the boy rebounded from his momentary funk. "Mom, did you know Corky keeps a full model train set up under his bed. It's really neat. And he's teaching me to whittle."

Dryly, Evelyn said, "Which explains why I've been vacuuming up wood shavings from your bedroom carpet. After I find the floor, of course. I was worried you were gnawing on the furniture in there because there wasn't enough fiber in your diet."

"Aw, it's not that bad, Mom. I sometimes do the vacuuming myself now."

His mother nearly snorted her water. "Uh huh, right. That's why it's at the repair shop. I hear they're still trying to get your sweatshirt out of it."

Tessa laughed. *I really like these two. The only other person we see on a regular basis is Alex. Sometimes I think he just hangs around for my cookies. Well, and to nurture his crush on Riley, poor guy. We don't go out with friends much anymore. Maybe I'm just lonely. I haven't seen Diana for a couple of weeks.*

"So," Tessa said, shaking herself out of that depressing train of thought. "We're driving to Vegas?"

Evelyn shrugged. "Have to. Just too expensive to ship my display and all those heavy books. Besides, it's always a good opportunity to bond with this rascal while sightseeing. Gives us some together time without clients and other distractions."

"Alex and I already have our tickets to fly in," Riley said. "I suppose I could see if I could get a refund so we can all drive down together."

"Really? You'd do that for me?" Tessa knew she was smiling from ear to ear.

Evelyn coughed. "I hate to be a party pooper, but think about it for a minute. Alex and I in a car together. For ten hours."

Riley paled. "Oh, right. I hadn't considered that. Okay, I guess we'll stick with our original plan then."

"We'll still beat you there," Evelyn said. "I like to get there early to set up before Cad."

"Cad's going to be there too? I wonder if he fired his clerk after the last fiasco."

"Of course he's going to be there. You think he'd miss a chance to push his stuff on people? I swear, that man is so full of himself. That's why I always ask for the booth across from his." She got a wicked grin on her face. "I love baiting him. He gets that bright red face and I can almost see the steam coming out of his ears. He's such a pompous ass. And his clerk? Denny is a dentist in Denver. He can't fire him. The man works for Cad for free, if you can you believe it."

"For free? What's he get out of it?" Tessa asked.

"To hear him talk, he does it all to get Cad's approval and beneficence. The man adores Cad."

Riley sniffed. "He needs a good therapist, if you ask me."

The women laughed.

Their server appeared with their pizzas. Kier began inhaling his, while the other three leisurely ate their pizza and continued to make plans for the conference.

Tessa took a bite and closed her eyes, savoring the rich, intense flavors. "Mmmm! This is so much better than what we get delivered."

Riley nodded, taking a drink of his soda. He pointed a finger at Evelyn. "I've got this idea to ask Cadwallader if I could regress him. According to you and Alex, Cad's from Xeres but neither of you can place him in one of the guilds. I thought if I regressed him, I could speak to his Xerian self and just ask him directly."

"You? Regress Cadwallader?" Evelyn's laughter pealed out, causing other diners to look her way.

"When hell freezes over, maybe."

Chapter 15

"You made good time," Riley said, kissing Tessa on the cheek.

"And we had a blast doing it," she told him, wrapping her arms around his neck. *Gods, I missed him! I hate being separated this long.*

Evelyn added, "We would have beat you boys here if Tessa hadn't wanted to stop every five miles to take pictures. We had loads of fun though."

Tessa laughed, still holding on to Riley. "Going the scenic route was wonderful. We drove through both Yosemite and Death Valley. After we crossed the mountains, the sunset was spectacular. The desert was beautiful at night, but it was even more amazing when the sun came up." She wiggled in his arms. "Riley, we've got to plan a driving vacation sometime so you can see all those beautiful vistas." *And make love under the stars,* she thought wickedly.

"I think I'm jealous," Riley grumbled. "All I got to see were the insides of airplanes and terminals. Hey, maybe Tessa and I should drive your car home and send you and Alex home on the plane."

"Right," Evelyn said, "though it'd probably take the sky marshals to get him on a plane with me!"

"Drat," Riley said, making a face.

"We just got in and haven't even unloaded the minivan yet. I'll go find a bellhop to bring the boxes in," Tessa said, pulling out of his arms.

"No, I'll grab a luggage cart and have Alex help me empty the van."

Evelyn's eyebrows rose. "He'd be all right with that?"

"As long as you aren't around, sure. Why don't you go check in to the hotel? Alex and I can unload the van and leave your things here with Tessa."

115

"You need someone to show you where we parked. How about I go with you and lend a hand?" Tessa proposed.

"Makes sense," Evelyn said, looking around. "I see Cad isn't here yet either. Since I can't harass him, I might as well deal with our room."

Evelyn tossed her keys to Tessa and went off toward the front desk.

Riley and Tessa found Alex perusing the overstuffed display of brochures trumpeting all the things to do in Vegas. The brightly-colored rack made Riley think of an abstract painting.

Alex spotted Riley and Tessa approaching and waved one of the brochures at them. "Hey there, Tessa. Long time, no see."

Tessa laughed. *Silly boy, it's barely been thirty-six hours since all three of us were sitting in my living room eating Chinese take-out.*

"There's a show I'm crazy to see," Alex continued. "Penn and Teller. I've always wanted to see them live."

"I'll bet there are several shows Tessa and Evelyn would like to see, too, right?" Riley asked, turning to her. "Maybe Saturday or Sunday night? We could make it dinner and a show?"

Alex grimaced. "Um, not for me, if Evelyn's coming along. Anyway, I ran into a couple of my friends from the last hypno con. I might be able to convince them to go with me."

Tessa sighed inwardly. *I hope he gets over this thing with Evelyn soon. Riley's exhausted from running interference between them. Besides, I like both of them too much to see them at each other's throats.*

Outwardly, she said, "I think dinner and a show would be good." She gave Riley a pouty lip and a pretend sniff. "Especially since you never take me anyplace fancy back home."

"Stop that," Riley said, rolling his eyes at her. "All right, you two, *we* have to unload Evelyn's van now. Ready for a workout?"

Alex groaned. "I thought conferences were supposed to be a break from work."

"Apparently not, if you're a vendor," Riley said. "Let's go."

The three of them worked together to unload the van into the vendors room. *Alex is jittery and sweating, and not just because he's working hard. He's desperate to get out of here before Evelyn arrives.* Watching the two men head for the door, she was surprised when Evelyn came up behind her.

"Ready to put this place together?"

Tessa turned. "Wow, you just missed the boys. That was great timing."

"No, I've been down at one of the other booths, waiting for them to leave before I headed over. No need to stress Alex out this early in the conference."

Evelyn opened the first box and began hauling out various objects that Tessa could only guess at their function. Over the next half hour, Evelyn handed Tessa a multitude of things with less than clear instructions.

"No, no, no," Evelyn all but screamed for the third time. "That doesn't go there. It goes over here.

Tessa set the box of books back down on the floor. "Somehow I missed out that being Xerian gave me psychic powers. I can't read your mind, you know."

"Okay, okay," Evelyn laughed. "I keep forgetting you're not Kier." She sighed heavily. "That boy knows where everything goes and hands me things even before I ask for them."

Shortly thereafter, Evelyn pointed behind Tessa, asking, "Hand me that box marked 'Sale Items', would you? They go over here on the bottom shelf."

Tessa slid the last box toward Evelyn.

"I think this is everything," Evelyn said, pulling a stack of books out of the box.

"Thank goodness," Tessa said, standing up and leaning back with her hands on her lower back. "And you do this for every conference? No wonder you bring Kier along."

"Oh, you should have seen my make-do display before he was big enough to help. Nothing more than a draped table, book piles, and a little thingy to hold my business cards. I've come a long way, baby!"

Tessa smiled. "Indeed you have."

They were gathering up their belongings to head for their room when they heard a commotion by the door.

"Figures," Evelyn said in a snarky voice. "He never can enter a room without pomp and circumstance."

Tessa saw a man making a grand entrance. *That must be the Cadwallader guy Riley and Evelyn talk so much about.* She watched as the older man greeted the other vendors with a two-handed shake. *He looks for all the world like a politician who's on the campaign trail. 'Hi, how you doing? Here, take my card and don't forget to vote for me.'*

She watched as he turned into the empty space across the aisle, paying absolutely no attention to the pair of luggage carts following in his wake. Another man toddled along, pushing one overloaded cart bearing large cases while towing a second one piled high with boxes.

Tessa watched in horror as the man rolled over his own heel with the trailing cart and nearly fell down. Before she could move to see if he was all right, Cadwallader yelled at him to be careful and to hurry up. *I feel sorry for that poor man.*

The harried-looking man practically flew around the space and had the booth set up in a matter of minutes.

Evelyn eyed it appraisingly. "Hmmm, not as classy as the last one, if you ask me. And a lot more work to set up. Poor Denny."

"Denny? Is that his name?" Tessa asked. "How does he ever stand being around that man?"

"Oh, he has his reasons. Until now. I'm seeing cracks in his façade that weren't there the last time I saw him. I figure he might last till the end of the conference." Evelyn snickered. "Then again, maybe not."

"Last?"

"I don't think Denny will take Cad's guff much longer. Denny does all the work while Cad reaps all the glory. Even a slave can only take so much before rebelling, you know."

"Well, it looks like this should be a very interesting conference then," Tessa said. "I've always wanted to go to one of Riley's cons. I guess I picked the right one."

They both jumped at the loud crash from the far side of Cadwallader's booth.

"Just wait," Evelyn muttered. "Watch this."

With that, the woman sailed across the aisle.

* * *

He'd better not break this *display,* Cadwallader thought as he supervised every move his clerk made. He couldn't let himself relax until the last piece had been assembled.

Finally! I don't know why that took him so long. He's lazy, that's why. He pointed at the cart holding his merchandise and raised his voice.

"Bring that over here and start unloading it!"

Denny looked up at him, arms braced on his knees and sweat pouring from his brow. "I just need a second to catch my breath."

"The room opens for business in fifteen minutes, you can catch your breath later."

Denny took a deep breath, straightened up and lumbered over to the cart. Pulling it into the booth, he accidentally snagged the corner of a neighboring display, causing the cart to tip sideways and empty itself into the other vendor's booth with a loud crash.

Denny screamed, "Oh, shit! No, no, NO!"

The vendor rose from the box he'd been unloading and yelled, "You lummox! Look what you've done to my display!" Banners and pieces of plastic pipe littered his space. "You're going to pay for this!"

After one horrified moment, Cadwallader walked over to the man, speaking in the calmest voice he could muster. "Now, now, it was an accident, good sir. Let us help you reassemble your display."

He turned to Denny, hissing between his teeth, "Danny, get busy!"

Standing behind his clerk, Cadwallader directed the recovery process, much to the annoyance of the booth's owner toiling beside Denny.

"You know, you could actually help with this rather than standing around looking for your next PR opportunity," said the booth's owner.

Sneering, Cadwallader turned to the man, "I don't—"

"Another mishap, Caddy?"

Cadwallader looked over his shoulder to find his chief rival and major thorn in his side standing at his elbow.

"Butt out, Evil-lyn. Nobody pulled your chain."

"Listen, son," she said, aiming a manicured finger at him, "there isn't a chain made that can hold me. Though maybe you need one to hold your boxes together. That's the second time I've seen your merchandise go flying. Too bad it isn't flying off the shelf as sales. I just wish I'd been there when you tried to light them all on fire. I've heard of fire sales, but that was a new one on me."

One of these days, she's going to push me too far and I'll have to take care of her. For good, he thought. *I haven't had anyone annoy me this much since...Elippa.* He straightened. *No, it couldn't be. She didn't survive—*

The vendor on the floor interrupted his chain of thought. "She's got a point there."

Cadwallader rounded on the man. "Look, your measly booth is back in the same condition it was when my oh-so-helpful associate knocked it over, so shouldn't you go back to whatever you were doing? I'm sure you have plenty you still need to do in the hopes of recouping your table fee."

The man huffed at him. "Well, I never."

Cadwallader dismissed the man from consideration. Turning back to Evelyn, he moved into her personal space, trying to intimidate her with his height.

She laughed at him. "What? You think you can scare me? I'm short. I'm used to people towering over me." He saw her glance down at his feet.

"Black and white striped socks, Cad?"

He followed her gaze. Sure enough, his pant leg had ridden up when he righted the cart. *Damn that woman!* He shook his leg, covering the offending sock.

Assuming a high, clear voice, she said, "You have no power here! Begone, before somebody drops a house on you, too!" With a wave of her fingers, Evelyn turned and strode back to her booth.

Cadwallader stared after her, fury filling him with a white hot rage. His eyes followed her the whole way back to her booth.

Hmmm. Who's the sexy dark-haired Latina beauty in Evelyn's booth? Funny, he thought. *I've never seen anyone but that annoying son of hers helping her set up.* He squinted, uncertain of what he was seeing. *Damn! She's another Xerian. I must find out who she is!*

Wheeling around, he found Denny standing beside the two carts, hands on his hips, glaring. Before the man could say a word, Cadwallader ordered, "Hurry up and get this set up; we open for customers in a few minutes." With that pronouncement, Cadwallader turned and stalked out of the room.

* * *

The undercurrent of sound in the vendors room dropped off as more and more sellers left at the end of the day.

I don't feel like I did very much work today, but, man, am I exhausted. Helping Evelyn is fun, but these people are intense.

Evelyn left to get ready for the evening's dinner and entertainment leaving Tessa to neaten up the displays. After she finished, she stepped back to inspect her handiwork.

Okay, everything looks like it's back where it belongs.

Satisfied, Tessa pulled her purse from beneath the skirted table. "Hi, there."

The voice, surprisingly close, startled Tessa. Popping her head up above the table, she found Cad's clerk standing in front of her booth.

"Uh, hello," she said as she straightened.

"I'm Denny Talbot." He gestured across the aisle. "I work for Dr. Cadwallader there."

Having heard about and now seen the relationship between Denny and Cad, Tessa had to suppress a laugh. *Work for? More like slave for, if you ask me. Poor guy.* "I'm Tessa Connors." She stood and smoothed the table drapery back into place. "Pleased to meet you." She rubbed her neck, then slung the purse strap over her shoulder.

"Long day, huh?" Denny said.

"Oh, yes. This is my first time working with Dr. Sloan. Have you been with Dr. Cadwallader long?"

"Jeez, it seems like ten years, but it's only been two."

"Oh? Don't you like working for him?"

"Well, he doesn't pay me. I sorta volunteered to work with him for the first few shows. After that, he expected me at every conference. And expected me to pay for all of it myself, my room, my meals, my plane fare, everything. The only thing he's *ever* paid for is my conference membership." The portly man had a sour look on his face. "It's not that I don't have plenty of money, I'm a dentist by trade." The man thrust his hands into his pocket and rocked on his heels after that pronouncement. "I just don't like working for free."

Tessa tried to look impressed. "A dentist? How'd you get mixed up with Dr. Cadwallader then?"

Edging around the table, Tessa started walking toward the door. A uniformed security guard stood there, tapping his foot and giving the evil eye to the last stragglers who were preventing him from locking up for the night.

Denny fell into step beside her.

Great. Just what I need, a puppy. If he gets any closer, I'm going to have to smack his nose.

"I've always been interested in hypnotherapy," he continued, "so I'd read all his books. When I started thinking about using hypnosis in my practice, I asked him lots of questions online. When I found he was doing a conference in Denver where I live, I was so excited that I volunteered to help him." He sucked in his lower lip and sighed. "I thought he was so wonderful, you see, so I began flying to his other

121

conferences, just to be around him."

Tessa nodded sympathetically. "And he started to take you for granted, didn't he? I saw how he treated you this morning. I felt sorry for you."

Denny's face reddened slightly. "You did? *He's* certainly never noticed how I feel," He paused a moment before continuing "To be fair, he's probably just preoccupied because of his financial problems."

"Really? He looks so well off. That display of his must have have cost a small fortune."

"It's new." He looked down at his shoes, his face reddening further. "I kind of broke the old one at the last conference. It was my fault." He scowled. "Well, mine and some brat that was hanging around. And then there was the fire."

"A fire? In the vendors room?" Tessa asked in alarm.

"No, at the book signing party in his room. He'd gone all out. Open bar, snacks, little tables. Somehow the curtains caught fire and the sprinklers came on. All of his books were ruined and the hotel charged him for the damages to the suite."

"How awful! He must have been crushed."

"No, he took it all out on me. Like I was the one who plugged in all the lights everywhere or something. I was too busy working the door keeping out undesirables like...like...." He stuttered to a halt.

Tessa wrinkled her brow. "He shouldn't have blamed you for that."

"I know. When I accidently broke the display the next day, it made everything worse." He grimaced. "I think if he'd had a whip, he'd have beaten me on the spot. He really scared me."

"Oh, you poor thing."

"I didn't let it bother me. But there sure won't be a party here. He's so hard up for money that I even had to pay for my own membership this time." He lowered his voice conspiratorially. "Between how he treats me and having to pay my own way, I'll probably have to stop helping him. It's just not worth it."

They'd passed the impatient security guard when Denny placed a hand on Tessa's arm, stopping her in the nearly empty hallway.

"Would you like to have a drink with me? We've both put in a hard day and we deserve it. My treat."

He put on a smile eerily similar to the one which she'd noticed

Cadwallader kept pasted on his face whenever a potential buyer entered his sphere. Inside, Tessa shuddered. Outwardly, she kept her own smile in place.

"That's very nice of you, Denny, but I could really use a shower and change of clothes before I do anything else."

Denny tried one last proposition. "You could join me afterward. We could even go someplace other than the hotel for dinner."

Yup, he's a puppy. Desperate for any attention, and loyal to anyone who will give it to him. Even if it's bad attention from Cad.

"I appreciate the offer, I just don't think my boyfriend would be very happy with me if I accepted."

"I just thought it would be nice to have a drink together," he backpedaled. "I wasn't trying to ask you on a date."

She put her hand on his arm. "I know. And it was nice of you to offer. But I've already made dinner plans. I need to hurry or I'll be late."

Denny's face fell. "Well, I guess. Maybe another time?"

She put on a sweet smile. "Maybe." *Sit. Stay. Good boy.*

With a little wave, she turned and headed for her room.

Yikes, I really do need to hurry if I want to get cleaned up before Riley gets done with his panels. Tessa quickened her pace, stepping up to the elevator and stabbing the up button repeatedly. *I wish I knew what he has planned for dinner tonight. He said it was fancy and I should dress up, but he was infuriatingly vague.* She sighed. *I really wish we were sharing a room, because I may not know what I'm having for dinner, but I sure know what I'd like for dessert.*

* * *

Alex watched Riley and Tessa's kiss go on and on. *Get a room,* he thought. *Oh, I bet they are doing, trying to make up for* not *having a room together tonight.*

"Ahem." Alex said, clearing his throat. "I hate to break this up, but I would really like to go to bed sometime soon."

The two opened their eyes and sprang apart.

"Alex, I didn't see you standing there," said Tessa, blushing slightly.

Riley nervously adjusted his jacket. *The poor guy's trying to regain his composure. It's not working. It's fun watching him squirm though.*

"Uh, Alex. We were just…."

Alex chuckled. "I've dated one or twice before, I could see what you were just."

"Well, you'd better go, Tessa," Riley said. "You and Evelyn have to get up early to open the vendors room, while I get to sleep in."

Tessa groaned. "Really, early?"

"Yup. You have to be there before any of the panels start at eight."

"What? Why didn't she tell me that when she hired me?"

"A, she didn't hire you, you volunteered. And B, you know how early the vendors room opens."

"Yes, but I've never worked there. It never occurred to me…"

Alex laughed at the woebegone expression on Tessa's face. "That'll teach you to read the fine print before you agree to do something."

Tessa shoved his shoulder. "Oh, you!"

"I'm going to leave you lovebirds alone. I'll be in the room, Riley. By myself." Alex tossed them a wave, turned his back, and strode away.

Several minutes went by before Alex heard the door open and close.

"*Mars Attacks* again?" Riley tossed his key card on the bureau, followed by the contents of his pockets.

"Yeah, isn't it cool?" Alex took a drink of his soda. "Found it running through the channels. I can't help it, I've had a passion for everything Mars since I was a kid." He grabbed a handful of potato chips and stuffed them in his mouth.

As Riley shed his jacket and tie, he glanced at Alex. "I see you didn't waste any time getting undressed. Good to see you're comfortable around me finally. Nice legs, by the way."

Alex glanced down and felt his face go warm. *I can't believe I'm sitting here in my boxers! What was I thinking? Tessa just gave him a passionate goodnight kiss, then he walks in and sees me sitting here in my underwear. Is he intentionally flirting with me or just wound up? Could he be interested? He didn't exactly reject me at the last conference.*

Pulling himself up against the headboard, Alex replied, "I can put on a shirt and a pair of shorts if it bothers you."

"No, no, that's not necessary," Riley said hastily. "It's just…well, I haven't really roomed with a guy since college. After what happened the last time we shared a room, and your confession and all, I feel like I need to clear the air a bit."

Riley flopped down on his own bed, avoiding Alex's eyes. "I think you are very attractive. I've fooled around with guys before, and it can be fun, but I don't really consider myself bi. It's more situational than emotional. I love Tessa and don't want to do anything that would mess that up. I really like you...."

Sensing Riley's discomfort, Alex swung his legs around till he was sitting on the edge of the bed.

"I understand. If you weren't with Tessa, you might be interested in me. Trust me, I don't want to do anything that would affect our friendship or jeopardize your relationship with her. After all, I like Tessa too. She's become one of my best friends."

Riley cleared his throat. "Uh, speaking of Tessa, you'll never believe what she told me over dinner about Cadwallader."

"I don't know what she said, but I overheard two panelists talking about him. Apparently he's not having a room party this time. They joked about how they usually shower before a party, not during. They were a couple of lushes, though. They mostly mourned the absence of his open bar. I'll bet Cad would have had a few choice words for them if he'd heard that."

"Well, Tessa said Cad's clerk hit on her after the vendors room closed."

"What? He hit on Tessa? I mean, she is a very attractive woman, but still...Denny? She's way out of his league."

"I know, right? She tried to politely refuse his offer. But Denny... well, Denny needed to someone to talk to. Tessa, being Tessa, couldn't help but listen. Do you know Denny has to pay his own way to the conferences? For the privilege of 'helping' Cad? And Denny's about fed up. Said he might even quit working for Cad entirely."

Alex's eyebrows rose. He sat forward, asking, "Why would Cad need to have free help anyway? He must make a mint with all his promotional stuff and workshops, not to mention his own practice."

"Denny said he was in financial bind. The fire and his display getting broken at the last conference must have been a serious blow to his finances."

"Still, he has his practice and sales. Wow! He really must be living beyond his means to be that deep in the hole."

Riley nodded. "Evelyn told Tessa that this is the first conference in years that he hasn't had some kind of room party. And according to her, his new display looks cheap compared to his old one. Though I doubt you've seen it, since you avoided the vendors room all day." Riley huffed.

"I know Evelyn makes you uncomfortable, but since Tessa's helping out in her booth, I've been spending a lot of my time there."

Alex grimaced. "Yeah, I know." He shook his head. "I really have to do something about not being able to be in the same room as Evelyn." He worried the corner of his lip. "I'm trying to work on that."

"I could try hypnotizing you, see if that helps," Riley offered.

Alex shook his head. "No thanks. That's what got me into this whole mess in the first place. I'd rather work it out for myself."

Riley laughed. "Well, all that aside, how was your day?"

"Oh, the usual. Some panels were gold, some lead. I've been hanging out with a few friends I made at the last conference. I think we'll be skipping the conference dinner tomorrow. I've convinced them to go with me to see Penn and Teller."

"That's a great idea. Maybe I should take Tessa and Evelyn out to a show, too. After all, how often do we get to Vegas? Hmmm. Tessa's always wanted to see that adult themed Cirque du Soleil show."

"Zumanity?"

"Yeah, that's the one." He reached for his phone. "I'll call her—"

Alex reached out an arm. "That's probably not a good idea," he said dryly. "They'll be asleep by now. Tomorrow will be soon enough, right? And you really don't want to deal with a grumpy Tessa, now, do you?"

"Oh. You're right. It is getting late. I should probably get a shower before I head to bed." Standing up, Riley took off his shirt and headed toward the bathroom. Stopping just outside the bathroom door, he slid his pants and underwear off in one fluid motion, and grabbed his toiletry kit.

Alex gaped. *Wow, naked butt. Nice!* When Riley disappeared around the corner, Alex shook his head. *I can't believe he just did that. That's something I won't soon forget. I wonder, did he do that on purpose?*

Chapter 16

Alex took the next-to-the-last seat in the room, the one closest to the door. Around him, the audience was getting settled, talking among themselves about the panels they'd attended that day. He eavesdropped on the conversation in front of him.

"My last panel was *the* most boring to date. At least this one promises to be interesting. Remind again me why we come to these things?"

"It's a tax write off vacation. Well, for me anyway."

"Do you believe in this past life regression stuff?"

"Nope. But it's in the program as a debate. So it should be interesting to hear the pros and cons clearly laid out."

A tall man passed behind Alex, heading for the only remaining open seat. Glancing up, he saw it was Cadwallader. *Why's he here?? Scoping out the competition? Hmmm, maybe this weekend we'll finally find out which faction he belongs to, since nobody seems to know.* He mentally shrugged. *Does it really matter?*

His eyes ranged around the room. He spotted his friends from the night before off to the left, near the front. *Riley's been stressed out all morning thinking Jake's better prepared than he is. And there's Tessa. Right up front. Hope she can keep him calm.* Alex shook his head. *Who knows, that might work.*

Wait a second. He sat up straight, his mind whirling as disparate facts dropped into place. *Tessa's upfront? She's sitting within arms reach of Evelyn. How can she stand being that close to her? Come to think of it, she's spent the last several days with Evelyn. She drove down here and is sharing a room with her. That's not possible. Evelyn's Klymurian, but Tessa's Bylantian like me. Isn't she?* Doubt filled his mind.

It just doesn't make sense. No matter how I twist the facts, Evelyn and Tessa shouldn't be able to bear being that near to each other, let alone as close as the two had been all weekend. Why didn't I notice that earlier?

He sighed. *Maybe Tessa just has a better handle on her emotions. If that's the case, maybe I can learn to control my reaction to Evelyn too. Definitely something to think about.*

Up on stage, Riley introduced himself and the other panelists. Evelyn went first, presenting the case *for* extra-terrestrial past life regressions, citing both her own cases and those of other hypnotherapists.

Riley then turned to Jake, who'd been shaking his head and muttering all through Evelyn's presentation.

"My turn," Jake said, leaning forward with a fierce grin. "First off, you're whole argument hinges on the belief that there *is* life on other planets, and that for some unexplained reason they decided to migrate here of all places. What, was Mars too cold? Or was Venus...."

Alex tuned him out after that. *It doesn't matter what Jake says, I know Xeres is real. I feel it in my bones.*

The person sitting next to Alex stood and pushed past him. Realizing he'd been daydreaming, Alex tuned back in just as the panel began wrapping up.

"Yes, you in the middle," Riley said, pointing to a man in a blue coat.

"What was the address again for the web forum you've set up to discuss this?"

"Our online forum for the discussion of past lives on other worlds can be found at our website Reincarnation Beyond Earth, www.reincarnate.net. These cards," He held up a stack. "have a link to the forum as well as my email address on them. Feel free to pick one up on your way out. My email address is docmezmer at gmail dot com. It's spelled it with a 'z' because the correct spelling was already taken." The audience chuckled.

Riley continued. "If you have any questions about the forum itself, email xeres@reincarnate.net and someone from my team will get back to you. That's Xeres, spelled X-E-R-E-S."

He smiled broadly. "Well, I think that's about it. I see the coordinator waving his arms at me, so I believe our time is up. Thank you, Dr. Sloan, Dr. Adams, for a fascinating debate."

Alex swam upstream to get to the front of the room, carefully staying out of sight on the far side of the group from Evelyn.

Riley was shaking Jake's hand, saying, "Thank you for being on the panel. Your arguments were great."

Jake huffed. "I still think you're crazy, but everyone's entitled to believe what they want. Evelyn's obviously on your side, though."

Evelyn stepped closer to the two men. "So you think I'm crazy too?"

The older man smiled benignly at her. "I wouldn't say that, at least not to your face. This whole thing unnerves me a bit. Shall we agree to disagree?" He began gathering up his belongings. "I'd better run or I'll miss my next panel."

"See you later, Jake. Thanks again." The big man nodded, then stepped down from the dais.

"Well, he certainly seemed to enjoy countering my points," Evelyn said, watching him depart.

"Yeah, he did," Riley chuckled. He turned to face her. "So, how do you think the panel went?"

"The audience had lots of good questions. I think we've struck a nerve."

"It seemed like every other question started a discussion that revealed some new tidbit of information. I was writing furiously, trying to keep up with the things people were saying. I had to get everything down so I can add it to my notes later."

As they headed for the door, Alex saw Tessa give Riley a hug.

"You did great, honey."

Riley smiled and his shoulders relaxed. "Yeah. It went even better than I hoped."

"And, wow, are these panels always so packed? I was worried that Alex wasn't going to get a seat. Where is he, anyway?"

"Here," Alex said quietly, forcing himself forward. Coming up behind Tessa, he gripped the small woman's shoulders, keeping her between him and Evelyn.

He couldn't help but notice how his sudden appearance affected Evelyn. First, she clutched the laptop to her chest so tightly he could see her knuckles whiten. Then, she backed up several paces, edging behind Riley.

Still staring at Alex, she said in a low voice, "Oh, my gods, Riley. I'm feeling such hatred toward Alex that I want to bash his brains in with my laptop. And I love this laptop."

"Yeah," Alex put in grimly. "Fun, huh?" He fought to stay behind Tessa. *I need to get away from her before I do something impolite, if not illegal,* he thought.

Tessa, taking pity on them both, changed the topic. "I don't know about you, Evelyn, but I'd like to see a show tonight."

"I'm gonna bail on the dinner thing tonight," Alex told Riley. "My friends are coming with me to see Penn and Teller."

Riley looked back and forth between Alex and Evelyn. "I figured as much. How about I get tickets for the rest of us to see the late show of Zumanity."

"Zumanity?" Tessa squealed. "I've wanted to see that show since it came out. Evelyn? Care to join us? I hear the tickets are kind of expensive."

"Okay by me," she said, glaring at Alex. "Just as long as it keeps me away from him."

Tessa exchanged a look with Riley. Then she turned to Alex and took his arm. "C'mon, I'll walk you out."

As they moved away, Alex tossed over his shoulder, "Great panel, you two."

* * *

Leaving the panel, Cadwallader stumbled into the hallway, lost in thought.

How did MacPherson manage to stumble on Xeres? Most people would just write it off as a delusion if their clients started talking about orange trees and blue leaves. Why did he believe them in the first place? And how has he been able to put together so many details? Damn, this is not good. I don't think I have any choice but to report this to Thierry.

Cadwallader was jarred from his disheartening thoughts when he ran into the man in front of him.

"Hey! Watch where you're going, buddy," the large man said, grabbing Cadwallader's arm.

"You watch out. It's your fault I almost fell. In fact," Cadwallader said, ice dripping from his voice, "you owe me an apology. You're the one who stopped without warning. You could have caused me bodily harm."

The large man released his grasp on Cadwallader's arm, his face suddenly contorted in rage. "If you had been paying attention, you

130

wouldn't have tripped in the first place."

Cadwallader reared back. *No. It can't be. I've only ever gotten that level of hostility from one of* them.

"I have places to be. I don't have time for you."

As he walked away, he heard voices behind him chuckling.

"You sure showed him, Ty," said one of his companions.

"You can calm down, Garrett, he's gone," said another.

Putting the incident from his mind, Cadwallader found a small alcove on the far side of the hallway, probably once used for a bank of payphones. Slipping into it, he leaned against the wall, waiting.

He hadn't been there long before he saw MacPherson's helper, Alex, leave with that woman who'd been assisting Evelyn. *What's her name? Oh, right. Tessa. Probably here to support Evelyn like a good little hanger-on. Why can't I have an attractive woman like that following me around instead of an oaf like Danny? Denny? Whatever.*

He watched as she hugged Alex, then sent him on his way. Once he'd disappeared into the crowd, she opened the door and yelled something back into the room. Moments later MacPherson and Evelyn emerged. MacPherson immediately grabbed Tessa's hand, then leaned in and kissed her.

Wait a minute. I thought she was just here to help Evelyn. She kissed MacPherson. He shook his head and let out an exasperated sigh. *Crap. Those two are a couple. I'll bet she's the person he talked about in the panel, the one who first told him about Xeres.*

Opening his awareness, he examined the hallway. Several figures stood out in his mind's eye.

There it is. They both have that faint overlay of Xerian energy. Tessa and Evelyn. I was right about that idiot, Ty Garrett, who almost tripped me. He's one of them too. And I'd bet money that the one I see moving away down the hall is MacPherson's assistant, Alex.

Well, at least that explains why he's investigating Xeres. Probably got his first hints by regressing her, and now he's surrounded by them. Alex, Tessa, Evelyn, and that brat of hers. Seems to be a cluster effect going on in San Francisco. Damn, I wonder how many more of them there are?

I've got to put a stop to his research, he fumed. *This could get out of hand if I don't. Maybe tomorrow I can dissuade MacPherson. This can't be allowed to get any bigger than it already is.*

He straightened, glaring at their backs until they disappeared through the doors to the casino.

Now I have to call Thierry, report this new development. He grimaced to himself. *After our last confrontation, I doubt he'll be happy to hear from me.*

Shaking his head, he turned and headed for his room.

* * *

Mezmer Notes - Update 68

Our panel was probably the most packed event of the day. I can't believe that this topic resonated so much with so many people. There were even a few people in attendance who weren't from the convention, they were just guests staying in the hotel! They saw the subject on the panel outside the event center and came in because they were remembering orange trees with blue leaves. I'm glad I made that part of the panel name because they provided some really interesting new information.

I feel sorry for Jake. He put up a good defense that this is all a delusion. But over half the audience either had a client who had talked about Xeres or they themselves had regressions or dreams about it. It was uncanny. There were people from all over the world in that room. I handed out almost all the cards I had printed up for the forum. If even half of them log in and start talking about this, the forum is going to explode. I need to have Alex make sure that we're ready for that many new users. I don't want it crashing right when we have so many people interested. If it goes down, they might not come back. This is such a great opportunity to gather information that we can't take any chances.

These are the new things I discovered today:

Animals:
- *Zelts are small russet rodents (a mouse or vole?).*
- *Jorgats are green songbirds.*
- *Sarters are predatory birds similar to eagles.*
- *Yimox are dove-like creatures that flap their wings like a hummingbird. They come in three colors: green, red, or blue.*
- *Thorats are insects that pollinate plants.*
- *There are large predatory amphibians described as a cross between a shark and a seal.*

Plants:

- *Siklin are annoying locust-like insects with clear wings.*
- *Sigbolg are kudzu-like plants that can move. It's a pest that people wear repellent to keep away.*
- *Vizet are flowering plants that are used in cooking.*

Clothing:
- *People wear a head covering containing an integrated communication device.*
- *Shoes sense the terrain and adapt to it.*

Transportation:
- *Vehicles don't have wheels.*
- *Vehicles in rural areas float on a cushion of air*
- *Vehicles in the cities don't seem to be individually owned.*
- *Mass transit is in group pods whisked through an intricate series of tunnels below ground.*
- *Most traffic above ground is pedestrian.*
- *There are functional bridges and tunnels between tall buildings, both to stabilize the buildings and to afford pedestrian access.*

Social:
- *There were two guilds, the Klymurians and the Bylantians.*
- *People from opposite guilds hate each other on sight.*
- *Before a person is regressed, they can be friends with an opposite guild person. Afterwards, the Xerian hatred for the opposite guild manifests.*
- *There used to be a third guild, the Tesham. They were completely killed off by the other guilds for inciting war.*
- *The Bylantians are scientists. Alex belongs to this guild.*
- *The Klymurians are mages. Evelyn and Kier belong to this guild.*
- *The Tesham were scientist-mages.*
- *Both Alex and Evelyn think that Tessa is a member of their guild.*
- *No one knows which guild Cadwallader or Bryce belongs to.*
- *Children are tested at a very young age to see if they have the correct aptitude (science or magic) for their guild. If they don't, they're killed.*

It's too much to take in. It boggles my mind. It's been less than a year since the first time I regressed Tessa when she mentioned orange trees with blue leaves. Now I've talked to dozens of people about this topic, hosted a public panel on it, and set up an online forum for other people to talk about it. I'm glad I brought Alex, Tessa, and

Evelyn into the loop on this. I think if I was still just dealing with this by myself, I would have gone crazy by now. I wish Jake wasn't so stubborn and could accept that this is real and be part of it with me. Working on the panel with him today made me realize how much I miss our weekly chats.

Saving…

Chapter 17

"Hey, you're the guy from the panel!"

"Uh, yes," Riley said, blushing.

Around them the vendors room muttered, squawked and beeped. Alex, at Riley's elbow, tried to hide his smile. *Riley's suddenly a celebrity and he doesn't like it. It's funny the way people have been interrupting us everywhere we go all morning. I know Riley wants to brush them off, but he's way too polite to do that. Besides, he really wants to see what these people can add to this world we're discovering.*

"I wasn't able to get into the panel. I got there too late and the room was full. Anyway, I've had several clients mention orange trees and blue leaves. I didn't know where the imagery was coming from either. Figured it was something they read as a kid or some online game maybe. I managed to talk to a couple of people who attended your panel yesterday. Wow! Extra-terrestrial past life regressions! Who'd have thought? So I was wondering, could I get one of your contact cards? I'll refer my clients to your forum. Heck, I might even log in myself."

Riley smiled at him. Pulling a card from his jacket, he handed it to the younger therapist. "I look forward to seeing as many people on the forum as possible. It's still new, but it's growing every day."

An older woman standing behind the young man spoke up. "I'm glad I got into the panel. Such an interesting new take on the field of hypnotherapy. I'm going to ask some of my friends if they'd like a past life regression. It would be fun if…."

Out of the corner of his eye, Alex saw a short man that he recognized from yesterday's panel running full tilt toward their little group. The man practically barreled into Alex as he cried, "I remembered something else! Last night I had another dream about the creature I told you about. The one that was kind of a cross between a shark and a seal? In my dream, it killed my little sister. I was calling out to her. I told her to look out for the eolipt."

Riley pulled out his phone and brought up his notes app. "Could you say that a little slower so I can try to figure out how to spell it?"

"E-o-l-i-p-t."

"Thank you. It's added to my notes." Looking up at the man, he asked, "You did get one of my cards, right?"

"Oh, yes. I can't wait to get on your forum!" There were murmurs about the forum from other listeners as well.

I've got to get Riley out of this.

Taking on the persona of personal assistant, Alex took Riley's arm, announcing, "Uh, sorry, folks. Mr. MacPherson has a luncheon starting soon, so we'll have to cut this short."

Riley blinked at him in surprise. Alex winked back at him.

As he escorted Riley out of the room, Alex shot him an amused look. "Bet you never thought you'd be so famous. Now everyone wants to talk to you. Before you know it, you'll give Cad a run for his money."

As they rounded the corner, Alex caught Cadwallader watching them.

Hmpf. Jealous, Cad?

* * *

Cadwallader watched as MacPherson and his aide disappeared from sight. *The man has groupies! All I have to show after years of coming to these things is Denny? Maybe MacPherson will be more forthcoming about Xeres over lunch.*

Calling across the booth, he said, "Danny, I'm going to lunch. Try not to break anything while I'm gone."

Denny shot him an evil look, but Cadwallader ignored him, turning away and surreptitiously following Riley and Alex toward the door.

Cadwallader chose a seat where he was sure to hear everything said at Riley's table, but off to one side so he could observe without being noticed. So far, neither Riley nor his assistant, Alex, had said or done anything interesting.

He was about to ask for his check, when he saw *that* woman and Tessa walk up to their table. Alex bolted upright, his face going ashen. Cadwallader watched as the man closed his eyes and took several deep breaths. Evil-lyn's face flushed with rage as she stared at the young man.

Ah, Cadwallader thought with amusement. *They must be from opposing guilds. Both Alex and Evelyn are remembering the animosity between their guilds. This should be interesting.*

As the two faced off, he noticed that Tessa had moved around the table. Wrapping an arm around MacPherson's shoulders, she gave him a light kiss on the cheek.

Wait. She isn't reacting to either Alex or Evelyn. I know she's from Xeres and MacPherson has obviously been regressing her, so why isn't she reacting to either of them? Maybe she's schooled herself enough to tolerate a person from the other guild. He shook his head. *No, she'd still exhibit some strain. She's not reacting at all. That's not possible, unless.... By the dark gods, she can't be!* His hand came up, covering his mouth. *She* has *to be a Tesham! We made sure the guilds wiped them all out! Hmmm,* he thought, *maybe some of them did escape. That would explain my encounter in the hall yesterday too.*

He watched avidly as the tableaux across from him unfurled.

Alex finally opened his eyes. He rose from his chair, nodded seriously to MacPherson. "If you don't mind, I need to be elsewhere right now. If you'll all excuse me...."

Cadwallader couldn't say Alex actually ran from the room, but it was clear the assistant was escaping. He saw Evelyn's eyes tracking the young man like a tiger following its prey. When he'd disappeared into the crowd, she turned back to the others, who were all staring at her.

"What?"

"Um," MacPherson said, "you looked like you wanted to eat him alive. I've never seen such a hungry a look on anyone's face." He licked his lips. "I seriously never want you to look at me that way."

"Amen," said Tessa.

MacPherson called a waiter, asking for the check, but Cadwallader had lost interest in them.

Damn, damn, damn! People from Xeres are starting to remember things. That blasted MacPherson and his ideas. He's beginning to annoy me. That damned panel of his has spread too much information about Xeres. And now he's going online with it. Why are all these Xerians clustered around MacPherson?

If it was just MacPherson and his ideas, I could kill him and that would be the end of the problem. But a Tesham? What a rat's nest. I have to tell Thierry about this. And soon.

Right now though, I need to do some damage control. Maybe I can talk

MacPherson into dropping this little quest of his or convince him that it will destroy his career.

He pulled out a few bills to leave on the table. His shaking hands sent one of them to the floor.

Eyeing the mutinous bill, he muttered, "Just stay there!" Then he turned and stalked away.

* * *

Early Sunday morning, Riley strode through the sparsely populated corridors of the convention center.

He groaned to himself. *Why am I up already? I didn't get to bed until late last night, no, make that this morning. I thought Evelyn would never leave. She finally headed off to bed around one AM. I'm glad we finally got a few minutes alone, even if it was just in the hallway. If Tessa ever comes to one of these things again,* he promised himself, *I will* not *be rooming with Alex!*

Still, Alex and Evelyn rooming together isn't feasible. Yet. Alex is making an effort, he had to concede, *though what Evelyn is doing to make the situation better I don't know.*

A heavy hand landing on his shoulder broke Riley from his reverie. Following the hand upward, he found himself facing the imposing presence of Matthew Cadwallader.

"MacPherson," he said. "I'd been hoping to find you before the panels began."

Turning, Riley leaned against the wall and crossed his arms.

"Oh? Why would that be?"

Cad rubbed at his chin. "That panel you did yesterday."

Just the thought of it made Riley smile. "It went over much better than I'd expected. And the feedback from attendees and even those who missed it has been great. I completely ran out of cards yesterday afternoon."

"But is that what you want to be known for?"

The serious, almost mournful look Cad was giving him made Riley raise his eyebrows.

"Huh? Known for?"

The man moved closer to Riley, pitching his voice in a conspiratorial whisper.

"I mean, do you want to be known as that crackpot therapist who believes we've been invaded by aliens? You'll lose standing in professional circles. You'll lose clients. You might even lose your practice altogether."

"That won't—"

"It could. I can't believe an intelligent professional like you would lend credence to such…mumbo-jumbo in the first place."

Riley felt his face heat up and his fists clench. *What right does Cadwallader have to judge me or my beliefs? He's got some nerve hitting me with that patronizing tone, too.*

With a conscious effort, Riley reined in his rising anger. *It's not possible that Cad has my best interests in mind here. What's in it for* him *if I drop this? After all, Cad's from Xeres. Maybe he's never had a past life regression, or never gone as far back as Xeres. Does know about Xeres, but wants to keep it covered up for some reason? Is he's doing his own research and planning a book? That would explain why he's trying to shoo me off the topic. He doesn't want the competition. It's all about money, as far as he's concerned.*

From over Cadwallader's shoulder, Riley heard a familiar voice. *Thank goodness, the cavalry has arrived.*

"Crackpot therapist? Isn't that *your* arena?"

Cadwallader stiffened. Standing directly behind him was Evelyn, arm in arm with Tessa.

"Ah, Evil-lyn," Cadwallader said, turning. "I don't believe anyone rattled your cage." Tipping his head at Tessa, he said, "Good morning, miss. I've seen you around, but I don't think we've been properly introduced. I'm Dr. Matthew Cadwallader."

"Tessa Connors." Withdrawing her arm from Evelyn's, she moved to stand beside Riley. "I'm Riley's fiancé."

"Don't listen to him, Riley," Evelyn said snarkily. "He's the last person you should be taking professional advice from if you hope to be taken seriously by your peers."

"Fine! Listen to her advice if you want to. But mark my words," he said, shaking a finger under Riley's nose, "if you keep pursuing this, it won't end well for you."

"Well," Riley said with a shrug, "I'm not worried about my name or my practice. But thank you for your concern."

"We'll see, MacPherson. We'll see." Head high and back straight, Cadwallader turned and stomped off.

Looking after him, Evelyn said sweetly, "Do you think it was something I said?"

Riley laughed. "You think?"

Evelyn joined in. When he realized that Tessa wasn't laughing with them, he tilted his head in inquiry at her. "Something wrong, sweetheart?"

"Um, I had the weirdest feeling when I came up beside you. I accidentally brushed up against Cad and…." Tessa's voice drifted off.

"What?" Riley and Evelyn asked in unison.

"I felt a rush of anger, like everything in me wanted to reach out and destroy him." She flushed with the acknowledgement. "I've always gotten along with everyone, no matter how insufferable, but him? Him I wanted to destroy. Not kill. Destroy."

Her entire body shook in one long quake.

"I don't like the guy either," Evelyn put in, "but 'destroy'? Isn't that a little harsh?"

Tessa shook her head. "I don't know, I really don't."

Yes, what is so special about him? Riley wondered, tucking the incident away for further consideration.

"Well, I'm starved," he said, taking Tessa's arm. "Enough with Cadwallader." Grabbing Evelyn's elbow with his free hand, he steered them both toward the restaurant.

* * *

"Pick it up, you clod!" Cadwallader thundered. "Can't you do anything right?"

Around them, the neighboring vendors went quiet, pausing in their packing.

Across the aisle, Tessa straightened from filling a box with books. *Maybe this thing will finally come to a head*, she thought.

When Denny didn't move, Cadwallader continued, "Don't you know how expensive that is? Remember, I had to fork out for a new display after you broke the old one."

"Pick it up yourself," Denny said through gritted teeth. "It's not like you're paying me to be here or anything. I had to pay for my flight, my room, *and* my membership. All for the glorious 'privilege' of doing your grunt work while you sit on your fat ass and take credit for everything. The least you could do is pick up one lousy piece of this shoddy display."

Cadwallader reeled back in shock. "What's wrong with you?"

140

Denny stepped back, placing his fists on his hips. "I'm fed up with you, your display, *and* your ego."

Oh, good one, Denny, Tessa thought, smiling to herself. She heard a slow clap behind her and turned to find Evelyn giving Denny a standing ovation.

"Bravo, Denny. About time you gave that pompous ass a piece of your mind." Evelyn was practically beaming. The rest of the room suddenly joined in, cheering and clapping for Denny.

The "pompous ass" turned on her indignantly. "You keep out of this!" He looked around at the other vendors. "All of you!"

Before Cadwallader could say anything more to Denny, the man dropped the tape gun he was wielding. "You know what? Pack it up yourself. Then your can load it and make arrangements for shipping it. Yourself. I'm through with you!" He paused, biting his lip and wrinkling his brow. "I used to think you were a hot shit hypnotherapist, so I helped you out, investing more and more of my time and hard-earned money to do it. Just hoping I could learn something from you. Well, I did finally learn something. You aren't hot shit, just full of shit."

Picking up his jacket, Denny turned his back on Cadwallader. Before leaving the room, he paused at Evelyn's table.

"Thank you for the support," he said to Tessa. "How about a farewell drink? To celebrate my independence?"

Cadwallader appeared like magic at Denny's elbow.

"You idiot!' he snarled. "Don't you know she's with MacPherson? She'd never be interested in the likes you."

Tessa gave Cadwallader a withering look. "I'd love to have a drink with you, Denny." Turning she saw Evelyn and realized that she couldn't leave all the work for her. "After I finish helping Evelyn pack out. It wouldn't be fair for me to leave before everything is loaded."

"Well, why don't I help you both?" he said, aiming a sneer at Cadwallader. "After all, I have a lot of experience. And I bet neither of you will yell at me."

Stalking back to his own booth, Cadwallader began slamming books into boxes. When part of his display teetered, he smacked it back into place.

As they listened to Cadwallader's grunts and complaints, Evelyn sing-songed, "Sounds like somebody could use a bit of therapy for anger management."

Chapter 18

When he heard Tessa come in the front door, Riley wiped his hands on a dish towel and hurried out of the kitchen.

Tessa placed her bags on the floor, a smile spreading across her face. "Honey, I'm home."

"I see that. Welcome home, my love." He spread his arms, waiting for her to give him a hug.

"I am *so* happy to see you!" Dropping her keys and jacket, she rushed to meet him.

Riley caught her up, spun her around, and kissed her soundly.

When they finally separated, he turned serious., "I've missed you, Tessa. And as much as I'd love to hear about your trip back, there's something you probably need to deal with first."

Tessa blinked. "What? You make it sound so ominous."

He shrugged. "Maybe. Your work phone's been ringing and ringing. I heard it chirp a few minutes ago, so you have text messages as well as voicemails. Maybe it's only a client who's losing his mind because he can't reach you to get carpet to complement his new Italian leather shoes."

She rolled her eyes. "Hand-holding. Just what I need right now. Wonder why Diana hasn't taken care of it?"

Riley followed her down the hall and into their office. "First things first," she said, going to the snake cages in the closet. "Hello, Meg. Hello, Calvin. How are you, my darlings?" The snakes both raised their heads and peered through the plexiglass wall at their owner as if to say, 'Hi, Mom! Where's our food?'

Tessa laughed. "Don't give me that look. I know you aren't due to be fed for another week."

Still chuckling, she heard a beep from the direction of her desk. "Right, phone, message, ugh."

Sliding into her chair, she unplugged her work phone from its charger. Seeing the name on the caller ID, her brow creased with worry.

"Riley, this's from Diana. I don't know why she'd be calling me so urgently though. She knew I was going to be out of town until tonight."

"Diana? What?" Riley asked.

As Tessa listened to her voicemail, her face grew ashen.

Riley went over and placed a hand on her shoulder. Tessa looked up at him, concern written all over her face.

"Riley, she's in trouble. She was crying so hard I couldn't make out much of what she was saying, but it's obvious she's had a serious blow-up with Bryce." She pocketed the phone and looked up at him. "I'm going over there to make sure she's ok. Would you come with me?"

"You couldn't stop me," he said grimly. "I'll drive."

Luckily, they found a parking spot right outside Diana's condo. Tessa didn't even wait for him to shut down the engine before bolting to the door and punching in the code to call upstairs. The intercom was still ringing when Riley caught up.

"She hasn't answered yet?"

"No and I'm starting to get worried."

At that moment, one of Diana's elderly neighbors Tessa recognized from previous visits arrived at the door.

"You're Tessa, right? You work with Diana in unit four. I saw you two going over that big book of fabrics a couple of months ago on the patio. Diana always seems happier when you're around." The woman's face hardened. "That creep of a husband of hers treats her horribly. You should have heard the yelling last night. It sounded like they were standing right outside my door, even though I knew they were down the hall."

Riley traded a look with Tessa. *Yelling? Yesterday?*

Tessa took the lead. "Um, could you let us into the building? Diana's not answering and we're concerned."

"Of course, dear." Juggling her purse and packages, the woman unlocked the door. Riley held it while the two women entered.

As soon as the elevator doors opened, Tessa and Riley heard raised voices from down the hallway. Tessa sprinted to the door, banging on it as hard as she could.

A sudden silence ensued. Then, Bryce's voice called through the door.

"Sorry, are we being too loud?"

Tessa rapped on the door again, rather than giving away her presence in the hallway.

The door cracked open. Bryce peered around the edge of the door.

"Where's Diana," Tessa growled.

"Diana's none of your business," the man shouted at her, trying to close the door in her face.

Riley was ready though. Shoving his shoulder into the door, he forced his way into the apartment. He pushed past Bryce, Tessa right on his heels.

"Tessa!" Diana cried, flying down the hall and into her friend's arms.

"What the hell do you think you're doing?" Bryce roared.

Riley turned on him, his anger flaring out of control. "Rescuing a woman from her abusive husband." When Bryce attempted to move toward Diana and Tessa, Riley threw an arm in his way. "I don't think so."

Bryce was so red in the face, Riley might have been concerned for his health. But it was hard to have sympathy for someone who abused his wife.

Diana raised her head in alarm, disheveled hair hanging in front of her reddened eyes and bruised cheek. "Don't let him get me!"

Keeping one arm around the woman's shoulder, Tessa stroked Diana's arm. "Shhh, it's all right. Riley won't let him touch you." She threw Riley a look.

Riley nodded. "Don't worry, he won't get near you."

He watched as Diana glanced at Bryce. His angry eyes and thunderous expression made her cower and duck her head into Tessa's shoulder.

He caught the look of pure fury Tessa cast at Bryce. *Sheesh, I hope I'm never on the receiving end of that!*

Pulling out his phone, Riley arched an eyebrow at Bryce. "Do I need to call 911, or will you leave of your own accord? I warn you, if the police come, with her visible injuries, you'll definitely be hauled off to jail."

Bryce sputtered. "*She* started it! If—"

Shaking his head, Riley cut him off. "Doesn't matter who started it. California law is very clear. Diana's the one with the bruises, so she's obviously the injured party. One look at her and you're spending the night in jail." Looking the man up and down, Riley fired off one last salvo. "I bet you'd be *really* popular there."

Bryce deflated. Shaking his head, he shoved Riley aside. Snatching up a set of keys from the basket on the counter, he stomped down the short hall and out the door.

As soon as the door closed, Riley went over to the women.

Concern lacing his voice, Riley asked, "Diana, do you want to go to the hospital? To get checked out?"

Practically spitting venom, Tessa suggested, "Or maybe to the courthouse to get a restraining order?"

That made Diana look up. "Restraining order? Oh, I don't know, that might make him madder." Riley saw a glimmer of hope come into her dark eyes. That hopeful look almost broke Riley's heart. "But it would keep him away from me, right?"

"Yes, it would," he said firmly. "If you get a restraining order and he shows up, you can call 911 and he'll be tossed in jail."

"Oh." She looked down at her ripped dress and shoeless feet. "I need to—"

Tessa said, "I know, sweetie. Let me help you get dressed."

* * *

Outside, sitting in his Lexus and staring at the windows of the condo he'd been forcibly evicted from, Bryce fumed. *Damn them. Damn them all, Diana, Riley, and especially Tessa. Gods, I thought I'd been so lucky finding one of them so young. It should have helped me in the organization, but no, I get stuck babysitting her all these years for...for nothing! And of all the people from Xeres that she could hook up with, it had to be that damn busybody Tessa, who just* had *to stick her nose in where it doesn't belong. Now Diana will never trust me again. All this work getting close to her, ruined. And there goes my chance of proving myself to Thierry by bringing in another person from Xeres. I'll never regain my position and get out from under that pompous ass.*

Pulling out his phone, he reluctantly dialed the number of the pompous ass in question.

Matthew Cadwallader.

* * *

"Dammit!"

Throwing his cell phone, Matthew Cadwallader scowled when he heard it shatter against the far wall of his office.

Standing and pacing, he shoved both hands through his hair. "That imbecile. He had one job. One lousy job. Keep an eye on Diana in case she made contact with others of her kind. And when she did, he blew it. Spectacularly! And, of course, Thierry's going to blame *me*."

Cadwallader pinched the bridge of his nose. *As if I didn't have enough to deal with,* he thought, *with MacPherson and his shenanigans. Xerians seem to be popping up all around him. And that damn girlfriend of his. A Tesham? If I reveal that to Thierry, he'll come charging in and take over. No, no. I need to keep that information to myself, my ace-in-the-hole in case things go wrong.*

He reached into his pocket for his phone, then frowned. Glaring at the pieces of metal and plastic littering the floor, he made a mental note to acquire a new one. *Damn! Another expense.* Sitting down in his desk chair, he took a moment to let the expensive piece of furniture do its job. After several minutes, he felt much calmer. Reaching for his desk phone, he looked at it in distaste. He hated to be tethered to the desk. Normally, he found himself much more focused if he paced while talking to Thierry.

"What is it now?" Acid dripped from each word Thierry spoke.

Uh-oh. Cadwallader wondered what he'd done to rouse Thierry's displeasure just by phoning him.

"Um, I have some developments that I need to report." *Maybe I can pique his interest.* He shuddered. *At least I'm not calling about money this time.*

"It had better be important. You are interrupting me at a very inopportune moment."

Behind Thierry, Cadwallader could hear the murmur of voices.

"I…Um, some interesting things happened over the weekend. There's been talk about orange trees with blue leaves at one of my hypnotherapy conferences. Dr. Riley MacPherson has been gathering information on people who 'remember' those things."

Thierry sputtered. "And you're just now telling me about this?"

In spite of himself, Cadwallader cringed in his expensive chair.

"It only came to a head this weekend when MacPherson gave a panel on extraterrestrial reincarnation. It was the talk of the conference."

"Go on," came the clipped reply from the other end of the line.

Cadwallader gulped. *If he's this upset already, I know he's going to hate*

146

what else I have to tell him.

"MacPherson has several Xerians in his inner circle."

"Several?" Thierry broke in. He wasn't angry now, Cadwallader noticed, though he couldn't quite put a finger on Thierry's new mood.

"At least four that I've seen. One of those is MacPherson's girlfriend, Tessa Connors. Another's his assistant. The last two are another therapist and her son. She's one of my competitors."

He paused, waiting for Thierry's reaction.

"And? I know there's more to this. Spill it."

"MacPherson's taken it online. He's invited people with memories of Xeres to post and discuss things in his online forum."

He'd been afraid Thierry would blame him, but his words met only silence. *Why is he being so quiet? That's not a good sign. Normally, he'd either be yelling or ordering me to do something by now.*

Finally, Thierry spoke up.

"What an excellent idea."

Cadwallader realized he'd been holding his breath. Air rushed into his lungs as he started breathing again.

"Sir?"

"Oh, yes. If this online thing attracts others Xerians, we'll have what we've been looking for all along, an unlimited source of energy."

"I…I'd thought that might be the case. So, um, what do you wish me to do here?"

"Just keep an eye on this forum. Send me a link as well. I'll have my techs monitor it."

Cadwallader drew a deep breath before pressing on.

"There is one other matter, sir."

"Not more money." The acid returned to the man's voice.

"Oh, no, sir," he rushed to say. "It's about Bryce Lundee."

Thierry answered in a flat, cold voice, "Yes?"

"He…he was caught physically abusing his wife. The woman's business partner and her husband threw him out of his own house. He's lost control of the situation. After all the years we've invested in him keeping an eye on that Xerian, and now he blows it? The man is incompetent."

"So? Quit whining and deal with it. He's your problem. That's why you're in charge of the West Coast, so *I* don't have to deal with these trivial matters. Besides, with MacPherson's online forum, we'll have plenty of Xerians without having to put in years of work. We know how to find Bryce's wife when we are ready."

He heard a click, then the line went dead.

Staring down at the dead receiver, he thought, *Well, that went better than I'd hoped. Maybe I'm not in that much trouble after all.*

With a self-satisfied smile, Cadwallader reached for his laptop to order a new cell phone.

* * *

"There's all these neat mods we can add to our website," Alex said enthusiastically. Scrolling down, page after page, he occasionally let out yelps of "I didn't know it could do that!" and "Wow! Neat!"

Not the technical wiz Alex was, Riley could only nod his head or ignore Alex's comments altogether. At the beginning of their session, Alex had addressed Riley's few quibbles, fixing a comma here, an apostrophe there. Once that was done, Riley felt like he'd faded into the background, with no access to whatever was so exciting to Alex.

Leaving the chair he'd pulled up so he could look over Alex's shoulder, Riley wandered over to Tessa's snake enclosure. It was a four foot tall rectangle of plexiglass, like a long aquarium set on its end. Riley opened the front panel and reached inside, gently hoisting Calvin off a heating rock.

"Look at this, Riley!"

Coming up behind Alex and peering over his shoulder, Riley paid no attention to the black, gray and white boa constrictor climbing down his arm.

"Hey! What's that...!"

Alex lurched sideways in his chair, trying to escape the advancing snake intent upon exploring his ear. Riley caught the snake before it could fall.

"What? You're not afraid of Calvin, are you? You've handled him before," Riley said.

"I'm just not used to him slithering up from behind and sticking his tongue in my ear! I reserve that for dates, not pets."

Riley smiled evilly. "He was just tasting you, to see if you were worth eating." He lifted Calvin up, wrapping the snake around his neck. "Now, what did you want me to see?" he said sweetly.

Alex moved gingerly back into his chair, adjusting the laptop he'd knocked askew.

"Uh, well, I found a mod that allows users to add words to their own custom dictionary. That was something you'd asked me about earlier and now it's there."

"Glad you found that. It'll make entering text easier for users. They won't get red underlines every time they type some odd word from Xeres."

Riley circled the mass of his and Tessa's conjoined desks, mindful of the snake he was carrying.

I love these snakes, but I'm always sure I'm going to drop one or hurt it in somehow. It's not fair of Tessa to call me Mr. Roboto. I'm not that stiff when I'm carrying one of them, am I?

Come to think of it, she has a lot of nicknames for me. He pondered. Doc, DocMezmer, Mac, Mr. Roboto. Is my name really that hard to say that she has to give me all these nicknames?

Opening his laptop, Riley checked his email. Calvin chose that moment to head for the desktop. Moving down Riley's arm, the snake flicked his tongue as he went, tasting the air. Riley chuckled to himself when he noted Alex eyeing the snake's progress.

"He won't bite you, Alex."

"I know, I know. It's just…a big snake."

"You are acting like you do toward Evelyn."

Alex's head came up. "I am not! Evelyn's…I don't know…." He ran one hand through his dark hair, leaving it spiked and messy. "I don't want to say loathsome, but that's close. I don't want to be near her." He stood up and began pacing the small office.

"Well, that's pretty much how she feels about you too, according to Tessa. But she's working on a way to get over it. I hear she's using self-hypnosis." After a moment, he asked, "Are you doing anything about it?"

Alex leaned over the desk on braced arms. "I'm trying, really. But this thing is really ingrained in me. I don't seem to have any control over how I react to Evelyn. What did you do to help Tessa get over this so she could be around Evelyn?"

"She never had any problems with Evelyn."

"But she's in my guild, so it makes sense that she feels the same as I do toward Evelyn."

"That's just it. Evelyn says the same thing. Tessa is in her guild."

"That can't be. She's in mine." Alex's eyes got big and round.

"That means...Tessa's a Tesham. Oh, my gosh! So they aren't extinct!" He sat back in his chair with a thump. "Man, does that change things."

"Yes, I know," Riley said dryly. "And I don't want that to become general knowledge, okay?"

"Oh, right."

Riley let him mull over the ramifications of this new information for a few moments, then said, "Getting back to our previous topic of your reaction to Evelyn? Have you tried self-hypnosis to get over your problem with her?"

"Tried that. It helped some. Now I can at least stay in the same room with her."

"Maybe I should try hypnotizing you. Make suggestions, help you get over it in stages."

Alex considered his options for a moment, then nodded. "Yeah, that is the next step, isn't it."

"Let's schedule a couple of office visits for you and explore the possibilities. It would be nice if we could all work together without this hanging over our heads," Riley said.

Alex returned to his laptop, leaving Riley to his own devices.

"Oh, this is cool," Alex said. "You can do email drafts. Aw, dang it. It doesn't want to load properly." He shrugged. "Oh, well. You can't have everything."

Riley looked up from his computer.

"Alex?"

"Yes?" he said absently.

"I just remembered something I forgot to tell you about, from the conference. About Cadwallader."

Now he had Alex's full attention.

"What?"

"The man had me buttonholed in the hall, trying to get me to drop the whole subject of Xeres. Said it was bad for my professional reputation. Tessa and Evelyn came along and rescued me. Tessa bumped into Cad and had a severe reaction. She didn't want to touch him or even talk with him. Afterward she said her instinct was to destroy him on the spot."

"Destroy him?" Alex asked, his eyebrows rising. "But if you're right and she's Tesham, *why?*"

"I don't know. I wasn't expecting anything that violent from Tessa either. I asked her, but she couldn't explain it. It's eerily similar to the reaction you and Evelyn have to each other, only much worse."

"Well," Alex said, "maybe there's a group that the Tesham hate like the Bylantians and Klymurians do each other."

Riley rubbed at his forehead. "A fourth guild? Another group?"

Alex chuckled. "Maybe they're door-to-door used car salesmen?"

* * *

"Yes, Latham?"

"Your private line has a priority call from Bryce Lundee. Shall I put it through?"

Thierry held his cell phone out in front of him, glaring at it as if it were alive and pissing on the carpet. *Those damned Americans. They are like misbehaving school children, requiring far too much of my attention.*

Shaking his head, he said, "I suppose. We still have a few minutes before we reach Renata's." He settled back, savoring the lavish appointments of the corporate limousine. Reaching into the liquor cabinet, he poured himself some Ardbeg Supernova 2009 in a crystal whiskey glass. He was savoring it's peaty taste when his cell chimed.

Hitting the speaker button he growled, "This had better be important."

Bryce's voice came through clearly. "Um, this is Bryce Lundee. There have been…incidents that I thought you should be made aware of."

Thierry frowned. *Why can those Americans not handle anything by themselves? I grow weary of them all.*

"And why are you bothering me instead of going through proper channels and speaking to your superior, Matthew Cadwallader?"

"I…he…I've been shackled to the Xerian woman, Diana, for several years…."

"That does not answer my question," Thierry said sharply "Why did you not take this matter to Matthew?"

"I have. Several times. He hasn't done anything about the situation, so I brought it to you."

"And what is so very important that you simply *have* to bother me with it?" Thierry didn't bother to keep his utter disdain for both American's out of his voice.

"Diana was supposed to be a stalking goat…bait to attract other

Xerians…and she did. One, anyway. I encouraged Diana to become partners with her. But lately, this woman, Tessa, has been interfering with the project. A lot. And now, she's encouraged Diana to leave me and take out a restraining order. Tessa's damned self-righteous boyfriend Riley served me with it this morning."

"I have already spoken with Matthew about your situation and as I told him, we know where to find Diana and her partner, Tessa, when we are ready for them." The quiet threat in his voice was crystal clear.

"Wait," Thierry said, as connections fell into place. "You said her partner's name was Tessa? And the boyfriend's name is Riley? Would his last name happen to be MacPherson?"

"Um, yes. Riley MacPherson and Tessa Connors."

"Matthew told me about the two of them, but not their connection to Diana. Very interesting. I am very glad you brought this to my attention. This changes things." *Damn Matthew! Why am I hearing this from Bryce? Matthew should have told me everything. What else is he hiding from me? He is quickly becoming more of a liability than an asset. There has been a sudden spike in Xerian activity being reported everywhere, but the United States' West Coast is the only place with problems. Matthew is useless. Perhaps it is time I got rid of him. For good.*

As the silence stretched out, Bryce said, "Ummmm, is there anything you want me to do?"

Thierry sat back, taking another slow sip of his whiskey, considering the offer. *Bryce was one of my lieutenants in his last life. Maybe it is time for him to be one again.*

Glancing out the tinted windows, he saw that the limo was nearing Renata's building.

"Not yet," he mused. "You have served me well before, and I may yet have work for you. Until then, keep me informed on Diana, Tessa, and especially this man Riley."

The door to the limo opened. Renata's perfume preceded her as his stunningly lovely fiancé slid into the seat beside him.

"But the restraining order—"

Thierry waved a hand. "That is your problem. Handle it." Thierry disconnected the phone, replacing it in his overcoat pocket.

Renata kissed him lightly on the cheek. "Those damned Americans again?" She pursed her lips in a pout. "Must they call you for every little thing? Can Matthew not deal with whatever it is? If he cannot, replace the incompetent buffoon."

Thierry nodded. "I just might do that. Soon."

Chapter 19

Riley watched as Meg, Tessa's red and cream boa constrictor, climbed the fake tree in her cage. *I know I should be working on my client notes, but it's the weekend.* The day was warm so he allowed himself a few minutes of mindlessly staring at the snakes.

He heard the chime from the doorbell in the living room. *Wonder who's at the door?* Riley started to rise, then thought better of it. *Tessa and Diana are in the kitchen working, they'll get it.*

Enough wool gathering, get down to business, MacPherson, he told himself sternly. You're way behind on your notes because you've been spending too much time on this Xerian matter. Still, he mused, *it is a puzzle of the first magnitude and I never could resist a good puzzle.*

He was opening a client's file when he heard Alex talking excitedly in the kitchen. *Any excuse to ditch the homework,* he thought, putting aside his papers. He stumbled out of the office and down the hall.

In the small kitchen, he found Alex pacing around and gesturing wildly. The two women looked on in amusement, their heads swiveling to follow him like spectators at a tennis match.

"You won't believe it!" he exclaimed. "We have more than a hundred and twenty new members on the forum and over two hundred discussion emails."

"Wow," Riley said, entering the kitchen. "That's great. I haven't had time to log into the forum since we got home from the conference."

Tessa broke into their conversation.

"Alex, I don't think you two have been properly introduced. This is my business partner Diana. She's staying with us for a while. Diana, this is Riley's assistant Alex." Alex nodded, offering his hand. Diana drew back, hesitant. Alex raised an eyebrow at Riley.

Riley cleared his throat. "Um, Diana's staying with us until she finds a place of her own. She recently separated from her husband." He allowed himself a sly smile. "I served him with a restraining order myself the other morning. That's why I missed our meeting."

"Restraining order? That sounds like more than just a simple separation." Concern was etched on his face.

"She decided that she didn't want to be his punching bag anymore," Tessa clarified through clenched teeth.

"Man, that sucks. You gonna be okay?"

"I hope so," Diana said quietly. "Right now, I don't feel safe with anyone except Tessa and Riley." She made a face. "My husband is back in our condo, while I'm sleeping on their couch."

Alex whistled. "That lumpy thing? You have my sympathies."

"Hey, I've spent many a night on that thing," Riley protested, "when Tessa got mad at me. It isn't that bad."

"Speak for yourself," Alex said. "How many times have I slept over after a game night? I'm always stiff as a board the next morning. You've just gotten used to it. I can't."

Riley threw up his hands in surrender. "Okay, okay, you win. Speaking of sleeping arrangements, how is your search for a new roommate going?"

Alex made a sour face. "My old roommate moved out last weekend. I've had a couple of people come by to look at the place, but the last applicant drank and smelled like an ashtray. The one before that brought his mother along for approval." He shook his head. "I'm beginning to get worried. I can't afford the rent on my own."

Riley and Tessa shared a look, then nodded in unison.

"You know, Alex," Tessa said, carefully looking down at the table where her finger was tracing circles on the plastic tablecloth. "I happen to know someone looking for somewhere to live."

Alex and Diana both turned to her.

"Well," Tessa said, "you have to admit, it would be perfect. For both of you. You're both friends of ours and we trust Alex implicitly. He spends more time here than he does at home some weeks. And you," she said, placing a gentle hand on Diana's arm, "need a safe place to live. Besides our lumpy couch, I mean."

Everyone laughed.

Maybe it has *outlived its welcome,* Riley sighed, *but Tessa doesn't want to spend a lot of money on something that 'won't go with the new house', whatever that means. Designers! I don't understand what the big deal is.*

Alex looked surprised. "Room with me? Hm, not a bad idea." He turned to Diana. "Drink or smoke?"

She shuddered. "I've been known to have a glass of wine now and then, but smoking? Ewww, no."

"And you don't have a boyfriend lurking somewhere?"

Diana blinked. "Just a soon-to-be ex-husband."

"Perfect." He told her what her share of rent and utilities would be.

She nodded. "I'm pretty sure I can manage that. You do have wi-fi, right?"

"Oh, you have no idea," he said with a laugh. "I have pretty much any computer gadget you might want to play with. Who do you think takes care of all of Riley's computer needs? He's pretty much useless for anything other than using it as a word processor."

"Hey," Riley protested, "I resemble that remark."

The whole room broke out in infectious chuckles.

Riley said, "Well, as long as that's settled, what's for lunch?"

Tessa glanced at Diana. "There's one other thing we should talk about if you're going to move in with Alex. Remember when we went to that fancy spa while Riley was out of town? You mentioned when you were a kid that you had dreams of wandering through a forest of orange trees with blue leaves."

"Yeah, I remember. It was only a silly dream I've had since I was little. What about it?"

Giving Riley a pointed look, Tessa said, "I just realized something. Is it a good idea for them to move in together? What if what happened with Evelyn and Alex happens with them too? They *are* both from Xeres, after all."

"Xeres?" Diana asked, furrowing her brow delicately. "No, I'm from Boston."

Riley shook his head. "That's not what we mean." He paused, searching for the right words to explain this massive undertaking. "It's a research project we're all involved in. Through past life regression, I've found several people reincarnated from the same planet, Xeres. One of the first links we found between them was the orange trees with blue leaves."

Diana stared at him in amazement. "Another planet? You can't be serious."

Alex pulled out a chair and sat down next to Diana. "No, we've definitely found a bunch of people from Xeres. We even have an online forum now. That's what I was going on about when I got here."

Pursing her lips, Diana looked at Tessa. "This is real?"

She nodded.

Diana scratched her head. "And all this comes out of one of your regressions?"

"Those and sometimes my clients' dreams," he said.

She was silent for a moment, staring at the tiled floor. Then she nodded. "I'd like a regression. Would that be possible, Riley?"

Alex jumped in, "I could do it for you, once you get moved in. After all, I've studied under Riley and I could use the practice."

Diana tilted her head to the side, eyeing him. "I"m not sure why, Alex, but I feel like I can trust you."

Alex grinned. "You know, I feel the same way." He chewed his lip. Glancing at Riley, he asked, "Do you think it's because we're from the same guild?"

"Probably. Otherwise she'd have run screaming at the sight of your face." He paused for effect. "Usually that's reserved for your ex-girlfriends."

"Ha, ha, very funny, Riley."

"Run screaming? Why in the world would I do that?"

"Don't worry about that just yet," Tessa said, patting Diana's arm "You'll understand after you've had a regression."

Alex pointed toward the door. "Would you like to go over and see the place? Get a feel for whether or not you'd even want to move in with me?"

Diana looked at Tessa. "We are at a good stopping place. Would you mind?"

Tessa laughed, folding her laptop closed. "No, go ahead. We can pick up this up again later." She made a shooing motion at her. "Go, go. Besides, Riley is probably famished by now. Must feed the animals, you know."

Riley looked at Tessa and growled. "Must feed bear now."

Diana laughed and stood up, joining Alex at the kitchen arch to wave goodbye.

"See you later," Alex said. "When you get a chance, Riley, get on the forum. I think you're going to enjoy the discussions."

He turned to Diana and offered his arm. After a moment's hesitation, she took it.

"So," Alex said lightly, "what's the deal with your soon-to-be ex-husband? Anything I need to worry about? He's not going to waylay me on the street and punch my lights out, is he?"

As they were walking out the door, Riley heard Diana tell Alex, "The hardest part of this whole mess is that I got myself into it in the first place. I'm way too smart to be so stupid, yet here I am."

* * *

Diana peered through the door of Alex's apartment. *Wow, I'm surprised at how light and airy this place feels. Neat too.*

"Oh, this is nicer than I'd expected."

"What, you thought I lived in squalor?"

She laughed. "I really didn't know what to expect. I've lived in condos with Bryce since we got married. I only have Tessa's place and my college apartments to go by."

"It *is* nice and that's why I need a roommate. It's way too expensive for one person alone."

"I can see that. I love the ceiling fans. We certainly need them with the summers we've been having lately."

"There are fans in the bedrooms, too."

Diana walked around the living room, looking with disapproval at the furniture. *Tacky, tacky, tacky,* she thought.

"I'm assuming these pieces came from your college days?"

Alex rubbed the side of his nose.

"No," Alex said, scrunching up his face. "Goodwill."

She laughed. "Let's see the rest of the place."

After Alex had shown her the entire apartment, they returned to the living room to discuss arrangements.

"Going through the kitchen to get to the bathroom seems a bit odd. Poor planning, at the very least," she said.

"I've been thinking on that. My bedroom's next to the bathroom now. There's no reason I can't move to the back bedroom."

"But your desk and all your computer stuff's in the big one."

"It won't be hard to move. I don't need all that space anyway, and

158

I can access the wi-fi from anywhere in the apartment. That's all that really matters to me."

"Oooh, you'd really do that? It would give me all that closet space, too. Still, I feel bad about making you move."

"It's really not a problem. I could fit everything I own, except for the computers, into a couple of backpacks."

She looked at him appraisingly. "Hmm, we'll have to do something about that, too."

Alex looked at her in alarm. "Not all of us have a lot of money. Remember, that's why I need a roommate."

"Ah, but I'm a designer. I have contracts with a wide variety of companies. I get discounts almost everywhere I shop. That even includes clothing."

He shook his head. "I don't need a makeover, thank you very much."

"Don't worry," Diana said, waving a small hand at him "You'll thank me later. When you have a girlfriend."

Wiggling his eyebrows, Alex grinned. "Or maybe a boyfriend."

"Oh. I didn't know." *Alex is bisexual, huh? Interesting.* "Well, either way, you need help if you're ever going to find someone."

Alex groaned. "We'll talk about it after you get moved in, okay?" Excitement coloring his voice, he asked, "So, when are you planning to move in?"

She pondered that a moment. "Well, I'd like to move in as soon a possible. No matter what he says, Riley's couch *is* lumpy. I'd have to call Bryce first and arrange a time when he's not around to get my stuff. Really, all I need is my clothes and a few other small things."

"I'll help," he offered. "I suspect you won't want to go there alone."

She shuddered. "Really? That would be perfect. To tell the truth, I'm scared to go there at all, let alone by myself. I could use some backup in case Bryce tries to violate the restraining order."

Her stomach lurched unpleasantly as she grabbed her cell phone from her purse and called an all-too-familiar number.

"Hello, Bryce."

"Diana! I was hoping you'd call. I miss you so much. I'm sorry I yelled at you. You know I love you, sweetheart."

He sounded so humble and beseeching that Diana's face softened.

"I know you love me and I know you're sorry you yelled—"

Alex waved his hand to get Diana's attention. He shook his head while mouthing, "Don't fall for it."

Straightening in the chair, she continued, "Look, I just called to see when you were going to be out of the condo for a few hours. I need to come by and pick up my stuff."

She held the phone away from her ear. Even Alex winced as Bryce yelled on the other end of the line.

"What do you mean, pick up your stuff? You're my wife. You can't leave me like this. I forbid it! If you want your things, you can come here and get them. I'm not leaving."

Diana stiffened. Through gritted teeth, she said, "No, you can't be there. The restraining order says you can't come within a thousand feet of me. You need to leave so I can get my things."

"I don't have to do anything, you bitch. This is my house. You already threw me out once, and I won't let you do it again."

"Calm down, Bryce. I'm trying to be civil here."

"Civil? You call this civil? After not talking to me for two weeks, you demand that I leave my home so you can get your things? I don't think so. Besides, where are you going to live, with Riley and Tessa?"

"It's none of your business where I live anymore. If you are still there when I show up, I will call the police and have your ass thrown in jail. Kind of hard to do business from a jail cell, don't you think?"

The volume of the cursing coming through the small phone went up several notches.

Raising her own voice to be heard over Bryce's temper tantrum, Diana shouted, "Shut the hell up!"

Instant silence.

After a moment, Diana smiled and continued at a normal volume. "You do *not* get to yell at me like that anymore, got it?" She tucked a strand of her hair that had fallen across her face behind her ear. "Make sure you are out of the condo between two and five PM this afternoon. I will come get my things, then you can have the place all to yourself from now on."

"Between two and five? You can't be serious. That would completely disrupt my day."

"It's an inconvenience for you? Well, I don't care. Just do it."

She heard him sputtering, trying to convince her to change her mind.

"Thank you," she said sweetly, ending the call.

Glancing at Alex, she smiled. "You know, that was very satisfying. Why couldn't I have done that before?" She shook her head, the strand of hair escaping again. "I can't believe I let myself get that much under his thumb. Well, that stops now."

"So," Alex said, raising his eyebrows. "It looks like we're moving you in today then." He grinned at her wickedly. "Let's go rob from the rich and give to the poor. Us."

* * *

Alex kicked his feet up on the end of the leather couch. *I really like Riley's new office. So much bigger than that old closet he had before.* He chuckled to himself. *At least I don't feel like I'm sitting in Riley's lap when I'm working with him now. Hmmm. Now there's an idea.*

"See, Riley?" Alex said. "I told you the forum's taken off. I think we've struck a chord with a lot of people. I mean, just think about it. They've all thought they were the only ones dreaming about this or having regressions. Now that they know they're not alone, they can't stop talking about it."

Riley nodded. "It seems there are more people interested in Xeres than we expected. Look, there are even people on here from some small town in Tennessee. How did *they* find out about us already?"

Alex covered his face with his hands before he answered. "Ummmm, I kind of posted about the forum to a couple of the Reddit groups that I belong to. Word must have gotten out from there."

"I thought the forum would be a few therapists and maybe some of their clients, but I never expected to reach this many people," Riley said.

Alex turned to him. "And look at this post from a guy named HotDoc."

> ‡*HotDoc: I had a client who mentioned these crystals. He said that they were once used in power plants, but that there were hardly any left anywhere because they'd all been mined. He said that whenever anyone found one, they kept it as a good luck stone. Sort of how we keep a rabbits foot.*‡

"That's interesting. Crystal, huh? Like Star Trek?" Riley asked. "I wonder what came after the crystals as an energy source?"

"I don't know, but whatever it was, it was clean and environmentally friendly. And it solved their energy crisis. Listen to this."

‡DemBones: I had dreams when I was a kid about working in this really odd building. I knew that it was some kind of power generating plant. I was always so proud because we'd solved the energy crisis and wouldn't have to ration our power consumption anymore.‡

‡Corny: @DemBones: I remember being a farmer. We used expensive electricity from hydropower plus wind turbines. Those damned turbines were always breaking down. We couldn't fix them ourselves. Had to call in really expensive techs. The turbines killed migrating birds too.

When the new energy source was available in our neck of the woods, we were so glad to give those turbines up. The new energy was clean, didn't harm the environment in any way. Our farm just bloomed after that.‡

"So they had an energy problem and when this new energy showed up, it was cleaner and better," Riley said, leaning away from the monitor. "If the first one was electricity, could the new one be atomic energy?"

Alex shook his head. "Not if it was clean and didn't hurt the environment. I can't think of any current technology that can produce clean, safe energy without some environmental side effects. Well, maybe fusion, but that's still a long way from being useful. Maybe they found a way to make it work."

A smile lit up Alex's face as he pointed to the screen.

"Oh, and you're going to love this: Cadwallader joined the forum."

Riley's eyebrows rose. "You're kidding. He warned me away from this line of research. What could possibly be in it for him? What's his angle?"

Alex huffed. "I can answer that. Clients."

"Huh? How?"

"Look here."

‡Spellbinder: I am indeed in San Diego, but I already have more clients than I can comfortably see in a week. I am booked solid for the next month and a

half. I could try to work you in sometime after that, if you'd like.‡

Riley looked at Alex. "Seriously? Spellbinder? That's what he chose as his name on the forum? Do you think he's telling the truth, about having so many clients? If it were, he wouldn't have any money problems, would he?"

"I don't know. Maybe. From what Denny told Tessa, I'd guess he's living beyond his means."

"I feel sorry for any of our members who actually go see him," Riley said, frowning. "I'd love to warn them off, but that's not polite. Who knows, they might get something out of it."

"There were four other hypnotherapists on that thread, including Evelyn. She even threw your name into the mix."

"That was nice of her. Still, he'll get anyone who lives close to San Diego."

"There's only three people on the forum from there. Statistically, I think we're safe."

"Thank goodness for small favors." Riley chuckled, but choked it off as his eyes fell on a different topic. He pointed to a message labeled *Let's Get Together?* "This could be trouble."

"Ouch! You're right," Alex said, leaning forward. "If they get together, they're going to need a referee, maybe even the police or a SWAT team."

"Here, let me post something." Elbowing Alex aside, he began to type.

"No," Alex said, yanking his laptop away from Riley. "I'm logged in. If you post something, it'll show up as me." He set his laptop back on the desk. "Here, let me log out, then you can log in." After a moment, he stood, offering Riley the chair. "There. All yours."

Riley sat down and began typing.

‡DocMezmer: I'd strongly advise against meeting up in person at this time.

There are extenuating circumstances regarding meeting in person which you are not aware of yet. We have found that people from the different guilds, even if they were friends prior to being regressed/having their memories of Xeres awakened, take an instant and visceral dislike to each other after regression/ awakening. We have no way currently to tell who is from which guild without a full regression where they are asked directly which one they belong to. I am deeply concerned that if several of you meet up, that it could lead to severe complications.

Please, I beg of you, do not pursue this at this time. Once we have a better idea if this can be surmounted, we will help arrange a get together for all interested parties.‡

"There. Hopefully, that will dissuade them." Riley's stress was evident in the tense line of his shoulders. He rolled his shoulders and twisted his neck. "I hope they listen."

Alex nodded, absentmindedly rubbing Riley's shoulders. "If they don't, things could get really interesting. Maybe I should tell them what happened between me and Evelyn. That might convince them."

* * *

"In other news tonight, two local college students at UC-San Diego have been reported missing. The two girls, on-campus roommates in the Village, went missing over the weekend. Friends of the girls say they realized something was wrong when they missed a study session on Wednesday night. One of the girls was seen leaving campus on Tuesday afternoon in a late model, dark blue Ford Taurus with California license plate 2XER454.

Viewers with any information are advised to contact the San Diego Police Department immediately."

Chapter 20

"Mr. LeRoux, we've been monitoring the subject's internet usage, as you requested. He's been spending considerable time on a website called Reincarnation Beyond Earth. Our agents on the ground in San Diego also report that he has had two after hours meetings with young women recently. Our agents saw the women meet with the subject, but did not see the women after their meeting. News reports have been issued about two local UCSD coeds who have gone missing. Sir…." The man in the well-tailored suit stood almost at attention. Only his eyes and the brief flick of his tongue betrayed his unease. "We believe that the subject may be holding the women somewhere. Should we search the subject's office and living quarters to see if we can locate the women?"

Across the wide expanse of polished marble, Thierry sat with his fingers steepled, deep in thought. Looking up at his head of security, he shook his head.

"No. I'll handle it from here, thank you." With a wave of his hand, he dismissed the man.

Cadwallader. Again. What scheme is the man up to now? Turning Bryce loose to remove this annoyance is looking better all the time.

Swiveling his chair to face the bank of windows, he reached into his jacket and retrieved his cell phone. A look of extreme distaste crossed his handsome face as he searched for the correct number. Stabbing it, he waited impatiently for an answer.

Finally, the other end picked up.

"Da?"

The coded message came easily to his tongue.

"Sheitan Protocol: Code Alpha Four, Beta Two, Charlie Six, Charlie Seven."

Silence.

It stretched on long enough for Thierry to start tapping his foot.

"Da. Recognized." The voice was guttural, harsh, like someone had sandpapered a normal voice. Sergei Antonov, aka Prizrak, was a man of few words. *Maybe,* Thierry considered, *spending so much time in the cold Russian winters has frozen any excess words he might once have had. That or the vodka.*

"I have a situation best handled by someone not connected to the company. One of my captains presumes too much power. I would have his online activity scrubbed clean before authorities catch a scent of his doings. Make sure that it looks as though he did it himself rather than an outside party. It must not be traceable to our organization."

"I can do. But you owe Sergei debt."

Thierry shook his head silently. That was always the way with his kind. One received nothing without paying for it.

"That is acceptable."

"Good. Send information and I do."

The line went dead.

Thierry gritted his teeth, wanting to hurl the sleek little phone across the room to shatter into tiny pieces, that he could then grind into dust with his elegant Italian loafers. With centuries of restraint, he carefully placed it into his pocket. Standing, he paced the gleaming marble floor from the Theodore Chasseriau painting to the bust of the screaming satyr Marsyas by Balthasar Permoser from the Baroque period. The tap-tap of his heels only served to increase his agitation.

Stopping mid-stride, he came to a decision. Pulling the offensive phone out, he gave it a wry look, then selected a number from his recent call list.

* * *

"Sir? How can I help you?" Bryce Lundee tried to keep the excitement out of his voice. *Thierry's calling me personally? I'm not the captain of this area anymore. Maybe Cadwallader screwed up enough that I'll finally get to take over as area captain again.*

"Regarding the matter that you brought to my attention—"

Bryce felt his insides freeze up. *Wait, am I in trouble for losing my hold on Diana after all? Could Thierry be blaming me for the whole situation?* For a moment he could scarcely breathe.

166

Interrupting, Bryce blurted out, "Sir, I have done everything I can to get Diana back." The next two seconds was the longest period he could remember.

"Diana?" The confusion in Thierry's voice was palpable. "No, no. We have more pressing problems at the moment."

Bryce let out a breath he hadn't realized he'd been holding. His body sloughed off his tension like a snake shedding its skin. Leaning into the phone, he waited, wondering if whatever Thierry was calling about could be twisted to his benefit.

"Matthew Cadwallader has stepped too far out of line. I have a report that he has most likely consumed two young Xerians he met on an online forum. I have gone to great expense to conceal his involvement. Now I need an operative to follow up and report back to me personally. You were the West Coast captain prior to Matthew Cadwallader. If things continue the way they are going, you may get the chance to reclaim that position."

Bryce sat down abruptly on his living room sofa. Holding the phone away from him, he gave it a look of astonishment. *At last! I'm finally getting the recognition I deserve. If only I hadn't died in that car accident and reincarnated ahead of schedule, I would never have lost the position in the first place. I'm almost positive Cadwallader arranged the accident so he could take over the West Coast operations. I had to wait twenty long years before I was old enough to investigate the cause of my car accident. After nearly ten years of research, I still can't prove Cadwallader was responsible.*

"I have always been loyal, sir. Anything you need, I am at your service." Bryce knew that he wasn't containing his excitement very well, but that couldn't be helped. *I would do anything to get my former status back. Anything! Even if it means eliminating Cadwallader. Especially if it means eliminating Cadwallader,* he amended.

"Good. You will log on to this website, reincarnate.net, and monitor things there. Contact me immediately if you encounter anything that needs my attention."

Bryce grinned. *Not only is he not mad at me, but I might get my old job and status back. And such a simple assignment.*

"Yes, sir, I can do that. I'll call you with any developments," Bryce replied smartly.

Thierry continued, "Also, start thinking of how we can permanently remove Matthew from the organization. Consuming two women without my permission puts our organization in jeopardy. This cannot be allowed. It goes without saying that whatever befalls Matthew can *not* be traceable to our organization. Do you understand?"

"Yes, sir. Certainly, sir." Bryce smiled wickedly. *Oh, how sweet it will be, getting my position back over Cadwallader's dead body. I could rid myself of Diana and finally be free to find a more compliant woman.*

"I think I know just how to deal with Cadwallader, sir."

* * *

The last few blocks to Bryce's condo, Cadwallader was still riding the high he'd gotten from the two coeds. The air of the Bay Area smelled fresher and the breeze through his open car window only heightened his mood. Even the heat of the day felt good against his skin. Colors were more brilliant. The whole world seemed newly created, just for him. *Why have I denied myself this pleasure for so long? Okay, LeRoux has rules against taking a Xerian without permission. So what? How would he ever know, anyway? And that forum? A prime hunting ground, just waiting to be exploited, and no one the wiser.* His thoughts took a darker turn. *It's too bad we'll have to shut it down eventually. It's just too dangerous to let all those Xerians wake up to their true selves.*

But first I have to deal with Bryce Lundee. The man has been a pain in my side ever since we got to Xeres. It won't do for him to get ideas of doing to me what I did to him. No, no. There won't be any 'accidents' in my future.

He drummed his fingers against the wheel in tune with the upbeat music on the satellite radio. He had it turned up so loud that he'd gotten the finger from a little old lady at one stoplight. Glancing at the speedometer, he realized he was speeding. A good mood could do that to you. He made himself slow down. It wouldn't do to hit a pedestrian on these urban streets, even if the only pedestrians around were hookers.

He pulled into an empty space near Bryce's condo. Frowning, he wondered why Bryce, who made buckets of money, would choose to live in such a dubious area. His own house was surrounded by other luxuriant homes and fenced against intruders. Unfortunately, his lush lawn, indeed, all the lush greenery that had once decorated San Diego's dry canyons and coast were becoming a thing of the past due to the ongoing drought.

Bryce answered the intercom quickly, buzzing him inside, out of the heat. The cool interior prickled on his skin like champagne bubbles, sending a pleasant shiver down his spine.

He was just leaving the elevator when a door opened down the hall.

"What are you doing this far north, Cadwallader?" Bryce didn't seem all that pleased to find him on his doorstep.

Cadwallader passed it off with a wave of his hand. "I thought it was time for a visit." Moving toward Bryce, he pushed past the man into the condo.

He looked around the spacious loft condo. Nicely decorated. Definitely a show place. It certainly fit the image the man liked to project. *Probably done up by that Xerian wife of his. The runaway wife,* he amended with a smirk.

Selecting a seat on the sofa, he laid an arm along the back and crossed his leg.

"I'm here to help you with your wayward wife."

Looking skeptical, Bryce perched on the edge of an over-stuffed chair.

"Oh? And you came all the way up here when you could have just called?" The man lifted an eyebrow.

Cadwallader frowned. *I don't like his tone. After all, I am the area captain. Still, I have my reasons. Better to placate him, for now, at least.*

"You called *me* looking for help, remember? I realized, belatedly, that I took your concerns too lightly. So rather than just phoning you, when I couldn't actually assist you, I came here in person to help you deal with it."

"Right. Well, I appreciate your time and expense, but I don't see what you can do about it. She took out a restraining order on me, so I can't even get close enough to apologize. I've tried calling, but she's blocked my number. And her damned partner, Tessa Connors, won't answer my calls either." He shrugged his shoulders. "I don't know what you can do about any of that."

Cadwallader's eyes blinked at the name. *It couldn't possibly be....* Steadying his voice so he wouldn't betray his interest, he asked, "Her partner's name is Tessa Connors? Might she be dating a hypnotherapist by the name of Riley MacPherson?"

Bryce answered through gritted teeth. "Oh, yes. That damned man and his girlfriend have taken Diana from me." He rose from the chair and began pacing. "Hell, I'll bet they put her up to getting that restraining order. I don't even know where she's living now."

Ignoring the man's ramblings, Cadwallader's mind was already putting the pieces together. *Bryce, Diana, Tessa, Riley. Of course, they're all interconnected. Maybe there's a way to get even more out of this trip than I thought. As good as it was to consume those two Xerian coeds, I could have a Tesham. It's been centuries since I've enjoyed that particular deliciousness. They're better than anything I've ever tasted. So sweet, so rich…. LeRoux's rules can go to hell. I must find a way to make her mine.*

But MacPherson's going to pose a problem. I need to find a way to take him out if I'm going to feast on that tasty Tesham of his. He's already asking too many questions. He's *responsible for waking the Xerians up in the first place. That won't be good for anyone, especially if the guilds start fighting again. History has an ugly way of repeating itself. And I've grown to like this planet.*

"Are you even listening to me?" Bryce's angry voice cut through Cadwallader's internal monologue. Looking up, he found Bryce standing in front of him, hands balled into fists.

"Of course I'm listening," he said. "And I understand your frustration." He bit his lip before continuing. "Hmmm. I actually know MacPherson and his Xerian girlfriend. We met at the last hypnotherapy conference. Perhaps I could talk some sense into him. Maybe convince them to let you visit Diana. To try and work things out."

Anger abating a little, Bryce returned to his chair and sat down. Leaning forward, he braced himself on his arms and knees.

"You really think you could mediate between me and Diana? Wait. Tessa? Tessa's a Xerian too?"

Cadwallader sat back. *Damn. Bryce didn't know she was Xerian? I hate giving the man new information, especially for free.* "Oh, I'm sure of it. I spotted her at the last conference. Her man, MacPherson, is becoming a thorn in my side. He's even started a forum for Xerians to connect with each other. It's helping them remember who they were before. And you know where that will lead. War."

"Does LeRoux know about this?"

"No, and if we handle this correctly, he never will. You know how the man hates to be bothered with minor problems. Well, this is a minor problem for the moment. If we eliminate MacPherson and his girlfriend, we can solve the problem before it gets big enough to concern LeRoux."

"So, what's your solution to this mess?"

Excellent. I've got him hooked.

Fairly thrumming with excitement, Cadwallader leaned toward

Bryce. In a conspiratorial voice, he said, "I propose we get rid of Tessa and frame MacPherson for her disappearance. That way, we can eliminate MacPherson and everyone will think he did her in, then ran away. No one would think to come after either one of us. And as an added bonus, with them gone, I'm *sure* Diana, devastated by the loss of her friend and business partner, would come back to you. And his damned forum would wither away and die without him there to keep it going."

Bryce nodded, then smiled.

Taking that for assent, Cadwallader rose. "MacPherson gave me his card at the conference. I'll go pay him a visit. Maybe I can find out something that can help you make your case with Diana. It's the perfect excuse to feel out this situation."

* * *

As the door closed behind Cadwallader, Bryce grabbed one of Diana's designer pillows and threw it across the room. When that didn't assuage his anger, he picked up another. Looking at it for a moment, he grabbed it with both hands and ripped it open. Stuffing flew into the air, settling on the carpet, sofa, chairs and table. He blinked at the mess for a moment. Sighing, he rolled his shoulders in an attempt to release the tension that had built up there. He sank into a chair and pulled out his phone. *Time to contact LeRoux,* he thought. *Maybe this will be enough to convince him to restore my authority. I* will *take back my area captaincy.*

"What?"

Bryce could hear the frown on his boss' face. *If I don't make this good, I'll squander the chance fate has offered me.*

"Cadwallader just left my condo."

"And what was he doing there?" LeRoux's voice betrayed nothing of what he felt. Bryce knew the man was focused on his every word.

"He *said* he was here to help me with Diana. I didn't believe that for an instant. I think he's plotting to take out Tessa Connors and Riley MacPherson. Said it would solve several problems for him and cause that forum of MacPherson's to go down."

Silence reigned at the other end of the connection. Bryce worried at his lower lip. *Have I somehow said the wrong thing? I thought LeRoux would be interested in this news.*

The voice, when it finally came, was cold, flat, and vibrated with an undercurrent of violence. "I will not have this. You must stop him. Neither of them is to be harmed and the forum must *not* go down. I have plans that depend upon them."

Bryce pumped his fist in the air. *YES! Finally!*

Carefully keeping the jubilation out of his voice, Bryce offered, "What would you like me to do, sir?"

Bryce could hear the barely controlled rage in LeRoux's cultured voice. "First, find a way to stop him. He cannot follow this plan to completion. If he does, it will be on *your* head."

"Of course, sir. Of course." Fear and jubilation warred within him.

Continuing on as if Bryce hadn't said anything, LeRoux said, "Second, find a way to return the favor that Mr. Cadwallader paid you at the end of your last life."

An ice-cold realization crept over Bryce as LeRoux's words sank in. *He knew that Cadwallader killed me all those years ago, but he didn't do anything about it. And he promoted the bastard to take my place. Am I nothing more than a pawn on his chessboard?*

"But make sure you aren't as sloppy as he was when your previous incarnation was killed. I had to step in and pay off several high-level officials to prevent it being traced back to our organization. I trust that you can handle such a simple task without my involvement?"

Bryce sat up straight, as much at attention as any soldier. "Yes, sir. You can count on me."

"I certainly hope so. Otherwise…."

The implied threat in LeRoux's words came crystal clear through the connection. *My very existence is on the line!* he thought. *Damn Cadwallader. The man has been causing me trouble ever since we arrived on Xeres.*

* * *

"Breaking news tonight. The bodies of two young women were found washed ashore at Dead Man's Point near Ruocco Park. Police believe the bodies belong to Sinthia Thorsgard and Belinda Kirk, the two UCSD students who went missing last weekend. The car they were last seen in was recovered earlier today in a downtown parking garage. Police report there were no signs of forced entry or struggle around the vehicle. We will update this story as more information becomes available."

172

Chapter 21

"I'm glad you understand the importance of shutting down that silly forum of yours. There's been lots of talk. None of it good. People think you're a crackpot, and that's not good for business," Cadwallader said, as Riley escorted him through the lobby to the front stairs.

Riley sighed. Same old, same old. "I'll take your advice under consideration. I'm flattered that you decided to stop by and see me while you were in town." He tried to keep his face neutral while lying through his teeth. Having Cadwallader "just drop in" wasn't high on Riley's list of the best ways to end his work day.

A door opened on the far side of the room.

"Well, look what the cat dragged in." Both men turned toward the new voice. "Thanks for taking out the trash, Riley." Evelyn was leaning against the door jam, hard eyes watching Cadwallader as if he were potential prey.

Cadwallader's face flooded red. Riley could practically see steam coming out of his ears.

"I didn't know you were sharing office space with this *harpy*. You really should work on your poor judgement."

"Um, actually, it's working quite well for me," Riley said.

The man looked down his nose at Riley, completely ignoring Evelyn. "Remember what I said about making good choices." Opening the outer door, he said, "I know where the stairs are."

When the door closed, Riley turned and braced his shoulders against the wall and crossed his arms. Smiling at Evelyn, he said, "Well, that was a fun way to get rid of him."

She gave him a wry grin. "Well, some people brighten the room when they enter it." She waved a hand towards the door. "He brightens the room when he leaves."

Riley couldn't help himself. Shoving away from the wall, he burst out laughing. "I do so love the way you and he get along. For my money, you always get the better of him."

"Don't I, though?" She joined in his laughter.

The door behind Riley swung open. *Oh dear god, he's back!* he thought with dismay. *Please, I can't take any more of the man.*

"Uh, what's going on in here? Did I miss something good?"

Alex stepped through, spied Evelyn, and looked pleadingly at Riley. "I...um...I need to show you something. About the forum. Could we...."

Recognizing Alex's discomfort, Riley waved goodnight to Evelyn and followed the man rapidly disappearing down the stairs.

Alex paused on the landing and looked back up at Riley. "Someone hacked into the forum. I wouldn't even have caught it if I hadn't broken something and had to restore from my backup. When I compared the two files, I noticed something odd. The number of users and posts didn't match up. I thought maybe someone had just deleted their account, but that should have left a record in the log. The log was clear. So I did a little digging and...." He trailed off.

"And?" Riley prompted.

"The missing user and the missing posts were connected. They were all about Cadwallader. The backups are at my place on my desktop computer, if you want to come over and see for yourself."

"That's odd. Cadwallader just stopped by, to 'chat' with me. Something's not right." He gestured for Alex to precede him through the glass door to the street. "Tessa's having dinner with a client this evening, so she's not expecting me home. Let's go."

It wasn't long before Riley found himself pacing around Alex's living room while he booted his computer. *It's easy to see Diana's hand in here. Looks good, too. Maybe I should let Tessa have her way with our place. It shouldn't cost that much.*

Alex's call pulled him out of his reverie. Riley pulled a chair from the dining table and sat down next to him.

"See here? It's just like I told you. Every post Spellbinder made or that even mentions him was scrubbed from the forum," Alex said, leaning back in his rolling chair.

"Can you tell who removed his stuff?"

Alex leaned forward, his fingers flying. *My fingers would tie themselves in knots at that speed.*

Alex's typing ceased suddenly. He stared transfixed at the screen.

"This doesn't make any sense." Alex turned to Riley, frowning. "It looks like the person who removed everything was Cadwallader himself. The intrusion came from the same IP address that he used when he signed up for the the forum. It had to be him, or someone using his computer."

Stroking his beard, Riley asked, "Why would Caddy remove his own profile and posts? He wants all the exposure he can get. He's probably trolling for clients here or maybe to sell some of his books."

Alex nodded. "You're right about that. Besides, he doesn't strike me as computer savvy enough to pull this off. He could have just deleted his posts and account. Why go to the extra trouble to hack the forum and remove everything from the log too?"

Riley ran a hand through his hair. "All that aside, the real question is, *why* would he remove them?"

"Why would who remove what?"

Turning from where they were hunched over the computer screen, the two men found Diana strolling across the living room towards them.

"Di. I didn't know you were home." Alex stood to give her a hug.

Returning the hug, she smiled down at Riley. "Good to see you too, Riley. I was working in the bedroom and heard you guys out here. So, who were you talking about?"

Riley answered. "Cadwallader. He's an author we know from our conferences."

"And pompous windbag, don't forget that," Alex added.

"Oh, Tessa mentioned him." She made a face. "Apparently she did *not* like him. She said he was a real pain in the ass." Laughing at Riley's raised eyebrows, she continued. "She likened him to a used car salesman. Strange, though. She said that when he touched her she felt an uncontrollable urge to kill him." She shook her head, dark hair swirling about her head. "That's just not like her. She likes everybody."

Alex turned back to his computer. He brought up Matthew Cadwallader's profile from his website. "This is the pain in the ass in question. See what she meant?"

"You know, he looks familiar. I think I saw him recently." She frowned in thought. "I know. It was when I stopped by for my mail this morning. He was coming out of our building. But I thought Tessa said he lived in San Diego."

"He does," Riley said, "but he's in the area for some reason or other. He stopped by my office this afternoon."

"Bryce is usually the only person in our building home at that time of day. I just assumed he was one of Bryce's clients." Diana pulled up another chair from the dining table and joined the gathering at Alex's computer desk.

"That doesn't make sense." Riley scratched his ear. "From what we've heard, Cadwallader's been having financial difficulties. Why would he have business with an expensive stock trader like Bryce?"

Alex, quiet until now, jumped in. "Riley, remember how in my regression I couldn't place which guild Cadwallader belonged to, and Tessa said the same thing about Bryce? What if they are from the same guild, some other guild besides the Bylantians or the Klymurians? Could they be Tesham?" Alex glanced significantly at Diana. He didn't want to reveal anything that she shouldn't know.

Riley shook his head. "Well, maybe. But Tessa reacted badly to both of them. I wonder if they are a fourth group we haven't heard about yet."

Alex held his head with both hands. "Oi! Just what we need, a fourth guild. This is getting so complicated."

Riley laughed. "You've *seen* the pages upon pages of notes that I have on all this. I can barely keep everything straight as it is. Whenever I go over my notes, I get a headache trying to juggle all the pieces."

"You know, Riley, I think that this is too much for you to sort through by yourself. We should all get together and go over everything we know. Maybe together we can make better sense of all this."

Riley nodded. "That's not a bad idea. How's Saturday afternoon sound?"

"This sounds fascinating! Can I come? I'd like to help, too," Diana said hopefully.

Alex looked at Riley.

"Um, I appreciate the offer, but I don't think that's such a good idea, Diana. There is something you're probably not aware of. People from different guilds don't react well to members of the other guilds."

"So? Alex is coping okay, isn't he?"

"I didn't, at first," he said with a wry grin. "Got sick to my stomach and wanted to hurt Evelyn. Bad!"

"And what did you do to conquer that?" Diana asked.

Alex sighed. "A *lot* of self-hypnosis and meditation. Took me weeks to even be in the same room with Evelyn."

Her face fell. "Oh."

Alex placed a reassuring hand on his roommate's arm. "I'm sure you can get over it in time, but not before Saturday afternoon. Sorry." Turning to Riley, he said, "Yeah, Saturday. Your place? I can load the forum backup on my laptop so we can show Tessa and Evelyn what we found."

Riley nodded. "I think that's best. At least we can all be comfy in my living room."

Alex gave him a wry smile. "Speak for yourself. Things are still a little tense with me and Evelyn, and I'm not on speaking terms with your lumpy sofa."

* * *

"Please, come in," Tessa said, smiling as she held the front door open for Evelyn. Closing it, Tessa took a seat on the sofa arm next to Riley.

Evelyn dropped her purse and jacket on the end table. Spying Alex, huddled with Riley on the couch, she felt an immediate spike of tension in the air. She took a calming breath. She knew she could overcome this. Hadn't it gotten easier every time she saw him?

Seeking a distraction from her slightly queasy stomach, she surveyed the drab living room and sniffed. *Well. This place looks like he just got out of college. It does sort of match his old office. Maybe he'll upgrade this next.*

Riley glanced up at her. "Hello, Evelyn. Did you see the post on the forum yesterday? One of our users says a couple of girls near her in San Diego have gone missing. She's worried that they are the girls who have suddenly stopped posting on the forum."

Riley pointed to the messages displayed on Alex's laptop. "I told WendyAnn we'd look into this. Alex, you're my resident computer expert. Can you find out anything?"

‡WendyAnn: @docmezmer, there was a news report that two girls have gone missing from UCSD. I'm concerned that it is @Vampgrrrl and @ThorRider. Do you have any way to look up their contact info and see if

they are the missing girls from here in San Diego? I think the police should know if that's the case. It's been all over the news, and I can't help but think that it might be them. Please put my mind at ease and let me know it isn't. Thank you.‡

‡DocMezmer: @WendyAnn Either myself or @OneEyedScoobie will look into that and let you know what we find out. I hope they are ok too.‡

Tapping a few keys, Alex brought up the administration panel and searched the user records for VampGrrrl and ThorRider.

"That's disturbing," Evelyn said. "I sure hope the missing girls aren't the same ones from your forum."

Circling the furniture, she looked for somewhere to sit. Unfortunately, the only place open was the overstuffed chair next to Alex.

As she approached, she saw Alex stiffen, then force himself to relax.

Good, she thought. *At least both of us are actively trying.*

Evelyn tried to make out what they were working on, but with them hunched over Alex's laptop on the coffee table, the angle was wrong. Hoping for a better view, she moved to perch on the sofa arm. Next to Alex.

"Riley, am I charging you too much for your office? I must be if you're still using this couch. It has to be from sometime in the middle of the last century. It's older than I am." She arched an eyebrow at him. "And I'm in better shape!" She ran a hand over her face, mentally kicking herself. *Being here and having to deal with Alex is sharpening my tongue. I'll have to watch that.*

Riley looked up, bewildered. "Huh? Couch?"

"See, Riley? It's not just me who thinks this couch is uncomfortable." Alex said, a big grin on his face.

Tessa, the color rising in her cheeks, leaped to Riley's defense. "We're saving up for the down-payment on a house. We don't want to get new things until we know what style we need for the new place."

Evelyn felt her face go warm. "Tessa, I'm sorry. I'm not usually like this. It's just—"

Alex broke in. "Yeah, I'm feeling the strain too."

Evelyn cleared her throat. "Well, if I'm through putting my foot in my mouth, can I say, this seating arrangement isn't working?"

She pointed to Tessa, on the other arm. "First, Tessa and I can't see the screen you two are so intent on. Second," she looked down at her perch, "this is damned uncomfortable."

Alex poked Riley in the ribs. "Told you so. I said we should sit at the kitchen table, but you had to sit on this damned lumpy couch."

Riley grimaced. He shot Tessa a look and she tilted her head toward the kitchen. Raising his hands above his head, he said, "I give up. Let's move to the kitchen table. I'll haul one of the chairs out of the office.

"Good idea." Evelyn commented, rising from the arm of the sofa.

"This way," Tessa said, heading for the arched doorway.

Evelyn stopped in the doorway. She took in the small table shoved up against the wall with its three mismatched chairs sitting one to a side. "Cozy, very cozy," she said slowly, pondering how to keep away from Alex but still be able to see his laptop's screen.

"I grabbed my laptop, too, just in case."

She started at Riley's voice behind her, then quickly moved aside as he rolled a desk chair into the kitchen.

"Okay," she said, taking the kitchen chair furthest from Alex.

Riley scooted his chair in between her and Tessa, then began filling her in.

"I know we were originally going to talk about other things, but with these girls going missing, we decided to make that a priority. Alex is looking into their records now."

Alex grabbed Riley's arm. "You know how I told you that the forum had been hacked and all of the posts involving Cadwallader had been deleted?"

Evelyn blinked. "Wait, someone hacked the forum?"

Alex nodded. "I discovered it when I installed a bad mod that crashed the forum. When I restored it, I found discrepancies. Looking into it, I discovered that anything connected to Cadwallader's alias had been deleted. But I just found something new. He had private conversations with both of the missing girls that were deleted too. Look."

They all bent toward his screen.

‡*Spellbinder: @ThorRider, I have a cancellation today at five, could you come in for a regression? I know that you and your roommate both want*

regressions, but I only have time today to see one of you. I wouldn't want to cause problems between the two of you, since you will get a regression and she won't, so if you want to wait until I have time for both of you, I'll understand. I promise I will let you know immediately if I get another cancellation so I can see your friend too.‡

‡ThorRider: @Spellbinder, I think I could just make it. I want my regression as soon as possible. You're right about her. She gets really jealous. She's always saying everything just works out for me when she has to work her butt off for everything. If I tell her, she'll get bent out of shape. I'm so excited to finally get a regression! Thank you thank you thank you! I'll be there shortly.‡

"Caddy had private conversations with *both* the missing girls?" Evelyn asked. She shook her head. *There's something fishy going on here.* "Yeah, he talked to the other girl the next day. See."

‡Spellbinder: @VampGrrrl I spoke with her on Friday afternoon. I had a cancellation so I offered for her to come in for a regression. The regression seemed to upset her pretty badly. She mentioned several things that I didn't understand, something about not trusting that lying bitch. I don't know. I have some free time this afternoon if you'd like to stop by. I can let you listen to the recording of the session and maybe you can make sense of what upset her. That might give you a clue where she's gone. I want to help in any way I can. I am beside myself to think that she's missing.‡

‡Vampgrrrl: @Spellbinder I think I might know what that's about. When we first discovered we both remembered Xeres, we remembered that we were both after the same guy. I never told her that I have had dreams where he and I hook up. I bet she found out about that and is pissed at me. Dammit, it was another life! She can't blame me for what happened then. I think I need to hear what she said. Maybe she's just avoiding me and I'm being paranoid. It will take me the better part of an hour to get to your office by bus. Will that be ok?‡

‡Spellbinder: @Vampgrrrl Actually, that will be perfect. I will have just finished with my last client of the day. We can listen to the tapes, and if you

think of where she might be, I can give you a lift to find her. I want to help you resolve this as quickly as possible. I hope the poor girl is just mad at you and not lost somewhere.‡

‡Vampgrrrl: @Spellbinder Ok, thanks for your help! I've been so stressed out worrying about her. No one else has done anything.‡

Silence reigned as everyone read over the messages. Then everyone began speaking at once.

"That makes it sound like—" Evelyn started.

"We have to show this to the—" Alex said.

Tessa protested. "Why would he.—"

THWEET!

Riley's ear-splitting whistle reverberated off the hard walls of the kitchen.

"Calm down everyone. I know this looks bad, but let's not jump to any conclusions just yet. It could all be perfectly harmless."

Alex nodded agreement. "I'm still confused about *how* Cadwallader removed all mention of himself from the forum."

"You're saying Cad's the one who hacked your forum?" Evelyn asked.

Their resident computer expert nodded. "It looks like it. At least, I traced it back to his IP address."

Evelyn's eyes widened. "I didn't think ole Cad had that kind of computer savvy. I mean, the man needs a map to find the bathrooms at conferences. And probably another one to know what to do once he gets there."

"Yes," Riley said, chuckling, "that's what I thought, too."

Alex raised a finger to get their attention. "If he didn't hack us, then who did?"

"I don't know," Tessa said, tension making her fidget. "But with two girls missing and the forum being hacked, I wonder if we should report this to the police?"

Evelyn said, "Or maybe we should take the forum down. At the very least, we should put out a warning. But what do we say? We don't have concrete proof that Cadwallader had anything to do with the missing girls. It's all circumstantial evidence at this point."

Riley rolled his shoulders. "Maybe we should—."

Boing!

Glancing at his computer, Alex read silently for a moment. Looking up from the screen, he said, "Uh, folks? We have a new user who just posted in this thread. He's a cop in San Francisco."

"Really? What does he say?"

> ‡*Tinman: I was referred here by my hypnotherapist, @HotDoc. (I can't believe he uses that handle.) I'm a cop here in San Francisco and apparently, I've been having dreams of Xeres too. Anyway, I just wanted to say that if anyone has any news on the missing girls, let me know, I can get it to the proper authorities in San Diego. I have friends on the force there who used to work with me here in SF.*‡

Evelyn broke the silence first.

"Should we just dump this all in his lap?"

Alex protested. "He's new on the forum. He could be anyone. Hell, he could even be the person who removed all of Cad's posts. He could just be pretending to be a cop."

"So we call and check out his story," Evelyn said impatiently. "See if he's really who he says he is. You have his name from his registration, right? Call the SFPD and see if they have an officer with that name. We could also contact this HotDoc person, too, and see if he is actually a patient."

Tessa interrupted. "I don't know about the rest of you, but my blood sugar is low and my brain's not firing on all cylinders. Let's figure out what to do over supper."

As everyone began gathering their things, Evelyn asked, "How does Ethiopian sound?"

Riley perked up. "Azhara's? You bet!"

"Let's take my car. It's right out front and it's big enough to fit everyone." She laughed. "Kier has a sci-fi convention coming up in a few weeks and I can load him and all his friends in, plus their costumes and gear, so fitting all four of us won't be a problem."

Evelyn stopped. Alex still sat rooted, staring at his computer screen.

"Aren't you joining us for supper?" she asked, puzzled by what looked like horror on his face.

"Guys, I just found a news article from San Diego. Police found the bodies of the two missing girls. They just released the names. They *are* the ones from our forum. It's VampGrrrl and ThorRider!

Chapter 22

The mood was subdued as the four made their way toward the restaurant.

"Thankfully we won't have to wait for a table," Tessa said.

The waitress pointed to one of the outside tables. "Is this all right for you?"

Riley checked around the group and found them all nodding.

"Yeah, we'll take that one." Riley pulled up a bench at one of the outdoor tables. "I love the smell of this place."

The others spread around the picnic table, each taking one of the wooden benches.

"Riley and I come here a couple of times a month. In the summer, though, maybe more often?" Tessa said, looking at Riley.

"Yeah. I enjoy dining outside. It's so…outdoorsy."

Evelyn tilted her head back, looking at Riley down her nose. "There are lots of places around here that have outdoor dining. This *is* California, you know."

Riley's face got red and he ducked his head. "You know what I mean. Remember, I'm from the Midwest. The season for dining outside isn't very long there and not always pleasant. Living here? I want to take every opportunity to eat outside. Can't exactly picnic at our place."

Evelyn chuckled. "Okay, Riley, I'll give you that."

After the waiter took their orders, Alex looked around the group. "So, what are we going to do about this disaster?"

"Disaster? I'll say it is," Riley said. "We'll certainly have to announce something on the forum. WendyAnn, at least, is on the edge of panic. And TinMan seems to be our best bet, if we want to report the connection to the police."

Evelyn cut in. "We don't know yet if he's legit. Unless HotDoc verifies it, I'm not willing to trust TinMan's post."

Tessa nodded. *At this point, I'm pretty sure we're all were seeing ghosts behind every lamp post and car.* Out loud she asked, "Maybe Monday Alex can track HotDoc down?"

"Actually, I can do that now." Alex pulled out his laptop and tethered it to his phone. His fingers flew across the keyboard.

"How——" Riley began.

Tessa laid a hand on Riley's arm. "Don't disturb the master while he's working."

"Trust me," Alex said with a devilish grin. "I have ways of making computers tell me everything I want to know."

"There," he said moments later. "So, looking through Dr. Garrett's files, that's HotDoc's real name in case you were wondering, it looks like James Cavenaugh, TinMan to those playing along at home, is definitely one of his patients. And——"

"You hacked HotDoc's files that fast? Crap. Is nothing safe from you?" Evelyn shook her head. "I gotta keep you away from Kier. He's too impressionable. I'd be bailing him out of jail by nightfall."

"Computers always came easy for me, though lately it seems almost as easy as breathing. Maybe some carryover from remembering Xeres? I was in the science guild, after all. Anyway, as I was saying, according to the SFPD, James Cavanaugh is a detective at Mission Station. So it looks like he's legit. Is that enough to satisfy your paranoia, Evelyn?" He looked up at her with a smug, self-satisfied look on his face.

"Well, thank you, Kevin Mitnick," Evelyn snarked.

"Well, well," Alex said, leaning back in his chair and putting his arms behind his head. "I'm surprised you even know who that is."

Evelyn waved a hand at him dismissively. "Yeah, yeah. Just because I don't live in a computer doesn't mean I don't know a thing or two. And yes, I'm happy."

Riley leaned forward, crossing his arms on the table. "Alex, can you get me TinMan's direct phone number?"

Evelyn objected. "Wouldn't it be better to talk to him in person? Or maybe email him for an appointment? You are the one who owns the forum, after all."

"You know, emailing him first is probably best. Otherwise, he might think I'm some kind of stalker. I don't want to give him a reason to distrust me when I'm coming to him with possible evidence in a murder case." Riley huffed a laugh. "He might even wonder if I'm somehow connected to the murders myself."

Tessa gave a low whistle. "Well, that takes care of TinMan, but it still leaves the question of Cadwallader's connection to the murders."

Evelyn spoke up. "I wish we knew more about Cad's Xerian connections. Both Alex and I pegged him as being from Xeres, but we still don't know what guild he belonged to. Could he be from that other guild, the supposedly extinct one?" She snapped her fingers. "Tesham, that's it."

Riley shook his head. "No. I'm fairly certain that Tessa is a Tesham. She doesn't react to either you or Alex, and you both think she belongs to your guild. From what I've been able to put together, Alex's guild were scientists, and your guild were magic users. The Tesham used both magic and science, so it makes sense that you would both see her as being in your guild. But neither of you can place Cad, so Alex and I think he may be part of some fourth guild that we haven't identified yet."

Tessa turned accusing eyes on Riley. *I'm a Tesham? Why didn't Riley tell me?*

She let out a slow breath. Unable to keep the thread of warning out of her voice, she asked, "Riley? Just when, exactly, were you planning on telling me that you thought I was a Tesham?"

Riley looked around at her, his eyes widening. "Uh, it was only speculation up till now. I should have told you before, but it never came up. Sorry."

"That's it, Riley. I need another regression," she demanded. "I have to know for sure if I was a Tesham and then maybe I'll know where Cad belongs."

Riley shook his head violently. "No, no, no. It's getting too dangerous. Two people are dead. And Cad just dropped in on my office the other day. He might still be in the area. I don't want you to risk…."

She rounded on him.

"I'm already at risk! I'm part of this. I'm the reason you started looking into this whole thing in the first place, dammit." She stopped to take a deep calming breath. "Look, we don't have a choice. We need more information and I might have it."

Riley took a deep breath, then slowly let it out.

"I think Alex and I should just take the forum down. Stop all of this before someone else gets killed. I'll turn everything over to this Cavenaugh fellow and we can just go back to how our lives were before I started looking into this damn mess."

Alex and Evelyn had both been quiet, watching the two of them argue. Tessa eyed them. "You two have a stake in this too. You don't get to sit there and say nothing."

"Leave me out of it," Alex said, waving his spread hands. "I know better than to get in the middle when mom and dad are fighting."

Evelyn snorted. "Me? I think you're right, Tessa. If Riley won't regress you, I will."

Riley rose, bracing his arms on the table. "She's my girlfriend. I just want to protect her," he said loudly.

The entire restaurant went silent.

Alex leaned in and whispered, "Uh, Riley? Everyone's staring at you. Maybe you should—"

"Riley, sit down!" Tessa hissed through clenched teeth. "You're making a scene."

Riley dropped onto his bench, grumbling under his breath.

Tessa leaned into him, putting a hand on his arm.

"Don't be that way, Riley. You know I'm right." She smiled at him, trying to diffuse some of his tension. "Look. I know you're worried, but knowledge is power. Somewhere inside me might be the answers we're looking for. We're pretty sure Cad's already killed two people. How do we know he won't keep doing it unless we find a way to stop him? The information you have so far for the police is circumstantial at best, so there's no guarantee that they would be able to convict him of anything. But maybe there's information in the past that can help us stop him now."

"Are you seriously suggesting that *we* stop him?"

"I'm not sure. I only know that we need more information. If we knew more about Cad, we might be able to figure out why he killed those two girls. And if we know that, we could give the police a motive. Then *they* can take care of him."

Riley put his head in his hands. "I'm just trying to protect you. That's my job."

She kissed him on the cheek. "I know, Riley, I know. But sometimes we have to take a risk in order to move forward." Tessa was silent for a moment before she asked, "So, will you do it?"

He sighed heavily. "You win. As soon as we get back home. Okay?"

She smiled at him. "Thank you."

Glancing up, she saw their server approaching with their dinner.

Alex rubbed his stomach. "Oh, good, the food's here. Now can we talk about something more pleasant, like ebola, maybe, or the bubonic plague?"

* * *

"Riley," Evelyn said drily, "if you're going to continue doing regressions at home, I suggest you get a new couch."

Alex, busily texting on his phone, snickered.

Rolling his eyes, Riley protested, "Tessa doesn't mind it." He looked over at her for confirmation.

"Well, I didn't want to mention it, but—"

Riley held his hands up. "Okay, okay. I give up." He grimaced. "Since we don't want to spend that kind of money, next time we'll do it in the bedroom."

"You will not!" Tessa said indignantly. "Not without a few days advance warning." She met Evelyn's eyes. "He still hasn't recovered from college dorm living, if you know what I mean."

Evelyn laughed. "I have a teenage boy, remember? I made him start vacuuming his own room so he'd get the idea of hanging up his own clothes."

"I'm not that bad, really," Riley protested.

"There." Alex said, looking up from his phone at last. "I sent a message to TinMan asking him to give us a call about the dead girls in San Diego. It's his work email, so he probably won't get it until Monday."

"And on that note," Riley said, "let's get back to Tessa's regression. If you're comfy, let's begin." He silenced the other two with a look. Evelyn, perched on the arm of Alex's chair, made a zipping-my-lips gesture. Alex just nodded.

"Tessa, I want you to relax. You will hear only my voice. I'm going to count backward. When I reach one, I want you to go back to Xeres." He leaned toward her. In a calm voice, he counted. "...three, two, one."

Riley thought a moment. *Perhaps now's the time to dig a little deeper into Tessa's personality on Xeres.* "Who am I speaking with?"

Alex snapped Riley a look.

Riley waved Alex's question aside. Returning his attention to Tessa, he waited for her answer.

"I'm Ezarra, of course. Who did you think I was?" Her voice was sharp, like a teacher answering a student's stupid question.

"Pardon me for asking the obvious," Riley said. "Pleased to meet you, Hexarra."

"No," she said impatiently. "My name is EZ-ar-rah, not Hex-ar-RAH. It's not that hard, please get it right."

Riley bit his lip to keep from smiling. "Yes, got it. My apologies. If you don't mind, I do have some other questions for you."

Tessa sighed. "Well, if you must. Proceed."

Riley paused a moment to compose his first question. He decided to jump right in and damn the consequences.

"Could you tell me, Ezarra, what guild you are in?"

She paused so long that Riley feared she wouldn't answer.

Finally her voice came, softer now. "I was born into the Klymurian guild."

Alex and Riley exchanged glances. Evelyn spoke the thought in all their minds. "That doesn't necessarily mean she's *in* the Klymurian guild."

Riley nodded. "You're right. Let me try something else."

"Tessa, do you get along with Bylantians?"

"Of course."

"And Klymurians?"

"Certainly."

He frowned and leaned forward. "So, what guild are you?"

She sighed. "I am Tesham."

Alex and Evelyn both jerked to their feet.

Almost in unison, the pair exclaimed, "But we killed off all of the Tesham!"

Alex looked sideways at Evelyn. "Well, at last we agree on something."

Evelyn gave him a wry smile. "Uh-huh. Now we have an enemy in common. Oh, joy."

"Worse," Alex said. "It's Tessa."

Riley held his hands out, palms down. "Calm down, you two. We're all professionals here. Deal with it."

Alex plopped into his chair. Putting his face in his hands, he said, "He really has no idea how hard this is on us."

Evelyn sat back down on the arm of the Alex's chair. "I agree, but he does have a point. We're both therapists and know all the techniques. I think it's a case of physician, heal thyself."

"Yeah, I guess," Alex agreed grudgingly. "Doesn't make it any easier."

"Hush, you two. We still have some business to cover."

Using his calm, professional voice, Riley asked Tessa, "Do you know the one called Cadwallader?"

Tessa cringed. "That one? Unfortunately, yes, I know him."

"Can you tell me what guild he belongs to?"

Her voice rose. "He's not in a guild. He's not even from Xeres. He's Sheitan!" She spit out the last word.

Riley blinked. "Sheitan? Who are they?"

"Demons! They came from the other side."

"Other side? What other side? Wait, not from Xeres?"

Tessa was beginning to show signs of distress. Riley didn't want to continue, but knew he couldn't stop now.

"The other side of the energy portal. He came through with the others. They rode the energy to our plane."

"Energy?"

Her voice sounded like she was lecturing again. That seemed to calm her, too.

"Our new clean energy source. We'd nearly used up all of our normal energy sources, and we were too far from our star to effectively use solar power. One of my lifemates stumbled upon a dimension of pure energy. We began tapping into it to solve our energy problems. It was free, clean, and unlimited, as far as we could tell."

Her voice hardened, bitterness creeping into her tone. "Or at least we thought it was clean. We didn't know that the Sheitan were coming through from wherever the energy originated until it was too late. My Tesham life mate, the one who discovered the power source, was the first one to detect them."

Her voice dropped almost to a whisper. "He was killed trying to stop them."

For a moment, Riley stopped breathing. *She sounds so terribly sad. I just want to scoop her up and hold her until the pain goes away.*

Alex gave a low whistle. "That's a turn I wasn't expecting." He stood and paced around the living room. "First we find out that the Tesham are still around and now we have a fourth group. Of demons, no less."

Evelyn leaned forward. "Riley, ask her if there are others, of these...Sheitan here."

"Good idea." He turned to her. "Tessa, do you know of any other Sheitan?"

"Only the one called Bryce Lundee," she spit out, her prone body tensing from head to toe.

"Diana's husband? Oh boy," Alex said, shaking his head. "I'm glad Diana's not here, she'd be freaking out right now."

"Who's Diana?" Evelyn asked.

Alex turned to her. "She's Tessa's business partner."

"The one who left her husband? Riley mentioned her, but not by name," Evelyn said.

"Yeah, she moved into my spare room."

"Oh." She looked at Riley. "Should we tell her that her husband's a demon? From what you've told me about her situation, that shouldn't be new information. He sounded just plain evil even before we found out he was a demon."

Riley nodded. "I have to agree with you there. Now, is there anything else we need to ask Tessa?"

Evelyn shook her head. "I think that's enough for one session. She's obviously distraught. If we go any further—"

Riley interrupted, waving a hand to her. "You're right, of course, even though I think we need more information on these Sheitan. I'm sure Tessa will want another session after she's rested. Hopefully, we can find out more about these Sheitan before we hear back from TinMan."

Turning on his professional voice, Riley said, "Tessa, I want you to return to the present. You will feel relaxed and refreshed, as though you'd just had a nap. You will remember what we talked about, but as if it had happened to someone else. Do you understand?"

Tessa nodded.

"Okay, I will count backward...."

* * *

Mezmer Notes - Update 126

The last few days have been a tornado of discoveries. I thought I had started putting the pieces together to figure out what happened on Xeres, but boy, was I wrong.

First, we discovered that two girls from our forum had been murdered. We think by Cadwallader.

Second, since neither Evelyn nor Alex knew which guild he belonged to, Tessa insisted that she be regressed to find out. We got so much more than we bargained for. I regressed Tessa twice, once Saturday evening and then again Sunday afternoon.

Just list the facts, deal with the implications later. That's gotten me this far, so here goes:

- *Tessa definitely was a Tesham. This fact severely freaked out both Alex and Evelyn.*
- *Her name was Ezarra.*
- *Ezarra's life mate discovered a dimension of clean energy and built a machine to harness it, solving Xeres' power problems.*
- *Energy creatures came from that dimension through the power portal.*
- *She says they are demons. She called them Sheitan.*
- *The Sheitan were discovered by Ezarra's life mate.*
- *The Sheitan consume the life energy of Xerians. Does she mean their souls?*
- *After consuming a Xerian's life energy, the Sheitan inhabited the bodies of their victims.*
- *Ezarra's life mate detected the Sheitan and began hunting them down. They found him first and killed him.*
- *Ezarra's life mate never reincarnated. She seemed very upset that he never came back to her.*
- *Cadwallader and Bryce are both Sheitan.*
- *Cadwallader probably killed the two girls in San Diego to consume their energy.*

This new information only brings up more questions:

1. *How many Sheitan are there on Earth?*
2. *Do the Sheitan prefer to consume Xerians' energy?*
3. *Do Xerians 'taste' better than humans? Is that why he killed those particular girls? He met them on our forum, after all.*
4. *What should we tell Diana? Let her know that Tessa identified her husband*

as a demon? They've been together since high school, so why hasn't he consumed her already?

5.   *How do I tell TinMan all of this without getting locked up in a psych ward? I'm sure Cadwallader was responsible for those girls' deaths, but how do I prove it?*

And as if dealing with all of that isn't enough to stress over, there's a new topic on the forum. I have to try to convince these people again *that getting together in person is a horrible idea. They're planning a big meet-up in a few weeks at a sci-fi convention here in the Bay Area called HydraCon. I've told them once already that it's a bad idea, but they are determined to meet anyway. Tessa's observation hit it right on the nose: 'Melee in the dealers room! Security, please respond! And the red shirts come running.'*

It's hard to believe it's only been six months since that first regression when Tessa told me about Xeres. And to think that all she wanted to know was if she had a past life with the Celts for her medieval reenactment group.

I'm really glad now that Jake isn't a part of this. If he couldn't handle the simplest information about Xeres, I know he wouldn't deal well knowing people have been murdered. Hell, I wish I didn't know about the murders.

I want my simple life back!

Saving....

Chapter 23

"I thought you were going to follow MacPherson and find out where he lives." Bryce barely kept the amusement out of his voice at Cadwallader's pouting expression.

"I did," Cadwallader all but snarled, throwing his rental car's keys onto the end table with more force than necessary. Pacing around the room, he continued. "I followed them to an apartment complex several miles south of here. His assistant, that Alex person, opened the gate when they arrived, so that must be where he lives. I waited outside on the street for hours, but I never saw MacPherson come out. I finally gave up and went back to my hotel room around 3 am."

Bryce bit his lip to keep from smiling at the man's obvious agitation. *I just love knowing things he doesn't. He's looked down on me ever since he killed my last incarnation. I'm really going to enjoy paying him back for that.*

"You know," Cadwallader said suspiciously, "it occurred to me while I was sitting out there half the night that you probably already know where MacPherson lives. After all, your wife is business partners with his woman."

Bryce leaned forward in his chair. "That doesn't mean I've ever been to their house. She and Diana mostly worked online and in coffee shops."

"I think you do. You're getting some sick enjoyment out of watching me run around in circles, aren't you?"

"Now, wait a minute," Bryce protested, leaping to his feet to face Cadwallader. "What are you accusing me of?"

"You've been trying to sabotage me ever since you came of age and regained your holdings. Don't try to deny it."

Bryce felt his face heat up.

"You're the one who came charging in here, supposedly to help me. All you've done so far is harass MacPherson and try to find out where he lives. Something tells me this 'visit'," He made air quotes around the word. "isn't about helping me at all. You're up to something."

They were practically nose to nose now. Bryce looked Cadwallader in the eyes and saw something he would never have expected.

Fear.

He is up to something. Why are MacPherson and his crowd so important to him? Have I missed something? Maybe something about Tessa or that assistant? When he leaves, I'd better report in to LeRoux. Maybe he'll have an idea why the man's so desperate to find out where MacPherson lives.

"You may be LeRoux's area captain now, but you know I've always been his first choice for that position, ever since we arrived on Xeres," Bryce said, clenching his jaw. "You only ever get promoted when I'm too young for the job. You never could accept that he trusts me over you."

"Oh, really?" Cadwallader returned, raising his eyebrows. "Then why am I still doing the job now, even though you're pushing thirty?" He smiled wickedly. "No matter how many times you've tried to take me down, I've always come out on top. Even back on Xeres, when you were much stronger, you could never beat me."

Bryce shook his head, a cruel smile escaping his tightly controlled emotions. "You've only ever won through deception. You're jealous that I win because I'm better and stronger than you are."

"Me? Jealous of you?" Cadwallader laughed. "You've got to be kidding. It's true that after we arrived on Xeres, LeRoux did make you his lieutenant. But wasn't it your bumbling that almost got us all killed when that damned Tesham found us?"

Bryce's eyes glazed over as his thoughts were pulled back through the eons to that fateful day on Xeres....

* * *

"I think someone has been following me," the man said nervously, catching up with his partner. The jitters he felt inside could be from the food this body required, but he doubted it. "I noticed a drone overhead last night and then today, I saw the same guy four different times as I was making arrangements for the meeting tonight."

Chuckling, the other man turned to greet him. "There you are. It's about time. Following you? You're just being paranoid, Byzoh. The Xerians have no reason to suspect that we are among them, so why would someone follow you?" He led the way to the empty warehouse. Inside they met only bare rafters and cement floors dotted with piles of refuse.

Dust and…possibly zelts, too, Byzoh thought with a shudder.

"I don't know. That's what worries me, Codin." He surveyed the area, checking for exits. "What if someone's found out that we're not who we say we are? What if one of the Xerians has discovered the existence of the Sheitan? We need to tell Anthery."

Codin swung around to face him. "Are you crazy? Take your suspicions to him and you're likely to lose your *special* status. You need proof."

The emphasis Codin placed on the word 'special' grated on Byzoh's already frayed nerves.

"What's wrong with you, Codin?" Byzoh glared at him. "Are you still angry that Anthery made me his lieutenant? Can't you let it go?" His voice softened. "You and I have been together as partners since long before we came here. You mean the world to me, but really, I couldn't pass up the opportunity when Anthery needed me to help keep us connected in this strange world."

Byzoh's face twisted in frustration. *Will he never be placated? Must I deal with this attitude for the rest of my existence?*

"You *could* have passed it up. But no, you enjoy being in charge too much." Codin pouted, pulling his lips into a thin line. "You love being at the center of everything that's happening."

"Jealousy doesn't suit you, my love," Byzoh said, laying a hand on Codin's arm.

Codin shook off Byzoh's hand. "You don't need to be so patronizing." He pivoted sharply, paced away, then whipped back around. "I *hate* that we ever came to this world. We were happy in our universe. But here? We have these gross physical shells that have disgusting necessary functions." He spit the last word out like a bullet, the echoes ricocheting around the empty warehouse. "Our people are becoming addicted to the sensations that they can get from these Xerian bodies. It's corrupting them…us. Especially Anthery. He revels in feeding off the energy that causing pain to these people creates. And you! You're becoming just like him."

Byzoh arched an eyebrow at him. "Funny, you seem to enjoy using that body of yours to seduce and bed anything that grabs *your* fancy." He heard Codin huff at him. "You don't think I know that you've been using sex to get close to some of the local leaders?" He aimed a finger at Codin. "I know how you think. You're up to something. You want to be the power behind the scenes. You don't like to be a target. You'd rather sit back and pull the strings and watch everyone dance to your music." Byzoh scowled at Codin, grinding his teeth.

"I am just enjoying this body," he said, smiling. "The reason you see ulterior motives everywhere is because you're the one who's always plotting and planning. I am innocent."

Byzoh snorted. "You? Innocent? You really expect me to believe that?"

Codin waved one hand at him. "Think whatever you want. You will anyway. You never listen to me."

Rubbing the side of his face, Byzoh sighed heavily. "I don't have time for this now. I still have four more people to contact about the meeting tonight. If Anthery weren't so worried that the Xerians would detect our activities, I could just send them a holo-mail. But no, I have to travel all over this huge, filthy place and contact each one in person."

"Okay," Codin waved two hands at Byzoh. "You run along then and do what your master wants. Maybe he'll give you a treat later, if you sit up and beg nicely like a trained patoo."

"Fine! Be that way." Byzoh turned and left the warehouse. Behind him, the door made a satisfying thud.

Several stops later, he approached the last of his contacts.

I've taken care of Holiza, Macap, and Azetala. Tarnet is the last on my list, then I can rejoin Codin at the meeting hall.

Byzoh rounded a corner, intent on his mission. The argument with his partner still irked him. He ran over their argument in his mind, but couldn't see any way to resolve their problems.

Shaking his head, he reached for the door when a bright flash illuminated the inside of the small shop, spilling from the viewports out into the roadway. Pushing open the door, he saw a figure kneeling beside Tarnet's prone body. The man looked up, quickly pocketed a oddly-shaped item, possibly a weapon of some kind, and fled toward the back of the store.

Thankfully, when he checked, Tarnet was still breathing. Rising from the fallen Sheitan, Byzoh chased after the intruder. He found the back door ajar, but there was no one in the alley.

The fallen man groaned, rolled over, and sat up.

"Tarnet? Are you okay?"

"Mmmmm." His head lolled to the side, his eyes unfocused.

Byzoh took the man's face in two hands, staring into his eyes. "Tarnet, talk to me!"

Shaking the man to get his attention, Byzoh searched his eyes for any sign of the man he knew. Icy fear danced across Byzoh's skin. The man had no energy pattern at all. Not the dark energy of one of his own people nor the bright energy of a Xerian.

With horror, he realized that this was no longer his friend, only an empty husk.

Byzoh gently laid Tarnet's body down. Around him, every shadow seemed to hold a potential assailant, ready to erase him from existence like it had poor Tarnet.

I've got to get out of here before I become the next victim of this crazed Xerian! Anthery must know that it isn't random accidents taking out our people. Someone has discovered our presence and is eliminating our people.

Peering around the front door, Byzoh found the street empty. Easing through, he shut it quietly behind him. Once he was on a busier street, he hurried across town toward the meeting hall, darting suspicious glances all around him for any sign of the assassin. At one point, he thought he saw the man from Tarnet's shop, but thankfully that person vanished into a nearby dining hall.

The way became spookier once he quit the lighted commercial area for the warehouse district. The shadows seemed deeper, darker, danger-filled. Several personal conveyances passed him, windows darkened. Though probably filled with Sheitan headed for the meeting, they could as easily be late workmen. Byzoh retreated into those dangerous shadows until each had passed.

He turned the last corner. Directly ahead, an open door poured light into the alley, providing a pale pathway to safety. He had almost reached the portal when he heard a sound behind him. The scrape of something on the pavement. A pebble gone skittering off. He paused, reaching for the access panel. His eyes searched the alley and tried to plumb the depths of its shadows.

Nothing rose up from the shadows, no Xerian with a bulbous weapon in hand to kill him. As far as his eyes could penetrate the black shrouded hulks of trash receptacles and derelict machinery around him, nothing moved.

He cast one last glance around the alley before ducking through the door. As the low murmuring of the crowd and the floating lights washed over him, he finally relaxed, bathed in the safety of his people.

Eyes scanning the crowd, Byzoh quickly spotted his mate talking to Anthery near the far end of the large open space. Making his way to them, he considered how to break the news to their leader.

"I'm glad you finally decided to join us, Byzoh," Codin said, voice overflowing with sarcasm.

"Yes," Anthery drawled. "The meeting was supposed to start some time ago. We have been waiting on you and Tarnet to arrive. Since you are here, we can get started."

Anthery began to turn, heading for the stack of pallets that was serving as a speaking platform. Byzoh reached out a tentative hand to stop him.

"Sir, I believe there is something you should know before we go any further."

Anthery turned, irritation and anger warring across his face. "What now? Can it not wait until afterwards?"

Codin sneered, "Of course, it can't wait. Don't you know that Byzoh is oh, so important, and anything that he thinks is important must be dealt with *first*? Let me guess, you were followed by a drone again. Or did you find the person who has been killing off our people? You're paranoia knows no bounds. You're afraid of your own shadow."

Byzoh ground his teeth together. *Codin set me up! Perfect. Now, no matter what I say, Anthery will chalk it up to paranoia. Damn the man!*

"Is watching Tarnet be murdered right in front of my eyes paranoia? Is seeing the assassin standing over his body with a strange weapon in his hand paranoia?"

Anthery frowned, his attention tightly focused on Byzoh. "Tarnet's dead?"

"As good as dead. His life energy was simply gone. All that was left was a hollow shell of flesh and bones."

"And you actually saw the killer standing over his body?" Anthery inquired, his eyes going distant. Behind those eyes, Byzoh could see the wheels within wheels turning. Anthery was plotting something. That never turned out well for anyone.

"Did he greet you? Give you his card, maybe?" Codin asked, skepticism oozing out of his words. "Or was he wearing a sign that said Sheitan Killer with tic marks to indicate how many kills he has?"

"No, damn you!" Byzoh shoved his partner away, causing Codin to fall unceremoniously on his ass. "Can't you be reasonable and supportive? Just once, Codin?"

Looking up, embarrassment clouding his handsome features, Codin opened his mouth for an angry retort.

"Shut up." Anthery snarled, cutting through their bickering. "Both of you."

Gesturing at Byzoh, he demanded, "What happened to the assassin?"

Cowering under the fierce gaze of his leader, Byzoh began, "He… he…he ran out the back door of Tarnet's shop before I could even register what had happened. I…umm…wasn't able to, that is, I checked on Tarnet and afterwards I couldn't find him."

"Why did you stop to check on Tarnet? The important thing is to catch the assassin. That's why we're meeting tonight, to figure out why some Sheitan have gone missing."

Codin, having recovered his feet, broke in, "Idiot! You've probably led the assassin right to us."

Rounding on his mate, Byzoh screamed, "Oh, so *now* you believe me? Now that you've found a way to make me look bad, of course you do."

Anthery's eyes narrowed, pinning Byzoh in place. "Well, did you? Lead the assassin to us?"

Feeling cornered, Byzoh answered, "I…don't think so. I was very careful."

Anthery swiped a hand down his beautiful face. "I can't believe how vulnerable you've made us. If the assassin did follow you, we're all in jeopardy." Turning his fierce gaze on Codin, he commanded, "Start the meeting. I need to consider how much to reveal before I speak. Inform them that someone has ordered the portals we came through to be shut off. Have everyone work their connections with the locals. Tell them to demand the power be reinstated. Use the anger that these people feel over having their access to the new power cut off." He stabbed several fingers at Byzoh and Codin. "If we do not get those portals running again, soon, we will not get reinforcements. Then our assassin can kill us off at his leisure, while we get weaker and weaker."

Byzoh drew his head back. *Things are even worse than I'd expected. And now Anthery's favoring Codin over me.* He felt his face heat up. *I hate feeling so powerless.*

Codin paused, looking Byzoh directly in the eyes. His smug look needed no words. Then Codin winked at him, turned and mounted the platform.

Waving at the crowd to quiet down, Codin began. "We have a lot to cover, so let's get this meeting started...."

Byzoh tuned Codin out, deep in thought about the assassin. He tried to remember every detail he could so that he would not be caught unawares like the other Sheitan.

"...and don't forget to work your contacts," Anthery was saying. "It's vitally important that we find out who ordered the energy centers shut down. Once we know who is responsible, we can take steps to remedy the situation."

Anthery was turning away when a voice from the far side of the room called out, "Does this mean we can't go home?"

Byzoh looked up sharply. No one had ever questioned Anthery. He cringed, wondering how the man would react.

"Now why," Anthery purred, "would you want to go home in the first place? Oh, I guess it was nice before we took on these bodies, when we could go back to our own dimension and check in. But now? When everything is going so well? We'll solve this little problem with the energy portal, then the others can join us here. There won't be any need to go back home, will there?"

The crowd muttered. Byzoh waited, hoping there wouldn't be any more questions.

A child in the front row piped up. "I know I'm not the only one who has this problem, but I hate being stuck in this small person. I didn't know that no one would listen to me, that I'd have to take orders from some damnable Xerian. If I did, I would have gone into a different body. I've tried leaving this body, but my true form is stuck in here. You've been here the longest, Anthery, how do I fix this?"

Anthery sighed, "You—"

The door to the left of the improvised stage exploded, twisted metal and plastic raining on the crowd inside. Tongues of flame licked the air for a moment where the door used to be.

The man Byzoh had seen earlier, the assassin standing over Tarnet's body, stood framed in the doorway, one of the man's hands still smoldering from where he had conjured fire to destroy the door.

"You want out? Let me help you." The man's voice, sounding clear and oddly calm, reached Byzoh over the screams of his people.

Doesn't he care about his own personal safety? He must be insane to think he can survive confronting a whole room of us.

Stepping inside, the assassin brought up the bulbous-shaped weapon and began methodically firing it into the crowd.

Several of his people crumpled to the floor, their life energy evaporated as though it had never existed. Byzoh backed away, taking refuge behind a pillar, hastily grabbing Codin's arm and hauling the man to safety behind him. At first Byzoh couldn't locate Anthery, but then he caught a glimpse of the man's boot behind another pillar.

Scanning the open area he'd just vacated, Byzoh saw the crowd surge toward the far wall, scrambling to get away from the assassin. The mad man charged through the warehouse, in pursuit of the panicked crowd. Byzoh watched, confused, as the man ripped something from his belt and lobbed it toward the wall, right into the crush of Sheitan.

A burst of searing light erupted from the center of the throng, momentarily blinding him. In the eerie silence, Byzoh rubbed his eyes, trying to restore his vision.

What was that?

When he had blinked away the spots in front of his eyes, what he saw horrified him. Everyone near the epicenter of the flash was lying in a twisted, lifeless mass on the floor.

The assassin, oblivious to the havoc he'd caused, spun, eyes seeking Byzoh's hiding place.

Terror froze Byzoh in place.

Codin grabbed his arm, hissing, "This is your fault! You led the assassin right to us! How could you be so stupid?"

Byzoh shook off his partner's hand. Whispering over his shoulder, he hissed out, "Would you shut up! Do you want him to find us?"

The few survivors of the explosion, shouting their hatred, charged their attacker.

From his hiding place, Byzoh saw shock, then fear, play across the assassin's face. The man glanced over his shoulder, weapon wavering. Pausing only a split second, he pivoted and raced for the shattered door frame.

As Byzoh and Codin moved to join the mob, Anthery caught their arms, yanking them back.

"You are responsible for this mess," Anthery snarled in Byzoh's face. "I expect you to get out there and keep him in sight."

Seizing the opportunity, Codin laid a hand on Anthery's arm. "I can get on the comm and have my contacts with the authorities help. I can tell them that the serial killer they've been hunting has struck again. Have them organize a search party immediately."

"We cannot let this butcher get away," Anthery said, his face inches from Byzoh's. "You! Stay in constant contact with Codin so you two can coordinate the search. Let me know as soon as you find him. He is mine to kill. Understand?"

Byzoh felt the heat of Anthery's gaze burn through him. He nodded, turned and raced to join the mob.

The first of the angry mob reached the hole in the wall mere seconds after the assassin disappeared. As the Sheitan wave broke against the wall around the doorway, Byzoh joined the outskirts of the mob, shoving his way to the front. Behind him, he could hear Codin barking into his comm, issuing orders to some hapless government functionary.

Byzoh maneuvered through the mob. Emerging on its leading edge, he caught sight of the assassin as he rounded the end of the block.

Waving his hand at the Sheitan behind him, Byzoh pointed toward where the man had disappeared, shouting, "Hurry, he's getting away. We can't lose him now!"

The hunt continued through the night. At one point, Byzoh's group lost the assassin. Just before dawn, a group of Xerians found the man and raised the alarm. Byzoh turned his followers toward the opposite side of the city. His group melded with the Xerians outside the city's main science center. Spotting Codin and Anthery conferring with several high ranking Xerians, Byzoh hastened to join them.

Anthery was speaking. "One of our people followed him to a lab on the second floor. I have men stationed outside the door in case he tries to sneak out. If you will have your men cover all the exits, I think my men can take him before he manages to escape again."

The government man scurried off to do Anthery's bidding.

Byzoh quailed under the expression Anthery turned on him.

"I should kill you for leading that damn Sci-mage to us. It is pure luck that his bomb did not destroy us all back in the warehouse. On top of that, you managed to lose him. I will deal with you later, count on it."

Byzoh staggered when Anthery switched his gaze to Codin.

"You, however, surprised me. That was fast thinking back there, getting the Xerian authorities involved and having them join in the search. If it were not for you, we would have lost him entirely."

Byzoh despised the self-satisfied smile that crossed Codin's face. Resentment rose within him, devouring the last few remnants of the love he'd once felt for Codin.

Anthery turned, dismissing both Byzoh and Codin. He motioned the Sheitan forward.

"Break down that door!"

* * *

Bryce looked up, startled, as Cadwallader snapped his fingers inches from his nose.

"Anybody home? Were you even paying attention to what I said? Now is not the time to be daydreaming. I have to be at the airport in just over an hour, so I don't have any more time to look for MacPherson. This entire trip was a waste of my precious time and a considerable amount of my money."

"And here I thought you came up to help me," Bryce snarled. "It looks to me like you haven't done anything but help yourself. As usual! For all your 'help,' I'm still no closer to getting Diana back."

"You haven't been very productive yourself. I still don't know where MacPherson lives." Cadwallader leveled his finger at Bryce, accusation heavy in his voice. "I don't believe you. I still think you know where he lives and are keeping it from me for some reason."

Bryce swallowed the smirk he felt rising inside at Cadwallader's words and struggled to maintain a bland expression. *Damned right I know where he lives, but I sure as hell am never telling you.*

Cadwallader spun about, pacing the carpet in long angry strides. Moments passed before he swung around to face Bryce.

"I have to go now or I'll miss my flight. I hate leaving this project unfinished due to your incompetence." He arched an eyebrow at Bryce. "And you wonder why you're not LeRoux's area captain anymore."

"My incompetence? Who lost MacPherson at his assistant's place? You." Bryce waved a hand at Cadwallader. "And the reason I'm not LeRoux's assistant anymore is that you had me assassinated. I may not be able to prove it, but I know you were behind my 'accident' thirty years ago."

"Are you still going on about that? Give it a rest. Contrary to what you believe, not everything is about you, Bryce. I hadn't even turned eighteen yet when that happened."

"When that happened? Like you couldn't have managed to arrange it. Eighteen or eighty, you have always been the biggest schemer I've ever known. Ever since the first time you connived to usurp my position with Anthery on Xeres."

Cadwallader moved toward the door, shaking his head. "I really don't have time for this." He picked up his keys and turned to face the other man. "Find out where MacPherson lives. I'll come back once you do and take care of him."

Bryce shrugged. "I'll try, but with the restraining order…."

Cadwallader's eyes hardened, his face flushing red.

"You'll get me the information I need, or else. You don't want to have another accident, now, do you?"

Chapter 24

"Yes, yes, of course I understand. What do you take me for, an imbecile?"

His phone's speaker was silent. Thierry was beginning to wonder if the international call had been disconnected when the Russian's gravelly voice grated out, "No, not take for imbecile. But if you good with the Internets, you would not call me to fix your little problem, no?"

LeRoux sighed. *Damn him, the man is too perceptive. If he wasn't such an asset to me....* "Are you sure Matthew has been expunged from that website?"

"Da. Completely. His account and mentions gone."

A light began blinking on Thierry's console, with that special urgency he knew he had to handle.

"Good, Prizrak. You have my favor for completing this little project. Use it carefully." He hung up before the computer hacker could say another word.

Reaching to the console, he pressed a button to stop the insistent flashing.

"What is it, Mr. Latham?"

"We have just been notified of the death of Herr Kahler, the Sheitan Rezzeal, in Berlin."

"Kahler? But he was in fine health the last time I spoke with him."

His Sheitan secretary's smooth voice replied, "I understand it was an accident."

Thierry frowned. *Accident? That is the third Sheitan killed in an accident in the past three months. Someone is making a power grab. I should inform Renata so she can find out who is responsible and deal with them accordingly.*

Pressing the intercom, Thierry ordered, "Have Mr. Somerset

report to me immediately."

"I have already taken the liberty of contacting Mr. Somerset. He is just entering the outer office. Shall I send him in now?"

"Ah, Latham, anticipating my needs as always. Make him wait five minutes and then send him in." Thierry allowed a cruel smile to play across his lips. *I do love making underlings wait. It keeps them in their place,* he thought with pleasure.

Thierry had cleared his desk to its expensive mahogany top before a slight blond man opened the door.

"Ah, Somerset. Good to see you. Tell me about Rezzeal."

"I have his file here." He tapped on his tablet computer. "His money is mostly in coal and steel, with an odd junket into the entertainment industry. He left behind a wife and three children." Somerset looked up. "We have all the documents ready for our representative to take over his investments in Berlin. It shouldn't take more than a month."

"Excellent. Send his portfolio to the financial division. They handle all investments for the Sheitan until we reincarnate and can contact them to reclaim our funds. Pay out his life insurance to the family so that they are taken care of. I caution you, do not forget to send a 'cleaner' to his house to remove any items that might reveal our presence to the humans. I am sure you remember what happened to your predecessor." *Gilcrest mysteriously 'fell' from the roof of the corporate offices in Berne. At least he was thoughtful enough to leave a suicide note,* Thierry thought grimly to himself. *'I'm sorry' covered a multitude of the man's sins against the Sheitan. Hopefully, he learns from this demotion and does not make the same mistakes in his next life.*

Somerset's face paled.

Thierry tapped a finger against his lip. "I have something else I want you to look into. Mr. Latham said Rezzeal died in an accident. I want you to send someone to look into his death. This is the third 'accidental' death in Europe in as many months. I want to know if it was indeed an accident or if we have a problem that needs dealt with."

Somerset nodded. "I've noted the seeming coincidence myself, sir. I'll have Security look into it immediately." He made a note on his tablet, then looked up at Thierry, who waved him off.

As the younger man hurried from the office, Thierry steepled his fingers.

207

Fools! Having to depend on whatever body fate throws their way, then waiting eighteen long, boring years before they can resume their place in our company. It was a happy accident that I learned the secret pattern of our reincarnation. We reincarnate into the nearest child born after our death.

Now I control my reincarnation. I refuse to bow to capricious fate. It is simply a matter of finding a woman, impregnating her, and making sure that she produces healthy offspring. Once I know that, I impregnate her again, then kill my current body the moment she delivers my child. That guarantees that I can reincarnate into my own offspring and protect my dynasty. Thankfully, modern technology allows me to be sure that my new body will be male. I will never be forced to live as a woman again. Ever!

Renata is such a good choice for a mate in this life. She runs our European holdings better than anyone else has in centuries. In her I have a strong, loyal Sheitan woman to keep me safe while I am still too young to run things openly. When I do resume control, it will be with a minimum of disruption.

His thoughts were interrupted by a buzzer. He sighed, reaching for the console. *I hope,* he thought dryly, *it is not another accidentally dead Sheitan.*

* * *

"You want me to what?"

"I will try to make myself as clear as possible, Bryce." Cadwallader's voice sounded like a college professor lecturing a particularly dense freshman class. "I can't get into the Xeres forum. I tried to login like normal, but it won't work. I tried to create a new account. I even tried using different email addresses. Nothing works. I'm completely blocked out." Cadwallader's voice, climbing into a near hysterical tone, suddenly dropped. "I need you to get on there and tell me what's happening."

Startled by the sudden change in Cadwallader's voice, Bryce sat up straight. "And why do *I* need to register on this forum?"

"To keep me informed about what MacPherson is planning. People on the forum were talking about getting together for some convention there in the Bay Area. I need to know if that's still happening. It might be our best chance to take MacPherson out."

I can't let him know that Thierry already ordered me to spy on the forum. I'm xdragonx, the mysterious dragon who lies in wait, ready to get revenge when you least expect it. I need to pretend to create a profile and get things set up or he'll be suspicious. After wasting enough time that Cadwallader was beginning to get impatient, he plunged into the discussion thread 'Anyone going to

HydraCon in Santa Clara, CA?'

"Well," said Bryce, "it appears that a lot of these Xerians are planning trips to this convention. I haven't actually counted the individual users who are going, but there're a lot."

A gathering of Xerians here? Bryce thought. *Wouldn't that be delightful. Maybe they'd react like on Xeres and actually fight, like they did after we turned the guilds against each other. Then we could harvest all the energy we wanted without getting caught.* Bryce smiled. *Good times.*

Cadwallader's voice came through the phone connection almost purring.

"Wonderful. I want you to register for the convention and reserve us a room."

Gods, the man sounds like a cartoon villain. I bet he's sitting there rubbing his hands together in glee.

"Wait a minute. Why me? This is your operation." *What the hell kind of twisted logic....* "Why should I pay for everything?"

"Because you wouldn't give me MacPherson's address. Thanks to you, I wasted all of my time and money coming up there."

"Humpf. I thought you said your visit was to help me with my problems. Typical," Bryce accused. "Following your own agenda, but trying to convince me that it's all for my benefit."

"You really need to let go of the past, Bryce. Quit blaming me for your failures. Not every problem you have is my fault, though I know it gives you some sadistic glee to think that it is."

No, not all of my problems, just most of them. Asshole.

"Fine, but still, why should I pay for everything?"

"Because, Bryce dear, you've taken great pains to tell me every chance you get how loaded you are. How much money you are making in this new life of yours. Now's your chance. Show me how rich you are. Unless it was all just a lie to make me jealous. Are you just pretending that your life is better than mine?

"Okay, you win," Bryce said, throwing up his hands. "I'll make the arrangements, but I don't have to like it."

"Excellent. I knew you'd see it my way—."

Bryce stabbed the disconnect button, cutting off Cadwallader's gloating. He sat for a moment deep in thought, then scrolled through his contacts to a familiar name.

"LeRoux Worldwide. Mr. LeRoux's office. How may I help you?"

"This is Bryce Lundee for Mr. LeRoux."

"Thank you, sir. One moment, please."

The phone spit out the standard bland hold music.

"Bryce. I take it you have news for me?"

Bryce was immediately suspicious. *Thierry sounds genial. That isn't normal. Is there more going on with Cadwallader than I know?*

"Yes. Yes, I do. Cadwallader's still intent upon taking out MacPherson. I managed to prevent him from finding MacPherson when he came here looking for him last time, but he has a new plan. He's making a move on MacPherson at a convention in Santa Clara."

"Convention? One of his hypnotherapy conferences?"

"No, a science fiction convention. Hydracon."

"Why there?"

"The online forum where Xerians are talking to each other? They've decided to meet at that convention. MacPherson thinks the two guilds will have a violent reaction to each other. He's tried talking them out of it, but they are adamant. Cadwallader plans to ambush him there. He's demanded I accompany him and assist him in taking MacPherson out."

"And what exactly are you planning? I have already informed you that MacPherson is important."

"Yes, sir. My plan is to lull Cadwallader into a false sense of security, then remove him from the picture. You needn't worry about it. I won't be messy or leave anything to tie it back to us. I plan to make it look like he committed suicide. Have him conveniently leave a note stating that he can't go on due to financial difficulties." Bryce knew that the big smile plastered across his face was probably evident to LeRoux, even through the phone, but he didn't care. *I'm finally getting back at Cadwallader. And disgracing him in the process is so much more satisfying.*

After a pause, Thierry responded. "I think that will be sufficient. However, I may wish to oversee this project. Personally."

"No, no, that won't be necessary," he said, rushing to reassure his boss. "I can handle it. And besides, it would be a waste of your valuable time." *Why would LeRoux need to be personally involved? Doesn't he trust me? And it's not like him to get personally involved in actual operations. He's much too important to get his hands dirty like that. After all, he has underlings for things like that.*

"Perhaps you are right. Just make sure that nothing, and I mean *nothing*, is traceable back to our organization."

* * *

Thierry hung up the phone and leaned back in his chair, steepling his fingers. After a moment's consideration, he nodded to himself. Extending one elegant finger, he reached out and hit the comm button on his desk.

"Mr. Latham, I need you to find out everything you can about something called Hydracon, in Santa Clara. Have that on my desk as soon as possible."

"Yes, sir. Right away, sir."

Thierry's eyes unfocused. *Given their history, it might be time to remove both Bryce and Matthew from the equation permanently. This is far too important to let those two screw up. Again.*

A Tesham. I can almost taste her. It has been far too long since I have indulged in the pleasure of consuming that energy.

Smiling broadly, he pressed the comm button again.

"Mr. Latham, please contact Renata. See if she is free for dinner tonight. I feel like celebrating."

Chapter 25

"I swear these people on the forum are blockheads," Riley muttered from his desk. He eyed Alex and Evelyn, sitting side-by-side on his office sofa, before continuing. "All three of us have told them what's going to happen when the two guilds get together. Do they believe us? Of course not."

Alex tapped a few keys on his laptop, then scratched his beard. "Riley, they're modern people, with jobs, families, kids, the whole mess. Taking an instant dislike to someone just isn't something they can relate to."

"Hunh," Evelyn said. "Well, they're in for a big surprise once they get to the convention then."

"There's also the possibility that we could find more people like Tessa who don't react to either side. We just have to make sure that no one figures out they're Tesham." Riley let out an exasperated sigh. "Then we'd have an even bigger problem on our hands."

Evelyn barked a laugh. "That's all we need, a riot in the middle of the convention. Security will love that. Usually the only thing they have to deal with is a drunken writer singing in the bar."

Perplexed, Alex asked her, "The writers hang out in the bar? Together?"

"No, that's just where they tend to wash up after the last panels are over," Evelyn said. "There's some connection between writing and drinking that's eluded the best psychologists for decades." She lifted a shoulder. "Maybe they're just lonely. I know when I'm in the throes of writing a how-to book, I've been known to stare out the bottom of a glass of wine or two."

Riley laughed. "You? I can't imagine."

Evelyn's eyes twinkled. "There's a lot about me you couldn't imagine."

Looking sideways at her, Alex raised an eyebrow. "Oh, really? Do tell. What—"

Riley cleared his throat. "Tessa and I decided to go to the convention. We talked it over last night. Right now, she's busy trying to figure out a costume for me for Saturday." Riley made a face. "So far, the choice seems to be a Hobbit or a superhero. Look at this body," he said, standing up and twirling. "Does this *look* like the body of a superhero? And spandex?" He shook his head. "No way."

"I don't know, Riley," Alex said, tilting his head. "I think you'd look good in spandex. You could go as Wolverine. You already have the hairy body."

Alex caught the evil eye Riley shot at him and laughed.

"*You* would think that," Riley said, plopping down in his chair.

Evelyn snorted. "Well, Kier and I already have tickets and a room. Though he's getting to the age where he's mortified to be sharing a room with his mother."

Alex ran a lascivious eye down Evelyn's body. Today, she was clad in a red designer dress and black heels. "Hmmm. If I had a mother that looked like you—"

She slapped him playfully on the arm. "You'd what? Sell tickets?"

"You know, that's not such a bad idea. I'll have to talk to Kier—"

Evelyn scowled over at Alex. "Don't you dare."

"Ahem," Riley said, interrupting. "That reminds me, we need to work with Kier, to get him used to being around people from the other guild before the convention."

Alex snapped his fingers. "Diana needs to learn that, too."

"Then why don't we get the two of them together?" Evelyn said. "Kill two birds and all that."

"I like that idea," Alex said, nodding. "Maybe she and I could share a room. That'd keep expenses down for both of us."

"The convention is only six weeks away," Riley said. "Will that be enough time, do you think?"

"Kier's been sitting in on my sessions when I've worked on getting over my issues with Alex. I think he's as prepared as he can be. We should introduce him to Diana as soon as possible. Over food. Nothing distracts Kier like a pizza."

Alex laughed. "Then I'll arrange a pizza date for the two of them. With supervision, of course." Closing his laptop, he stood. "I'm heading home. After I talk to Diana, I'll give you a call to set a time and date." Walking out the door, he chuckled, picturing a defenseless restaurant invaded by two angry Xerians sparring over a meat lover's pizza.

He was still in a good mood when he got back to their apartment. Closing their front door, he sang out, "Home, I'm honey."

Diana poked her head out of her bedroom. "I don't care how many times I hear that, it still makes me laugh." She ducked back into her room, coming out moments later carrying her laptop. "Thanks, I needed the laugh. It's been a rough day. One of my clients emailed me the wrong code so I ended up ordering the wrong sample. I've been his whipping post for the last hour about my 'serious lack of work ethic.'" She shook her head and made a face. "I only barely resisted informing him where he could put his work ethic."

Alex laughed at her sour look. "Bring your laptop into the dining room while I start supper. Mac and cheese all right?"

Diana smiled. "Mmmm, my favorite. With hot dogs?"

"If you insist. I was going to use Spam—"

"Ew, gross! Don't you dare ruin my mac and cheese with that foul-tasting stuff."

"All right, all right. Hot dogs it is."

He began assembling the ingredients, whistling slightly off-key. While he waited for the water to boil, he pulled a chair from the dining room, mounted it backwards, and rested his chin on his folded arms.

"My, my," Diana said when he remained silent. "You look so serious."

"Huh? No, just trying to figure out where to start."

"So just tell me. What came out of your meeting with Riley and Evelyn."

Alex drew a deep breath. "Well, for starters, we're all going to a science fiction convention in Santa Clara."

Her eyebrows rose. "What does that have to do with the forum? I thought your problem had something to do with that."

"It does. A whole bunch of Xerians are going to this HydraCon convention, no matter what we say."

"Won't that be—"

"Yeah. A disaster," Alex finished for her. "And I don't want to leave you alone in the apartment while I'm gone." He looked up at her. "Want to come along? We could share a room. Save expenses?"

"So, let me get this straight," she said, tapping her lips with one finger. "You're inviting me to have a front row seat at a disaster *and* you want me to foot half the bill for the privilege?"

Alex choked and felt his face warm clear to the hairline. "No... well...yes...I mean...."

Diana laughed at him. "I understand what you meant. But you have to admit, the way you worded it sounded pretty bad."

"Um, yeah. I guess." He rubbed the back of his neck. "But I meant it, about not wanting to leave you here alone. Especially after you let your restraining order against Bryce lapse. I don't like the idea of spending the whole weekend worried that he might show up here and... and..."

"That won't happen. We both signed the papers today. I'm divorcing him." She raised her chin. "He has no claim on me. Not anymore."

Alex clapped his hands slowly. "Good for you." He sobered. "But there's something else you should know about. I've been meaning to tell you, but I didn't want to worry you while you were still dealing with Bryce. We found out recently that two women from our forum were murdered in San Diego. We think someone might be stalking people from the board."

Her eyes grew wide. "And you think I might be in danger?"

"It's possible. That's another reason why I'd really rather have you at the convention than all alone here." He hastened to add, "Riley and Tessa will be there, as will Evelyn and her son Kier."

The stove began sizzling as the water boiled over the rim of his pan. Alex jumped up, almost upsetting his chair, and began fixing their dinner. Over his shoulder, he continued, "Tessa's making a costume for Riley and I know Kier's already working on one."

Diana nodded. "I'll talk to Tessa, see what she suggests I wear. I've never been to a science fiction convention before, but she's told me about them. They sound like fun."

Alex shrugged. "I never have to worry about costumes. I just wear whichever of my t-shirts is appropriate."

Diana laughed. "You mean like the one that says 'I aim to misbehave' or the one that says 'Trust me, I'm the Doctor'?"

He laughed. "Yeah, those." After adding sliced hot dogs and macaroni to the boiling water, he returned to the table. "Which reminds me. You and Kier are from different Xerian guilds, so you'll both need training before you meet people from the other guild. Like Evelyn and I have."

"I suppose that would be helpful. You'll need all the help you can get dealing with the people from the forum getting together." She furrowed her brow. "How exactly do we do that, though?"

"We get you and Kier together." He pulled out his phone. "Bring up your calendar and I'll call Evelyn. Apparently Kier learns better over pizza."

* * *

"Hey, guys," Diana said, answering the door and grabbing the other woman's arm. "C'mon, Tessa, let's go." With that the two women were out the door and gone.

Riley turned and waved goodbye to Tessa's rapidly disappearing backside.

"Diana sure seemed to be in a hurry."

Alex shrugged one shoulder. "She's just nervous about having dinner with Evelyn and Kier. We told her what meeting someone from the other guild can be like, so she's worried she'll react badly and cause a scene. To hear her tell it, she practically threatened Tessa with bodily harm if she didn't go with her for moral support."

"Well, for the record, Tessa didn't mind. She saw how hard it was for you and Evelyn and she's always been supportive of Diana." Riley grabbed a chair from the dining table and pulled it up to Alex's desk. "Now, what was it you wanted to show me?"

"I just wanted to go over some things about the forum with you. You've been MIA for the last couple weeks, so I figured you hadn't seen the latest developments with the group that's coming to HydraCon."

Riley picked up a bone-shaped hand exerciser from Alex's desk and began absentmindedly squeezing it. "Speak."

"Woof! What next? Sit, stay, roll over?"

"Play dead." Riley punched him in the arm. "You know what I mean. Get on with it."

"Fine, be that way. So, what you've missed...." Alex logged in to the forum and brought up a message thread.

Riley leaned forward to read the messages on Alex's screen.

‡Scullyluver: I just suggested over in the thread about the missing girls that maybe you should hold a memorial for @VampGrrrl and @ThorRider at the convention. They were part of our community and if a bunch of people are getting together, I think it would be nice to at least light a candle for them. Wish I could be there to join you, but I have another commitment that weekend.‡

‡WendyAnn: You bet I'm coming! I can't wait to meet you folks! Plus, I like the idea of a memorial for @ThorRider and @VampGrrrl. Maybe Sunday morning?‡

‡Vino: I really like @ScullyLuver's suggestion of having a memorial service for our two fallen forum members. If you need a room, I'm offering mine. I'll have my forum name on my badge. Find me!‡

"That's a nice thought and all, but they didn't really know either girl and I'm a little worried about putting that many of them in the same space."

Alex turned to him. "That's not the point, Riley. The girls were part of this little family they've created on our forum. Even not knowing the girls personally, they still need some kind of closure." Alex sighed. "We can't keep using the same excuse for not letting them get together. They will, no matter what we say."

"As much as I hate to admit it, you're probably right." Riley sat back in his chair, diddling with a plastic dinosaur. "I think the best we can hope for is to do damage control."

Alex stared pointedly at the dinosaur in Riley's hands. After a moment, Riley put the toy slowly back on the desk.

A few clicks later, Alex brought up a different set of messages on the board. "And then there's this."

‡MileHigh: Hey guys? I got enough for the membership but not the wheels to get there. I'm in Boulder, Colorado and winter's comin' on. Time for me to relocate to some place warm. LIke southern Cal. Hey, @RoadRanger29 & @Amazon - either of you close enough to pick me up? Otherwise, I'm thumbing it to California.‡

‡Amazon: Hey, MileHigh, looks like I'll be up your way before heading for the con. Send me a private message and we'll make arrangements. Can't have you thumbing when you could be cruising in my luxury rig!‡

Riley held his head in his hands. "He's hitchhiking with one of the truckers? What if they're from different guilds? Just the thing, road rage neatly contained in one huge, fast moving juggernaut. I don't know what we can do about it though."

Alex rubbed the bridge of his nose. "Yeah. Explain that to the cops."

"Here's hoping that if they are from opposite guilds, Amazon just leaves MileHigh high and dry." Riley coughed, trying to hide his laughter.

Alex groaned. "You did not just make a joke, did you?"

"Who, me? I don't know what you could be talking about." This time, Riley didn't even try to hide his grin.

"Still, he's a big boy and can take care of himself. He already said on the forum that if he can't get a ride with them," Alex pantomimed sticking out his thumb and showing a little leg in the classic hitchhiking pose, "he'll just hitch a ride."

"I remember when I used to do that. In college. My poor Wisconsin parents were appalled," Riley said.

Alex sat forward, almost dropping his laptop. "The question remains, what are we going to do at the convention with a bunch of Xerians, half of whom hate the other half?"

"Good question," Riley said, shaking his head.

"Anyway," Alex said with a sigh, "Cavanagh, you know, the cop from SF who offered to help us with the missing girls? He's going to the convention too, so I told him he could stay with Diana and me, but he turned me down. He said he'd already gotten his own room. He acted kinda weird about me offering it to him."

"You dolt," Riley said with a grin. "He probably thinks you and Diana are a couple and he'd be a third wheel, sleeping on your floor."

"Diana and I? Really? Why would—"

"Because he doesn't know you. Or her for that matter." Riley laughed. "You just asked a relative stranger if he wanted to bunk with you and some woman. What did you expect him to think?"

Alex felt his face warming. "Uh, I'd never…Diana and I don't…."

Oh my god, Alex thought. *I can't believe I didn't see that. How do I face this guy at the convention? He's going to think I was trying to seduce him into a three-way with my girlfriend or something.* Alex pondered a moment. *Well, it's not like I haven't done something like that before, but I don't have that kind of relationship with Diana.*

Riley laughed, clapping a hand on Alex's shoulder. "I know that, but he doesn't."

Alex coughed. "So…um…anyway, Cavanagh has offered to be our 'private cop' for the convention. We should probably connect with him early on and bring him up to speed on our plans."

Riley picked up another one of Alex's toys, a light-up ball. "That's a good idea. Do you want to message him and set up a meeting? You've already been talking to him, so it's probably best that you be the person that follows up with him."

No, Alex thought, *I don't want to follow up with him. Not now. He already thinks I'm trying to get into his pants. I don't need to embarrass myself further.*

"Yeah, I can do that," he said out loud with just a hint of a sigh. *Just be professional. Handle it like Riley would and pretend like nothing happened. Maybe I should wear nicer clothes when I go see him so he sees a professional, not a perv.*

After watching Riley turn the ball on and off several times, Alex slapped his hands. "Stop that! You're going to run down its batteries."

Riley gingerly put the ball back on the desk.

Apparently he finally got my message, Alex thought wryly. *Leave my toys alone!*

"There was one more thing that I wanted to show you." Alex clicked a few times, bringing up yet another message on the forum.

‡*GoldenOldie: Hey, guys? Could you put your forum name on your con badge? It would sure help the old memory of mine! It'd be a lot easier to find our folks at the convention, too.*‡

Riley nodded. "Yeah, I like that idea. That'll make things a lot easier for us too."

"Especially with how many of them are planning on coming."

"Many? How many? There's a lot of them?"

Alex couldn't help but laugh at the panic-stricken look on Riley's face.

"According to the poll Aurora12 started, there'll be thirty-nine people from the forum there." Alex shook his head. "That's a lot of folks to keep under control."

"I've been chewing on that problem myself. Tessa's the one who came up with the coolest idea though. Since we know that half the people are going to have problems with the other half, she thought we should put out a message, asking each of them to come by our room after they get checked in. We'll have you and Evelyn waiting in the room. Once we see which one of you they react to, we can give them a badge ribbon for their guild."

"What if one of them is a Tesham?"

"We've got that covered too. Everyone will get a ribbon that says 'Xerian Ambassador' on it, plus the one for their guild. Anyone we find who's a Tesham will just get the Xerian one. We'll need to have a long talk with any Tesham we find and explain what it means that they don't react to either guild. That way they don't reveal themselves and cause even more problems." Riley made a face. "That's just what we need, for two groups who hate each other to have a common enemy."

Riley pulled a thick pen-shaped object from a mug of writing implements.

Alex snatched it out of Riley's hand. "Leave my sonic screwdriver alone!" *Dammit, man, I thought you'd finally learned your lesson.*

"Sorry." Riley looked down at his now-empty hands. He brought them together in his lap and began twiddling his thumbs. "I'm a little on edge. I haven't had much free time lately, with all the new patients I've picked up." He shook his head. "Being in Evelyn's office has certainly been good for business. And while that's great for my wallet, it's not so great for having any free time."

"Free time I've got by the bucketful. Maybe I could take on some extra work. Pick up a couple of your hypnotherapy clients, once I get my certification in a couple weeks."

Riley looked at him. "You know, that's not a half bad idea. We'll talk."

* * *

The bedroom lights went out and Tessa slipped into bed beside Riley.

Riley yelped. "Your toes are like ice!"

"Blame the hardwood floors. You wanted them, so stop complaining." Tessa snuggled into Riley's embrace, fitting her head beneath his chin. "Are you ready for this?"

"The convention? We're as ready as we can get, I think."

"We have everything packed for tomorrow. The ribbons finally came yesterday. I was really sweating that they weren't going to arrive in time," Tessa said.

Riley was silent for a few moments. Tessa was thinking maybe he'd drifted off to sleep when he finally spoke softly.

"What have we started, Tessa? Where is this Xerian thing leading us?"

In an amused voice, she said, "Isn't it a little late to be questioning the whole issue, Mac?" She shrugged. "It just grew. Now all we can do is let it play out, right?"

Riley sat up abruptly, pulling the bedspread over his bare shoulder. Tessa propped herself on one elbow, staring up at his pale face in the dark.

"I mean, two of the Xerians we found are dead. I feel sort of responsible for them."

He sounds so sad, she thought, reaching out and patting his arm. "You aren't," she said adamantly. "Just get that idea right out of your head. The only one responsible is whoever killed them." *He's got enough to worry about already. He doesn't need to shoulder that burden too.*

"I followed a thread that interested me and put up the forum. hey were targeted because of something I did."

"But if you hadn't done that, all those people would still think that they were going crazy. Now they know there are others like them who remember Xeres."

Riley peered down at her. "Like you?"

She nodded. "Like me," she said in a softer voice. "I've been remembering more things lately too."

"Like what?"

Tessa bit at her lip. *I really don't want to tell Riley about this, but now I don't have any choice.*

"About my mate being killed by the Sheitan."

"Mate? As in, husband?"

"No," she said, searching for the right words. "Mate seems to be

221

the best word. Like, people pairing up wasn't the norm. I think it's three people in a marriage."

Riley whistled softly. "That's a new twist. You need to put that up on the forum and see what others remember."

She huffed. "You're not jealous? Just a teensy bit?" she teased.

"Of someone who died who knows how many years ago?"

"Kind of. What if I meet my other mate at the con? Or worse still, I meet another Sheitan?"

"Are you scared of the Sheitan?" Riley probed.

"I'm not scared of them, but my mate was the only one who knew how to kill them permanently."

"What do you mean, permanently?"

"You can kill the body they are inhabiting, but they just come back in a different body. My mate was the one who discovered that they were among us in the first place. He figured out how to kill them for good. But they found and killed him before he could share that information with the rest of us." She shivered. *Am I being paranoid? I'm remembering demons who are out to get me. Maybe I am circling insanity after all.*

Riley slid back down next to her and took her in his arms.

"I'm sure there won't be any Sheitan there. Even if one happens to show up, I'll protect you."

She looked up at him, his face shrouded in shadows. "But who's going to protect you?"

He laughed softly. "I'm human, remember? I don't need protection. They're after Xerians, not humans. You're *my* mate now, so it's my job to protect you."

He kissed her on the forehead. Snuggling down under the covers, they spooned together.

I feel safe in Riley's arms, but still…what could he do against a Sheitan? And what about all the other Xerians coming to the convention? How do we keep them safe?

Riley nuzzled her ear. "There's another interesting thread on the forum. Folks have been wondering where Xeres is, astronomically speaking. Any insight?"

"In space?" Turning her head, Tessa spoke over her shoulder. "Haven't a clue. Maybe if you'd asked me that during a regression…."

They went silent, both drifting toward sleep.

…Around her, Tessa felt the presence of the rest of her class, but her eyes were held by the speaker in front of the huge star map.

"Here we have our solar system. Nine planets around our yellow star, five terrestrial planets and four gas giants. We have detected life in various stages of evolution on three of the other worlds, all within the inner terrestrial bodies. No intelligent life exists on these others beyond simple plants and animals....

"Tessa?"

She felt someone shaking her shoulder. *Did I fall asleep in class again?* she wondered through the fog of sleep.

"You were talking in your sleep. Something about planets?"

Riley! That's who's with me. I'm on Earth, not....

"I remembered! Riley, I know where Xeres was...at least I think so."

"What? Did you get turn-by-turn directions in your dream? Like intergalactic Google Maps?" Riley said playfully.

She smiled. "Something like that. I was a student and the teacher was talking about our solar system. Nine planets, yellow star, five terrestrial planets and four gas giants."

"You mean, *our* solar system? Xeres was, what, Mars?" Riley paused for a moment, then chuckled. "Oh, my gods. I can't wait to tell Alex. I'm sleeping with a Martian!"

Chapter 26

Diana, juggling her luggage, asked Tessa, "Is it always this chaotic?" Around them, clots of newly-arrived convention-goers greeted each other like long lost friends.

Tessa laughed. "Yeah, pretty much. A lot of these folks only get to see each other once a year at this con."

"But," Diana protested, "they're all on social media, aren't they?"

"Oh, yes. Meeting in person is still special though." Tessa reached over to relieve Diana of a couple of her bags.

Watching the crowd, Diana finally spotted Alex pulling an overloaded luggage cart through the glass double doors.

"The guys are here," Diana said, pointing them out to Tessa.

The women steered their way across the flow of traffic to where Alex and Riley stood panting against the cart.

Eyeing the black shirt Alex was wearing, Tessa giggled. "You're so silly. 'Aliens are real.' Where did you find that shirt?"

He shrugged. "I've had it for ages. There's more on the back. Look." He twisted around.

Tessa read the neon green lettering, "'Ask me about my little green men.' Cute. You always seem to have just the right shirt for any occasion."

Riley sighed heavily. "Yes, and he loves showing them off too." He shoved the cart over to the seating area, out of the way. "Come on, Alex. Let's check in."

The two men left, moving like eels through the evening crowd.

As Diana made her way to an unoccupied chair, a masked convention-goer clipped their overloaded cart, almost knocking her into Tessa. Giving the the cart an irritated look, the man kept going.

"Well, excuse you!" Tessa called sarcastically after him. "You give fans a bad name."

As the boys returned, Diana stood and gathered up her luggage.

"We're checked in, so let's get out of the lobby before you get run over again. Good thing we were early, too. Look how much that line's grown already." Alex said, offering Diana a key card.

"Where exactly am I supposed to put that?" Diana asked, glancing down at her overloaded arms.

"I can think of a few places," Alex said, waggling his eyebrows.

She threw her bags and suitcase down, narrowly missing his feet. "Smartass." Snatching the card from his hand, she shoved it into her bra.

"We're on the fifth floor, in adjoining rooms. It's not far from the elevator, either," Riley said. "Let's get our stuff put away, then explore the convention."

"Good idea," Diana said, bending to pick up one of the bags she'd just dropped.

Alex pointed over the women's heads. "Elevators are over there."

"OneEyedScoobie!" A deep peremptory shout made them all turn.

"TinMan," Alex said, shouldering past the women and almost knocking Diana over.

Diana saw Alex smiling at a tall, slender man with reddish hair cutting through the crowd toward them. *He looks familiar,* Diana thought. *And that voice....*

When Alex met the man, they shook hands and Alex towed him along toward their group.

"Guys, this is TinMan, the San Francisco cop from the forum. His real name's James. James, this is Riley, he's on the board as DocMezmer. This is his girlfriend, Tessa, aka SnakeGrrrl, and my roommate, the charming WWLives, Di—"

As soon as the man's eyes met hers, everything clicked.

"Diana? Princess?"

"Jimmy B?" she asked in disbelief.

Oh, now she remembered that voice. It sent shivers down her back.

Starting forward to greet him, she said, "I can't believe...." In her haste, Diana tripped over her suitcase and fell, scattering her luggage across the floor. Strong arms caught her.

"Oh, sorry. I—"

"No problem, Princess."

She found herself looking up into his intense blue eyes. Being in his arms again felt right somehow.

He set her on her feet. Suddenly, Diana couldn't think of anything to say. She blushed, turned her back on him, and began picking up her things.

Alex looked from one to the other. "Uh, you two know each other?"

"Well, duh," Tessa said, bending to help Diana with her bags.

"Um," TinMan said, "we grew up together. In Boston."

"Really? And you're meeting here, in San Francisco? Small world, huh?" Alex said.

"Indeed," TinMan agreed, bending to help Diana. "We've known each other since second grade."

Diana nodded, smiling. "Yeah, all the way through graduation. We drifted apart in high school. He and I didn't run in the same circles."

She saw Jimmy B's face take on a closed look.

"Right. I wasn't one of the popular kids. Or dating one of them." The bitterness in his voice surprised her.

Her brows rose. "Oh? I don't remember it that way. We were always friends."

"You're right, we were. It's just...I don't know, that guy you dated seemed to take you over in high school. He walled you off like a treasure trove he didn't want anyone else to touch. I wonder whatever happened to him?"

"Unfortunately, I married him."

His eyebrows rose. "Oh. Sorry."

Diana laughed. "No need. I'm in the process of divorcing him."

"Oh," he said, surprise on his face. "Then you're...?"

"Free as a bird," she said lightly.

The smile that lit up his face warmed her heart.

Moving the cart toward the elevators, Riley piped up, "Move it, folks. We gotta get settled and back down here to intercept any Xerians who show up early, before they start a fight."

"I still need to get checked in, so I'll catch up with you all later." Jimmy B started to turn away.

Tessa stopped him. "James, why don't you join us for dinner in, say, half an hour or so at the restaurant?"

"I'd like that. Very much," he said, giving Diana a look. Then he waved and moved off.

Diana watched him go. *We've just met for the first time in years. Why does it feel like he's taking all of the warmth in the room with him?*

Half an hour later, the four friends headed down to the restaurant.

"Has anyone heard from Evelyn? She's supposed to be here already." Riley pushed the lobby button, holding the door as three more people shoved in, separating Alex from the rest of the group.

Mashed into the corner, Alex said, "She just called. They're on the elevator heading up to their room. They'll meet us in the restaurant after they drop their stuff off."

"That's good. They'll get to meet Jimmy B too." Diana, sardined between Riley and Tessa, felt her face get warm. "Umm, James. Sorry, old habits."

Tessa gave her a quizzical look. "So, what's the story with you two, anyway? Why haven't you mentioned him before?"

"It was a long time ago. We lost touch after graduation. I married Bryce right out of college and we moved to San Francisco for his job." She shrugged. "You know how it is."

The elevator door slid open, blissfully releasing them from their forced intimacy. While Riley waited for Alex, Tessa took Diana's arm and started toward the restaurant.

"Is it going to be that crowded all weekend?" Diana asked, trying to keep the panic out of her voice.

"That? No, that was roomy, compared to, say, after the masquerade or the dance," Tessa replied with a smile.

Diana blinked, not believing her friend. *How can things get worse than that?*

Tessa's smile disappeared. "Oh, sweetie, I'm sorry. I forgot that you don't like crowds."

Diana schooled her face to hide the panic she felt in the pit of her stomach.

"That's okay. Looks like I'll be getting plenty of exercise this weekend taking the stairs."

"Just a warning," Tessa said. "You might encounter people making out or monsters on the stairs."

"Monsters?" Diana said, eyes widening. "Like trolls under the stairs?"

Tessa giggled. "Lots of people wearing costumes, I mean."

"Oh." Diana sighed, relieved. "I'll be careful, then." She spun to face her friend. "Wait. People making out? Really?"

Tessa shrugged. "It happens. When you don't have much money, you end up having to share a room with three or four people. That isn't conducive to having a private place to make out with the hot guy or girl you just met. And since so few people take the stairs...."

Diana felt her face reddening.

Tessa chuckled. "It's been awhile since I've been around a con-virgin. Even Riley didn't get this embarrassed when I dragged him to his first sci-fi con."

"Con-virgin? Now what the hell does that mean?"

"It just means you're new to the convention scene. Everyone starts out there."

"Look at the line. We're going to be waiting awhile for supper," Diana said, scanning the restaurant.

She went still. She couldn't believe what she was seeing. Over at the check-in desk stood Bryce.

What's he *doing here? Is he following me? Why would he do that?* She took a deep breath. *Calm down. Maybe he's here on business.*

A small woman with a waterfall of sleek auburn hair approached him. He put his arms around her.

Diana gasped softly. *He's meeting a woman? She looks just like me! Is he having an affair?* She felt a wave of jealousy. *How long has this been going on?*

"Earth to Diana. You coming?"

Evelyn, with Kier at her elbow, was waving a hand in front of her face.

Diana's thoughts veered from jealousy to anger in an instant. She took a step back, away from the other woman.

Get a grip. You've been working with Kier to get over these impulses. You can do this. Closing her eyes for a moment, she ran through the mental exercises she'd learned. *There. That's better.*

"Oh. Hi, Evelyn. When did you get here?"

Evelyn grinned at her. "Don't worry, it gets easier with time. And we got here a few minutes ago. Our table's ready. Coming, dear?"

"Right. I must have been daydreaming." Diana turned, hurrying to catch up to the group.

They were still sorting out seating when Jimmy B appeared.

Riley shook his hand. "Hey, TinMan. Thanks for joining us."

"It's James. Or Jimmy," he said, smiling down at Diana. "Sorry I'm late. I checked in with con security. I always do, in case they need a real cop. I also warned them about possible dust-ups this weekend. Can't have the Red Shirts getting caught off guard."

Diana caught the *look* Riley and Tessa exchanged, when Jimmy B held her chair for her, then quickly grabbed the seat beside her. She bit her lip to keep from smiling. *I feel like I'm in high school again. And the hottest guy in the room is showing interest in me. Is it wrong to hope Bryce sees us together?*

"Red Shirts?" Diana asked, looking at Jimmy.

"Convention security. Comes from the original Star Trek series. Security wore red shirts and were always the first to die."

"Oh." She wrinkled her brow. "Does security often get killed at the convention?"

The rest of the table laughed.

"No," Tessa said, wiping away tears of laughter. "They're all volunteers and no one gets killed at sci-fi conventions anyway."

Riley spoke up. "James, this is Evelyn Sloan and her son Kier. They're Hypnotique and KidCosmic on the forum. I work out of her office in Oakland."

Diana tuned out for a moment. *It's so nice to see Jimmy B again, though I guess he goes by James these days. James Brendan Cavenaugh. Sounds so grown up. Maybe we'll have some free time to catch up this weekend.*

"Nice to meet you both. James half rose from his chair, reaching across the table to shake hands with Evelyn and Kier.

"Pleased to meet you."

"Uh, Evelyn?" Tessa said, a funny look on her face. "Did you feel anything when you shook James' hand?"

Evelyn raised her eyebrows. "No. Why? Does he have cooties?"

Instead of answering her, Tessa turned to Alex.

"How about you?" When Alex shook his head, she turned to Riley. "Tesham. We've got another Tesham."

James looked from Tessa to Riley.

"Another what? Tesh-Shum? What's a Tesham? And who else is one?"

"I'm the only other one we've discovered so far."

Their server showed up, interrupting further conversation.

When he had taken their orders and gone, Tessa continued, "You know how there are two guilds from Xeres who are in conflict with each other?

James nodded.

"Alex told you about the Sheitan, right? Well, there used to be a third guild...."

* * *

"You're in room 419, sir," the clerk said, handing Bryce the key card. "The elevators are located right behind you on the far wall. Enjoy your stay with us, Mr. Lundee."

Bryce had turned toward the elevators when he heard a familiar voice.

"Bryce, is that you?"

Turning, he smiled. "Jessica!"

She stepped in close, wrapping her arms around him.

He returned the gesture, momentarily lifting her off her feet, her dark hair spilling over his arms. Gently setting her back down, he asked, "What are you doing here? It's been ages."

She shrugged. "I'm here for the convention, of course. Aren't you?"

"Yes. Of course. The forum."

"Yeah, I'm BunnyFuFu there."

"BunnyFuFu? That's so...innocent, and so not you. You're one of the most dangerous people I know. I mean, you have a black belt in karate, you're a private investigator.."

She chuckled. "But all anyone sees is this petite little woman. They never see me as a threat."

"Ah, so BunnyFuFu is just part of your camouflage. Got it."

"I'm here because I figured I might get some information that would get me in Cadwallader's good graces. Can you believe he's still mad at me for what happened during the Gold Rush? I mean, come on, it's been over a hundred and seventy years. Let it go already."

He sighed. "He's always been one to hold a grudge. Hell, he's still mad at me for things that happened on Xeres."

"Really? That's harsh."

"You know what they say about a thin line between love and hate."

A hand fell on Bryce's shoulder. He turned, his eyes following the arm to a stocky, sad-eyed man with a droopy mustache.

"Mel?" Bryce said. "Are you here for the convention, too?"

"When I saw Jessica was coming, I decided to tag along. We're sharing a room and checking out the smorgasbord."

Bryce frowned at the older man. "You know as well as I do that Thierry would have our heads if we actually ate someone without his permission."

The other man waggled his eyebrows. "What Thierry doesn't know can't hurt me."

"Yes, but his brown-nosing 'Area Supervisor'," he accentuated his comment by making air quotes, "is coming in tonight. And I have the distinct pleasure of collecting him at the airport in," he glanced at his watch, "about twenty minutes. I need to get these bags up to my room first. Catch up with you both later?"

Jessica shook her head. "Oh, definitely, you can't be late. He'd just add that to the tally against you."

Waving as he headed to the elevators, Bryce shot back, "Don't I know it."

Chapter 27

"Good afternoon and welcome to the Xerian Embassy. I'm Tessa, SnakeGrrrl on the forum," Tessa said with a grin.

"Nice sign," the young woman said, stepping through the door Tessa was holding open. "I'm HouseofMouse. I've already checked in for the convention. I ran into DocMezmer there and he told me to come up here. Now what?"

"Now, I'd like you to meet a couple of people."

Tessa ushered her into the room where Evelyn and Alex waited. He rose and offered his hand.

"Hi, I'm Alex, aka OneEyedScoobie."

The woman looked at his hand with naked anger and balled up her fists.

"Um, I…My mother told me to be polite to strangers, but I'm sorry, I just want to—"

Evelyn chuckled. "I'm Hypnotique, though my friends call me Evelyn. Just ignore him. He's Bylantian and you're obviously not."

Relief evident on her face, she shook Evelyn's hand. Tessa collected the appropriate ribbons from the box and handed them to HouseofMouse.

"Here," Tessa said, handing her the orange and blue Xerian Ambassador ribbon and the purple Klymurian ribbon. "With these on your badge, you can avoid anyone with Bylantian red ribbons. We're having a meeting of Xerians on Saturday at nine, before the panels start for the day. HankT and I will be teaching the Klymurians how to overcome their problems with us, while DocMezmer and Alex teach the Bylantians in a different room."

HouseofMouse nodded, grinning wryly and shooting a dark look toward Alex.

"I can see now how important that would be. I never realized—"

Evelyn interjected, spreading her hands apart. "Heh, we tried to tell you all, more than once. But you were so sure it wouldn't be that bad. OneEyedScoobie and I had already gone through this and knew what we were talking about. To say the least, it's unsettling to meet someone and take an instant dislike to them."

Tessa looked up as James appeared at the door. He was wearing olive drab slacks, a blue shirt, a brown leather vest, with a dark green duster covering it all. The final touch was a dark green fedora on top of his blond head. She thought it looked vaguely familiar, but she couldn't place it.

"Morning, James. Who are you supposed to be?" she asked with a smile.

He spread his arms wide. "I'm the TinMan. You know, from the TV mini-series?"

Nodding, she said, "Oh, now I recognize you. Aren't you supposed to have a gun?

"Yeah, but I can't wear the shoulder holster and pistol. Hotel policy."

"SnakeGrrrl, um, Tessa, has my roommate stopped by yet? UFOLuver?"

"Ah," Evelyn said, "that was the next thing on our list, roommates."

Alex looked up from his laptop, "Nope, UFOLuver hasn't checked in yet. We're keeping track of everyone's guilds and their roommates to make sure they're staying with someone from the same guild." He looked up. "Can I have your cell phone number, so we can notify you if there's a problem?"

Curling her lip at Alex, she reeled off her number through gritted teeth, then added the panel info into her calendar.

"Is that all, Tessa? I'm meeting friends in the coffee shop in a few minutes."

Tessa smiled slightly at the woman's response to Alex. "Yeah, that's all. See you at the panel tomorrow?"

"For sure. Meeting people from the other guild is way more uncomfortable than I ever imagined."

"Just remember, if you see someone wearing a red ribbon that says

'Bylantian', you might want to avoid them."

"Trust me," she said over her shoulder as she headed for the door, "I will."

Tessa noticed James staring intently at Alex. Finally he asked, "What does your shirt say?"

Alex stood up, tugging his shirt down to make it easier to read. "In my past lives, I was a huge skeptic of reincarnation."

James chuckled. "Good one." He grabbed the desk chair, turned it around backwards and straddled it. He looked up at Tessa. "Are all of the introductions that awkward? 'Cause, I have to agree with HouseofMouse, I thought you guys were exaggerating how bad the guild reactions were."

"That," Tessa said, motioning with her chin toward the door, then shaking her head, "that wasn't bad. Earlier we had someone try to strangle Alex. It was just a lucky coincidence that I noticed something off right before he jumped at Alex so I was able to intercept him."

Evelyn spoke up. "It was the weirdest thing, too. I could have sworn that Tessa's eyes had a purple glow about them for a second there. But it had to have been a trick of the light. The sun reflecting off the purple cloak the girl was wearing, right?"

Tessa shrugged. "Purple glowing eyes? Seriously? We're on Earth now, not Xeres. Magic doesn't work here."

Quirking his mouth, James asked, "Magic, huh. I never thought about that." He shook his head. "Anyway, so why don't they react to you or me like that? You said that the other guilds almost wiped our guild out. Wouldn't they hate us even more than they hate each other?"

Tessa perched on the edge of Evelyn's bed. "As near as we can figure, it's *exactly* because they think our guild was wiped out that they don't react to us physically."

"Okay. So, what ribbons do I get then?"

"Hunh. We just planned to have them wear the Xerian Ambassador ribbon and claim we hadn't figured out which guild they were in yet."

"But won't they realize that nobody is reacting to me?"

"Alex and Evelyn got along great until they were regressed and started remembering more about Xeres. That's when their problems with each other started. Just tell anyone who asks that you only recently started having dreams about Xeres and haven't been regressed yet."

"So, all the Xerians here have been regressed?"

"No, not all, but most have, or they've been having dreams for awhile. Anyway, that's how we planned to explain my non-reaction. We thought that finding another Tesham was unlikely. I guess we were wrong." She shrugged.

James smiled. "Well, at least I'll get along with everyone and can help stop any confrontations. By the way," he asked, looking around, "where's Riley?"

"He's stuck down at registration making sure there aren't any Xerian confrontations before we can get people sorted out up here."

James rose, returning his chair to the desk. "He's been down there all morning? How about I go down and relieve him so you guys can get some lunch?"

"Really? You'd do that?" Tessa said gratefully. "Diana's right, you *are* a jewel! I was going to pick up something and take it to him, but I'm sure he'd rather sit down and relax for a bit."

Tessa escorted him to the door. "Could you ask Riley to come up here once you relieve him?"

"Sure," he said, stepping out into the hallway and heading for the elevator.

Tessa glanced down the hallway and noticed two young women approaching from opposite ends. Registering that they wore identical angry looks, Tessa stepped out into the hallway to intercept them.

"Hi, I'm SnakeGrrrl. Welcome to the Xerian Embassy." She pointed to one of the girls. "Would you please go in first?"

The red-haired woman cast a furious look at the other before entering. Tessa guided the second one into the room, making sure to keep them separated.

"My handle's UFOLuver," said the redhead. "Just got in from Florida."

"I'm IrisArch," the other one said from behind Tessa.

Evelyn rose, extending her hand to UFOLover. "Hypnotique here."

The young woman shied away from Evelyn. "Don't touch me!"

Alex sprang from his seat on the bed and stepped between the woman and Evelyn. "Hi, there. I'm OneEyedScoobie. Let me help you." He grabbed a couple ribbons from the boxes on the desk and handed them to the woman.

Looking at the ribbons, she said, "Bylantian, huh? Isn't that the science guild?"

Rescuing his laptop up from where he'd unceremoniously dumped it on the bed, Alex nodded, "Yup. So, do you have a roommate this weekend? And can I have your phone number in case we need to contact you."

"Uh, I'm rooming with HouseofMouse—."

Alex looked up from his laptop in alarm. "Warning, warning! Danger, Will Robinson! That's a bad idea!"

"What? Why?"

"HouseofMouse is Klymurian. So," he consulted his spreadsheet, "you'll have to room with someone else. This is the third room switch we've had today."

"Um, Alex?" Tessa interjected. "I think I have a solution to UFO's problem." She turned to look at the woman behind her. "Check the spreadsheet. If I remember right, IrisArch is supposed to be rooming with Vino. If so, she's in the same boat."

He bent and consulted his laptop.

"Yep, you're right." He looked up at UFOLuver. "Let me give you Vino and HouseofMouse's numbers, so you can arrange the room swap among yourselves."

"I already have House's number. What's Vino's?"

Tessa interjected, "Iris, you'll need those numbers, too."

"Great," said IrisArch, pulling out her phone.

After both women had all the information they needed and their respective ribbons, Tessa escorted them out of the room, keeping her body between them until they were all outside in the hall. The women shot off in opposite directions, obviously eager to get away.

Shaking her head at the near collision, Tessa turned and re-entered the hotel room.

"Phew!" Evelyn said. "I really hope *that* doesn't happen again."

Tessa sighed. "It's bound to, especially this evening when most of the people will be arriving."

"Goodness," Riley said from the doorway, another man coming in right behind him. "You all look like you've just been through a hurricane. What did I miss?"

"Just another pair of mismatched roommates," Evelyn said, shaking her head.

"Just?" Alex said, raising his eyebrows. "We nearly had a blowup. Two people from opposite guilds came in at the same time. The only thing that prevented it from erupting into something bigger was Tessa's quick thinking. She jumped between them and kept them separated until we could get everything sorted out." He shook his head. "That's the second time this morning she's managed to head off a problem. She kept me from getting strangled earlier."

Riley turned and gestured to the man behind him. "Everyone, this is HankT. I met him at the hypnotherapy conference in Seattle. He was the first person I ever heard talk about orange trees with blue leaves other than Tessa."

HankT moved the rest of the way into the room. "Hi, Dr. Henry Thompson. Hank to my friends. Like Riley, I've been interested in this ever since my first client talked about it. Two of my clients are from opposing guilds, so I've seen the problems firsthand. That's why I contacted Riley about helping you out this weekend. I'm human like him, so nobody reacts to me."

Evelyn stood and shook Hank's hand. "Thanks for helping out. We can use all the help we can get."

Alex chimed in up from the bed, "Ditto."

Riley turned to Tessa. "I think I should take you to lunch, for being so resourceful. But can they survive without you?"

Smiling at the suggestion, she glanced at Alex and Evelyn. "Will you two be okay without me for an hour or so?"

"We were planning on going get lunch too," Evelyn said. "Diana and Kier should be here any minute to relieve us." She got a worried look on her face. "I don't want to leave them here alone, though, not after the morning we've had already."

HankT spoke up. "I had an early lunch. I could stay with them and help out if you like."

Evelyn laid a hand on his arm. "You'd do that? Thank you." She looked at Riley and Tessa. "If you don't mind then, could Alex and I join you there?"

Tessa laced her arm through Riley's. "Sure, see you downstairs in a few. Try not to get into any fights on the way."

* * *

"This seems adequate, Miss Donahue," Thierry said as they

entered the hotel suite behind the assistant manager. Latham directed the porter in the disposition of their bags.

"Is there anything else I can do for you, Mr. LeRoux?"

He waved her off. "No, that will be all. I think we can manage from here." Pacing to the windows, he swept open the curtains.

He sniffed his dissatisfaction. "Marvelous. A view of the airport. I always hate these pedestrian accommodations."

"I agree, sir," said his majordomo. "I have already texted our suite number to your operatives. They should report in within the hour. Shall I order you a late dinner?"

"Yes. See to it. Bring Melvin and Jessica to me as soon as they arrive."

"Certainly, sir. I also have some paperwork that requires your attention. Shall I leave it on the coffee table?"

Thierry was still going over the prospectus for the company he was considering taking over when he heard a soft knock at the door. Latham, ever vigilant, glided out of the bedroom and down the hall to the door. Thierry heard muffled voices, then footsteps.

Latham entered the room, followed by his two operatives. "Jessica Coney and Melvin Ashcroft to see you, sir."

"Nice place you got for yourself, Mr. LeRoux." Jessica moved to the white sofa and sat down, curling her legs under her. Melvin stood uncertainly for a moment, then choose an armchair.

Thierry looked at Jessica coldly. No matter that he'd known them both for millennia, that hardly excused her for being so informal.

"I was not aware that this was a social call," he said, tilting his head to the side. "I thought you were here to deliver a report."

Responding to his tone, Jessica uncurled swiftly, planting both feet on the lush carpet.

"I am. Matthew and Bryce are both here, sharing a room on the fourth floor." She emitted a low, throaty chuckle. "Just like old times. Gods, they just need to kiss and make up and have sex with each other. This tension between them is not good for business."

Thierry raised an eyebrow. "I could not agree with you more," he said dryly. "Do they know that you are here?"

Melvin spoke up. "Um, we've both made contact with Bryce. He thinks we're here for the convention, but I'm the only one who's made contact with the Xerians." He pointed to his badge. "They've given these ribbons to the Xerians so they can identify each other. I pretended to be Klymurian when I went to the their room for sorting. I even flirted with the older woman there. I plan to use her to keep me informed about their activities. She seems to be one of the people running this little get-together."

"I made sure we got the room next to our star-crossed lovers." Jessica rolled her eyes. "I might regret that. The walls are pretty thin. While I might get some information that way, I really won't enjoy listening to them bitch at each other all night."

Thierry closed his eyes and shook his head. *Those two will end up bringing down our entire organization if I don't do something. Their rivalry has been useful to motivate them in the past, but it has gotten completely out of hand.*

"They're really that bad?" Melvin asked. "I haven't been around the two of them together in centuries. I've only dealt with whichever one was running the West Coast at any given time."

"Lately, it's been worse than ever," Jessica said. "I think it has something to do with Matthew killing Bryce off this last time." She sniffed. "I don't know why *this* time should be any worse than the last time or the times before that. They've been sparring forever."

Thierry broke in. "That is enough. Do you have any idea what Bryce is planning?"

Jessica shook her head. "Nothing definite. Personally, I don't think he *has* a plan."

"Tsk, tsk. How unprofessional of him." Turning his gaze to Melvin, Thierry asked, "And the Xerians?"

Melvin answered, "They're meeting Saturday morning. Something about getting both guilds comfortable with each other. I don't see how, though."

His phone began to dance across the coffee table. Picking it up, he sighed. *Bryce.*

He speared the woman with a glance. "Do not let either of them know I am here. Make sure you report in daily. Understood?"

Melvin visibly gulped as he straightened to attention in his chair.

"Yes, sir," they said in unison.

Thierry waved them toward the door, ending the interview.

Latham appeared and ushered them to the door. Once they were out of range, Thierry thumbed the answer button.

"Yes?"

"It's Bryce, sir. I'm at the convention with Cadwallader, as you requested. He still seems hell bent on killing Riley. I tried to reason with him, but he's made up his mind and nothing can change it. You know how he is."

"Riley must not die. His work is bringing the Xerians into the open after centuries of being hidden. It is too important to let Matthew foul things up."

"Yes, sir. I agree, sir. I plan to stop him." Thierry could practically see the man bowing and scraping through the connection.

"And your plan is…?"

"Ummm, well, uhhh…I thought it would be best to let him make the first move, then.—"

"So basically, you have no plan," Thierry deadpanned. "Typical."

From the other end of the line, Thierry heard Bryce draw in a breath.

"I—"

"Save it." Controlling the anger in his voice, he continued. "I am tired of your incompetence. Matthew's, too." Thierry stood and began pacing the floor. "Both of you are a disgrace to our kind. This little feud between the two of you was funny once upon a time, but that time has passed. There are other operatives that would be delighted to remove you and take your place in my favor. Fail me again, and I will let them."

Thierry ended the call, unwilling to listen to any more of Bryce's feeble excuses.

He raised his voice. "Latham?"

"Yes, sir," the man said, peering around a corner.

Thierry dropped back onto the overstuffed sofa and brought his free hand up to cover his face. Shaking his head, he barked out, "Get me a drink. And where is my dinner?"

Chapter 28

Alex set the box of t-shirts on the floor next to the table and looked around.

"Well, this is cozy."

"We didn't really need a large room," Riley said, throwing his jacket over one of the chairs behind the speaker's table. Reaching into the inner pocket, he pulled out a tent sign reading "DOCMEZMER" and placed it on the table in front of his chair.

Noticing the box beside the table, Riley asked, "You're really going to sell those shirts here?"

Alex glanced up. "I didn't hear you objecting before."

"I didn't think you were serious," Riley said, shaking his head. "It seems so commercial."

"Hey, you earn your rent money your way, I'll earn mine my way."

He draped one of dark blue shirts over the edge of the box facing the audience, then joined Riley at the table.

"Do you think this room is too small?" Alex asked, sitting down.

"We should have around twenty people in each room. They're all the convention had left, that's why I was able to book them on such short notice," Riley said.

"Where's Tessa?"

"Right here," Tessa said, coming in the door. "I just checked up on Evelyn in the other room. HankT is all set to help her run that room. They already have a few Klymurians showing up."

"I'm glad he's here. It's hard to believe it's only been nine months since I first talked to him about all this." He laughed. "Nine months? No wonder I feel like I'm about to give birth."

"Well, dear," Tessa said with a sly smile, draping an arm around his shoulder, "we don't know how the Xerians mated, so maybe the *men* carried the babies." She patted his stomach. "You *have* put on a little weight in the last few months."

He glared at her pointedly, protesting,, "That's just *someone's* good cooking and a very full schedule. My practice has almost doubled since I moved my office in with Evelyn's."

"Too many fast food drive-thru windows, you mean," she teased.

The room had started filling up.

"Hey, guys," Alex said, waving a hand in front of them for attention. "Business, remember?"

"Oh, right," Riley said, glancing at Alex. "We already covered what's expected, didn't we?"

"Yes," Tessa said, raising an eyebrow, "but what if some of the Xerians haven't checked the forum and seen our warning about Cadwallader? Do we announce that he's here before we start?"

"That shouldn't be necessary," Alex said. "Since I already had everyone's numbers, I texted them all last night with the same warning. They should all know by now not to be alone with Cadwallader."

Tessa nodded. "I thought Evelyn was going to explode when she heard Kier and Diana had run into him at registration." She laughed gently. "For a professional therapist, Evelyn certainly lets Kier wind her around his little finger. If she had her way, Kier would be glued to her hip for the whole convention."

James, in his TinMan outfit, eased through the door with Diana following. As they made for the speaker's table, his eyes lit up.

"Alex! Where did you get that shirt? I gotta get me one."

Diana came around him, reading the shirt's words. "I reincarnated from Xeres and all I got was this lousy t-shirt." She giggled. "Alex, you told me you had shirts made up to sell, but that is priceless."

"Well, James," Alex said rubbing his hands together, "I was planning on selling them for twenty bucks, but I'll make you a deal." He raised an eyebrow. "Ten?"

"You're on," James said, reaching inside his duster for his wallet.

A squeal from behind James made them all turn.

"Oh! Look, girls! We have to have one for each of us." Three young women in Anime costumes ran up, shoving past James.

Alex peered at their nametags, each sporting 'Xerian Ambassador' and 'Bylantian' ribbons.

"Uh, hello…um…Chai19, Latte12, and…" he leaned over to peer at the last girl's name tag, "Java27. Wow, you three must really love your coffee or come from Seattle."

Chai19 reddened. "Guilty on both counts. Do you have the shirt in extra small?"

Riley watched in amusement as Alex appreciated the cleavage their scant costumes revealed. *Good to know I'm not the only one he's got eyes for.*

"Extra small? How are you going to get those boo…." Alex's face turned crimson. "Ummm, never mind. Yes, I have two extra smalls."

Several other participants came forward to purchase shirts as well. A commotion in the back of the room grabbed everyone's attention. Riley searched for the cause. At the center of the maelstrom stood a tall, salt-and-pepper-haired man in a very out-of-place business suit. As he took a seat in the back of the room, those nearest him began whispering, their barely audible message rippling out, person to person, until the whole room was abuzz.

Riley raised his arms for their attention.

"Folks? Could we settle down please? We have a lot to cover and only two hours to do it in." He waited a couple of minutes for the hum to die down.

"Thank you. First of all, welcome to the Xerian Embassy's first panel."

That got a few titters from the audience.

"Second, we have a famous guest among us. The acclaimed hypnotherapist and author Dr. Matthew Cadwallader has graced us with his presence. He's even been active on our forum as Spellbinder." Riley beckoned. "Won't you come forward and say a few words?"

There was an audible gasp from the audience. *He probably thinks they know him and are suitably impressed, not scared half to death of a probable double murderer. Come up here so everyone can get a good look at you and know who we've warned them about,* Riley thought grimly.

Cadwallader smiled beatifically. "Of course, I'd be happy to, Dr. MacPherson."

He ambled up to the speaker's table. Leaning in on Riley, he whispered, "I'm glad you got over whatever it was that made you block me from your forum. We're both professionals, after all. Jealousy is such an ugly emotion."

Turning to the audience, he nodded to Riley and said, "Thank you, Dr. MacPherson, for your kind words. I'm just here to be part of this incredible undertaking. I have to admit, when Dr. MacPherson first approached me with the idea that people were reincarnating from another planet, I thought he had gone off the deep end. I see now that there is some merit to his theories.

"And I'd like to add my own support by offering free, private past-life regressions in my room, all weekend." Cadwallader looked around the room. "That's room 419."

Fear radiated from the audience at Cadwallader's suggestion. Riley turned to look at him, worried that the man would realize they knew he was a Sheitan and a murderer. But one look at Cadwallader's face erased all his fears. *He looks surprised, not angry. He has no clue they're afraid of him. He can't figure out why they aren't jumping at the chance to have a regression with a famous author.* Riley chuckled inwardly. *His ego knows no bounds.*

At the back of the room, James stood up. "Hey, how about we get a picture of our two famous hypnotherapists together?" He marched to the front of the room, pulling out his phone and launching the camera app.

Riley barely had a moment to register what was happening before he was momentarily blinded by the flash from James' phone.

TinMan sounded almost gleeful as he said, "Oh, man the other group is going to be so jealous that we had Dr. Cadwallader in our session. I've got to send this to Dr. Sloan in the other panel. She'll be furious that she missed out."

Riley watched in amusement as Cad made a face at the mere mention of Evelyn's name. *I can't wait to tell her about this later!*

"Thank you, Dr. Cadwallader." As Cad went back to his seat, Riley began, "Now, let's get to work. For those of you who didn't meet me yesterday in the lobby, I'm DocMezmer, better known as Dr. Riley MacPherson. With me is OneEyedScoobie, aka Alex and SnakeGrrrl, my lovely girlfriend Tessa. Our esteemed photographer is James, TinMan on the forum." He looked around the room to see if he'd missed anyone else.

"Okay, down to business. I want everyone to close their eyes and relax." The audience shifted around in their seats. "Well, as much as you can on these hotel chairs." He drew a laugh which eased the tension in the room just as he'd hoped.

"We're going to start with some meditation and visualization…."

* * *

Thierry pushed back the plate, empty save for the steamed black mussel shells on it. The attentive waiter deftly removed it, replacing it with a Tuscan white bean soup. Around him, the muted sounds of diners and the occasional gust of laughter was a pleasant change from the silent dining he'd endured for the past two days. He huffed to himself. *Trying to remain inconspicuous at this…convention, has become tiresome. I am glad Renata was busy elsewhere. I fear she would have considered this restaurant slumming. At least they have one of my favorite desserts.*

Halfway through his soup course, he spotted Jessica and Melvin weaving their way through the tables toward him. He'd chosen an isolated booth, safely out of hearing range of other diners.

"So," he began. "Your report?"

Melvin glanced at Jessica, grimaced, and began his report.

"Um, well, uh, someone took Cadwallader's picture and showed it to all the forum's attendees. And, ah, they were all warned to stay away from him. On the forum, it was, um, suggested he might be responsible for the deaths of the two girls in San Diego."

Thierry dropped his spoon into his nearly-empty soup bowl, splashing the last of it onto the shiny black table. He looked down at the spill, then back up at Melvin, his ire rising.

The waiter appeared, deftly retrieving the soup bowl with one hand while wiping up the mess with the other. As quickly as he had appeared, he vanished.

Melvin opened his mouth to say more, but the waiter returned too quickly, bearing Thierry's wild organic arugula salad. Before Melvin could say another word, though, Thierry erupted.

"That imbecile! All the trouble I went to to cover that up for him was wasted. His exposure could lead the Xerians back to our organization. I have not spent centuries building our prestige to have Matthew tear it down by running us afoul of both the Xerians and the human authorities." He sat back in his seat while consciously reining in his temper. Then he stabbed at a bit of his salad.

"There is one bright spot, however," Melvin offered. "We've identified at least one, possibly two, Tesham."

Thierry's head came up.

"Was one a small Hispanic woman?" he asked.

Melvin queried Jessica with a raised eyebrow, then shook his head.

"No, sir. The one I saw was a stocky blond man with a fedora. Jessica…?""

"The one I saw was a well-built, tanned young man. Barbed wire tattoo on his upper arm."

Thierry paused, his fork suspended in mid-air. *More Tesham? There are several Tesham here? Oh, how delicious! I did not expect this development.*

Placing his fork carefully on his plate, he ordered, "Keep an eye out for other Tesham. I want to know who they are." He snapped his fingers. "Send me pictures of them. I will have a team research them."

Taking a bite of his salad, Thierry motioned for them to continue.

Melvin shifted in his chair.

"Uh, the Xerians seem to be…well, getting along, is the only way I can think to say it. Apparently the meetings MacPherson and Sloan held this morning had a calming effect. There have still been a few isolated scuffles, but nothing major."

Jessica spoke up.

"I've heard," she began, "some Xerians saying they're afraid of Cadwallader. Someone suggested they should pair up for the rest of the convention."

Melvin put in, "In the meeting—"

Thierry smiled as the waiter interrupted Melvin again. The man whisked his now-empty salad plate away and replaced it with a tastefully arrayed rack of lamb.

Savoring the first bite, he nodded to Melvin to continue.

Melvin cleared his throat, then reddened as his stomach growled loud enough for all of them to hear.

That's right, remember who is in charge. You will eat when I am done with you, and not a moment sooner.

Melvin began again. "In the meeting, Cadwallader offered free past-life regressions, in his hotel room, for the entire weekend."

"That cannot be allowed," Thierry said, shaking his head sharply.

"I wouldn't worry about that, sir. The Xerians are all too afraid to be alone with him after that warning was passed around."

Thierry pondered this news for a moment before turning to Jessica.

"And what news do you have about our bumbling area captain?"

Jessica nodded. "I overheard the same thing, that the Xerians are scared of him. They're worried that they might be his next victim. But oddly, when they interacted with him, they seemed to be hiding their fear from him. I think MacPherson and his people are up to something. If they think he killed those girls, why haven't they talked to the police? One of their people is a cop from San Francisco and he seems to be in on it too. I can't figure out their angle."

"Good question. What *are* they up to?" Thierry paused to take a bite of his lamb, enjoying the succulent morsel. "Keep following Matthew and see if you can dig up any more on what he is planning."

"I did manage to place a bug in their room." She smiled. "I went in right behind the cleaning woman. If he discusses his plans with Bryce, I'll bring it to you right away."

Thierry nodded. "Also, make sure that he doesn't slip up and consume another Xerian. He has already jeopardized our operations with his rash actions. We cannot allow him to further imperil us."

He took another bite, then stopped, eyeing Jessica.

"You are well aware of what he is like, Jessica. His hunger makes him sloppy and he loses control. He never can seem to just snack on their energy, he always has to gorge himself. Witness the two dead girls. It is imperative he not be allowed to misbehave here. It would be nearly impossible to cover up."

"Yes, sir," Jessica hastened to agree. "You're right, sir."

"You both have your orders. See that you follow them. Make me aware of any new developments immediately." He made a shooing motion in their direction. "Now go. Let me finish my meal in peace."

As if on cue, his waiter arrived to clear the main course.

"Would you like your dessert now or would you prefer to have coffee first, sir?"

"The dessert, please. Chocolate molten lava is a favorite of mine." *Though I rarely allow myself to indulge,* he thought.

"Right away, sir."

Thierry's mind meandered back through the centuries he'd spent alternately mediating between Matthew and Bryce and pitting them against each other. *Like all good tools, they must be honed to perfection. Sadly, I have learned that you cannot hone defective blades.*

The waiter set the steaming dessert in front of him. The rich chocolate aroma broke him out of his reverie. Thierry looked up, nodding to the waiter, who bowed and withdrew. He was reaching for his fork when a commotion at the door drew his attention. A young dark-haired man had just joined a group of people waiting to be seated and had tripped, barrelling into the maitre-d's podium. The smile of amusement that began to form on his lips abruptly died away as he recognized the energy emanating from one of the members of the group.

Impossible! You cannot be standing there alive! I consumed you on Xeres. I felt your energy fade away.

Thierry sat back in his seat, throwing his napkin over his untouched dessert.

"Waiter. Check, please."

* * *

"Alex! Do you always have to make such an entrance?" Riley asked, helping his assistant to his feet, while the hostess picked up the scattered menus.

"Come on, man," Tessa said, grabbing him by the other arm. "I didn't think you were quite that hungry."

Beside her, Evelyn chuckled. "Have you seen my son eat? He'll even eat vegetables, if that's all the food he can get."

Diana looked around for Kier. "Isn't he joining us?" She smiled. "I've really taken a liking to him since our 'adjustment' sessions."

"Your what sessions?" James asked at her elbow.

She turned toward him. "You know, getting used to someone from the other guild." She crinkled up her eyes at him. "Oh, right, you didn't have to deal with that. Kier was my partner. We mostly met over pizza."

"Which he dearly loved," Evelyn put in. "He wants to have a pizza party when we get back, one of those make-your-own kind of parties."

The hostess waved them forward, leading their party to one of the larger tables. On the way, Tessa noticed a well-dressed man eyeing them. She shivered briefly at the cold look on the man's face. She caught the hostess' attention. "That man back there? Any idea why he's...?"

Their hostess glanced in the direction Tessa indicated.

"Him? Some high powered CEO or something. Heard he's staying in the penthouse suite." She shrugged. "He gets his own waiter, not one of us ordinary mortals. I heard from the chefs that him and his manservant...." She snapped her fingers. "Latham, that's his name.

They've been driving the kitchen nuts all weekend." The young woman confided in Tessa, "Maybe he doesn't think the rest of us mortals should be breathing the same air."

Tessa looked the man's way again, but he had disappeared. She thought she caught a glimpse of him heading toward the elevators.

They sorted themselves out, with Riley and James taking the seats at either end of the table.

Tessa cast an amused glance their way. *I doubt James will hear much of our conversation, the way he's watching Diana. If he wasn't such an intimidating man, I'd say he was mooning over her. He must have had it pretty bad for her in high school.* Tessa ducked her head to hide her smile. *I would love it if Diana finds someone as solid as James. Hmmm, maybe I should help things along.*

The blonde hostess dealt out the menus like an oversized deck of cards and returned to her station, where the line had spread into the walkway.

Opening her menu, Tessa scoped out the prices with alarm.

"Riley? Are you sure we should be eating here? This place is way above our usual pizza and Ethiopian dine-outs."

He glanced at the menu, then up at Tessa. "I know we've been saving every penny, but we deserve to splurge once in a while, right?"

She heaved a sigh. "I guess. Still," she said, getting a determined look on her face, "the food better live up to these prices."

Alex laughed at their exchange. "It had better. My budget's strained as it is."

"Speaking of which," Tessa asked. "How did your shirt sales go?"

"Great! I'm completely sold out. Between what I sold in our room and what Kier sold for me in the other room this morning, they're all gone." He got a crafty look on his face. "Maybe I could put them up for sale on the forum."

"I don't think so," Riley said sternly. "The forum is there to help people connect, not to supplement your income."

Tessa socked his arm. "Don't be that way, Riley. You know he wasn't serious."

"I wasn't?" Alex said, blinking. "My bank account needs all the help it can get."

"Oh, by the way, Alex," Evelyn began. "Thanks, for sharing your profits with Kier. He was over the moon to have more money to spend in the dealers room. He went off with his friends to buy a wand that he's had his eye on for a while now."

Riley reached over and took Alex's arm. "Dinner's our treat, Alex, for all the work you've done getting things ready for this weekend. We couldn't have managed all this without your help."

Alex colored, looking pleased. "You're welcome, of course." He sat back in his chair, laying the menu down. "You know, it felt good that you trusted me to handle everything on my own. I felt like what I was doing was important, not just pushing papers around like I used to do."

Riley frowned slightly. "I'm sorry you ever felt like you weren't useful to me——"

Seeing Riley's discomfort, Tessa broke in, deftly changing the subject.

"Alex, what happened that you were running so late? Literally running, even."

"Just breaking up a little scuffle between our guilds. Nothing major."

"Scuffle?" Riley asked, concerned. "Hopefully not a physical fight."

"No, not physical, just heated words. I was able to calm them down by reminding them to practice the meditation we taught them earlier. It could have been much worse. There was a pretty big crowd of our people around. Most of them seemed to be ok." Alex shook his head. "MileHigh and RoadRanger29 were arguing over something. I never did find out what. Meeker and Blinks were trying to break it up when I arrived."

"Hey, look on the bright side, Alex," Evelyn said from her side of the table. "It looks like the techniques you and I came up with have calmed down most of our Xerians. Maybe MileHigh and RoadRanger are more volatile by nature than the rest. If we only have one scuffle, I'll count ourselves extremely lucky."

"Good point," Riley said with a smile.

Their waiter showed up and took their orders.

Tessa watched with amusement as Diana and James chattered quietly, all but ignoring Evelyn. Catching Evelyn's eye, Tessa indicated the two and grinned. Evelyn rolled her eyes, mouthing, 'Young love?' Tessa shrugged. *It's too soon to tell, but I'd bet money they're going to be together for at least the rest of the convention.*

At that moment, Alex caught on to Tessa and Evelyn's silent

conversation. Turning to Diana, he nudged her arm.

"Earth to Diana. Anyone home?"

James' head came up and Diana blushed.

"Oh, sorry," she said. "Did we miss something?"

The others laughed.

Tessa took pity on them.

"You two seem to have a lot of catching up to do. Maybe you should find someplace quiet after dinner."

James and Diana looked at each other and nodded.

"We never expected to run into each other after high school, especially not on the opposite side of the country." He looked at her tenderly. "Maybe we were just fated to come together again."

"You know," Riley said, raising a hand and pointing at James, "there might be something to that. I mean, think about it. The Tesham were supposedly wiped out on Xeres, right? Yet we have six of you here at this convention alone. Who knows how many more of you are out there."

Tessa leaned forward. "You think we are drawn to each other for some reason? Maybe it has something to do with how we survived the purge on Xeres."

"Yes, how exactly did you survive?" Evelyn asked.

"I don't know, but that's a very good question. I think once we get home from the convention, we should schedule a few more regression sessions and see if we can figure that out."

Their drink order arrived. As James reached across the table for his, Tessa caught a glimpse of a tattoo, barely visible where his shirt sleeve rode up.

"Oh, you have a tattoo?" Diana asked, her eyes widening.

"Yeah," James said, glancing down at it. "I got it after I got out of the military. I'd been dreaming of this symbol since I was a kid. I used to doodle it on everything when I was growing up. Don't you remember?" he asked, raising an eyebrow.

He pulled up his shirtsleeve, exposing the tattoo.

Three separate gasps rocked the table.

"What?" he asked in surprise. "It's just this weird gear-like wheel with four spokes and a hole in the middle."

"Tessa...?" Riley and Diana said in unison.

"I can't...It's not possible. How?" Tessa said, bewildered.

"Ok, what am I missing here?" James asked.

Tessa pulled on the collar of her shirt, exposing an identical tattoo directly over her heart.

James went white. "But...wait...how?"

Tessa shook her head. "I don't know. It's like you said, I doodled the image on all my notebooks. When I turned eighteen, I got it tattooed on me. It felt...I don't know, like it was supposed to be a part of me."

James nodded. "Yeah. I felt that way, too."

Alex shifted in his chair. "This is getting spooky. Do you suppose —"

Evelyn interrupted him. "I wonder if it has something to do with you both being Tesham? Like the fish the Christians used to recognize each other to avoid getting captured by the Romans."

"I don't know, but I definitely want to be included if you do more regressions," James said. "This symbol has been haunting my dreams for years. I want to know what it means."

Tessa watched James with a new-found fascination. *What does this symbol mean? Is it a connection to our shared Tesham past or something darker, say, a brand that marked us, like the pink triangle that gays were forced to wear in World War II Germany?*

Chapter 29

"Don't wait up for me, Alex," Diana said as the group neared the elevators. She shook her head at the long lines waiting at each door.

Alex smiled knowingly. "No problem. I guess you two have a lot of catching up to do." He looked around at the streams of fans rushing in every direction. "Good luck finding somewhere quiet enough to talk, though."

"Oh. Ummm, Tessa, you know your way around these sci-fi conventions. Is there someplace quiet where James and I can talk?"

"At this time of night? With the masquerade and the dance going on? You could try the fireplace in the lobby or the bottom of the staircase. I've had lots of long discussions in the stairwell," she said, smirking sideways at Riley. "If you don't have any luck with either of those, you might look for an empty panel room."

She looked at James. "The lobby fireplace?"

"Sounds good. How about we start there?"

As Alex, Tessa and Riley got on the elevators, Alex called after the pair, "Don't do anything I wouldn't."

Diana and James got separated twice trying to ford the streams of intense and wildly costumed fans before they managed to exit the convention freeway into the relative peace of the fireplace area. Glancing around, James saw two overstuffed chairs to one side and managed to snare them before another couple could.

"Gee, Tessa wasn't kidding," Diana said shakily, coming up behind him and slipping quickly into her seat. "This place is swarming with people."

He shrugged. "This isn't so bad. Try going to a convention that has outgrown its hotel and refuses to upgrade. Now, that's crowded. I went to one where they had to empty all the con panel rooms and the lobby to reset for the masquerade. Empty, as in, you all go outside." James made a face. "It was March and raining, with no parking garage. I think half the convention came down with colds."

Diana laughed delightedly. "You know, Jimmy, I've missed this. You always could make me laugh, even when I was in tears."

He smiled at her, tilting his head to one side. "You know, in all these years since high school, I've never had a friend like you. Combat buddies, guys to catch a beer with, and a shaman I met online. I'll have to introduce you two sometime. But no real, honest friends like we were."

She nodded. "I know what you mean. Bryce and I got married shortly after we graduated college. We moved here almost immediately after that. I'd really only had acquaintances until I met Tessa. We just clicked somehow."

"You two are in business together, aren't you?" he asked, leaning forward and resting his elbows on his knees. *It feels so right,* he thought, *finally being alone with her. Has it really only been two days since we reconnected?*

She nodded, her dark hair spilling around her dainty face.

"I studied graphic arts in college, then took up interior design when we moved here. As a hobby, you know? She and I met at a trade show and really clicked. It wasn't long before we decided to take our relationship to a professional level and started our own business." Shaking her head, she added, "I was positive Bryce would object but he actually supported the idea. He's always been as possessive as he was in high school." Diana shifted in her chair. "When he started getting abusive, Tessa helped me get away. She and Riley and Alex have been wonderful, helping me through this."

James bolted up straight in his chair. Anger flared in his chest. He caught his hands reflexively clenching into fists. *Abusive? Why didn't she tell me sooner? I'd have…But I wasn't around, was I? If only….*

* * *

Diana was in tears, drooping against the cold metal locker behind her, that long auburn hair he so enjoyed almost veiling her face.

"He says I can't see you anymore. Says you're a bad influence, that I should only associate with my own kind." She reached up and brushed her hair aside, peering up at him. "According to him, you're just friends with me because my family is rich and you're poor. I don't believe him, but he's convinced my dad, and now dad's forbidden me to hang out with you too."

Jimmy B thought, It didn't seem to matter to anyone before now. So why does it matter now that we're in high school? He'd been as confused as all the other freshmen at first, but then he'd watched as they'd all drifted into established cliques based on race or wealth. I never thought my friendship with Diana would be affected.

"Why are you letting 'Beautiful Bryce' dictate who you can see? Until recently, he wouldn't have given you the time of day."

She winced. "I know, but he's changed. He's so attentive, including me in all their activities. He's up for class president, you know, and it looks like he'll win."

Jimmy didn't like the way her face lit up when she talked about him. Bryce came into high school the center of a large clique of rich kids, then he swept up all the other well-off students like a vacuum cleaner. Now, his group is one of the most popular on campus. I even heard one of the teachers say that his clique was becoming a real nuisance, demanding special privileges.

"You don't have to do everything he wants you to do, Princess. He doesn't own you." He was starting to get angry now.

She laid her small hand on his arm. "Don't be that way. You know he's good for me. I have lots of new friends now."

"Oh, I see. So you don't need your old friends anymore." He felt his face flush. Please let her think that I'm just angry. I'd die if she found out I've had a crush on her since we were little. She's happy. I should be happy for her, not jealous of Bryce. Why couldn't I tell her how I felt before she met Mr. Perfect.

He spun around and began to walk away.

"Jimmy, I'm still your friend." He voice barely carried over the noise of students rushing to class all around them.

He didn't turn back, just shrugged and kept walking.

"Okay. If that's what you want. I gotta get to class. If I get another demerit, my dad'll ground me for sure."

He slid into the passing stream, not risking a backward glance until he was far enough away that she wouldn't see.

His last view of his friend was heartbreaking. Bryce stood, towering over her, bracing his arms on either side of her. Diana was chatting animatedly with him, a love-struck smile on her dainty face.

"Hey, watch out!"

Jimmy's head swiveled back. "Sorry, I was distracted."

Standing in front of him was one of the most attractive girls in his class.

"Well, if you're going to run over me, we should be properly introduced. I'm Cathy Norcross."

"I know who you are. You're family's kinda famous in Boston."

"Yeah," she said, making a face. "Unfortunately. My mom is always trying to set me up with some rich, snotty brat or another. I can't stand most of them." She flipped her long stylish blonde hair back. "I'd rather have someone who likes me for me, not for my money."

"Then you're safe with me," he said. "I don't have any money. Everyone in my family is a cop or wants to be."

"Oh, so you're a tough guy, huh?"

He straightened into a Superman pose, fists resting on his waist, shoulders back, and chest puffed out. When she giggled, he deflated. "Well, I try, anyway."

She frowned at him. "Are you okay? You look like you just lost your best friend."

He glanced back over his shoulder, but couldn't see Diana or Bryce. Facing her again, he sighed.

"Yeah. I think I just did."

Cathy peered around him. "Oh, then I guess it's a good thing we ran into each other. I'm told I make a very good friend."

She looped an arm through his and smiled. "You wouldn't mind walking me to history class, would you?"

* * *

James felt something slap his face, jarring him out of his memories and back to the present.

"Oh, no! I am so sorry." The young woman, wearing what could only be described as a skimpy angel costume complete with eight foot wide wings, hurried up to the fireplace. "I didn't mean to hit you with my wings. It's really cold outside and I just needed to get warm."

James rubbed the side of his head. "Your feathers aren't as soft as the real ones, are they?"

The girl smiled ruefully. "Poster board. The only thing I could afford that was strong but still be light enough to wear."

"It's okay. Though I should cite you for indecent exposure for that outfit." He gave her a wide grin so she'd know he was just teasing.

She peered at his tin badge. "Why, thank you, sheriff. I guess I should be glad you didn't see the devil costume I was wearing earlier. You'd have arrested me on the spot. Wait, I recognize you. You're TinMan. Oh, I am so sorry. You deserve a proper apology." She pulled him up into a hug, kissing him and rubbing her ample chest into him.

James stood, stunned. *How do I get out of this gracefully?*

Diana interrupted the woman's flirtation before James could react.

"Hey, remember me? We were talking, you spaced out, now you're fondling an angel? How's a girl supposed to compete with that?"

James flushed. "Yeah, right," he said, disengaging himself from the angel's clutches. He looked at Diana. "Um, maybe we'd better find somewhere else to chat. Maybe a little more private?"

"I'm sorry I interrupted you and your lady friend. I didn't know you were taken or I wouldn't have flirted with you," the angel said, looking between the two of them. "But if you need someplace private, the San Francisco room is empty. My crew and I were assembling my costume in there earlier. It's probably still empty."

"Hey, thanks." Diana stood up, grabbing James and towing him down the hall in search of the empty room.

The San Francisco room looked like an emergency drill had exploded all over it. The comfy executive-style black chairs had been rolled every which way and there was glitter on nearly every flat surface.

James spied a trash can full of more sparkly stuff that must have been debris from the angel's costume. "This must be the place," he said, wheeling two chairs up to the narrow table on one side of the room.

Diana attempted to brush some glitter off her chair and then sat down, laying her purse on the table.

"So, now you know I've been with Bryce since high school. What have you done with your life?"

James drew a long breath and leaned back, rubbing the side of his face. "Um, high school. You probably heard I married Cathy Norcross."

"I heard. That was just before Bryce moved us out here."

"Well, our marriage didn't go over so well with her family. They thought I was beneath her. It was hard for us. My family loved her, but she didn't know how to be part of such a sprawling Irish family. I wanted to get a degree, but we could barely afford rent, so I enlisted in the

Marines. Afghanistan."

He was silent for so long, Diana leaned forward and touched his arm. "You don't have to talk about it if you don't want to, Jimmy."

His head came up. "I don't talk about it with anyone. Well, except for my shaman friend CLion and my therapist. Trust me, you don't want to know about what happened over there."

Absentmindedly, he rubbed his hand over his upper arm. After a moment, he continued. "I got wounded four months into my second deployment and was discharged on disability. When I got home, Cathy was eight months pregnant." He shook his head. "All those months away and she hadn't even told me. When I asked her why, she said that she wasn't sure she wanted to keep it."

"That's awful, Jimmy. Did she have the baby? Are you a father?"

Jimmy smiled. "Oh, yes. I have a son. His name's Morgan. He's a great kid, bright, friendly, active as hell." Images of his son flashed across his mind like home movies and album snapshots. Then his face fell.

"He's with Cathy. In Boston."

"I'm confused. Why are they still in Boston?"

"After the baby was born, her parents took her back into the fold. Me, not so much. I was still the poor relation to them. They helped us financially while I went to school, but I knew it was because of Morgan, not because they wanted to help me out." He sucked in a lip, thinking of those years. *How can I tell Diana about my problems without scaring her off?*

"That had to have been rough. Going to school is hard enough without all that hanging over your head too."

He looked at her gratefully. She'd always been empathetic, at least with him.

Taking a deep breath, he plunged on.

"I also came back with PTSD. I have really bad nightmares. I rarely sleep more than three hours at a shot. That's one reason I got a room by myself this weekend. No one needs to be rudely awakened when I come out of a nightmare screaming." He rubbed his chin thoughtfully. "Though given the thinness of hotel walls, I'm sure the people in the next room are convinced someone's being murdered."

That got a tiny smile from Diana.

"And how did Cathy handle your nightmares?"

He felt his face stiffen into the mask he'd seen often enough in the mirror.

"Anyway, by the time I finished my degree, we were sleeping in separate rooms. It wasn't that big of a surprise when she filed for divorce two months after I graduated."

He felt a knife twist in his gut. *Now, I have to tell her about Rory. I've almost managed to pack that pain into a neat box, but it breaks open far too often.*

"You remember Rory? My kid brother?"

"Oh, yes! He had the biggest crush on me when he was seven."

James smiled, remembering. "Yeah, he did. You're right. Used to follow us around even when we didn't want him to." He couldn't help himself, his smile drifted away. "He joined the police force, with Kevin and Finn and Killian. He'd only been on the force a few months when he was killed. A robbery gone bad, they said. I was never so sure." He shook his head, trying to clear the memory of Rory's funeral, the long lines of blue-clad policemen standing at attention to honor him. It hadn't helped his family or him.

"That was after the divorce. I couldn't stay in Boston. I wanted to get as far away as I could." He looked up into her eyes. "I ran. Ended up here in San Francisco. I joined the police force, bought a houseboat, and now here I am." He paused, keenly feeling the empty places in his heart where his family should have been. "The hardest part of leaving Boston was leaving Morgan. For awhile, all I had of him were the occasional pictures that Cathy would send me. Now she lets me Skype with him, when she's feeling generous." He began rubbing his arm again.

"I'm so sorry, Jimmy. About Rory and your marriage." She gave a wry smile. "We're quite a pair, aren't we? We had to come all the way across the country to meet up again." She reached out, grabbing his arm and stopping his unconscious motion. "Is that where you were wounded? I've noticed that you keep rubbing your arm when you're stressed."

"Huh? What? No, that was a chest wound. Why would you think…" Realization dawned on him. "Oh. One of the things that my therapist, HotDoc actually, suggested I do to handle my PTSD was to have something to focus on to help me calm down. Something not connected to my stressors. I figured, why not use something I always have with me, no matter what. My tattoo symbol. Funny, with what we learned tonight, it's kind of stressing me out now too."

"It'll be okay. So it's a Tesham symbol. Personally, I think it's cool that you and Tessa have the same tattoo. It means you belong to something greater. Something bigger than yourself. I'd find that idea pretty calming."

"Hmmm, I never thought of it that way." He considered for a moment, then nodded. "Yeah, I think you're right. Like I just discovered that I had an extended family I never knew about."

"Well, I've known Tessa for years. I've learned to trust her and Riley. They'll figure out what the symbol means. For both your sakes."

He took her hands in his. "Thanks, Diana. You always did know just what to say to calm me down." He sighed. "I wish you'd been around when I came home from Afghanistan. I probably wouldn't still be having nightmares eight years later."

Chapter 30

"I can't believe I'm up this early on a Sunday morning," Alex grumbled. "Hell, I haven't seen eight AM in years."

"This was the best time to have the candlelight vigil. Everyone else is either at church services or asleep. There's less chance of being interrupted." Riley made a wry face at Alex. "And do you think that's an appropriate shirt to be wearing today? At this?"

Alex looked down at his t-shirt, pulling it out at the bottom so he could read it upside down. "What's wrong with my shirt? 'You need a lover with lifetimes of experience. I've reincarnated. A lot!' What's wrong with that?" He shot Riley an aggrieved look.

Riley sighed. "You're incorrigible. What would you wear to a funeral? 'Newly single? I'm available!' or maybe a tie-dyed outfit?" He shook his head. "Tacky, tacky, tacky."

Alex sniffed. "I'm a free soul and you're…you're stodgy. Lighten up, Riley."

"Who's stodgy? Riley? I could have told you that," Tessa chimed in as she approached the pair. She carried a brown paper sack which she set down on a chair near the door.

"What is this, gang-up-on-Riley day?" he protested.

Tessa laughed, kissing Riley lightly on the cheek. "And what day isn't, dear? Besides, I thought you liked group scenes…." She giggled when Riley blushed.

"Oh, really now?" Seeing the exasperated look on Riley's face, Alex smoothly changed the subject. "What's in the sack?"

"LED candles and batteries. In separate boxes. Get busy. Everyone will be arriving soon."

"I thought WendyAnn was running this," Riley muttered, pulling out several long skinny boxes and beginning to unpack the candles. After he'd freed each one from its packaging, he passed it to Alex to insert the batteries.

"She was," Tessa said, nodding. "I messaged her on the forum. She was going to bring real candles until I told her the hotel has an open-flame ban. I offered to bring these." She pulled the last of the boxes from the sack. "They were left over from a Halloween party Riley and I threw a couple of years back."

Alex said, "Well, that would explain them being black."

She shrugged. "Beggars…choosers, you know the story."

"Good morning." The two young women coming through the door were a study in contrast, one tall and willowy, the other one shorter and Hispanic.

Tessa looked up. "WendyAnn, Vino. Good morning to you too. I brought the LED candles we talked about. Would the two of you like to hand them out as people arrive?"

The women brightened up. "Sure. That way we get to talk to everyone before the vigil." The taller one, WendyAnn, started gathering the candles up. "We can explain our plan so we can all start on the same page."

Vino, the shorter one, asked, "Do you want to say a few words, DocMezmer?"

Riley nodded. "I would, yes. But, towards the end, I think."

As the pair moved away, Alex nudged Riley and pointed to the doorway. Cadwallader stood there uncertainly. Frowning, he thought, *Oh, this should be fun.* Then he noticed James coming up behind the man.

Cadwallader accepted the candle WendyAnn handed him with a sour look on his face. Alex could hear the disdain in his voice as Cadwallader lectured the girl.

"Black candles for a vigil? Or is this a black mass. Oh dear, and I forgot my robes and sacrificial goat." He tossed her one last withering look and began making his way to a seat at the back of the room.

When Alex glanced back at the doorway, two things stood out. The look of dismay and hurt on Vino's face and the look of pure hatred smeared on James' face.

Alex moved quickly to intercept him. "Morning, James. How are you today?"

"Huh? Oh, hi, Alex." James shook his head. "What just happened?

I was fine, but when I bumped into the man in front of me, I suddenly wanted to kill him. I've been fine with everyone all weekend, so why should someone set me off like that?"

"It's because he's not a Xerian. He's Sheitan," he whispered. "You Tesham don't react to Bylantians like me or Klymurians like Evelyn. But your reaction to the Sheitan makes what we feel look like a disagreement over what to have for dinner."

"I can believe it. That was intense. I barely touched him and I had to stop myself and take deep breaths to keep from beating him senseless right there in the doorway."

Alex nodded. "I can sympathize. Tessa had the same reaction to Cad the first time she met him. Just use the techniques Riley taught in yesterday's panel."

James looked confused. "You guys told me Cadwallader might have murdered those two girls in San Diego, but you never mentioned he was anything other than a Xerian." He thought for a moment. "Wait, he was in our panel yesterday. Why didn't I—"

Alex interrupted. "But I bet you didn't get close to him, did you?"

"No, Tessa had me sitting on the other side of the room. Even when I took his picture, I didn't get that close."

"That's why you didn't have a reaction. Apparently, you guys have to come in contact before you react."

The other man sighed, scratching his chin. "I'll have to remember that and avoid that man like the plague."

Riley walked up. "Avoiding someone like the plague? Oh, you must have touched Cadwallader. Sorry, I forgot to warn you about that."

"Which reminds me," Alex said. "If you ever meet Diana's soon-to-be ex-husband, he's one of them, too. Just a heads up."

"Bryce is one of *them*?" A horrified look spread across James' face. "How—"

Tessa spoke up from the front of the room. "Okay, everyone, we're about to start. Please take a seat."

Glancing around, Alex noticed Cad, sitting in isolation at the back of the room. The Xerians had given him a wide berth, leaving several chairs empty around him.

"Uh, Riley, I think I'd better go babysit Cad. I don't want him getting suspicious that no one will sit near him. Plus I can keep an eye on him."

Riley nodded. "Good idea. I need to be up front, with Tessa. James?"

"Yes?"

"Did you want to say anything? About the investigation? I'm sure it would help put people's minds at ease. Just don't mention anything about you-know-who."

"Voldemort, you mean?" James chuckled. "Sure. Be glad to."

As the other two went toward the front of the room, laughing the whole way, Alex maneuvered to take the empty seat beside Cadwallader.

The man looked up at Alex in surprise, but remained silent.

"I see I'm not the only one who likes sitting in the back of the room," Alex said by way of explaining his presence. "I had enough being on display yesterday helping Riley out. It's nice to not be in the spotlight for a change,"

Cad nodded.

"I understand. I decided to sit back here after that embarrassing photo op yesterday." He cleared his throat. "This is MacPherson's show. I wouldn't want to upstage him and make him feel like I'm trying to take over."

"Well, you are very famous. I bet everyone here knows who you are. That's probably why no one sat by you, they were too intimidated."

Alex suppressed a laugh. *The reason they all know who you are is because we warned them about you, asshole.*

Riley addressed the group. "Thank you all for coming. The vigil will be lead by WendyAnn and Vino, who you met at the door. Vino, can you turn down the lights?"

"Thank you, DocMezmer," WendyAnne began. "If everyone would please turn on your candles...."

Alex was so focused on keeping an eye on Cadwallader that he barely paid any attention to the service. When the lights suddenly came back up, he blinked, trying to clear his vision.

WendyAnn and Vino planned a nice service. I wish I'd been able to relax and pay more attention. I know there was singing, and a prayer, but for the life of me, I have no idea what either was about. I do like that they'd printed some pictures of the two girls to hang on the whiteboard in the front of the room. It's sad though that this is the only way we get to meet them

As the audience sat back down, James strode to the front of the room. Alex thought he looked authoritative in his khaki and tan costume, even without the fedora.

"I expect you all know me by now. I'm James Cavanaugh, TinMan on the forum. I'm with the San Francisco police department. With Riley and Alex's help, I sent the San Diego police a list of everyone the two girls talked to on the forum. I wanted to let you all know that, in case anyone gets a call from them."

Beside Alex, Cad stiffened. *He seems nervous. Anxious about something. Is he worried about the information James gave to the SDPD? Maybe he suspects we recovered the messages he deleted.* Alex made a mental note to talk to James about it later.

"If there are any new developments," James said, "I will post to the forum to let everyone know. I've requested they keep me in the information loop." He looked around at the people in the room. "If any of you has information you'd like me to send to the SDPD, you can tell me in person or message me on the board."

Riley stood up, thanked James, and turned to address the group.

"I'm happy to see all of you in the same room finally. I know yesterday's sessions were intense, but it looks like everyone has managed to overcome your guild compulsions. We owe a big thanks to Alex and Dr. Sloan," he said, gesturing at each of them as he said their names, "for perfecting the techniques that enabled you to progress so far so fast. However, that said, I can't help but notice, looking out over the room, that you are almost perfectly split by guild. We have a few rogue people sitting with their opposite guild, and to those I say, congratulations. Now I'd like to challenge you all to integrate more. Mix it up. Go ahead, move around, change seats." Riley glanced at his watch. "I'll wait." With that, he crossed his arms and stared at the gathered Xerians.

For a few moments, nothing happened. Then the murmurings began. MileHigh was the first to stand up. He looked across the center aisle and asked, "Yo, someone want to trade with me?"

Aurora12 stood up. "Okay by me." She sidled out of her row and MileHigh moved in.

After that, chaos broke out as half the room tried to migrate to the opposite side. Those who stayed in their own seats had to contend with the ones trying to get to new seats. Alex, an immobile spectator, didn't even try to hide his amusement when the non-moving Xerians were stepped on and yelped in pain.

He turned to Cad. "I don't think we need to move, do you?"

Cad gave him a scathing look without commenting.

Sheesh, he really needs to lighten up. Casting a sideways glance at Cadwallader, Alex reevaluated his thought. *Nope, what he really needs is to get laid. That might remove the stick up his ass.*

"Okay, everybody, settle down," Riley said, waving his hands. "Good job, everyone. I think you've stirred the pot up enough." He waited for the crowd to quiet down, then smiled like a proud parent. "See? Everyone was mingling and no fights broke out. Well done."

From the middle of the room, a hand shot up.

Riley pointed to the woman. "Yes, UFOLuver?"

She stood. "Do you know why we felt this way toward each other? Don't get me wrong, Doc. It's nice to have gotten over it, but I wanna know what caused it in the first place."

There were several agreements from the crowd. Other hands shot up.

Riley looked surprised, but Alex was nodding. *We haven't given everyone a chance to ask questions. It's not like we've regressed everyone for answers.*

"That's a good question. We aren't really sure. Nothing in any of the regressions we've done has explained why the guilds hate each other. But that's a good question to follow up on." Riley looked at the scattered hands raised around the room raised around the room. "Saxman?"

"If the two guilds hated each other so much, how did they manage to live anywhere near each other? I mean, did they self-segregate on Xeres?"

"Another good question." Riley looked around the room at the other hypnotherapists. "HankT? HotDoc? Evelyn?" They all shook their heads. "That doesn't seem to be something any of us have asked yet."

Beside Alex, Cadwallader huffed a breath. *He's probably wondering why Riley didn't ask him,* Alex thought, biting his lip to keep from laughing.

CardShark stood next. "What was their economic system like? I mean, did they have a barter system or universal credit?"

"A valid question," Riley said, nodding. "I'm sure there's a lot about the Xerian society we'd all like to know."

The noise level in the room spiked as several people began asking questions simultaneously. Riley raised his hands, motioning for everyone to calm down.

"One at a time, please." Gesturing to the large woman covered in tattoos and wearing a plaid shirt. "Amazon?"

The woman stood, looking around the room at the gathered Xerians. "What I really want to know is what started the war and what happened that we all ended up here?" Many people were nodding their heads or verbally agreeing with her.

Riley nodded. "Yes, I remember that thread from the forum. You know, we've been so focused on perfecting a means for the guilds to get over their aversion to each other that we haven't had time to delve into all the questions you've raised on the forum."

Alex saw Evelyn, HotDoc, and HankT putting their heads together. When they finally looked up, Riley raised an inquisitive eyebrow at them. "I know that look, Evelyn. What?"

She stood, turning to face the crowd.

"Maybe we should have a mass regression. With the whole group. We could ask all your questions and try to get you some answers."

Alex sat back, startled. *Why didn't we think of this before? This could be our only opportunity to regress so many Xerians at one time. Maybe with all of us being regressed at once, we can finally piece this puzzle together.*

Beside him, Alex noted Cad's tenseness. *What is he afraid we'll find out?*

In the front of the room, Riley queried Tessa. "Do you know if there are any other panels in this room this morning?"

Tessa pulled out her pocket schedule for the convention. "Ummm…. It looks like the next panel in here is at noon. Let me go check with convention operations and see if we can stay in here until then."

With that she was out the door.

Alex took the opportunity to try again to strike up a conversation with Cadwallader.

"I'm curious. Riley told me you didn't believe any of this stuff was real. He said you encouraged him to drop it before he made a fool of himself in front of his peers. So it makes me wonder, why did *you* join the forum. And why did you come this weekend?"

Cadwallader was silent for a moment, then said, "After the last convention, I checked out that website he put up. There were a lot of people that claimed to be one of these 'Xerians.' I wanted to see for myself if they really are aliens reincarnated on Earth or just a bunch of people in need of serious therapy."

Alex burst into laughter, startling Cadwallader.

"What is so funny?" Cad demanded.

"Xerians...need serious therapy? Xerian, serious? I thought you were intentionally making a joke." Seeing the dour expression Cadwallader turned his way, Alex explained, "C'mon, Xerians, serious, they sound alike. Surely you meant that as a joke...."

Cadwallader huffed, turning his head away.

Fine. I thought it was funny, anyway, Alex thought, leaning back in his chair and crossing his arms. *Evelyn's right, the man has no sense of humor whatsoever.* He was about to ask Cad another question, just to needle him, when he noticed Tessa slip back into the room.

"Ops says we can use the room till noon."

"Okay, folks," Riley said. "What we're suggesting is a mass regression, right here." He glanced at the other therapists. "I think we need a fifteen minute break, to reset the room and to get our act together."

"Uh, Doc?"

"Yes, uh, OldFart?" Shaking his head, he smiled at the man. "You gotta get a better handle. I feel like I'm calling you names."

The white-haired man laughed. "Yeah, didn't think of that when I chose it. Anyway, I think some of us need more time, to pack up and check out. How about thirty minutes?"

"Good point. Okay everyone, be back here in thirty minutes. Oh, and when you come back? Have some questions written up that you'd like us to ask."

Alex got up and followed Cadwallader as he exited the room. *I think I'll just keep an eye on old Cad, make sure he doesn't get any of our folks alone.*

Just outside the door, Cad stopped dead in his tracks, staring at an older man with a Fu Manchu mustache.

"Melvin? What are you doing here? How did you find out about this gathering? Did Thierry send you to spy on me?"

Alex ducked behind a cardboard cutout display of some large robot hoping he wouldn't be noticed eavesdropping on the pair.

"Cadwallader! Wow, I haven't seen you in person in what? Eighty years?"

Alex drew in a sharp breath. *Eighty...? I read Cadwallader's bio in one of his books. He's only in his late forties. Meeker can't be older than his mid-fifties. How could they have known each other eighty years ago?*

Cadwallader hissed, "Careful, you fool. One of the Xerians might overhear you. How would you explain knowing me for that long?"

"Sorry, sir," Melvin said, lowering his voice. Alex strained to hear. "I was just surprised to see you here."

"Of course I'm here." He gave the man a withering look. "It's my job to know about any and all matters relating to Xerians in my territory. I am the Area Captain for the West Coast, after all." He paused momentarily. "You didn't answer my question. How did you find out about this gathering?"

"I found a message online that talked about Xeres, so I investigated and joined their forum. I go by the name Meeker on there. I wanted to gather as much information as possible before I made my report to you. I know you're very busy, so I didn't want to waste your time if it was a dead end."

"As you can see, I am fully aware of what the Xerians are doing. And do you really expect me to believe that you are here gathering information on my behalf? I imagine you thought you could grab a snack with me none the wiser."

I can just picture Cad peering down his nose at the old man. He must be some kind of underling. Wait. I thought the only underling Cad had was Denny. And that's past tense. Cad said he was Area Captain. What the hell does that mean?

Cad continued, "You know that Thierry has banned us from consuming Xerians."

Meeker winked at Cadwallader. "Well, I won't tell if you don't."

Cad's voice was full of longing when he replied. "It *has* been a very long time since I've had a Xerian—"

"Really?" the older man said doubtfully. "Because I couldn't help noticing that the two missing girls we just had a candlelight vigil for were from San Diego, which just happens to be where you live. Now, isn't that a coincidence."

"Are you suggesting—" Alex saw Cadwallader leaning toward the man.

"Of course not," he said hastily. "I just believe in sharing my meals with my friends."

"I haven't violated any rules," Cad's voice growled. "I've half a mind to report you to Thierry myself for even suggesting that we share a Xerian against his express orders. It would be much better for your continued health if you drop it. Now."

Meeker waved his hands in front of him. "No, no. I'm sorry I ever suggested that you would violate Mr. LeRoux's orders. Please don't report me."

The two men moved off, continuing their squabbling. Alex, overwhelmed by the new information, wandered over to a circle of comfortable chairs and plopped down in the nearest one.

Meeker is a Sheitan. He isn't actually a Klymurian like he said he was. Dammit, how many of them are there? Cadwallader, Bryce, Meeker, and this Thierry LeRoux they mentioned.

Breaking out of his daze, Alex went in search of his friends.

* * *

"Sir, I have to say, I don't know why you have me following Cadwallader. He's just going to these damn panels and hanging around with the Xerians." Jessica wrinkled her nose in disgust. "It's like he's playing with his food. And Bryce? He spends all day sleeping in his room. And let me tell you, that man snores like a freight train. Then he spends the entire night roaming the convention space and the rest of the hotel. I have to say, it's hard for me to be inconspicuous when I'm wearing a suit and the only people in the halls are dressed in costumes. People must think I'm part of the hotel staff, because they keep asking me if I can open their rooms for them. And that's not to mention the drunks lurking in every other doorway." She shuddered delicately. "They're just gross."

So Bryce is scoping out the hotel, is he? Probably planning Matthew's demise. Matthew, meanwhile, is stalking that human hypnotherapist and his Tesham girlfriend. He shook his head. *This is sounding more and more like an obsession. Obsessions are not good for business.*

"Ahem." Latham entered from the hall, Melvin Ashcroft behind him puffing like he'd been running. While the man found a seat next to Jessica, Latham asked, "Mr. Ashcroft, Miss Coney, would either of you care for a beverage?"

"Sure, I'll have...." Melvin's voice tapered off at LeRoux's look.

"They are both fine, Latham. You are dismissed."

Why am I surrounded by incompetents? Thierry wondered. Returning his gaze to Melvin, he said, "You are late."

"I know, sir. Sorry. The vigil ran late, then Cadwallader stopped me in the hall."

"Interesting. What did he want?"

"Well, he threatened to tell you I was here stalking Xerians," he

270

said, running his words together.

"Accusing you of what he himself is most likely doing? That is his style," he said, nodding.

"I do have some vital news, however. The Xerians are planning a mass regression in," he glanced at his watch, "twenty minutes. They hope to find out what started the war between the guilds and why they hate each other so much."

A feeling he hadn't experienced in millennia rushed through him. Fear.

"What? They cannot...."

Why are they doing this now, after all this time?

"Sir? What would you like me to do? I have to go back down there. If I don't, I might be missed."

"Of course you should go back down to this regression. I want you to feed them false information. Anything you can do to distract them and keep them from figuring out our part in their war."

"Yes, sir. I'll report back after the event." The man stood and headed for the door.

Thierry barely registered Melvin's departure. He was already lost in his own roiling thoughts.

I am sure this has something to do with the damned Tesham I saw last night in the restaurant. They can detect us. That one even built a weapon that can destroy us as well as our host body. We turned the populace against them and thought we had wiped them out entirely. The Tesham were created from the mating of the strongest of each guild, so by driving them apart, we insured that no new Tesham could come into being. Then we started the war to keep the Klymurians and the Bylantians forever separated.

Pulling himself from his thoughts, he straightened.

"Jessica!" The little woman jumped like he'd barked at her. *Good.*

"Sir?"

"I need you to prepare dossiers on the core group of these Xerians. The ones running this mess. Full background checks, personal history, everything."

Jessica drew out her smartphone and began a list. "Hmmm, that would be Riley MacPherson, Tessa Connors, Alex Wilson, Evelyn Sloan, and the new one, James Cavanaugh."

"Include Bryce's wife Diana. She is mixed up in this too."

She frowned and rubbed her face. "Sir, that could take hours. I can't do that and follow Cadwallader around. Plus, Melvin and I have to be out of our room by noon."

Thierry pondered a moment.

"Latham?"

The man appeared as if by magic.

"Sir?"

"Take Jessica's room key and retrieve her and Melvin's belongings from their room."

Looking slightly bewildered, Jessica handed Latham her room key.

"And you, my dear, can take over Latham's room. He has a desk and a printer you can use to compile the reports I have requested.

The majordomo's face twisted briefly into a scowl, but he recovered quickly. Bowing, he vanished from the room.

Jessica stood, grabbed her laptop bag and headed into the bedroom.

Thierry sank back into the sofa, shaking his head. *I have worked too hard for too many years to lose control now. There are too many players. Too many wildcards. Too many things I cannot control.*

His phone rang. Glancing at the display, he sighed, pleasantly surprised to find it was from Renata. *Finally, something I can control.*

Smiling, he hit the answer button. "Your timing is perfect as usual, Renata, darling. I need a distraction from this damn Xerian business."

Chapter 31

As Cadwallader entered the room, he found it buzzing with conversation. He noticed the Xerians were filling the chairs without regard for guild. *Damn! I cannot believe he has managed to undo centuries of our work. In a weekend. MacPherson's good.*

Melvin arrived with the last stragglers. Cadwallader watched as he joined a group of Xerians making themselves comfortable in the back corner. *He's out of breath. Just from running up to his room to check out? He's let himself grow too old. Plus, he already suspects I was the one who murdered those girls in San Diego. Maybe it's time for him to move on to his next life. I can certainly help him with that.*

He caught Melvin's eye and smiled at the man. The look of fear that slid across Melvin's face was exactly what Cadwallader needed to lift his spirits.

MacPherson stood up in the front, waving at them all to quiet down.

"First, does Tessa have all your questions?"

A few hands shot up and Tessa moved to collect their slips.

While she was doing that, Cadwallader approached the man.

"Good morning, MacPherson. I see you have a good turnout for your regression. May I offer my services, to help you?"

The man blinked. "Help? Uh, no, thank you. Dr. Thompson is assisting me. Right Hank?" The other man nodded. "We've already worked together this weekend. I think we can handle it on our own. Thank you anyway."

Tessa came up and handed the slips she'd collected to Thompson. Before leaving to get comfortable herself, she tossed a look at Cadwallader of pure hatred.

Shit! I forgot for a moment that she's Tesham. She's reacting to me. I can't let her remember anything about the Sheitan.

"Have it your way. I'm only trying to help. I know I didn't believe you about this at first, but you've made me a believer. Well, I'll be right over here if things get too complicated for you."

Pulling an empty chair from the front row, he turned it around so he could view the whole room, adding himself to MacPherson's group.

I can't believe he turned me down, he fumed to himself. *I have more years of experience as a hypnotherapist than the two of them combined. Besides, I already know all the answers to the questions they have. I know exactly what questions to ask because I was there. Ungrateful human.* He had a sudden thought. *Oh, that's an idea. Maybe I'll just ask a few questions anyway. Show him that he made a mistake by not accepting my help in the first place. And if Tessa puts enough pieces together to remember the Sheitan, then her fear will be like a fine wine complementing her energy when I consume her.*

He felt a warm glow of anticipation as MacPherson stood to begin the regression.

"Okay, everyone. Get comfortable. You can sit in the chairs or on the floor…"

Cadwallader saw several people pushing chairs aside and lying down on the floor. *Yuck. You couldn't pay me to lie on these floors. They're disgusting.*

"…or, hell, I guess lie on the floor, if you want to. Whatever you need to be comfortable for the regression." He waited while they sorted themselves out. Soon, the neat rows of chairs began to look like children had been building forts without sheets.

Once they were settled, MacPherson ran them through the relaxation steps to get them into a trance state.

Gods, this is the part of this job I hate most. Having to get them relaxed enough to actually talk. Blah, blah, blah, blah.

As Riley droned on, Cadwallader's mind wandered on to his plan to get rid of MacPherson and his tasty girlfriend.

First I have to get that delicious Tesham alone. Her fear will make consuming her a delightful experience. Then I'll plant her body in their room to make it look like he killed her. Once he finds her body, he'll be so distraught, he won't even see me coming. Humans aren't as tasty as Xerians, but he'll make a decent dessert. Then I just have to wait for the police to show up and I can act positively horrified. Show them the fake file I created for MacPherson. I'm so sorry, officer. I suspected my patient

274

might be homicidal, but I didn't think he'd kill his girlfriend and then himself.' With what looks like a murder-suicide on their hands, they'll have no choice but to believe the story I've spun for them.

Cadwallader glanced at his watch. *Fifteen minutes of white light and you're protected. Get to the questions already.*

"...now I want you to go back to a previous life, when you were Xerians, before the guilds split. You are only watching the events of that time. They cannot harm you or affect you in any way. You are safe."

Finally!

"What is it like, between the guilds?"

HouseofMouse spoke up with an unsettling gravelly voice. "I don't trust the Bylantians anymore. They're taking too much power for themselves. More everyday."

Saxman piped up in a bright, girlish voice. "Yeah. I had to leave my old school. The new one only has Klymurians in it."

Chai19 scoffed, "Well, of course you should be separated in school. How else will you improve your inborn skills?"

SgtCox said, "It's only natural for the guilds to separate. We're so different."

"But hadn't you been coexisting together just fine for a long time?" MacPherson asked. "What started you fighting?"

"We got along fine for an eternity, before they turned on us and started fights. They started killing Bylantians," GeekSheik said.

"No, the Bylantians started the fights," said OldFart, sounding like a man in his prime. "They were the ones who started killing Klymurians. We just responded to it. We had to defend ourselves, didn't we?"

MacPherson probed deeper. "When did the fighting start? Was there some specific incident that caused it?"

"It was gradual," said UFOLuver. "At first, it was just disagreements that got out of hand. I thought it was something in the water, to be frank."

"Or in the air," Chai19 put in.

"Were there people who were stirring things up? Was it the same people who were starting the fights?" MacPherson asked.

"Well," said GoldenOldie, "at first is was so...random. One day your friend just picked a fight. I mean, about nothing. Next thing you know, everybody's swinging. Fights broke out at gatherings, on the street, everywhere."

"No, it was always one guild against the other," said FoxTotem. "The Bylantians hated that we had magic and they didn't. They were jealous. Their science wasn't able to do things that we could with magic."

"Yeah, for no reason. My brother picked a fight with my husbands and wrecked our house," said MileHigh, sounding miffed.

MacPherson stepped in again. "So, in the beginning, the quarrels weren't between different guilds, but among…citizens?"

Several voices around the room answered, "Yes."

"How can you be sure that the citizens who were fighting weren't from different guilds? Do you have some way of telling one guild from the other?" MacPherson asked.

The man is feeling his way through the facts and supposition being presented, Cadwallader thought. *I've underestimated him. He's moving faster than I thought possible. He's gotten the guilds to get along, now he's uncovering information at an alarming rate. I was right, he needs to be stopped immediately.*

"Of course," Evelyn answered. "Each Xerian is unique, but depending on your proficiencies, it feels different. We Kylmurians are warm, like the natural elements that fuel our powers. "

"And we Bylantians," Alex added, "feel cool, like the metal and gadgets we love. That how we recognize each other."

Let's see how he handles this curve ball, Cadwallader thought smugly. "Are there just the two guilds, then?"

The room erupted. The reaction was everything Cadwallader had hoped for. MacPherson's expression was priceless. His eyes were sending daggers at Cadwallader, while his jaw was clenched in a tight line.

"No! There was a third—"

"Those damn Tesham—"

"…we killed them all—"

"Whoa, folks. Settle down now. Remember, these events are in your past. They have no control over you now. Let's just focus on the Bylantians and Klymurians for now." The Xerians muttered for a bit before quieting.

Cadwallader couldn't resist pouring fuel on the fire he'd started.

"So what happened to this third guild, the Tesham, I believe you called them?"

BrightBlue's voice was flat as she spoke."We killed them. All of them. They'd gone crazy." She shrugged. "Probably the combination of science and magic in them caused it. Everyone knows that the two systems are incompatible. Trying to use both at the same time? It was bound to happen eventually."

Diana nearly screamed, "They are murderers! I was visiting relatives in a different city when I found out that the Tesham had killed my whole family. It all started with the one who found the new energy source. He was sneaking around killing people randomly. We later found out he'd killed an entire warehouse full of people. He wasn't just a serial killer, he was a mass murderer."

Avilla picked up the story from there. "I was there when we finally cornered that Tesham, Jember, in his lab. He may have been the first Tesham to go crazy, but he sure wasn't the last."

"Honestly," said Ogre6, sounding very young and girlish, "we should have seen it coming."

"Yeah, but we didn't," chimed Lyocel. "Then there was the thing with the new power stations...."

Evelyn's brat chimed in next. "Yeah, things got really out of hand after the power stations were shut down. A lot of people were angry about having to go back to power rationing."

Amazon's voice boomed out. "Yeah. The Tesham were the ones who took away the new energy source."

"That's what really got me, too," UnderBloke said. "First the Tesham discovered a new energy source and installed those generators. We had more clean energy than we knew what to do with. It was amazing! But they didn't want to share. They wanted to keep the power to themselves." There was real venom in his voice.

"They shut down the power stations to try to put us Klymurians in our place," Melvin said, interrupting. "They wanted to show that we were more dependent on their technology than they were on our magic."

What's Melvin talking about? Cadwallader thought, dismayed. *That's not what happened at all. We started them fighting. It was never about jealousy. He was there, he knows that. Why is he misleading them?*

Several voices began shouting at once.

"We couldn't run all our—"

"Jealous? Hardly—"

"It was so nice there for a few months, being able to use—"

"Why'd they have to take the power away? Tell me that."

MacPherson gestured for quiet, but of course they couldn't see him. *Such a rookie mistake,* Cadwallader thought smugly.

"Quiet, please, everyone," MacPherson said loudly.

When they'd all gotten quiet again, the man asked, "How long before things settled down?"

WendyAnn answered that one with such hatred in her voice. "Not until all the Tesham were gone!"

There was a murmuring around the room as others agreed with her.

Blinks spoke up, sounding like an gossipy housewife. "It took about ten years, I think, before we couldn't find any more of them. Everyone thought they were all dead, but, just between you and me, I suspected all along that they'd just gone underground. Pretended to be one of us."

"Well, since they were all killed off, let's stop talking about the Tesham and get back to finding out why the guilds separated," MacPherson said.

Hmmm, Cadwallader thought, stroking his chin and eyeing the man. *Do you know that your girlfriend is a Tesham? Is that why you don't want the Xerians talking about them? Have you figured that out already? Very interesting. What else have you found out, MacPherson?*

Thompson tapped MacPherson on the shoulder. "I have a question I'd like to ask the group."

MacPherson gestured for him to proceed, then moved aside.

"Let's skip forward." He looked at MacPherson, who nodded. "Say twenty years. What are things like between the two guilds?"

"We're at war. There is constant fighting. Each guild has claimed one of the large land masses and set up their own capitals," Java27 said in a hushed tone.

"We never know when there'll be another attack," said Latte12.

Thompson drew in a long breath, then exhaled loudly. "When did the fighting turn into all-out war? What changed?"

Jedi165 spoke up from the back of the room, his voice slow and meditative. "The Bylantians set off an explosion that destroyed half of the old capital city. It was a massacre."

"No, the Klymurians were responsible for that bombing!" Vino said, almost rising off the floor.

Jedi 165 countered that. "It felt like after we had eradicated the Tesham, we just turned on each other. All of our anger and frustration boiled over. Once the bloodshed began, it didn't matter anymore who started it. It became all about who was going to finish it."

"Yeah," Avilla said. "Every time we built a better machine, the Klymurians came up with a better spell. The tide of war went back and forth for a long time."

"Let's move forward in time again." Thompson moved to MacPherson's side. Some silent communication between the two made Cadwallader wonder what was coming next.

Finally they reached an agreement and both nodded.

Thompson turned back to the crowd.

"Let's move forward again to when the war on Xeres ended."

He never got to finish his suggestion. The room filled with raised voices. Some people even began crying.

"The ultimate weapon—"

"They didn't give us a choice—"

Vino's deep voice cut through the chatter in the room. "I hear the Klymurians have one, too. What happens to us if they use their ultimate weapon?"

"My cousin says that the Bylantians have an ultimate weapon that they are going to use on us if we don't surrender," FoxTotem said, his fear sending ripples through the room.

MacPherson grabbed the box full of the LED candles from the previous session and lifted it high above the table before dropping it. The resounding crash still managed to startle Cadwallader, even though he'd watched it happen. *I can't imagine the impact it will have on these regressed Xerians. These people are probably going to need therapy for PTSD after that demonstration. What was he thinking? Damned amateur.*

The sudden silence was almost deafening.

MacPherson smiled. Resuming control of the session, he said calmly, "That's better. Now I have one last question. What happened to Xeres? How did you all end up on Earth?"

No one spoke for several moments, then Melvin's voice broke the silence. "Some of us from both guilds got tired of the constant fighting. We decided to leave Xeres. We reincarnated on a different planet to get away from the fighting."

What the…? What is Melvin doing? Cadwallader thought with dismay. *He makes it sound like they just started reincarnating here on Earth from Xeres. He knows that they physically moved before they started reincarnating.*

MacPherson looked puzzled.

"Both guilds came here together? They actually worked together?"

Melvin answered, "Yes, some of us collaborated to get here."

Why is he misdirecting them like this? It's obvious, to me at least, that he's not actually regressed like everyone else. He sounds like a bad actor pretending to be in a trance.

"But after we got to Earth," Melvin continued, "the old animosity came up all over again until we started fighting here too. We eventually went our separate ways, agreeing not to interfere with each other. Then somewhere along the line, we forgot about where we came from. Until now, at least."

Cadwallader could practically see the crocodile tears spilling from his eyes. *He's really laying it on thick. I need to find out what game he's playing.*

Melvin's voice became shrill. "I wish you'd never woken us up. I hate remembering all the fighting."

Voices rose in agreement from other parts of the room.

Thompson looked at MacPherson. They both nodded.

MacPherson took over again. "Feel the white light surround you. You have nothing to fear. You are floating back to the present…."

* * *

Around them, the Xerians were hugging and saying their goodbyes. By the panel room's door, SaxMan, OneNoteWonder and Valves were loudly planning to meet up soon. Riley had heard about their 'get together' last night in the bar. Apparently, their live jamming on saxophone, percussion, and trumpet had drawn quite a crowd.

A group further down the hall caught his eye. OldFart and GoldenOldie were exchanging phone numbers with FoxTotem. On little paper slips. Riley saw Blinks shaking his head at his companions.

"Guys. Just put the numbers in your phones."

The other three looked sheepish as they pulled out their iPhones and began tapping at them.

Tessa tugged at Riley's elbow, interrupting his thoughts.

"Huh? What?"

"Riley, I need you. Now."

"But—"

"This can't wait." She pulled him away from the crowd, leading him toward the elevators.

They passed a row of the hotel's charging stations. Amazon and RoadRanger, their two truckers, sat at one of the desks, heads together, comparing routes on their laptops. At another desk, SgtCox and Jedi165 were peering intently at their phones, arguing about which military Space-A flight would get them home the soonest.

When they got off on the eighth floor, Riley said, "This isn't our floor. What's going on? I thought we were going to pack out, then have lunch."

"I finished packing our stuff up during the break and put it in Evelyn's room. She always gets late check out. It gives Kier more time with his friends and lets her stay in the dealers room longer. Right now, we're going to Starr's room. We Tesham have been talking, comparing notes, and we want you to regress us all together."

Riley stopped in the middle of the hall, protesting, "By myself? I should get Evelyn to help."

She shook her head, pulling him on. "What we want to look into, we didn't want anyone else involved. We decided we just wanted you, by yourself."

He raised an eyebrow at her. "Should I be flattered?"

Tessa punched his arm in mock annoyance. "You can catch Evelyn and Alex up on the results later."

Starr opened the door at Tessa's knock. Inside, Riley was surprised to find the remaining four Tesham also present: GirlAUWatch, HotDoc, Lyocel, and TinMan. Starr slipped past them, folding himself to sit on the floor by the window. Tessa joined GirlAUWatch on one of the queen sized beds, with HotDoc and James reclining on the other. Lyocel occupied the comfy chair in the corner of the room. Riley nodded to them, then rolled the office chair in front of the armoire before sitting down.

"Anyone care to enlighten me why I was kidnapped and brought here?"

GirlAUWatch turned to Tessa. "You didn't tell him?"

Tessa shook her head. "Didn't have time." She looked pleadingly at Riley. "We all know there's more to what happened than the other Xerians are aware of. We want you to help us find out what really happened."

From the other bed, HotDoc said, "Like, why did the other two guilds really turn on us? That thing with the power stations couldn't have triggered it."

From the floor, Starr added, "Tessa told us about the Sheitan, and we want to know more about them."

"Well, personally, I want to know about the tattoo Tessa and I share," said James. "That's really been bugging me."

HotDoc turned to James, asking, "What tattoo? This is the first I've heard about a tattoo."

James slid his sleeve up to reveal his tattoo. At the same time, Tessa tugged the collar of her t-shirt down, exposing hers.

"You have one, too?" GirlAUWatch gasped. Twisting, she pulled up her t-shirt, revealing a smaller version of the gear just above her waist.

From the corner, Lyocel piped up, "I have one, too, just like yours, Tessa." She blushed. "It's just not in a place I'm prepared to show you all."

"Mine's public enough. You just haven't seen it." Starr held up his arm, pulling on the cuff of his hoodie to reveal his right wrist. "See?"

HotDoc reddened. "I've got one also. Excuse me if I don't strip. Mine is below my navel and to the right."

"Ah," said Starr from the floor, "you're no fun."

The general laughter released some of the tension that had been building in the room.

They all have the symbol tattoo somewhere, Riley thought. *It's not just that they were all drawn to that symbol, but they felt compelled to permanently add it to their bodies. It's really important somehow. It connects them together. From what James and Tessa said, it comforts them too. What does it mean that they all have it? I need to get to the bottom of that.*

"Okay, folks, I get the drift of what you want to know. Shall we begin?"

"One second, Riley," Tessa interrupted. "Does anyone else notice that all of our tattoos are in places we normally keep covered up? Even Starr's." She looked at him. "I don't think I've seen you without your hoodie or a long sleeve shirt all weekend."

Starr considered for a moment, then pointed at Tessa. "You know, you're right. I almost always wear long sleeves in public. Either my hoodie or some other jacket."

"And the images, well, the ones I've seen, anyway, are all pretty much the same. That's not a coincidence," HotDoc said.

After a moment's silence, Riley tried again. "Now that we've had show-and-tell, may I start the regression?"

They all nodded. James put in, "And definitely ask about the symbol, what it means. There must be a reason we all have one."

"Okay, folks, get comfortable…."

Riley walked them through the steps to get back to their Xerian lives after the guilds had split. Then he began questioning them.

"Where did the Sheitan come from?"

"One of our top researchers discovered they were among us. He hunted them, trying to rid them from our world," James said. "They found him and killed him, but not before he had warned one of his mates. She spread the word and told us what to look for. Soon we all knew."

"It was one of my mates the Sheitan killed," Tessa said, tears running down her face. "When he discovered them, he started working to eliminate them."

Riley couldn't keep from asking his own question.

"*One* of your mates? As in, you had, like, two husbands?"

Tessa brushed the question away with a wave of her hand. "We don't have binary genders like you do. Our mating…." she paused, considering. "Any one of us can be the receptive partner. When we wish to have a child, two partners work together to inseminate the third. It takes all three of us to produce a child. That's why we have triad marriages. Besides," she said, smiling, "everyone knows that a three-sided structure, like a triangle, is the most stable in nature. So any combination of three people who love each other works."

Riley's head was spinning with this new information. *There's so much I want to ask them. So many questions that I would love to get answers for. But no. I'm doing this for them, not to satisfy my own prurient curiosity. Mental note to self, follow up on this group marriage thing with Tessa.*

"Didn't you try to warn the authorities?" Riley said, changing the subject.

HotDoc answered. "When we tried, they wouldn't listen to us." His voice turned bitter. "We watched as the Sheitan rose in power. As they started rumors about us that set the other guilds against us. As the mobs came after us."

"Why did the Sheitan turn the other guilds against you?"

"We were the only ones who could detect them," GirlAUWatch said. "Something about our unique abilities with both magic and science allowed us to detect them. Their energy was on a wavelength that we could see, but the Klymurians and Bylantians couldn't."

Lyocel picked up the story. "They knew we were a threat because we could see them, so they set out to eradicate us. First through discrediting us, then by accusing us of atrocities," she paused, taking a deep breath, "and finally through genocide."

"They thought we were completely wiped out," said Starr, slyly. "But at first the Sheitan didn't know that we Tesham don't just come from the mating of Tesham triads. The way that our guild first came into being was through the union of Bylantians and Klymurians. Any child of a mixed pairing had the potential to be a Tesham. How gifted they were depended on how gifted the parents were. Once the Sheitan realized that, they drove a wedge between the guilds to prevent any new Tesham from being born."

Oh, my gods, Riley thought in horror. *Starting wars to prevent your enemy from even being born.*

"That's why they instituted testing for all young children," Tessa said sourly. "To weed out the ones who had any aptitude for the other guild's specialty, whether magic or science."

"Then how did the Tesham survive?" Riley asked.

GirlAUWatch spoke up. "We had to go into hiding, after the other guilds turned against us."

"After the Sheitan turned the other guilds against us, you mean," said Tessa bitterly.

"We went underground," James said. "Pretended to be either Bylantian or Klymurian. We kept in touch, though. We developed the gear symbol so we never forgot who we really were."

"What does the symbol itself mean?" Riley asked.

James spoke as though he were lecturing. "It's a toothed gear with four spokes and a small hole in the center. The gear itself represents our Tesham science side. The four chambers created by the spokes represent the four elements of our magical side, Earth, Air, Fire, and Water. The hole in the center represents our Spirit, which unites both sides of our nature."

Lyocel added, "It became the symbol of the Tesham. We used it to identify each other secretly."

"Like a secret handshake. If someone is wearing the symbol, we know they can be trusted," HotDoc clarified.

Riley nodded. "I understand. I have one last question for you all that has been bugging me since this all started. How do the Klymurians and Bylantians recognize each other here on Earth?"

James picked up the lecture. "The guilds have been fighting so long that they have developed an aversion to each other's energy. They can sense that energy, no matter what vessel it's in. It's the same with us and the Sheitan. We've been bitter enemies so long that we react violently when we detect their energies. But it's easy for that energy to get masked by a crowd. We have to be close to recognize each other. That's part of the reason we hid among the other guilds, camouflage."

Riley paused, checking his memory of the Teshams' questions. Then he glanced at the clock on the nightstand. *Yikes! Where did the time go? I need to wrap this up.*

He quickly walked them through the steps to bring them back to the present and back into their own bodies.

"…when I count backwards from three, you will awaken. You will remember everything we have talked about here today. You will be relaxed and at peace. Three, two, one." Riley checked in with each of them, making sure they didn't have any lingering issues from the regression. When he was sure they were all doing okay, he turned to Tessa.

"Look at the time. We've got to get our things out of Evelyn's room so she can check out of the hotel."

Lyocel protested, rising from her chair. "We can't just leave. Not now. There's so much to discuss."

Tessa went to hug her. "I know, dear. But we just don't have the time. Not today." She glanced around the room. "We can get together on the forum. Have private chats. Okay?"

The others reluctantly nodded.

GirlAUWatch sighed. "Yeah, I guess that'll have to do. But I don't have to like it."

Tessa and the others laughed. "I know." She grabbed Riley's arm. "Come on, Doc, it's time to go."

Riley and Tessa caught up with Kier just before they got to Evelyn's door.

"Hey, guys, where did you run off to? Mom and Alex have been looking everywhere for you."

"We had business to take care of after this morning's session," Tessa said. "Where *are* Evelyn and Alex, anyway?"

"They gave up on you two and went for a last pass through the dealers room."

"Then could you let us into your room? We need to take our luggage to the car."

"I just got back from taking mine and mom's down. I can take yours to your car if you want," Kier offered.

"No, we can get it," Riley said. "I wouldn't want you to have to lug our stuff around."

"I don't mind. All of my friends are already gone and I've spent all the money Alex gave me for helping sell his shirts."

"Tell you what," Riley said. "I'll give you ten bucks for taking our stuff to the car. That way you'll have some money for anything else you want in the dealers room."

"Really? Sweet!" Kier's eyes brightened. "That would give me enough for two expansion sets for the card game I play. Thanks, Riley."

Riley handed him the keys to his car and told him where to find it in the parking garage.

"Well," Tessa said, grabbing his arm, "that gives us time to check out the dealers room ourselves." She gave Riley a sly grin. "I've been eyeing this kilt that would look great on you."

* * *

"That's the fourth Sheitan killed in Europe in as many months!" Thierry slammed a hand on the coffee table, making his phone bounce toward the edge.

Latham, standing beside him, reached out to rescue it.

"Um, am I interrupting?" Jessica asked, entering the living room.

Thierry glanced at the small woman. "No. Do you have the information I requested?" He beckoned for her to join him on the sofa.

"It took a while, but yes, I have everything you asked for on MacPherson's group."

She handed over several folders, each one neatly labeled.

Thierry glanced at the first two, finding them meticulously detailed. He nodded.

"Will there be anything else, sir? Melvin and I are due to fly out in just over an hour. I can stay if you want, but I would need to rebook my flight."

"No, this is exactly what I needed. You are dismissed." He stacked her folders on the table, selected one and began to read.

286

Jessica gave a slight bow, then went back to Latham's room. Shrugging into her jacket, she placed a call.

"Melvin? I've got our luggage. Have the front desk call us a cab." She sighed wearily. "I'm more than ready to head home. I can't wait to sleep in my own bed again."

Chapter 32

Around Kier, the parking garage stretched cold and empty. He heard faraway voices, probably fans like him, loading out. Then, closer, he heard a familiar voice, though he couldn't catch all the words.

"…kill MacPherson…."

He stopped, startled. *What? Someone wants to kill Riley?*

He moved silently toward the voice. Rounding a panel truck, he saw Cadwallader arguing with someone over the phone as he paced.

"…you're supposed to be helping me, not getting in the way…."

Kier ducked back behind the truck. *Yikes! Cad wants to kill Riley? And who's supposed to be helping him? I gotta tell mom!*

Hurrying down the next aisle, he found Riley's car. Opening the trunk, he shoved the suitcases and bags in. He was reaching up to close the hatch when a hand clamped down on his shoulder.

"What are you doing here? Where's MacPherson?"

Kier, shocked by Cadwallader's sudden appearance, could only shake his head mutely.

"He has to be here. It's important. There's no more time," he said, though Kier got the impression he was talking to himself.

The man grabbed Kier's shoulders and shook him hard. When Cad released him, Kier fell back into the open hatch of Riley's Prius. Pain flared through his lower back where he fell on the luggage. Levering himself out of the hatch, Kier nearly tripped when he stepped on a large flashlight that had tumbled out of the car.

Catching himself, Kier glared at Cadwallader. *You think I'm helpless, don't you? Think again, prick. I remembered my magic years ago. Now I get to practice on* you.

Kier straightened. Bringing up his hands between himself and

Cadwallader, he felt for the wind currents moving through the garage.

"Get your hands off me, Sheitan!" he yelled. Gathering the strands of wind together, he pushed with his hands, shoving the compressed air at Cadwallader.

The man staggered across the aisle and into a van. Catching his balance, Cadwallader lowered his head, glared at Kier, and began advancing.

"Oh, so the little boy thinks he's a man, huh?"

"I'm not some helpless kid," Kier shouted. "I've been remembering my life on Xeres for over two years now. I remember my magic, too."

When Cadwallader kept coming, Kier hit him with another blast of wind. This one caught him full force and sent the man flying through the air. He landed in a heap against the far wall of the garage. *Take that!*

Cadwallader stirred. Kier watched in horrified fascination as the man unfolded himself, rose and began stalking back towards Kier.

Why can't he just stay down, he thought desperately. *What else can I use against him?*

Kier heard Cadwallader's voice, eerily hollow, floating across the concrete toward him.

"Oh, even better. It's no fun if you don't fight back. Besides, I owe your mother for all the years she's tormented me. I just wish I could see the look on her face when she finds your cold, dead body."

The man's words froze Kier in place for a moment. Glancing around for something else to fight with, his eyes caught on the overhead lights. Summoning up his will, Kier began pulling the energy from the exciters on each fluorescent bulb like he had the wind currents.

He could see the electricity as it built, causing the lights to sputter. Cadwallader looked up in confusion.

Kier gestured, pushing the built-up electricity toward his enemy.

Lightning began arcing from one fixture to the next, blowing out the fluorescent bulbs in a cascading shower of glass that rapidly advanced on Cadwallader.

The bolt arced one final time, grounding itself through Cadwallader's body.

The last thing Kier saw before the end of the garage plunged into darkness was Cadwallader's body, haloed in light, crumpling to the ground.

"Kier? Kier! Where are you?" His mother's voice came from behind him.

He turned, yelling. "Mom? I'm over here!"

Evelyn rushed up to him. "Kier! Where have you been? Riley said you were taking their stuff to his car. It's been twenty minutes. What's taking you so long?" She looked around. "What happened to the lights?"

I can't let her know about my magic. She'd make stop me using it. And that Sheitan? He'll kill her!

"Mom, you can't be here. Cadwallader—"

The man himself came rushing out of the dark like a charging wraith. He grabbed Kier's arm.

Unngh. Hurts. His hand's so cold. It burns, Kier's mind keened.

The pain drove him to his knees.

He screamed, "Mom, help! Make it stop!"

As he writhed in Cadwallader's grip, Kier caught a flash of something flying over his head and a sound like something breaking in two. Cad's hold on his arm loosened enough for Kier to break free. He quickly rolled to his feet and backed away until he came up against another parked car.

He saw his mom standing over Cadwallader, a bag from one of the convention vendors swaying in her hand. There were flecks of blood on the bag that matched the splatter on the side of Cadwallader's head.

Mom clocked Cadwallader! She's wanted to do that for years. Go Mom! he thought, fist pumping into the air.

Cadwallader rose up, blood across his face, looking like some unstoppable horror movie villain.

Damn, he's still coming!

The smell of sulphur hit Kier like a wall. His mouth gaped as his mother started to glow.

"What's going on? What are you doing to my mom?" he demanded.

But Cadwallader looked as surprised as Kier did.

Fire enveloped his mother's body.

"Noooo!" Kier wailed.

Evelyn lifted her hand and pointed it at Cadwallader. A jet of flames surged from her finger, hitting Cad in the chest. His coat began to smolder, then caught fire.

Cadwallader slapped at the flames for a moment, then tore the jacket off and threw it away from him.

Kier shook his head, not believing what he was seeing.

Whoa! Mom's got magic too! Flames? Too cool.

"Mom, how…?"

Evelyn looked down at her hands in confusion. "I don't know." Looking up, she barked an order at him. "Go! Get help. Find Riley or James."

Kier paused, torn between doing what she told him to and trying to help her.

Evelyn raised her hands and directed another stream of fire at Cadwallader, shouting over her shoulder, "Kier, GO!"

Without looking back, Kier bolted away. As he hit the stairs, he heard his mom screaming at Cadwallader, "So, you thought you could threaten my son…."

Arriving out of breath at the dealers room door, Kier scanned the crowd until he spotted Riley. Shoving aside late buyers, he finally reached his friend.

"Mom…Cadwallader…garage…HELP!" he panted, clutching Riley's arm.

"What? Slow down. Breathe," Riley told him.

Kier took a deep breath, held it a moment, then exhaled loudly.

"Cadwallader jumped me when I was taking your stuff to the car. We fought. I used magic on him, but he kept coming. Mom found us." Kier's voice cracked. "They're still fighting. She told me to find you. Come on. Hurry!"

He pulled at Riley, but the man stood firm, biting his lip and frowning.

Coming to a decision, Riley told Kier, "Stay here with Alex."

Turning to Alex, he ordered, "Call James. Tell him to meet me in the garage."

Shaking off Kier's hand, Riley raced toward the door.

* * *

From his vantage point inside his car, Bryce could see Cadwallader pacing back and forth in the parking garage. He ended the call, thinking, *You always were so easy to bait. When you let your emotions run away with you, you get sloppy. And that, my dear, makes you an easy target. After all this time, I will finally be free of you, once and for all.*

291

Bryce opened the car door and stepped out into the dank air of the parking garage. Reaching back inside, he grabbed a large piece of white material. Silently, he inched toward where he could hear Cadwallader fuming and cussing. When he rounded the end of the row though, Cadwallader was nowhere to be seen.

Where has he gotten off to now? Hold still so I can kill you, dammit.

He heard raised voices further down the line of cars. Peering out from behind a minivan, he saw that Cadwallader had grabbed a young Asian boy and was shaking him. As he watched, Cadwallader threw the boy into the open hatch of the vehicle he'd obviously been loading when the big man accosted him. The next thing Bryce saw was Cadwallader stumbling backwards, slamming into the cars on the far side of the aisle.

Wow, that kid must have shoved Cadwallader pretty hard to send him flying like that. Funny, he doesn't look that strong. Maybe Cadwallader's getting weak in his old age. Good. It'll make my job that much easier.

Cadwallader started back toward the boy. When the man reached the center of the aisle, a fierce wind blasted Bryce in the face, knocking him back against the pickup behind him. He watched, astonished, as Cadwallader sailed past his hiding place. Peeking around the pickup, he was astonished to find Cadwallader collapsed against the cement half wall.

As Cadwallader went stalking back toward the boy, the lights overhead began to flicker. When the fixture over his head burst, Bryce covered his head with his arms. He looked over in time to see Cadwallader, enveloped in light, crumple to the garage floor.

Then all was darkness.

Interesting. Ah, yes. That boy must be a Klymurian magic user.

Bryce heard voices shouting. Glancing that direction, he saw a petite African-American woman standing next to the Asian boy. He heard footsteps shuffle past his hiding place.

Cadwallader? Alive? I thought that blast of electricity would have saved me the trouble of killing him.

Bryce edged closer to the action. He was only a few cars away when he heard the boy scream.

Things began happening too rapidly for Bryce to process. The small woman hit Cadwallader with something and he went down. When the man started to rise, the woman began glowing and caught fire.

Another damned Klymurian? And this one's a fire mage! Haven't seen one of them for a really long time. Maybe she'll *take care of him for me.*

He watched as the woman set Cadwallader's jacket on fire. While he was tearing off his jacket, the woman screamed at the boy to run and get help.

Now's my chance, Bryce thought gleefully. *While he's distracted.*

As he moved closer, he could tell the woman was unaccustomed to using magic. Her flames were already dwindling.

As if on cue, Cadwallader turned on her, grabbing her shoulder. Even with his human eyes, Bryce could tell that Cadwallader was consuming her energy.

He's feeding on her. He's so focused, he'll never see me coming.

Pulling the white pillowcase from his jacket pocket, Bryce grabbed either end and hurriedly twisted it into a makeshift garrote. Easing up behind his prey, he crossed his arms before looping the cloth over Cadwallader's head and settling it under the man's chin. Then he pulled with all his strength.

Cadwallader was so caught up in his feeding it was several seconds before he registered the threat. He dropped the woman and clawed at his throat.

But it was too late. Bryce felt the man's weight shift as he slipped into unconsciousness.

The woman, now free from her attacker, raised her arms, sending a gout of flame up Cadwallader's body. The heat singed the hairs on Bryce's hands, startling him into releasing his hold on the pillowcase.

Without Bryce supporting his weight, Cadwallader slumped forward, falling face first onto the concrete floor.

The woman rose from the ground. In a quavery voice, she said, "Whoever you are, thanks. I thought I was a goner." She started to move away.

"Not so fast. I'm afraid I can't leave you around as a witness," Bryce snickered menacingly.

The woman backed away from him, but in her weakened state, she couldn't move fast enough to evade him. Grabbing both of her arms, Bryce took his first taste of her energy.

Mmmmm, Bryce thought, electric fingers running up and down his spine. *I'd forgotten how delicious Xerian energy is. It's been far too long since I indulged myself. After years of being so close to Diana and being forbidden to even taste her, this is heavenly.*

He was so involved with the woman that he almost missed it when Cadwallader stirred and began to rise. He hastily dropped her.

Casting about for a suitable weapon, Bryce's eyes landed on a large flashlight lying on the ground next to him. Grabbing it, he swung with all his strength, connecting with Cadwallader's temple.

The man folded, sprawling across the woman.

"Dammit! I'm done with you causing me headaches!" Bryce said through gritted teeth. "This is the last time!"

Reaching down, Bryce placed his hand on Cadwallader's shoulder, then paused.

Wait! What am I doing? Thierry ordered me to do this, but Cadwallader's still my mate and a fellow Sheitan. Killing him? That's easy. I've done that many times before. But eating him? We don't eat our own.

A lone tear ran down Bryce's face. He shook his head and straightened. *I have to do it, dammit. If I don't, Thierry will just have someone take us both out. Better he dies the final death than both of us.*

Feeling his former lover's energy rise beneath his hand, Bryce closed his eyes and began draining Cadwallader's life force.

Bryce's eyes flew open when he felt Cadwallader stir. The other man was struggling to get up. Their eyes locked. He saw realization flicker in Cadwallader's eyes. *He knows what I'm doing.* He watched as horror and terror warred in his former lover's eyes.

Stop looking at me like that, he begged silently. *This is hard enough for me already. I can't….*

Bryce had to stop that look. He couldn't take it. Raising his hand, he was startled to see that he was still clutching the bloody flashlight. He swung, catching Cadwallader in the temple a second time.

The man collapsed, his outstretched hand falling limply upon the small woman's face.

Bryce reached for Cadwallader's shoulder, needing to complete his assignment before he lost his nerve. He spent the next several minutes draining the life energy from his fellow Sheitan.

Oh, no! he thought suddenly. *My prints are on the flashlight. I need something to wipe them off with.* Flicking on the flashlight still in his free hand, he scanned the area for anything he could use. Spying a piece of his makeshift garrote, he released his hold on Cadwallader. Hurriedly, he swiped at the flashlight, trying to wipe it clean.

Fear raced through him at the sound of running footsteps. Rising, he glanced at the tableaux laid out around him.

Someone's coming. They can't catch me here with two dead bodies like this. I'll be in prison for the rest of this body's life.

Dropping the flashlight beside the two bodies, he tossed the material under the next car. Slinking back into the shadows, Bryce buried himself in the darkness.

From the shadows, he saw Riley MacPherson run up the ramp and squat to retrieve the lit flashlight that had rolled under the back edge of an SUV. Bryce watched as Riley panned the light across the ceiling, then shone it on the floor, exposing the bodies of Cadwallader and the black woman.

I can't risk him seeing me with blood on my jacket, Bryce thought in panic. He was creeping toward the upward ramp when a large panel van rounded the corner above him, lights illuminating the darkened section of the garage. Diving between two cars, he fervently hoped the driver hadn't seen him. Once the van was past him, he fled the garage. From behind him, he heard the squeal of brakes, then a woman's scream.

Perfect, he thought jubilantly. *Who better to pick up the murder weapon than MacPherson. That's payback for helping Diana leave me. Hope you like prison, asshole.*

Slipping into the hotel, Bryce bypassed the elevators and headed straight for the stairwell, climbing toward his floor.

No one uses the stairs anymore. This way no one has a chance to see the blood on my jacket. And if they do, I can say it's fake, part of my costume for this damned convention.

He was almost to the fourth floor and safety when he heard a stairwell door open above him. Shrinking against the right hand railing, he waited. When the person rounded the bend, he was surprised to see Diana. *What is she doing here?* Fury at her presence overcame him.

All those years wasted. Waiting, watching her, but never allowing myself to even taste her. He came to a sudden, blinding conclusion. *What's one more dead body at this point?*

He saw shock and fear wash over her face when she caught sight of him. She raised a hand to her chest.

"What are you doing here? I saw you with that, that clone of me at the front desk," she spit out. "Tell me, how long have you been having an affair with her? Was I playing the part of the timid wife you took your frustrations out on while you were running around screwing some cheap whore?"

Momentarily stunned by her words and tone, he could only stand mute. *Clone? Front desk?* The light dawned. *Oh, Jessica. They do look somewhat alike. I hadn't really thought about that before now.*

Putting her hands on her hips, she stared at him defiantly.

He drew in a breath to explain, but before he could say anything, she launched into another tirade.

"I'm glad I'm divorcing you," she said coldly. Then she leveled a fierce look at him and tossed her head, dark hair swirling about her shoulders. "And I've met someone too. I ran into an old friend from Boston this weekend. Remember Jimmy B? Remember how you forced me to stop talking to him? Well, he's back in my life and there's not a damn thing you can do about it."

Rage welled up in Bryce. Something snapped.

Racing up the intervening steps, he grabbed her shoulders with both hands, shoving her back against the wall of the landing.

"Listen to me, bitch!" he roared. "I own you! I've spent most of this life doing nothing but babysitting you because you were a damn Xerian. I was just supposed to watch you, so you could lead us to more of your damned kind. Well, not anymore."

Before he get out another word, she twisted in his grip and kneed him in the balls.

Bryce folded over in pain.

"Nobody owns me, you bastard!"

He felt Diana shove past him, heading down the stairs, her pounding footsteps beating in time with the red pulses of pain washing over him.

Chapter 33

James swerved to avoid several people with slow-moving luggage carts as he raced through the halls toward the dealers room. He saw Kier and Alex standing outside, their heads together.

"...jumped me. I fought him off twice, but he kept on coming. Then mom showed up. She clocked him upside the head. Then she threw fire at him! It was so cool."

"Evelyn threw fire at someone?" James said, coming up behind the boy.

Turning at his arrival, Kier said, "Yeah, at Cadwallader. She set his coat on fire."

"Cadwallader? The Sheitan?"

Kier started moving toward the parking garage, talking and gesturing as he went.

"She fought him off and told me to get help. Riley went to the garage to help her." Kier tugged at James' coat sleeve. "We need to hurry and make sure they're okay."

They sped across the driveway, then up the stairs of the garage. Emerging on the second floor, they heard a woman screaming.

They ran faster.

Heading up the ramp, their eyes were momentarily dazzled by the headlights of a vehicle stopped at the top.

What the hell's wrong with the lights? James thought. *It's dark as pitch up there.*

Shielding his eyes with his hand, James squinted into the glare, trying to piece together what he was seeing.

Stiffening, he shouted to Alex, "Call 911! Tell them we need an ambulance. Now!"

Racing the rest of the way up the ramp, James passed Riley with barely a notice before dropping to one knee beside the bodies. Checking Evelyn first, then Cadwallader, he sighed with relief. *They're both alive, though their pulses are weak.*

Noticing blood on his hands, James searched the fallen man until he found Cadwallader's head wound. Stripping off his jacket, he wadded it up and used it to stop the heavy bleeding.

"Mom!" wailed Kier, rushing up next to James and kneeling beside the fallen woman. The boy looked up at James, pleading, "Help her!"

"Don't move her, Kier," he cautioned the boy. "She may have broken something. The EMTs are on the way."

Kier began to sob, repeating, "Mom. Wake up, mom."

Looking up at Riley, James began, "What happ...."

He cut himself off as he registered what he was seeing.

Riley stood frozen in the van's headlights, holding a large flashlight in one hand. James saw blood splattered all across it. As he watched, a drop fell from the flashlight's lens, joining the pool next to Cadwallader's head.

Snapping into full cop mode, he kept his voice calm as he asked, "Riley, tell me you didn't do this."

Riley appeared to come out of his daze. He looked at the object in his hand, eye widening. "I...." he began. A look of horror came over his face and his voice quavered, "Are they dead?"

James shook his head. "Not yet. Alex is calling 911." Looking around, he spied Alex trying to calm the screaming woman. James noticed that he kept stealing glances at them, obviously more concerned for his friends than the driver of the van.

He brought his attention back to the stunned man standing before him.

"Riley, can you tell me what happened?"

Gotta keep him talking. If he goes into shock, he'll be worthless helping me figure out what happened.

"I...I don't know. I came up here looking for Evelyn and found them like that."

"Where did you get the flashlight?"

"The flashlight?" he asked in a daze. *He's forgotten he's even holding it,* James thought to himself. "It was over there. On the ground. Under that

298

car. It was dark. The light was on. I picked it up to look around."

"And you didn't hit anyone with it?"

"What? No! I wouldn't—"

"There's blood on your arm and on the flashlight. Is it yours? Are you hurt?"

Riley looked at the object in his hand in confusion. "I'm not hurt. Blood?" He started when he registered the blood for the first time. "Oh, my gods!" He dropped the light. It hit the cement floor and rolled in a semicircle, until it came to a stop, the beam spotlighting the pool of blood from Cadwallader's head wound.

Dammit, he's going into shock, James thought, frustrated. *I've got to get him calmed down. Keep him coherent. I need him to tell me what happened before the local police arrive. It isn't a coincidence that this involves a Sheitan and a Xerian.* He grimaced. *I can't very well explain* that *to the unit that shows up.*

He heard voices approaching.

A murmuring voice floated toward James. *A cop on his shoulder mic,* he thought, then groaned. *What am I going to tell them?*

A large man in a black police uniform carefully edged around Riley and into James' view.

Nodding to James, the policeman demanded, "Tell me what happened."

"James Cavanaugh, SFPD. I was one of the first people on the scene. Nothing's been moved." He gestured with his chin toward the two prone bodies. "They're both alive, but barely." He indicated Cadwallader. "This one's got a nasty gash on his temple. Bleeding badly." Glancing at Evelyn's still body and her sobbing son, "She's not hurt, as far as I can see." Nodding at Kier, he said, "The boy is her son."

The policeman waved a hand at Riley. "And this one?"

"Riley MacPherson. As far as I can tell, he came upon the scene after the assailant had fled." Honesty and training compelled him to add, "Though Riley was holding the probable weapon used in this assault."

The cop looked at Riley speculatively. "Is that so?" Turning, he called to his partner. "Leary? Take charge of this one," he said, pointing at Riley.

A tall, stick-thin policeman emerged from the shadows. Placing a firm hand on Riley's arm, he steered the man off to one side.

Watching his friend move away, James felt the large cop's gaze on him.

"Sgt. Carson, here. Person Crimes is on its way."

"No, we're here," said a low feminine voice from behind the big man.

James turned his head to appraise the Asian woman in a black pants suit coming toward them. Behind her marched three others, all men, in similar suits.

She motioned to one of them. "Get some uniforms in here to direct traffic. Lock down all exits from this garage until we know what happened. And get me some better lights!" One man pulled out a cell phone and began speaking quietly into it. The other two began processing the scene, taking pictures and stringing yellow crime scene tape.

"Detective Zhou," said Sgt. Carson, nodding his head toward James, "this is Officer Cavanaugh, SFPD. That one over there," he gestured toward his partner and Riley, "is Riley MacPherson. He's a possible suspect."

"Cavanaugh? SFPD?" She got a pensive look on her face, one finger tapping against her cheek. "Aha. You were Guerrero's partner, before you made detective. I'll need to check your ID when you're, uh, less tied up."

"You know Javier?" James brightened. "I meant to give him a call while I was at the convention, but," He shrugged. "well, things got in the way."

She gave him a dry look. "Uh-huh. Like bodies in a parking garage?"

"Yes, ma'am."

Two paramedics bustled onto the scene, pushing James aside and taking over. He stood, moving out of their way. Detective Zhou motioned for him to follow, then walked a few steps away.

Joining her, James pulled his wallet from the back pocket of his jeans, presenting his badge and ID for the detective to check.

"Thanks. I appreciate that. I believed you," she said with a wry grin, "but you know the drill."

"Yeah," he said, nodding. "Gotta go by the book."

"So far, we've got the flashlight and this half-burned cloth. It looks like a pillowcase from the hotel...." she continued.

He knew he should be listening to her, but he was watching the paramedics, anxious about his fallen friend and her son. After their initial

300

examinations, they called for another ambulance.

"Kier…." Alex stepped up beside the boy, laying a gentle hand on his shoulder. "Let's move back. Let them work."

Kier's look of utter loss broke James' heart. He wanted to go to the boy, reassure him, protect him. Instead, he watched as Alex and Kier moved across the aisle.

Finally, he pulled his attention back to Detective Zhou, who was speaking to one of her men.

"…need to search the victim's room, if it hasn't been cleaned yet."

"Do you mind if I go with you?" James asked. "I have a personal interest in this case and might have insight that could help."

This guy is a Sheitan. You're good, but you won't know what to look for. Hell, I'm not sure if I will, but at least I know to look. If I tried explaining it to her, she'd think I'd lost my marbles. Huh. Now I know what Alex must have felt like when he first approached me.

Giving him a measuring look, the detective replied, "Sure. Be glad for the assist. Guerrero says you're one of the best detectives in the SFPD."

Alex tapped James on the arm, momentarily diverting him.

"They won't let me ride in the ambulance with Kier. The police are impounding Riley's car, and Evelyn's keys are in her purse, which the police put into evidence. We can't just leave the kid alone at the hospital. I called Tessa and Diana. Tessa's on her way out to be with Riley. Diana didn't answer, so I left her a message to call one of us."

James could see the man was seriously stressed out.

"We're headed for the front desk," he told Alex. "Keep trying to contact Diana."

Alex nodded miserably, his eyes following the two ambulances as they proceeded around the corner.

As James approached the police line with Zhou, he heard a familiar voice raised in anger.

"I have to get through! My boyfriend's in there!"

"Please stay back, miss. This is a crime scene." The beat cop edged Tessa further back from the yellow tape, his breath fogging in the suddenly frosty air.

James, holding the crime tape up for Detective Zhou, asked her, "Ma'am, that's Mr. MacPherson's girlfriend. Could you let her through? She'd be a lot of help keeping Riley from going into shock."

Zhou considered, then nodded. "Officer Castle? Escort that woman to Officer Leary. She's the girlfriend of our possible suspect. See if she can calm him down, but no direct contact with the suspect, hear?"

"Yes, ma'am."

As the officer raised the tape for her, Tessa looked over at James. "Thank you. Alex called and told me that the police were holding Riley. I rushed right out here. I didn't even stop to tell Diana where I was going, I just took off."

He nodded. "Don't worry, I'll give her a call and let her know you're out here."

The detective looked at him with a raised eyebrow.

"Do you know everybody involved with this crime?"

James huffed a laugh. "Well, most of them. The big man with the head wound is Dr. Matthew Cadwallader. The woman is Dr. Evelyn Sloan. Her son's name is Kier. Riley you met. That woman was Tessa Connors. She lives with Riley somewhere in the East Bay. The other man is Alex Wilson, MacPherson's assistant." At her look, he raised his hands. "Look, I just met them all here at the convention."

Inwardly he groaned. *Please, let's not involve the forum in this.*

"Convention?"

"HydraCon. It's a science fiction convention held here every year. I'm surprised you haven't heard of it. It's the biggest one of its kind on the West Coast."

"And you came down here just to go to a convention?" she asked as they entered the hotel.

He laughed. "You don't understand this kind of convention." He swept his hand in an arc. "A lot of these people come from across the country to attend. Some even come from other countries." He smiled. "It's a big deal for us."

"Us?" She raised an eyebrow at him.

"Yes, us. I take in five or six science fiction conventions a year, though none of them is as big as this one."

As they approached the desk, a woman hurried out to meet them.

"I'm the assistant manager, Edie Donahue. How may I help you?"

Detective Zhou introduced them both. Then she said, "We would like to find out what rooms Evelyn Sloan and Matthew Cadwallader are staying in."

The woman led them to the desk, then slipped behind it. Shooing the desk clerk aside she began typing. "Evelyn Sloan is in Room 529, but it shows she's already checked out. The other name was what? Matthew Cadwallader?" She frowned.

"Yes. What room is he staying in?" Zhou asked.

"I'm very sorry, ma'am, but there is no guest staying here under that name."

Zhou fished a plastic bag from her pocket. Removing the card from the bag, she handed it to the assistant manager who ran it through the scanner.

"This card is for room 419. It's registered to Bryce Lundee. He hasn't checked out yet."

Hearing the name, James audibly gasped. Zhou arched an eyebrow at him.

"Another friend of yours?" she asked neutrally.

As they headed for the elevator, he said, "No. Not this time." He shook his head wearily. "It's complicated."

* * *

Their journey to Bryce's room seemed to stretch out. Time slowed to a crawl as James sorted through everything that had occurred over the weekend.

I found Diana after all these years. I made new friends. I learned new things about myself and about what my tattoo means. I thought that was a lot to take in, but now I'm mixed up in a case that involves it all. My head is spinning. But they are all counting on me to sort this out so Riley doesn't get sent to jail. He rubbed his eyes. *Please, no more crazy surprises. I don't need to have a PTSD episode in the middle of an investigation.*

He was pulled from his somber thoughts by the manager.

"This is the room," the woman said to Zhou.

When the detective raised her hand to knock, James motioned for her to stop.

"Yes? Do you have an objection to my knocking? Are you going to be all chivalrous and demand to knock for me?"

He shook his head once. "No, not at all. I just think that I should wait down the hall. You'll probably find him much more cooperative if he doesn't know I'm here."

She tilted her head. "Does this relate in any way to my crime scene in the garage?"

"No, it's ancient history. I just don't want my presence making your job harder than it needs to be. I'll listen from the hallway."

"Right," she said. After a beat, she turned back to the door while James backed around the corner.

She knocked.

Between two of Zhou's detectives, James saw the door open, revealing a well-built, tanned man in nothing but a towel.

Well, he's certainly changed. I remember him as a slender kid in black. He obviously works out. He must be proud of his body. I mean, who answers a hotel door in a towel?

James ducked back before Bryce could notice him.

"Mr. Lundee?" Zhou asked.

"Yes?"

"I'm Detective Zhou. Is Matthew Cadwallader staying with you in this room?"

He could hear the surprise in Bryce's voice. "Cadwallader? Yes, but he isn't here right now. I don't know when he'll return."

"I'm afraid Mr. Cadwallader's been involved in an accident. He's been sent to the trauma center at Santa Clara Valley Medical."

"Please, come in. Make yourself comfortable while I get dressed."

The assistant manager laid a hand on Detective Zhou's arm. "Would you like me to open Mrs. Sloan's room when you're done here?"

"No, my men will go with you now." Turning, she waved two of the officers off with the assistant manager. She motioned the remaining officer into the room. Holding the door open with one hand, she nodded to James.

Realizing she meant for him to stay near, James slid along the wall until he was next to Zhou.

She smiled at him. "I'm going in. I'm guessing you still want to hear what he has to say, so I'd suggest you don't let the door close."

Returning her grin, James nodded.

When Detective Zhou entered the room, James stuck his foot out, preventing the door from shutting. He heard the bathroom door open and could almost picture Bryce making sure all eyes were on him as he entered the room, just like he had in high school.

His voice sounded smooth and cultured. "Now, what is this about Mr. Cadwallader?"

Zhou's voice. "How do you know Mr. Cadwallader?"

James detected an uncertain pause before Bryce replied.

"Matthew contacted me and mentioned he was attending a convention in this hotel, and since I had client meetings here this weekend, I offered to let him to stay with me to save him some money." There was a degree of snark in the man's voice as he went on. "He's an old family friend and he's been having money problems, so I thought I'd help him out."

James stiffened, then opened the door, striding in.

"Old family friend, huh?" James said, catching Bryce off guard. "I didn't know Cadwallader was from Boston too."

Bryce gaped at him for a moment, like a fish on dry land.

"Jimmy Cavanaugh? What are you doing here? In my room?"

Bryce and James glared at each other.

Zhou said dryly, "All right, boys, high school's over. Dial it down a notch." She focused on Bryce, saying, "Mr. Lundee, we'll need to look through Mr. Cadwallader's things."

Bryce broke off his staring contest with James, then pointed to a suitcase on the luggage rack on the far side of the room.

"And that's his messenger bag hanging on the back of the desk chair. The black Dell is his, too."

Zhou's man began going through Cadwallader' things, looking for clues.

Fishing a notepad out of her tailored jacket, Zhou continued with her questioning.

"When did you last see Mr. Cadwallader?"

"Um, yesterday, I believe. My client is only in for a few days from Greece, so we've been meeting from midnight until seven AM to accommodate his normal work schedule. Matthew had left by the time I got back this morning. I just woke up a few minutes ago."

"Uh, sir? I think you should see this."

Zhou moved to the desk, where her man had a file spread out across its faux-wood surface. She bent, reading silently for a few moments.

James saw her eyes harden. Her tone was flat as she said, "This changes things." Looking up at Bryce, she said, "Thank you for your time and cooperation, Mr. Lundee. I think we have all we need."

Motioning for her man to gather up all of Cadwallader's belongings, she grabbed James' arm and marched him into the hallway.

"Did you know your friend Riley MacPherson was a patient of Dr. Cadwallader's?"

"What? Seeing Cadwallader? First I've heard of that."

She waved the file folder. "According to this file from his messenger bag, Mr. Cadwallader has been having video counseling sessions with Mr. MacPherson for several months. Mr. Cadwallader states in his notes that he feared Mr. MacPherson was a danger to those around him. He even diagnosed Mr. MacPherson as homicidal. He states that Mr. MacPherson did not react well when Mr. Cadwallader discontinued his treatment and threatened to 'make all of you pay'. His final entry says that he feared for his own life."

James shook his head. "That just doesn't gibe with everything I've observed this weekend. Riley strikes me as a very caring individual, concerned for others' well-being. That file has got to be a fake."

"Well, you're a detective. What would you think if you came across this evidence? You have to admit that it puts a different complexion on the assault, don't you agree?"

Reluctantly, James nodded, muttering, "*If* it's true."

One of her officers rushed up. "Detective, we've just gotten word from the hospital, Mr. Cadwallader is dead.

She looked at James with a touch of pity in her eyes. Pulling out her phone, she punched a number.

"Officer Leary? Arrest Riley MacPherson for the murder of Matthew Cadwallader."

Chapter 34

"Roger that," the black-uniformed policeman said into his shoulder mic.

Tessa, Riley, and Alex watched the man expectantly. When he turned toward them, the expression on his face made Riley's stomach flop over.

"Riley MacPherson, I'm placing you under arrest for the murder of Matthew Cadwallader."

"Cadwallader's dead?" Tessa asked.

The man pulled out his handcuffs, snapped them around Riley's wrists, and read him his Miranda rights.

Riley stared at the cuffs, unable to process the fact that he was being arrested. He vaguely heard the policeman ask if he understood his rights, so he nodded.

"You can't seriously believe Riley had anything to do with Cadwallader's murder."

He raised his head. Beside him Tessa had assumed her I'm-about-to-hurt-someone stance.

"Tessa, no. It's okay. The officer is just doing his job."

He saw her visibly take her anger in hand and force it down.

I'm supposed to be the one protecting her, not the other way around, Riley thought. *I pity the poor cop if she goes after him.*

Alex faced the policeman as well.

"Are the cuffs really necessary?" he demanded.

The officer answered Alex in a calm voice. "Yes, sir, procedure." Turning to Riley, he said, "Please, come this way. I've been ordered to transport you to the station."

"I'm coming, too!" Tessa demanded.

The man shivered in the frosty air. "I'm sorry, ma'am, that's not allowed. Just Mr. MacPherson."

"But—" Tessa protested.

Alex put a hand on her shoulder.

"The man's only doing his job, Tessa." Looking up at the tall policeman, Alex asked, "Where are you taking him?"

"To the Temporary Holding Center at the station." Taking Riley by the elbow, the man explained, "He'll be held there for twenty-four hours while he's in processing. After that, he'll be transferred to the county jail while the investigators gather evidence."

As the officer marched him away, Riley heard Tessa and Alex calling after him, but he couldn't understand their words.

Jail? I've never even been in a police station. They think I murdered Cadwallader? The guy was an ass and a Sheitan, but I couldn't kill him. Well, maybe if he attacked me or Tessa I could, but he didn't. Was Cadwallader trying to kill Evelyn when she hit him with the flashlight? Knocked him unconscious and he fell on her, knocking her out?

The ride passed in a blur for Riley. Hours later, he found himself in an empty interrogation room. Riley was startled out of his fugue when the door opened.

"Hello, Mr. MacPherson," Detective Zhou said as she entered.

Riley's eyes riveted on the two covered coffee cups she placed on the table before taking her seat across from him. The promise of something warm inside him sent shivers down his spine.

She smiled, pushing one toward him. "I know how chilly those white jumpsuits are. I thought you'd appreciate a cup of coffee."

She opened the file folder she'd had under one arm and spread out a number of pages.

Sipping the black coffee, Riley swung between delight as the warmth went down and annoyance at the bitter, burned taste. He grimaced.

Zhou laughed. "Yeah, that's the way I feel about the coffee at the station too. I usually bring my own." Her face went serious. "Now, let's get down to business."

She held up one page. "So, about your therapy sessions with Mr. Cadwallader."

His head snapped up. "My what?"

"Therapy sessions, online, with Mr. Cadwallader." She kept her voice calm, but that didn't keep Riley from rising from his chair.

"I've never had therapy sessions with Cadwallader, online or in person." He frowned. "Why would you think that?"

She gave him a commanding look. "Sit down, Mr. MacPherson."

He did.

"Where is this coming from?" Riley asked, this time restraining his shock.

"We found this file in Mr. Cadwallader's possessions. It says you had a number of online sessions with him. It also says you have anger issues and concludes that you are homicidal. He states in here that you threatened his life."

Riley took a deep breath before he answered.

"First, I've never had a therapy session with the man. Second, I've only met the man a handful of times. The only interaction we had online was maybe an email or two. I can't remember. Check my computer, if you don't believe me."

She nodded. "Your computer is being processed as we speak."

Riley rubbed his eyes wearily.

"All right, let's put that aside for a moment." She shuffled her papers, then looked directly into his eyes.

"So why did you attack Mr. Cadwallader? Were you defending Mrs. Sloan or yourself? Did he attack you? Did your temper get the better of you?" She fired off the questions like machine gun bullets.

"I don't have a temper," he said, pounding the table with his fist.

She arched one eyebrow at him.

"Oh, really?"

He sagged in his seat, closing his eyes.

Well, that didn't help my case at all, did it? he thought. Falling back on his hypnotherapy training, he mentally recited a mantra to calm himself down.

When he opened his eyes, he found Zhou watching him patiently.

In a calm voice, he began again. "As I've already told your people, I found them like that. The lights were out at that end of the garage when I walked up. I saw the flashlight shining out from under a car. I grabbed it and looked around. That's when I saw Evelyn and Cadwallader on the ground." He swallowed at the mental picture of the two of them sprawled on the pavement. He felt his stomach start to roil. "I had barely registered what I was seeing when the van came around the corner and lit the whole place up with its headlights." He waved a hand. "The next thing I knew, James, Officer Cavanaugh, was there and I could hear a woman screaming."

"So you didn't notice blood on the flashlight when you picked it up?"

"Honestly, no. Not until James pointed it out. There really wasn't much time between when I picked up the flashlight and he showed up. Everything happened so fast."

"So you expect me to believe that, what, Matthew Cadwallader just happened to have documents in his possession that show you had been seeing him for anger issues and that you had threatened his life? What did he do, just make it all up? Why would he do that?" She leaned toward him, stabbing a finger onto the file. "Are you saying it's just a coincidence that he wrote that you threatened his life and then you were found standing over his dying body with the murder weapon in your hand?" The woman leaned back, crossing her arms over her chest.

The woman's dark eyes accused him. Riley's shoulders slumped. He shook his head.

"I have no idea why he had that file, but I swear to you that those sessions never happened. And I never threatened him. Like I said before, we've barely had any interactions at all. Maybe he planned to frame me. …"

"Frame you? For his own murder? I doubt that."

"No, not for his murder." Riley rested his chin on his hands, fisted on the table. After a few moments contemplation, he made a decision and pressed ahead. "He might have been planning on framing me for the murders he committed in San Diego."

"Oh, so now our victim is actually a murderer. This just gets better and better. I suppose you have proof?"

He nodded. "Yes, as a matter of fact, I do." He looked around the bare room, looking for a power outlet. There wasn't one. "I'll need my computer to show you, though."

"My techs are still processing your computer. You can't use it."

He shook his head.

"Fine. Any computer will do."

She thought a moment, then nodded. Rising, she said, "Okay, I'll humor you." She knocked on the door to the interrogation room. When a uniformed officer opened the door, she barked, "Get me a laptop."

It was only moments before the door opened and the officer handed Zhou a laptop.

Opening the case, she slid her finger across the trackpad and clicked a few times. "What URL should I go to?"

"The forum is at www.reincarnate.net."

"Do I need to create an account so I can see these messages you're talking about?" she queried.

"No, you wouldn't be able to see them. You'll need to use my login." He told her his username and password and watched as she typed them in.

"Now what?"

He walked her through the steps to access the administration features, then had her pull up the member profiles, pointing her to Cad's profile on the forum.

"All right, so you've proven that Mr. Cadwallader had an account on your website. That doesn't indicate that he's a murderer."

"I just wanted you to see that the user Spellbinder was actually Cadwallader first." He directed her to another section of the admin panel and had her bring up the saved private conversations between Cad and the two deceased girls. He sat back, letting the detective read over the messages, hope and fear warring within him.

What if she doesn't believe me? What if she dismisses the evidence altogether? What if this implicates me *in those murders?*

The woman sat back, laying her hands in her lap. "So he planned on meeting with these women to perform regressions on them. The man was a hypnotherapist, so I don't see how you make the jump from there to murder."

He directed her to the message thread about the missing girls. After she'd read it over, he continued, "One of our users, WendyAnn, wondered what happened to the two girls when they stopped posting suddenly. Then she told us about the news report from San Diego about two missing college students. We thought we'd put everyone at ease and asked Detective Cavanaugh, who is also a member, to look into it for us. We provided him with the names of the girls from the forum and he contacted the San Diego police. While we were waiting to hear back from them, my associate, Alex Wilson, found the news article from San Diego that revealed the murdered girls' names. That's when we knew that they were the ones from our forum." He huffed out a breath. "At about the same time, Alex noticed that some messages had been deleted from the forum. Thankfully, we had backups. When he restored the messages, we found Cadwallader's email exchanges with the girls. According to the timing of the missing persons reports, Cadwallader was probably the last person to see both of them alive."

He could see the gears turning as Zhou digested all of the data. She rubbed her hand over her eyes, then pinched the bridge of her nose.

"So you're suggesting that Cadwallader murdered those two girls? Why? What was his motive? And why didn't you contact the police?"

"We did, through James."

She nodded slightly.

"Well, at least we can verify that information anyway," she said. Raising her head, she looked at Riley. "You've certainly given me a lot to consider." She closed the laptop and began to rise. "I think we're done for now."

Half-rising from his chair, Riley pleaded, "Please, can you tell me how Evelyn is doing? And Kier. Is somebody with them?"

She stopped, one hand raised to knock on the door.

"The boy's at the hospital. I don't know his mother's condition. Child Protective Services is taking care of him." Zhou knocked and was let out of the room.

Riley subsided into his chair. Taking his head in his hands, he closed his eyes.

Where are Tessa and Alex?

* * *

As he left the hotel elevator with Detective Zhou, James noted that the lobby was quite a bit emptier than when they'd first come in. So empty that he easily spotted Tessa storming through the double doors that led in from the parking garage. He barely noticed Alex following in her wake like a dinghy behind a war ship.

Apparently Zhou sighted her too.

"Um, Detective Cavanaugh, I'll be on my way. MacPherson will probably beat me to the station as it is."

He looked down at her and said dryly, "I'm sure he would rather be here." Gesturing at Tessa bearing down on them with a glare that promised havoc, he continued, "And I think Tessa would rather have him here, too."

Grimacing, Zhou told him, "I'm sure she would. If you get any more information for me, please call." She fished her card out of her suit pocket and handed it to him.

Nodding her head to Tessa and Alex, she walked away, leaving Tessa, one hand raised, gaping after her.

Turning her glare on James, she spit out, "They arrested Riley! For Cadwallader's murder!"

He made a shushing movement with his hands. "I know. She got the call that Cad died while we were upstairs. Did you know he was sharing a room with Bryce?"

Tessa and Alex both gave him a confused look.

Alex surfaced first. "What? Bryce is here?"

James shrugged. "Claimed he was meeting a client from Greece. Thought he'd help an 'old family friend' out by letting Cad stay in his room." His fingers made air quotes around the phrase. "Bryce and I grew up together in Boston. I don't believe that he knew Cadwallader from there. I called him on it, but he didn't back down."

Tessa laid a hand on James' arm. "What's going to happen to Riley?"

"He'll be processed, given a jumpsuit to wear, then interrogated, probably by Zhou," he recited matter-of-factly.

"Jumpsuit?"

"They'll take his clothes into evidence."

She shook her head. "Poor Riley. Nothing like this has ever happened to him. I wish I could be there with him."

"I doubt they'd let you see him, even if you went to the station," James told her, hoping to calm her down. *Tessa looks like she wants to clobber someone. Hopefully not me. I'm just the messenger here.*

Apparently Alex agreed, saying, "Tessa, we don't even have a way to the station, unless we take a cab or rent a car. I don't know about you, but either option would strap me."

Tessa tilted her head, looking around the lobby.

"Where's Diana? I haven't seen her since this morning's panel."

"I've tried calling her. Repeatedly," Alex said, shaking his head. "It keeps going to voicemail."

James groaned and pulled out his phone, suddenly concerned for Diana. "Shit, I was going to call her and tell her you were in the garage with Riley. When I found out Bryce was here, I forgot all about that. Let me try her now."

His call was picked up on the second ring. A quavery voice answered, "Yes?"

"Diana. Where are you," James asked, relief and fear warring within him.

"In…in the bar."

"We'll be right there."

Steaming ahead of the other two, he was first into the bar. Her white dress with its red flower pattern almost glowed in the gloom. She looked up just as he reached her. Seeing the look on her face, he pulled her into a fierce hug, holding onto her until he could convince himself she was safe.

Coming up behind him, Tessa demanded, "Where have you been? We've been calling and calling." She shook her head. "You have no idea what's been going on."

James remained standing beside her while the other two took bar stools.

"I'm sorry." She shivered. "After this morning's sessions, I got into a conversation with HankT about design stuff. When he left, I went up to Evelyn's room, but no one was there."

Tessa fairly shook with suppressed anger. "That's because the police arrested Riley. Evelyn and Cadwallader were attacked in the garage. The police mistakenly think Riley was the one who assaulted them. Cad died on the way to the hospital, so they arrested Riley for his murder."

Diana held a fist to her mouth. "Oh, dear! Poor Riley!"

James reached for her hands. "He's safe. What happened to you? You're shaking." He slid his hands up to rub her arms. "It's chilly in here, but you act like you're freezing."

She shifted her focus to him. "When I couldn't find anyone," she let out a short sob, "I started downstairs to see if you all were in the dealers room." Diana took a ragged breath. "I was in the stairwell when I ran into Bryce." She started shaking again. "He shouted at me, then grabbed me. He seemed so upset, I was afraid he was going to throw me down the stairs."

Alarmed, James put an arm around her shoulders. She looked up at him gratefully.

After a moment, he asked, "What happened? What did you do."

She looked into his eyes, a tiny smile tugging at the corner of her lips. "I kneed him in the balls."

James heard Alex make the same sharp intake of breath he did at that pronouncement. "Ouch." He gave her shoulders a squeeze. "I'm proud of you, Diana. He deserved it."

Wait. She ran into him on the stairs? When did this happen? He said he'd just gotten up and was taking a shower when we arrived. Something doesn't add up. I was in Bryce's room not five minutes ago. How could she have run into him on the stairs and gotten to the bar in the time it took me to take the elevator down from the fifth floor?

"How long ago was this?"

She shook her head helplessly.

"I don't know. Sorry. Is it important?"

He looked away. "I don't know yet. We'll see."

"Diana?" Tessa said, concern lacing her voice. "Are you all right?" When she reached to touch Diana's arm, James could have sworn Tessa's eyes glowing. "There's blood on your arm. Did Bryce hurt you?"

"No, he only shook me. Blood?"

Confused, Diana peered down at her sleeve.

James rotated Diana on the stool until she faced him.

After a brief examination, he told her, "You have dried blood on your dress. On both sleeves." Pulling the fabric into her field of vision, he asked, "Is this where Bryce grabbed you?"

Diana nodded mutely.

Sucking in his lower lip, James considered a moment.

"I think Detective Zhou should see this. As soon as possible." He glanced at Tessa. "This just might help Riley."

Diana looked shocked. "You don't think he killed Cadwallader, do you?

"I don't know yet. It's possible." He shrugged. "Either way, we need to tell Zhou."

Alex spoke up for the first time in awhile.

"What about Kier? He went to the hospital in the ambulance with his mom. I tried to go with him, but the paramedics wouldn't let me."

"He's alone at the hospital?" Diana demanded. "Oh, the poor kid. Someone needs to go there, to be with him." She pulled her purse open, rummaging inside.

"Aha!" she said triumphantly, holding up her keys.

Handing them to Alex, she ordered him, "Take my car. Get down to the hospital. He shouldn't be alone right now. Not if his mom is hurt."

Alex grabbed the keys. "Good idea, Diana." He paused in mid-stride. "Wait. I'd better call Maeve and tell her what's going on too. Evelyn told me once that Maeve took care of Kier whenever she was out of town. He'll need someone to take care of him until his mom's home from the hospital."

James nodded. "Good idea, Alex." Looking around, he said, "The rest of us can take my car to the station."

Pulling out his phone and fishing in his pocket for Zhou's card, James punched in her number. "Detective Zhou? You've got the wrong man. I think I know who really killed Matthew Cadwallader."

CHAPTER ONE

Chapter 35

"She's in a coma. As far as we can tell, her only injury...."

The short Indian woman was talking quietly to Kier, next to a vast white gurney where Evelyn lay like a broken doll in a child's bed. The doctor stopped speaking as Alex entered.

Kier's face lit up when he spotted Alex. It pained him to see the boy's face change from gray despair to sunshine hope. *Damn! Why couldn't they have let me go along with him in the ambulance?*

"Alex!"

Kier broke away from the doctor, flying across the room to throw his arms around Alex. It took Alex a second to remember to embrace the boy, but it felt good, too. Like they'd somehow forged an instant bond.

Holding the boy away from him, he saw dried tear tracks on the boy's face. Alex asked, "How are you doing, kid?"

"F...fine," Kier said with a quaver in his voice. He turned his head to look at his mother. "She just won't wake up. I don't—"

The doctor's soft voice interrupted him.

"Kier, is this a family member?"

Kier gave Alex a tiny smile. "Yes, ma'am. He is."

"Well, then, shall I fill him in on what's happening?"

"Please?" said the boy.

"I'm Dr. Parvell. You are?" the woman asked as she held out her hand.

As Alex shook her tiny hand, he said, "I'm Alex Wilson." Glancing over her shoulder at Evelyn, he asked, "How is she?"

"As I was saying to the young man, Mrs. Sloan is in a coma. We've found some head trauma, probably caused when she fell. Other than that, there's nothing physically wrong with her. She's breathing on her own and her pupils react to light. We'll be running a CAT scan to determine why she isn't awake yet." She smiled gently at Kier. "He's welcome to stay here until we know more."

The harsh voice devoid of warmth came from the doorway, causing all three of them to turn.

"I'll decide that, doctor."

A short, heavy-set black woman strode into the hospital room, her severe red pantsuit and minimal jewelry proclaiming her no-nonsense attitude. *Oh, dear gods. She's one of those types. She believes she has to be harder than her male counterparts in order to succeed.*

"I'm from Child Protective Services. I'm here to take custody of Kier Sloan until his mother recovers."

The boy looked at her in horror. Alex placed a protective arm about his shoulders.

"What do you mean, custody?" Alex asked.

She looked at him like he was an idiot. "I mean," she said haughtily, "I'm here to remove him to our custody."

Alex protested. "You can't seriously be thinking of taking him away from his mother. He needs to stay with her, at least till she wakes up."

As the woman shook her head, Kier clutched at Alex's arm, blurting out, "Call Maeve! She'll straighten this out."

"Good idea," Alex said, laying a hand on top of Kier's. "Do you have her number?"

Kier did. Alex dialed her number, growing concerned as he listened to the ringing go on and on. His own spirits had begun to sag when a wary voice answered. "Maeve O'Malley here. To whom am I speaking?"

"Maeve, it's Alex Wilson. Riley's associate?"

Her voice warmed instantly. "Alex. Nice to hear your voice. What can I do for you?"

"I'm afraid I have some bad news. Evelyn's been in an accident." He heard her gasp. "She's in a coma and CPS is here at the hospital wanting to take Kier into custody." Alex saw the hope in Kier's eyes. "Can you help us?"

Maeve's voice took on the business tone she used in the office. "I most certainly can. Let me talk to this CPS person."

Alex handed his phone to the woman, who scowled at him before speaking.

"I'm Co—" she began. Her mouth hung open for a few seconds before closing. Then she started to nod. "I see…. Yes, of course…. You have legal cust—medical power of attor— Yes, I'll stay with him till you arrive." She handed the phone back to Alex. "She wants to speak to you."

"Maeve—" he began.

She cut him off. "Text me the hospital's address. I'll pack up Corky and our bikes. We should be there in an hour and a half. You just stay there and keep that woman from abducting Kier. You hear me?"

"Yes, ma'am. I sure will. You don't have to worry—"

"Gotta run. Text me the address." The line went dead.

Alex lowered the phone and looked at it a moment before turning to Kier.

"Maeve and Corky are on their way. An hour and a half, she said." The boy was almost in tears. Alex hugged the boy to him, murmuring, "It's going to be all right."

"I'll be back later, sir, ma'am," the doctor said, moving toward the door. Aiming a frown at the other woman, Dr. Parvell patted Alex's arm. "I'm glad the boy is in good hands."

Within moments, orderlies arrived to take Evelyn for her CAT scan.

Kier grabbed one of the orderlies' arm. "How long will the scan take?"

"We should have her back here in half an hour or so," the man said kindly.

"Come on, Kier," Alex coaxed as the two men wheeled Evelyn out. "Let's get you some food."

The boy's eyebrows rose.

"Food? I haven't eaten since breakfast but I'm not really hungry." He thought a moment, then shrugged. "I probably should eat something."

Alex laughed gently at him. "Now I *know* you're not doing well. To hear your mom tell it, you're always hungry." He pulled the boy close. "Don't worry, they'll take good care of her. You heard the doctor, there's barely a scratch on her. I'm sure she'll wake up soon."

The woman from CPS stood, clearly intending to follow them to the cafeteria.

Alex fixed her with an icy glare. "We're only going to the cafeteria and I doubt we need an escort." He scowled at the CPS lady. "That okay with you?"

Though her face was a study in disapproval, she nodded. "I'll stay right here until you return."

"You do that. Come on, Kier. First food, then I'll tell you what you missed."

The cafeteria had an amazing variety of dishes, from which Kier chose more than Alex thought was healthy. Still, he couldn't deny the boy anything he wanted right now. Thankfully for Alex's wallet, Kier had his own debit card to pay for the banquet.

Between bites, well, shovels really, of food, Kier told Alex about riding the ambulance to the hospital and waiting all alone for anyone to tell him what was happening to his mother. *It's not right to make a kid his age have to be alone at a time like that.*

Talking around a mouthful of chocolate cake, Kier said, "Some cops showed up here and asked me to tell them what happened with mom. I told them everything I knew, but I didn't see much. I...." Kier put his fork down. Alex thought the boy looked a little green. *Maybe he's eaten too much. Maybe I should have stopped him from getting so much food.*

Patiently, Alex waited for Kier to speak.

"It's my fault. I...made the garage dark. Before. When Cadwallader first attacked me."

"Made? How did you 'make' the garage dark?"

Kier swallowed and sat back, his dessert forgotten.

"I'm not sure how it works, but I've known I had magic for a couple of years now. It just sorta...showed up. I found I could shove things, like, with wind. I tried that with Cadwallader a couple of times. I knocked him all the way to the end of the garage. I only wanted him to stop, you know? When he didn't, I just, I don't know, pulled the electricity out of the lights and shoved it at him." His glum face brightened. "I zapped him good. But he got back up and was hurting me. That's when mom showed up. Cad attacked her too." His eyebrows went up. "But she's got magic like me. She started to glow, then threw fire at him. It was awesome."

Alex, trying to suppress his shock, asked, "Fire? Real flames? Didn't she burn herself?"

"No. She balled it up and threw it. Like a baseball."

"Whoa. Knowing how your mom feels about Cadwallader, I bet she enjoyed that." Alex loved seeing the smile that played across Kier's face as they both pictured Evelyn gleefully toasting Cadwallader like a marshmallow. Sobering, he continued, "Then what happened?"

Kier's face crumpled. "I ran." He looked shamefaced. "She told me to run. To get help. Then I found you and Riley and…. Well, you know the rest."

Alex rushed to reassure the boy.

"You just did what your mom told you to do. There's nothing to be ashamed of about that."

"But if I'd stayed…?"

"She sent you away for help and to keep you safe. It was her decision, not yours. You did the right thing."

"You sure? Maybe I could have—"

"No," Alex said firmly, shaking his head. "If you hadn't left to get help, it could have been both of you on the ground unconscious or dead. Cad would have gotten away without any of us knowing what happened." He saw the boy's head coming up. "You did the right thing, Kier."

"I guess," Kier sighed, reaching for his fork. He ate a few more bites, then said, "Wait a sec. Why didn't Riley come down here with you? Where's everybody else?" He frowned. "Don't they care about my mom?"

Alex bit his lower lip. "Um, Cadwallader died on the way here. The police think Riley killed him."

Kier's eyebrows vanished into the bangs spilling onto his face. "Riley killed Cad? He'd never—"

Waving the boy's protests aside, Alex said, "Yeah. I know that and you know that, but the police just deal with facts. I'm sure they'll come to their senses. Meanwhile, I'm here with you and the others are at the station, trying to help Riley."

Kier dropped his fork and pushed his plate away. Shaking his head wearily, he said, "This is all messed up." Then he turned to face Alex. "Can we go back upstairs? Mom's probably back by now."

"Sure. I think the cafeteria could use the chance to restock, now that you've cleaned them out."

In the hall, Alex pulled out his phone and called Tessa.

"Hey. Yeah, I'm here with Kier. Evelyn's stable, but unconscious. They're still running tests to figure out why. Maeve is on the way to be with Kier."

Alex took a deep breath, preparing himself for bad news. "What's the word on Riley?"

* * *

The barred metal door clanged shut behind Riley. He stood still for a moment, the realization of where he was and why threatening to overwhelm him.

This is really happening. I'm in jail. For murder! What am I going to do?

A deep, gruff voice spoke up, startling him.

"What are you in for?"

Riley looked up, taking in the small bare room and its lone occupant. On a bunk attached to the wall sat a large Hispanic man wearing the same white jumpsuit that the officers had given him when they'd taken his clothes away. The material felt like paper coated with plastic.

This feels so thin. Gods, I hope it doesn't rip. The stress of the whole situation caught up to him and he couldn't help but laugh at himself. *I've already been arrested on suspicion of murder, I don't need to add indecent exposure to my rap sheet.*

Riley realized his cell mate was staring at him waiting for an answer. *Cell mate. I have a cell mate. This is surreal.* He cleared his throat. "Ummm, murder?"

The man let out a low whistle. Shooting an eye at the guard walking past their cell, the man shook his head.

"Wow. You got me beat. I'm here because my wife and I got into an argument. I found out she was cheating on me so I grabbed her to get her to tell me who she was screwing. We struggled, her hand came down on the electric burner, and she got burned." He shrugged, raising his hands palms up. "She called the cops and here I am."

"Wow, that sucks," Riley said, sitting down on the other hanging bed. "At least your stove works. My girlfriend and I live in an old building in Oakland. Our cranky old gas stove's from the eighties. We have to use a match to light it 'cause the built-in lighter gave up the ghost years ago. The super just ignores our complaints."

"Yeah, just my luck. The stove's the only thing that works in my apartment." The big man stuck out his hand. "Dante Alvarez."

He took the man's hand.

"Riley MacPherson."

"So, murder?" He raised an eyebrow. "Who'd you kill?"

Riley flung himself down on the mattress, hands behind his head. "I didn't. They think I killed a guy named Matthew Cadwallader."

"Cadwallader, huh?" He paused a moment. "Now that's not a name you hear very often. You do it?"

Rearing up on the bed, Riley protested, "Hell, no! I picked up a flashlight that had his blood on it." He settled back, tension ebbing. "While I know a lot of people who didn't like him," he said pensively, "I have no idea who'd want to kill him."

"Well, I hope you get out of it."

Riley noticed the man was watching him carefully. *I'm probably the only entertainment this place has,* he thought ruefully. *I'm a therapist. Might as well get to know him.*

"So Dante, what do you do?"

The man got a sly, happy grin on his face.

"I blow shit up."

Riley felt his eyebrows travel up his forehead.

"Blow things up? As in bombs?"

The man laughed, a big booming sound that reverberated off the hard bare walls.

"Former marine special ops. Demolitions. These days, I bring down old buildings so new ones can go up in their place." He quirked an eyebrow. "You?"

Riley grinned with a wry twist of his mouth. "I'm a therapist. I talk to people about their problems."

"No shit? A shrink? Maybe if they say I need to see a shrink for my 'anger issues,' I can come see you, man." He chuckled good-naturedly.

Riley felt some of his tension ease as he joined the man in laughter.

"Well, these days I mostly do hypnotherapy. You know, quit smoking, lose weight, that sort of thing. I've been doing a lot of past life regressions, too."

"You believe in that shit?"

"I didn't originally, but lately—"

"Mr. MacPherson?"

Riley hadn't noticed Detective Zhou walk up to their cell.

323

Warily, he asked, "Yes, detective?"

"You'll be happy to know that your story checks out. We couldn't find any evidence on either your or Dr. Cadwallader's computers that you had been seeing him. Also, your friends showed up with some revealing evidence that points to someone else being responsible for the murder."

The guard unlocked the door and swung it open. Zhou motioned him out of the cell.

Riley rose, his jaw hanging loose as it dawned on him that he was being set free.

"Looks like you're getting out of here. Lucky you," said his cell mate. "Hopefully, my wife won't press charges so I can get out of here soon. It was an accident. I'm not a violent man."

One hand on the cell door, Riley looked back. "It was nice to meet you…?"

"Dante," the Hispanic man supplied.

"Right, sorry. Stress and lack of sleep are catching up to me. I'm usually much better with names."

"Yeah, I get that. I guess it's not every day you get accused of murder. That would throw off anybody's game."

Riley tossed a goodbye wave to Dante, then turned to Zhou. "So, who killed Cadwallader then?"

As they walked toward the exit, Detective Zhou said the last name Riley expected to hear. "We have an arrest warrant out for Bryce Lundee."

Riley stopped in his tracks. "Bryce? Bryce Lundee? Diana mentioned that Bryce knew Cad, but…. Wow."

They exited the holding cell area and passed through a sea of desks. All around them, officers were taking statements or hunkered down filling out forms on their computers.

She ushered him into the same interrogation room where he'd been questioned.

"Wait here. I'll have someone bring you your clothes." She shook her head. "Sorry, but we'll have to keep your jacket in evidence."

Half an hour later, Zhou escorted him through one last door out into the waiting room.

"Riley!" he heard, right before Tessa flew into his arms. *Damn,* he thought. *It feels so good to be back with her. It's only been a matter of hours, but it's like we've been separated for months. One of these days, I'm going to ask her to marry me.*

Zhou's voice interrupted their reunion.

"You're released, Mr. MacPherson, but please don't leave the area. You can pick up your car downstairs at the impound lot."

"By area, do you mean Santa Clara, or can I go home to Oakland?"

She gave him a thin smile. "Oakland will be fine." She rubbed at the bridge of her nose. "We're working with the Oakland PD, so it shouldn't be long before we have Mr. Lundee in custody."

"Detective, a moment of your time, please."

Riley had been so focused on Tessa that he hadn't noticed James and Diana behind her.

James continued, "If it's not too much trouble, could you keep me in the loop regarding Mr. Lundee's arrest? I'm concerned about Diana's safety with him on the loose. He's already hurt her once. I don't want to give him the chance to do it again."

The detective nodded. "I don't think that should be a problem, Detective Cavanaugh."

"Call me James," he said with a smile.

"Okay, James." She smiled back at him. "You can call me Lee."

"Lee?"

"It's short for Leslee. I use it because I get more respect when people see Lee and assume I'm a guy." She shrugged. "But that's the reality of this business."

James nodded. "Sad, but true. Thanks again, detective."

Coming down off the adrenaline that had kept him going so far, Riley half fell into a hard plastic chair.

"Looks like my friend is about to collapse," James said. "It's been a long night. I should probably get them home before they all crash. I'm used to pulling an all-nighter, but they aren't."

Tessa pulled Riley to his feet as James ushered them all out the door.

It feels good to let someone else take responsibility for everything for a change. I'm so tired of leading this expedition. Mission? Whatever it is, it's getting way too complicated for me. I just wanted to have fun playing at past lives with Tessa. How did I end up being mixed up in two girls getting killed in San Diego, Cadwallader's murder, and Evelyn in the hospital? Tears welled up in his eyes, threatening to spill over. *I wish I'd just left all this alone.*

As they made their way to the impound lot to retrieve their car, James filled Riley in on what had happened while he was in police custody.

"You won't believe this. After the police took you away, we found Diana in the bar. She'd had a run-in with Bryce on the hotel stairs. Tessa's the one who noticed the blood on Diana's dress." He shook his head. "I still don't know how the hell she saw the blood with the red patterns on that dress. I'm trained to notice these things and I completely missed it."

Diana chimed in, "Also, the police found a pillowcase was missing from one of the extra pillows in Bryce's room. He'd evidently used it to strangle Cadwallader before he hit him over the head."

"Zhou told me that she'd been suspicious of Bryce after the way he acted when she and I visited his room," James said. "She remembered that when she told Bryce that Cadwallader had been in an accident, he shrugged it off. He wasn't surprised at all. He didn't even ask what happened. She thought it was strange at the time, but then she found Cad's fake notes, and, well, you know what happened after that."

Tessa looked at Riley. He could see the worry in her eyes.

"Enough about all that. What happened to you, Riley? Are you all right?"

Riley sighed. "It wasn't that bad, actually. I spent most of the night answering questions in the interrogation room, wearing one of those thin paper jumpsuits. Then they put me in a cell with a guy who helped cheer me up by making jokes. He even told me he might look me up later...."

Chapter 36

"Your table is ready. Please follow—"

The hostess stopped, nimbly shifting her attention from the couple she'd been assisting, then hurried up to Thierry.

"Good evening, sir. Right this way."

"But we were here first," the man behind her complained.

"I'll be right with you, sir," she said over her shoulder.

As Thierry stepped past the dumbfounded couple, he gave them a look he usually reserved for an unwashed homeless person on the street. A small smile escaped Thierry's lips as he watched the man's face fall. Dismissing the couple from his consciousness, Thierry slid behind the large corner table. Within moments, his appetizer appeared.

For being only a three-star hotel, the waitstaff are very well trained.

He opened one of the files Jessica created and began to read. When the waiter arrived with his wine, Thierry's attention was drawn to the lobby beyond the restaurant's half walls. People were stopping and pulling back. He was startled to see several uniformed policemen stride through.

Beckoning to his waiter, Thierry demanded, "Why are there police marching through the lobby?"

The waiter raised his eyebrows.

"I'm sure it's nothing, sir. Could I get you some more wine?"

Thierry wasn't fooled by the waiter's ruse. The beads of perspiration that studded his normally reserved waiter's forehead told him all he needed to know. The man was lying.

Thierry waved the man away. Moments later, his sharp ears and suspicious mind caught a snippet of conversation between the waiters.

"...don't mention anything to Mr. LeRoux...murder in the

garage...."

Murder in the garage? Has Bryce finally completed his assignment? The real question is, did he put an end to Matthew for good, or is their rivalry going to start back up again in twenty years when Matthew comes of age? I sincerely hope the presence of the police does not indicate he botched the job. I do not wish to deal with covering up for his incompetence. Again. Thierry put his head in his hands, rubbing at his temples. *I do not need the headache of all the political maneuvering that would occur amongst the Sheitan if I have to select a new Area Captain for the West Coast. That is all I need on top of my current problem concerning my impending marriage to Renata. Plus, someone is still killing off the European Sheitan.*

He had pulled out his phone to call Latham when the waiter appeared with his main course. As soon as the waiter left, he stabbed the button.

"Latham. There is a commotion down here regarding the police and the garage. Look into it." He hung up.

Putting the matter out of his mind, he picked up his utensils and deftly sliced into his prime rib. He had just pushed his plate back when his phone vibrated.

"Sir. It would seem that Mr. Cadwallader was involved in an assault in the parking garage, along with Mrs. Sloan from the files Miss Coney provided you. I am told Mr. Cadwallader passed away en route to the hospital. The police are currently holding Mr. MacPherson for the murder."

"Excellent. Is there any mention of Bryce?"

"No, sir. Mr. MacPherson is the only suspect."

"Perfect. Keep me informed." He returned his phone to it's proper place in his jacket pocket while a waiter cleared his plate.

A tiny smile teased at his lips as his usual waiter promptly appeared to place his dessert in the recently vacated space.

Good news is like a delicious aperitif. What a lovely way to finish the meal.

The next afternoon, as Thierry was gathering up Jessica's files in preparation for leaving the hotel, he heard Latham clear his throat from the doorway.

"Sir, I hate to be the bearer of bad tidings, but I just received an update regarding the death of Mr. Cadwallader."

Annoyance colored Thierry's tone. "Yes?"

"It seems that there has been a new development in the case. According to my sources with the Santa Clara police department, they have evidence linking Mr. Lundee to the murder. They have released Mr. MacPherson and issued an arrest warrant for Mr. Lundee."

Thierry felt cold fire flaring up within him.

Damn the man! He has had centuries of practice, so how the hell did he manage to screw this up?

Shaking his head, he clamped down on his temper. Snatching up his cell phone from the table, he dialed furiously.

Thierry didn't even give the man a moment to speak. As soon as the call picked up, he shouted, "What the hell were you thinking? Two dead bodies? I distinctly told you not to do anything that could be tied back to us. And yet, there is a warrant out for your arrest. Leave. Get out of the country before they find you. Now!"

"Warrant? How—"

Thierry heard a loud pounding coming through the connection.

"This is the Oakland police. We have a warrant for the arrest of Bryce Lundee. Open up or we will be forced to break the door down."

Thierry heard a crash and rushing footsteps, then the connection went dead.

Thierry shook his head. "Latham."

"Sir?"

"Begin the process to remove all mention of Bryce Lundee from the company. Have our contacts erase any connection between him and LeRoux WorldWide."

"Yes, sir. Ummm...."

Thierry eyed the man in annoyance. "Is there something you wish to say, Latham?"

Seldom had Thierry seen his aide uncomfortable. When he didn't immediately answer, Thierry became impatient.

"Out with it, man. I do not have time for dissembling."

"Please excuse me, sir, but I'm afraid I need to clear something up. Mr. Cadwallader is indeed dead, but Mrs. Sloan, the other assault victim, is still alive, although she is in a coma."

Thierry's face screwed up in a mask of disapproval. "See that you are more precise in your reports in the future."

"Certainly, sir."

The man turned stiffly, striding toward his bedroom. Thierry heard the musical tones of the man's cell phone, then, "No, Mr. Leroux is busy. I'm afraid...What? You did? One moment."

Latham strode briskly into the room until he stood in front of Thierry.

Handing over the phone, he explained, "Sir, I have a call from headquarters that has been routed to me through the Sheitan network. One of our local operatives has some information I believe may be of interest regarding the current situation.

Still annoyed by Latham's incompetence, Thierry scowled at him, then took the phone.

"And who is this?"

Thierry heard the deep authoritative voice respond, "I'm Dante Alvarez, sir. Normally I report to Mr. Cadwallader, but since he's dead, I didn't know who else to call."

"How can you be aware of Mr. Cadwallader's death already?" Thierry asked suspiciously. "It only happened yesterday."

"That's the thing, sir. I was in the same jail cell as the man they originally arrested for his murder. I was in on a bum rap. My damn woman mouthed off and I had to show her who was boss. She called the cops on me. You know how women are."

"Get to the point, Mr. Alvarez."

"Sorry. Anyway, this guy, MacPherson, said they had arrested him for killing Cadwallader. I couldn't believe my ears. Cadwallader dead?" The man paused briefly, letting out a low whistle. "When they let him go, this female cop said they had evidence that Bryce Lundee had killed Cadwallader. I overheard her tell him that the police were on their way to arrest him. I didn't know how to get in contact with Bryce, so I called the main office and used the Sheitan codes to get through to you. I know how important it is to keep our organization secret."

Thierry raised his head, spearing Latham with look. Then he mouthed, 'Get me all the information you can on Dante Alvarez.' Latham turned and headed for his bedroom and his computer.

While he waited impatiently for Latham to access the information, Thierry let Alvarez prattle on about his situation.

Why can I not have competent people working for me? It has been millenia, you would think they would be more cultured. But no, they all seem to prefer acting like the savages we found when we first came here.

Latham returned with his tablet.

Taking it and glancing through the dossier, Thierry smiled.

What perfect timing. You have no idea, Mr. Alvarez, but you could be the solution to my current problems.

Interrupting the man's rambling, Thierry said, "Mr. Alvarez, I have a job for you, one that utilizes your unique skills. I want you to find the man who shared your cell. Then I want you to kill him and his girlfriend. Make sure you kill them both."

The silence on the other end of the line stretched out so much that Thierry began to wonder if the call had disconnected. Then he heard a deep, throaty chuckle.

"Well, I did tell Riley that I'd look him up when I got out of jail. Guess it'll be sooner than either of us suspected."

* * *

"What did you pack in here, bricks? I don't know how Kier got this in the car without help," Riley said as he grabbed the second of Tessa's suitcases out of the car.

"That's the suitcase that has all my chainmail-making stuff in it."

Riley hoisted the offending bag to the curb, joining the quartet already there. He was about to slam the hatch when his phone went off. Digging the phone out of his pants pocket, he muttered, "I miss my jacket. Dammit! Why'd the police have to keep it, anyway?" Tessa's laughter pealed out from the sidewalk.

She giggled. "So, you would have worn a bloody jacket home?"

He shot her a dirty look, earning another round of laughter, and answered the phone.

Riley sobered. "Hey, James. Any news?"

"Yup. The Oakland police arrested Bryce and took him into custody. At his house."

"So, it's over?" Riley said hopefully.

"Well," James said thoughtfully, "maybe for you. Santa Clara PD has your statement. With all the physical evidence, I doubt you'd be called for the trial. Diana, maybe, but not you."

"I'll bet Diana is relieved."

James laughed. "You have no idea. We got the news just before I dropped her off at her place. Alex is still at the hospital. He insisted on staying with Kier, even after his guardian showed up."

"That's Maeve O'Malley. She's his mom's receptionist and Kier's unofficial grandmother." Riley smiled at the thought of anyone calling Maeve 'grandmother.' That would probably get them hit with her purse.

"Does this mean I'm off the hook with Detective Zhou?"

James sounded amused. "I wouldn't go that far. Not yet, anyway."

"Thanks for the call, James. We finally made it home. The traffic was horrible. We're just unloading the car now."

"You don't have to tell me about the traffic. I'm still stuck in it, trying to get home to San Francisco. I'm eternally grateful my houseboat is close to the station."

"Then I'll let you go. I'm getting speed-it-up gestures from Tessa."

As he hung up, Tessa grabbed a couple of bags and set off for the door. Riley let out a heavy sigh when he noticed she'd left the chainmail bag for him.

Later, as they were unpacking, he paused, a handful of dirty socks held absently in his hands.

"Tessa?"

The concerned look on her face when she looked up made him realize just how dispirited he must have sounded.

"Honey, what's wrong?"

He flung the socks toward the hamper, then sat down heavily on the edge of the bed.

"How do I go on now? Can I ever get back to normal? Whatever that is. I mean," he said, pulling her into his arms, "how do I put getting charged for murder into the past? And what about the Xerians and the board? What do I tell them?"

She huffed a laugh into his hair. "You'll be fine, sweetie. You just need to take it one step at a time." She hugged him tighter. "I have faith in you, even when you don't."

Riley felt his eyes begin to burn.

What did I ever do to rate such a wonderful woman?

He sighed. "I know. You're right. It's just——"

"It's just that there are so many others involved in this whole mess and you're taking all their problems on your own shoulders." She pulled back and looked him in the eye. "I have an idea. Let's get everyone together and work this out."

He thought a moment, then nodded.

"You're right. We haven't had time to process everything as a group. We've been too spread out." He felt like a weight had been lifted from his shoulders. "I'll call and see if we can meet tomorrow, after everyone gets settled."

He kissed her then, a long, sweet kiss that promised more, many more, to come.

"You know," Tessa said, drawing back, "we don't have to unpack right this second."

Chapter 37

"You look tired, Maeve," Riley said as he entered the office.

Maeve looked up and gave him a smaller-than-usual greeting smile.

"If you were in my shoes, you'd be tired too." She abandoned the notepad she'd been using and folded her arms across her chest. "We didn't get back to Berkeley till after midnight. This morning, I started calling Evelyn's clients to let them know she will be unavailable indefinitely. Thankfully, the other tenants here have offered to pick up some of her clients, at least for the time being. We're all hoping that Evelyn comes out of her coma and gets back to work soon."

"I couldn't agree more," Riley said. "Getting everyone here to take care of her clients is a good idea too. I could pick up a few of them, if needed. I'd be happy to help out." He sat down in one of the chairs across from Maeve's desk. "How's Kier holding up?"

"That poor boy. He's not taking this well. Oh, he tries to put on a good face, but it's his *mother* in a coma. He was only five when she adopted him, but he remembers his life before that. I'm sure he's feeling like that abandoned child again, wondering what'll happen to him without her."

Riley nodded his agreement. "That's gotta be hard on the kid. But," he said, pointing a finger at Maeve, "you know how resilient kids are in general and how well adjusted Kier is. He'll be okay, especially with all of us here for support."

That earned him a tired smile from Maeve.

"You're right. Perhaps I'm worrying too much. But then, that's my job, to take care of Evelyn and Kier." Her face sobered. "I just didn't think I'd be caring for Kier all by myself. He's a teenager. Corky and I…

we're senior citizens. It's one thing to babysit, but quite another to take full responsibility for him."

"Ah, you beat me in," came a voice from the doorway.

Alex plopped into the seat next to Riley.

"So, what's on the agenda, boss?"

Riley laughed in his face.

"You think *I* know what's going on? Right now, Maeve is in charge and we do what she says."

"Gee, thanks, Riley," Maeve said sourly. Squaring her shoulders, she ripped a couple of pages out of her notebook, rose and handed one to each of the men. "Riley, take this sheet. Alex, here's one for you too. You can use my desk. Call these clients, tell them the situation, and have them call me this week to make appointments with another therapist in our building."

She pulled a sweater off the back of her chair and folded it over her arm.

"I'm driving Kier to Santa Clara. We're arranging to move Evelyn to a facility up here for treatment and Kier wants to ride along." She rubbed at her forehead, then took her purse from one of the desk drawers. "We'd rather have her here in Berkeley than trying to drive Kier down there every day." She gave them a weak smile. "He decided this morning that he was going to read the Hobbit to her."

Both men chuckled.

"That sounds like Kier," Alex said.

Riley put in, "Yeah. I think she'll enjoy that. It'll keep her mind busy trying to psychoanalyze the characters."

Maeve laughed outright. "You're right, she would. Okay then, I'm off. We'll be back this afternoon in time for your meeting. For now, you're in charge." With that, she was gone.

Alex got a lopsided grin on his face. "Well, that's another thing you're in charge of. I hope our little get-together this afternoon helps us untangle this mess. You need to relax and let us help with this burden you're carrying. You aren't going to do anyone any good if you burn yourself out."

Riley smiled ruefully. "You're right. Tessa said the same thing. Well," he said, rubbing at the tightness in his neck, "we'll see this afternoon, won't we."

* * *

Riley groaned with pleasure as Tessa massaged this neck and shoulders. He glanced up as Alex entered the office and deposited himself next to Diana on the couch.

Alex took in the way Diana was curled on the couch, asking, "How can you curl up like that and still work on your laptop?"

Looking down at herself, she shrugged. "I just do. I've curled my legs under me since I was a kid. You mean you can't?"

Alex chuckled at the idea. "Only if you move a chiropractor in with us–permanently."

"Sorry I'm late," James said from the open door. "You wouldn't believe the paperwork that piled up while I was in Santa Clara."

"That's okay. Maeve and Kier are still en route," Riley told him. "It'll be a few minutes before they get here."

He watched as James covetously eyed the end of the couch Alex was occupying. Alex was completely oblivious to the look he was getting until James cleared his throat.

"Oh." Alex said, jumping up from the sofa. "Guess I'd better move or the cop will arrest me for loitering next to his girlfriend."

The room filled with laughter as Diana blushed and James glowered at Alex, hands on his hips.

"Come on, do you really think it's a secret?" Alex said. "You two have been making googly eyes at each other since the first day of the con. I thought I was going to have to get a new room or risk walking in on something."

Diana shot daggers at Alex, who raised his hands in surrender.

"Okay, okay. I'll shut up," he said, relocating to another seat.

"You'd better," she said darkly.

"What'd we miss?"

Kier pushed through the waiting room door. Behind him, Riley could hear Maeve still on the stairs. *The kid looks tired,* he thought. *Wow. I don't think I've ever seen him less than bouncing with excess energy. Must be hard, seeing his mom like that.*

"Nothing," Tessa said, coming around the corner of the desk. "Just Alex and James fighting over who gets to sit next to Diana."

"Oh, that," Kier said with a wave of his hand. "I think Alex lost that fight a long time ago." He thought a moment. "Friday, I think. Besides," the boy said, pointing at Alex, "he prefers guys."

336

Alex rounded on the boy. "One, I like guys *and* girls. Two, how the hell do you know that?"

Kier smiled impishly. "Mom told me. She overheard you flirting with Riley one day. She said she thought you had a crush on him."

Alex's face turned scarlet. He stammered, "I didn't…. I just like teasing…. I think I should just quit while I'm behind." He hung his head.

"Whose behind, Alex?" Tessa teased with a grin. "Just remember, Riley's mine."

Motioning to Diana, Alex pleaded, "Can I borrow your laptop? There's something I need to research right away. Like, how to make myself disappear."

Riley cleared his throat. "Ahem. Moving right along. Maeve. Hi!"

Maeve gave Riley a look, then advanced on him. "Up, son. My desk."

Riley sprang up, offering Maeve her chair with a flourish of his arms. "Yes, ma'am. Of course, ma'am."

She swatted playfully at him. "Don't you 'ma'am' me, you whippersnapper." While everyone laughed, she took her seat and put her purse away.

Sitting back up, she clasped her hands on the desk. Singling out Riley and Alex, she demanded, "So, boys, did you get your homework done while I was gone?"

Riley and Alex looked at each other, then both of them stood and came to attention before her desk. In unison, they saluted her.

"Yes, ma'am! Of course, ma'am!"

Her mock stern face broke into a smile. "That's better." She made a shooing motion with both hands. "Return to your seats."

Kier had a big grin on his face.

"That's just the way she treats me. And Corky, sometimes." His face became solemn. "Mom's being moved up here tomorrow. By ambulance. I wanted to be with her, but they said she'd be safe, so I'll be there to meet her when she arrives."

Diana rose and rushed to hug Kier

"You're not alone in this," she said. "We're all here whenever you need us." She looked around at the others. "Right, guys?"

Riley spoke up before anyone else could. "I think I speak for all of us when I say that we care about you, Kier, and we are here for you if you need anything at all. You and Evelyn have become like family over the last few months." Riley watched as Kier looked around the room. He saw the effort the boy was making as he stood straighter and pulled out of his slumped pose.

With barely a quaver in his voice, Kier said, "I know. Thanks, everyone."

He's had enough problems for one day. Let's give the kid some space. Riley pulled a chair over to Maeve's desk and motioned for them all to sit down.

"Ok, everyone, now that that's settled, shall we get down to business? We've had an eventful few days, I think you'd agree."

Maeve snorted. "Eventful? Catastrophic, I'd say. Not only is my Evelyn in a coma, but I learn that you all are people from another planet."

Riley piped up, "For the record, not all of us are. I'm human like you."

She nodded. "I have to say, I didn't believe it when Kier told me, but after he shorted out the engine in my car, I had to believe him." She glanced sourly at Kier. "Thankfully, I had jumper cables and a gentleman at the hospital was nice enough to help us or we would still be there."

Kier squirmed in his chair. "I said I was sorry." Looking at Riley, he continued, "I was just trying to show her that I could make the electricity jump from the battery to my hand. I didn't mean to ground the battery out."

James shook his head in disbelief.

"Kid, you're lucky you weren't electrocuted."

Kier ducked his head. "Yeah, I know. Working with electricity is still new to me." He raised his head. "I'll get better, though, with practice."

Tessa jumped into the conversation.

"No, Kier, not by yourself. It's too dangerous for you to experiment without adult supervision."

Muttering to himself, Kier said, "I've got more experience working with magic than any of you. Why do I need adult supervision all of a sudden?"

Maeve spoke up. "Because your mother trusted me to take care of you if anything happened to her, and I will *not* have her wake up and have to tell her you've electrocuted yourself. On. My. Watch."

Ducking his head, Kier capitulated. "Okay, I give up. I'll only experiment when there's an adult around. Satisfied?"

Maeve eyed him warily, but finally nodded.

"Now that that's settled," Riley said, "let's discuss what we know."

"Well, for one," Tessa began, "we know that at least two Sheitan were at the convention with us. Cadwallader and Bryce."

"Yeah, but both of them are out of the picture now. Cad's dead and Bryce is in jail," James said, leaning his elbows on his knees. "And I doubt he'll be getting out anytime soon."

"There *was* another Sheitan at the convention," Alex interrupted. "With everything that happened, I forgot to tell you guys."

The sudden silence was deafening.

Alex licked his lips.

"It was between the memorial and the mass regression. I'd been keeping an eye on Cad during the memorial since everyone else was too scared to sit next to him. I followed him out of the room to make sure nobody went off alone with him." Alex paused, looking around at the others. "He was talking to one of the older Xerians, a Klymurian." Alex snapped his fingers. "Meeker, that was his name. I overheard him tell Cad that they hadn't seen each other in eighty years." Alex shook his head. "There's no way that either of them could be old enough for that, unless they were talking about a different lifetime."

"Wait a minute," Tessa said. "The Sheitan remember their past lives? Then they probably remember everything about Xeres too. It sounds like they don't forget like we do. That can't be good."

Alex continued. "That's not all I overheard. They talked about another Sheitan, called him their boss. A funny, foreign-sounding name. Let me think. Thierry...Roux, no, LeRoux. That's it." He looked around at them all. "That name ring a bell for anyone?"

"Not for me," James offered, "but I can find out who he is easy enough."

As he pulled out his phone and moved to rise, Alex grabbed Diana's laptop.

"I'll find him." He looked up at the others and shrugged. "It's what I do." A few minutes later, he looked up, his eyes wide.

James, reading over his shoulder, whistled. "Damn, that dude's seriously rich."

"You can say that again," Alex said, turning the screen around so they could all see a picture of the man. "He's the CEO of LeRoux Worldwide, one of the biggest holding companies in the world."

Riley felt his eyebrows rise. "He's the leader of the Sheitan?"

James locked eyes with Riley. "We're screwed."

It was several moments before anyone spoke.

"Why?" Kier asked, breaking the silence. "I mean, why would he be dangerous to us? To mom?"

Maeve looked at the boy. "Honey, someone with that kind of power and influence could have us erased without breaking a sweat."

"Does he even know we exist though?" Diana ventured.

Riley felt sick to his stomach at the news. "It's a pretty good bet he does. Between Cad's death and Bryce's arrest, if he didn't know about us before, he most certainly does now. I think we all need to lay low for awhile. Hopefully, it'll all blow over and we can go back to our normal lives."

Alex was shaking his head. "We have to warn the other Xerians, the ones on the forum. What happened to those two girls could happen to more of them."

James eyed Diana, then nodded. "You could come home with me. It'd be safer."

She laughed. "I don't need a knight in shining armor to rescue me."

"But," James protested, "you could be in danger."

"And I could get hit by a car when I leave here tonight. I've lived in fear for too many years with Bryce, and I refuse to do so anymore."

James held his hands up. "Okay, okay. I get the picture. Just know that I want to keep you safe and I'm here if you need me."

Diana reached out and patted his arm. "I know, Jimmy B. I know."

Kier's stomach growled. He blushed. "Sorry. Maeve and I didn't have time for lunch."

Maeve glared at him. "And whose fault is that, young man? Maybe the boy who shorted out the battery causing us to waste a half hour getting a jump start?"

"Fine. It's my fault. I'm still hungry!"

Tessa snickered. "From everything I've seen, you're always hungry." She looked around at the gathered friends. "But I'm getting hungry too. How about we all head back to our place and I'll fix up

340

enough spaghetti and meatballs to feed an army."

General agreement broke out.

After conferring with Tessa, Riley turned to Diana. "Can you take Alex and James and run by the store? We have everything we need for the spaghetti, but some garlic bread and a salad would be nice to go with it."

Diana agreed, but asked, "What about Kier and Maeve?"

They all turned to Maeve.

"I still have some work to do here tonight," she said, shaking her head. "Besides, Corky's fixing ribs tonight."

Kier wrinkled up his nose. "Maeve, you know I don't like barbeque. I'd rather have spaghetti. Can't I go with Riley? Pleeease?"

Maeve queried Riley with a raised eyebrow. He smiled at her and nodded.

"Well, go on then. Riley'll have to bring you home, though."

"Great," the boy said, bouncing on the balls of his feet. "Can we go now?"

Riley laughed. "From the sound of his stomach, he's about to starve. I think we'd better hurry."

The trip to Riley and Tessa's apartment was punctuated by Kier's eager questions about the type of meatballs they had and whether or not they made their sauce from scratch.

As they approached their door, Kier continued his interrogation. "What about dessert? More of those great cookies you make?"

As she unlocked the door, Tessa said, "Sure. There's some in the ___"

Riley had started to push past her through the half-opened doorway when she blocked his path.

"Wha—" he said, looking into her upturned face.

What the hell? Her eyes! They're glowing. They're shining with purple light.

Before he could ask any questions, she shoved him back, grabbed Kier and pushed them all back towards the stairs.

"Run! We've got to get out of here. Now!" Tessa screamed.

Instinct took over. Riley snatched Kier up, sweeping the boy off his feet and into his arms, barrelling down the hallway and through the doorway to the stairs with Tessa hot on his heels.

BOOM!

Chapter 38

"My babies!" Tessa screamed, scrambling over Riley and Kier. Both of them made a grab for her, but she shook them off, rushing back the way they'd come.

She found their apartment door lying in charred pieces all over hallway. Flames reached out for her from the door frame, making it impossible for her to enter without setting herself on fire. The sprinklers had activated, but they barely made a dent in the flames filling the apartment.

Kier rushed up beside her. "Here, let me help."

He raised his hands and made a shoving motion.

It seemed to Tessa that a great wind erupted from Kier, forcing a curtain of water and smoke across the living room. She watched in astonishment as Kier used more wind to direct the spray from the sprinkler heads to put out the fires.

"Tessa? Your eyes are glowing."

Tessa turned to face Riley. She had been so consumed with concern for her precious snakes that she'd completely forgotten he was there.

Raising a hand to her face, Tessa touched her temples. "My eyes are tingling. I thought it was just the smoke."

"Let's worry about finding Calvin and Meg first. We can talk later."

Kier yelped, "Tessa, help! I can't contain the fire. I'm not strong enough." Tears were running down his face, lines of strain scoring his cheeks.

Kier went down on one knee, hands planted on either side to stabilize himself. His supernatural wind, previously directing the sprinkler water, died.

Raising her own hands, Tessa felt something well up inside her. *I could see him moving the wind. How could I do that?* She reached out with her awareness. *I can feel the water too.* Instinctively, she reached out and gathered up the falling water, directing it like a fire hose. In a matter of seconds, she had drowned all the remaining fires.

As she lowered her hands, she gazed, stupefied, around what had once been her living room and kitchen. The back wall of the kitchen was gone, along with much of the side wall into the next apartment. The furniture was charred or in ashes. Their sofa, still smoking, lay against the near wall.

It's all too much, she thought, tears running down her cheeks.

Then she remembered her snakes. *Meg! Calvin!*

Dashing through the living room, she passed the bathroom. The wall closest to the kitchen had been reduced to rubble, but the wall shared with the office remained intact. Her heart soared. *Maybe the snake cages survived. Maybe....* She couldn't allow herself to think of the alternative.

Rounding the door frame into the office, she jerked to a stop at its almost-normal appearance. Riley's desk was just as cluttered as always. The small window had shattered outward. The only things out of place were the books scattered across the floor.

Fear clutched her throat. She turned toward the closet. She felt Riley come up behind her, but couldn't spare him any attention. Stepping carefully across the book-strewn floor, she shoved at the closet door.

The bifold door refused to open. *It's off the track and wedged shut,* she thought with dismay as she began to wrestle with it. *Come on, move, damn you.*

Holding her breath, she pulled one final time, wrenching it away.

Inside, a shelf had fallen across the top of the cages, but she could see that both were intact. *The plexiglass held!* she rejoiced.

Riley squeezed past her. "I'll hold the shelf up. Grab Meg and Calvin."

Tessa reached inside and gathered up the traumatized snakes. Placing Meg around her own neck, she gently wrapped Calvin around Riley's.

"I'll get something to put them in," she said.

Dashing out into the hall, Tessa grabbed two pillowcases from the linen closet.

She lifted Calvin from Riley's shoulders and deftly slid him into the first one. Handing the second one to Riley, she unwound Meg from her shoulders and slipped her into the open mouth of his pillowcase. They hastily tied knots in the open ends to prevent either snake from escaping.

Kier called from the living room, "Are they all right?" He looked over his shoulder toward the devastation that used to be her kitchen. "All the fires are out, but there's still a flame in the kitchen. I've been trying to put it out, but can't."

Riley rushed past the boy, scanning the kitchen.

"Don't put that one out, Kier. That's the gas pipe. It's acting like a pilot light right now. If it goes out, we could have another explosion."

"Oh," Kier said in a very small voice.

Tessa came up beside the boy.

"It's not safe here. Think you could take care of my babies while we rescue some of our things?"

As she'd hoped, Kier's fascination with the snakes distracted him from the near catastrophe.

Minutes later, as they were struggling out the ruined doorframe with their luggage, James, arms weighed down with grocery bags, cleared the stairwell.

"What the hell happened here?"

"Our apartment blew up!" Tessa shouted. "I felt something was wrong when I opened the door. Things were out of place." She shook her head. "I just knew we were in danger. I practically threw Riley and Kier back into the stairwell."

James dropped his bags and strode quickly toward the empty doorframe. He brushed past Tessa and entered the apartment, saying, "Let me take a look around. Where are your neighbors? You'd think this kind of thing would attract some attention."

"This time of day, I'm usually the only one in the building. Everyone else is at work," Tessa said.

Hearing a noise at the stairwell behind her, Tessa turned to see Alex stumble over the bags James had dropped. He would have fallen if Diana hadn't caught his arm.

"Oh, my," Diana gasped as she took in the scene.

Alex stood there a moment, his eyes widening.

Rushing to Riley, Tessa, and Kier, he demanded, "Are you guys all right?" He glanced at the boy. "Kier?"

When Kier nodded, Alex looked around at all the suitcases and bags they were holding.

"Where are you going?" he asked.

"I thought it best," she said, looking over her shoulder at the ruined apartment, "to pack a few things before the firemen showed up and doused everything with their hoses."

"I have the snakes," Kier said, holding up the weighted pillowcases.

James emerged from the apartment and grabbed Tessa's arm, pulling her and Riley back inside.

"Did you leave a lot of stuff on top of the stove? Pots and pans, that kind of thing?" he asked.

Bewildered at the question, Tessa blinked, peering into the kitchen. "No, I keep them hanging on the wall. Why?"

"Look at the ceiling, Tessa."

Tessa gazed upward. Arrayed across the ceiling and along the walls were her pots, pans and skillets embedded in the plaster, most of them crumpled and twisted beyond recognition.

"How is that possible?" Riley said.

Glancing around, James replied, "It isn't, if they were hanging on the wall. But if they were placed on the stove to become projectiles, they'd look like that."

Placed? Someone placed them on the stove? Who? Why? Then it dawned on her. *Someone tried to kill us! Was that why I felt something was wrong when I opened the door?*

She felt Riley put an arm around her shoulder, only then realizing she was shaking.

James voice was soothing, almost enough to calm her.

"It looks like someone rigged the stove to explode when you opened the door. They probably turned the oven and gas burners on, but didn't light them. Then they rigged a wire or string to strike a spark and set off the gas that had filled the apartment. My guess is, the gas wasn't on long enough to spread throughout the entire apartment, or this whole side of the building would have collapsed."

That did nothing to calm Tessa's nerves. Quite the opposite. She felt an icy calm descend upon her, falling to near absolute zero. *Whoever set an assassin against me and mine is going to pay for this.*

James was looking at her strangely. Riley hastily pulled his arm off her shoulders.

"Tessa?" Riley queried, his breath pluming in the sudden chill. "Calm down. Your eyes are glowing again and you're ice cold. Think, Tessa. There's no enemy here for you to direct your energy at. Save it till we find out who did this."

From outside, she could hear the sound of sirens rapidly approaching.

Tessa wrenched herself out of the swirling maelstrom of her thoughts. Blinking up at Riley, she nodded shortly.

"You're right. Later," she said grimly.

"We need to get out of here," James said urgently. "We can't be here when the fire trucks arrive. If someone's trying to kill you, standing around talking to the police and fire department will make us sitting ducks."

Suiting his actions to his words, James shepherded them into the hallway. Gathering up the rest of their group, he drove them down the stairs and out of the building.

They barely made it to their assorted vehicles before the fire trucks began to arrive.

Tessa, sitting in the passenger seat, distractedly noticed a very expensive car parked directly across from their building, looking very out of place.

I feel sorry for whoever owns that, she thought. *In this neighborhood, a nice car like that is begging to get broken into.*

* * *

James grabbed Alex before he could put his key in the door. "What—"

"Your place could be boobytrapped too. Everyone, move away from the door. Let me check things out before we all go in."

Behind James, Tessa spoke up.

"I'm going in with you." When James started to protest, she shushed him.

"Who do you think detected the last trap? Let me help."

James took a deep breath, then exhaled. "All right. Just be careful not to touch anything, okay?"

346

Taking Alex's keys, James unlocked the door and inched it open. When nothing happened, he gently swung it open and he and Tessa entered.

Moments later, Tessa poked her head out.

"All clear."

Diana was first in.

"I don't have enough spaghetti for everyone, but I can do macaroni and cheese, if that's ok?"

Kier stepped up beside her.

"Right on. Can I help? I know how to fix that."

Diana laughed at his enthusiasm, but was familiar enough with his appetite to understand.

She turned toward the kitchen. "Sure. Come on."

Alex placed the cloth shopping bags on the dining table and began emptying them, careful not to set anything down on the lumpy pillowcases containing Tessa's snakes. Meanwhile Riley, Tessa, and James were conferring in the living room. He called over to them, "Hey, don't start without me."

Hanging the now-empty bags on a chair back, he walked over in time to hear Tessa say, "…we have to leave the country."

"What? Why?" Alex protested.

Riley turned to catch Alex up on their conversation.

"If we're right that the person after us is this Thierry LeRoux guy, we need to disappear. If we stick around, we're liable to end up dead."

James let out a heavy sigh. "It's not just you two that are in danger. We have no idea how much this Thierry person knows. None of us could be safe."

Kier's head popped around the corner from the kitchen.

"You mean my mom's not safe either?"

James glanced up at the young man, a sad look crossing his face. "Probably not, kiddo."

"Then it's a good thing we're moving her up here tomorrow. I'll protect her." He got such a look of fierce determination on his face that they all smiled.

"I think," James began, "I'll have a talk with the Oakland police. Just in case you need some help. You have to sleep sometime."

Kier nodded. "Okay."

From the kitchen, Diana called, "Hey, get back here. You said you were helping me."

Kier ducked back into the kitchen.

Alex turned back to Riley and Tessa. They were sitting on the futon, whispering, with their heads together.

"…can't leave the country," Riley said, exasperation coming off the man in waves. "I don't have a passport. I don't even know how to go about getting one."

Alex shook his head. "Dude, how can you not have a passport? After 9/11, you need one just to go to Canada."

Alex went to his computer and began researching. Moments later, he swung his chair around, putting his hands behind his head and leaning back.

"You can apply for the passport online. Then you chose how soon you want it. Standard processing is four to six weeks. Or you can pay an extra sixty bucks to expedite it. That cuts the time down to two to three weeks. You can bring that down to five days if you go to an office in person and have a pressing need. And they tack on a twenty-five dollar execution fee." He made a face. "Execution fee? I really don't want to think about executions right now. Anyway, that brings the total to a hundred and ninety-five dollars." He made a motion like he was wiping sweat from his brow. "Phew! Kinda pricey for a little blue book of blank pages."

"Don't you need to send in a copy of your birth certificate?" Tessa asked. "I've had my passport for awhile now, but thankfully, they're good for ten years."

Alex shook his head. "Nope, you have to send the original, not a copy. Plus you need a copy of your driver's licence and have proper photos when you go in."

"I don't have my birth certificate. My parents have it. In Wisconsin. It'd take a week just to get them to send it to us."

"Well, Riley," Alex said glancing back at his screen, "you could go there and pick it up. There are local passport offices in Minneapolis and Chicago."

Tessa brightened. "I guess this means you're finally taking me home to meet your parents?"

Riley smiled ruefully.

"I'd hoped it would be under more pleasant circumstances. Like, our engagement."

Tessa's eyes widened. "Engagement?"

He ducked his head. "Um, um, that is, whenever we decided to...."

As Riley's face turned red, the others laughed.

"I know what you mean, Riley," Tessa said, letting him off the hook.

"But how can we afford it?" Riley protested. "Going out of the country, even for a few weeks, is going to be really expensive."

"Well," said Tessa with a sigh, "we do have all that money we've saved to buy a house."

Diana came around the corner. "The mac and cheese will be ready in just a couple minutes. Did I hear you right? Are you guys really going to leave the country?"

"Yes, we decided that was the safest thing for us to do." Tessa gestured to include the rest of the group. "The rest of you should probably think about leaving the area too."

James nodded. "I agree. Staying here only puts us in harms way." He thought a moment. "I could go back to Boston. Probably get a detective's job with my brothers."

Diana nodded. "As long as I have my laptop, I can work from anywhere. I have family in Boston too, so I could go with James." She pondered a moment, then grimaced. "Though my family wasn't happy when Bryce moved us to California. Things are still kinda strained between us."

James shook his head. "So you have to face the wrath of Caan to get back in your family's graces?"

Diana huffed a laugh. "I forgot that's how you referred to my dad."

"For a short guy, he has a really big presence."

Kier got an anxious look on his face. "But what about me and mom? Where can we go? I can't ask Maeve and Corky to move just because of me and mom."

I'd love to take care of him, Alex thought, *and his mom. The kid has really grown on me. But I can barely support myself, let alone a teenager.*

Alex caught James and Diana conversing with their eyes. Then they both nodded.

"Well," James began, "you could come to Boston with us, if Maeve's okay with that. Your mom's in danger too, so we could have her transferred to a facility there. I know of one that specializes in brain injuries. They might be able to figure out what's wrong with her."

Alex saw the boy's eyes light up. *It's probably for the best that they take him. We'd end up living on mac and cheese and pizza until we were both the size of blimps.*

James stood up and went to Diana.

"If we're going to do this, I need to beat feet to the City. I have to talk to my captain and deal with my houseboat." Over her protests, he said, "That way, I can talk to Maeve and make arrangements. If she agrees, all three of us can leave for Boston tonight." He kissed her on the forehead. "You pack some things here. When I get back, we'll take Kier to Berkeley for his things, then head East."

Diana sighed. "You're right. It's just that I've barely gotten settled in here. I really dislike the idea of moving again. But I see your point. And there's Kier to consider." She patted him on the shoulder. "Go on, git! The sooner we're out of here, the safer we'll all be."

James said goodbye to the others and left. Diana stared at the closed door for a moment, then turned back to the kitchen, muttering, "We still need to eat."

Tessa had been staring at Alex for several minutes. *Why is she staring at me like that? I feel like I'm under a microscope.*

"What?" he said, trying to look affronted.

"Exactly! What are you going to do, Alex?" Tessa went over to him, standing firmly in his space. "If we leave and Diana moves out, that means you won't have a job or a roommate anymore."

Alex looked up at her. *Gods,* he thought, *she's magnificent. She'd face a dragon with a teaspoon to protect anyone she cares about!*

"I know that," he said patiently. "I've been trying to figure out where I can go or what I could do to help everyone else." He shook his head. "I could go stay with my dad; he lives in Vancouver. We've never really gotten along, but I'm sure he'd let me stay with him for awhile. Besides, you're all going to need my computer skills to help you stay ahead of these people. Finding information and manipulating computers is what I do."

Riley and Tessa shared a long look. Tessa broke the silence.

"It's decided then. You're coming with us."

"What? Why? I don't have any money," Alex began.

"But we do, and you're right. We do need your skills to stay ahead of the people who are after us." Tessa smiled. "Besides, you're family."

Family? Family's always been something that throws you out, not takes you in. But they care about me. I don't know why, but they do. Is it just as a friend or…? Tessa said that Xerians mated in triads. Could she be thinking of me as their third? No time for those thoughts now. Later. If there is a later, he thought sourly.

Alex flew into his room, grabbing his favorite t-shirts, a couple pairs of jeans, and a few other necessities. Coming back into the living room, he paused at his computer, taking a few of his favorite knick-knacks and stuffing them in the bag with his clothes.

Looking down at his computers, a cold realization dawned. *Oh shit. I can't take my computers. I've spent so much time building and working on them, what's going to happen to 'em?*

Diana came up behind him and put her arms around his shoulders. "I know how much you love your computers. I'll hire movers and have them put all of it in storage with the rest of our things. Hopefully, this'll all blow over and we can get them back to you."

Diana turned her head and raised her voice.

"Kier, get those snakes off the dining table. If we're all going our separate ways, then we're going to do it on a full stomach, damn it."

* * *

Even knowing there was going to be a blast, Thierry started when the apartment windows blew outward, raining glass on the alley beside the building. Sitting in the back of the Tesla Model S across the street, Thierry felt the shock waves created by the explosion.

From the front seat, Latham commented dryly, "That should take care of your problem."

"Why didn't the explosion take out the whole building, though?"

Latham shrugged. "Poor workmanship, perhaps?"

Another car pulled up, pulling in directly behind Thierry's car. Two men and a woman climbed out, colorful bags dangling from one man's arms.

Latham pointed to them through the tinted windows.

"Those are some of MacPherson's friends, from the convention."

"I'm not blind, Latham. Of course I recognize them from Jessica's files. They must have stopped to pick up food." He sighed. "We'll have to take care of them separately."

He saw Latham raise a finger to the bluetooth receiver in his ear, carry on a short conversation, then tap it again to end the call. The man turned, laying an arm on the seat back.

"Sir, I've just received word from my contact at the hospital in Santa Clara that Mrs. Sloan is to be moved to a facility in Berkeley tomorrow.

"Excellent." Thierry settled back, relaxing comfortably into his plush seat. "It will be much easier to arrange for someone to eliminate her once she is out of the hospital and in private care. We can't have the damned woman waking up and identifying Bryce as Matthew's actual murderer. The police already suspect him. We don't need an eyewitness."

Thierry's eyes drifted back to the still smouldering building. *Now that those two are out of my hair,* he thought, *I can—*

Several people spilled out of the building, some carrying luggage and a child holding what appeared to be pillowcases.

Peering out the car window, Thierry stiffened. "It's MacPherson and Connors! How did they escape the explosion?"

He went silent as the six people split into two groups, each going to one of the cars bracketing his own. Through the window, he caught a snatch of the young boy's conversation.

"…be dead if Tessa hadn't sensed something was wrong."

As the two cars pulled away, Thierry ordered, "Follow them. Discreetly."

Latham started the vehicle, following their quarry at a safe distance. He tailed them until they pulled into a gated parking lot. Latham gracefully maneuvered the Tesla into a free slot across the street from the gate.

"This is as close as we can get, sir."

Thierry waved a well-manicured hand at him.

"This will have to do."

Shortly, he saw the gate open and one of their vehicles exit. When it passed under a light, Thierry recognized the police officer from San Francisco, Cavanaugh.

Where is he off to? Are they splitting up?

Retrieving his cell phone from his suit pocket, he placed a call.

"Dante. Why am I sitting outside an apartment in San Leandro staring at people who are supposed to be dead already?" He silenced the man's protestations. "I don't have time for your excuses. I gave you a job

352

to do, see that you complete it. Mr. Latham will get you whatever supplies you need. Finish the job. Or else!"

An hour later, Cavanaugh returned, parking his car right outside the front door of the complex.

Why is he just sitting there? Is he not going back inside?

Moments later, MacPherson's car emerged, stopping just outside the gate. Thierry watched as first the young boy, then Bryce's wife, got out of MacPherson's car. They grabbed luggage and joined Cavanaugh in his vehicle. Windows rolled down on both cars and goodbyes were exchanged.

They are running. Damn!

As Thierry's watched, the two cars pulled away, crossing under a street light just as they passed his car. He growled as he got a good look at their faces.

Damnation. Will I never be rid of you, you cursed Tesham? I will kill you again. This time, permanently."

Epilogue

The pounding on the door grew stronger by the minute. *I can't keep the Sheitan out much longer. Their mob has already broken through my shield spell. It won't be long before they get through the remaining physical barriers.*

He began racing around the lab, desperate to complete his preparations. *Everything* must *be done before they break through or our entire civilization will be destroyed.*

He made the final connections before starting the ritual. Closing his eyes, he took a deep centering breath. An involuntary sob briefly escaping his iron control.

And it's all my fault.

* * *

Jember unlocked the storage cabinet and began tossing the various components he needed onto his workbench. Around him, the lab was eerily silent. After months of hyperactivity, it was odd to see the lab deserted. Looking down, he realized that wasn't completely true. Their mascot, Perti, was winding around his ankles, begging to be fed.

"All right, you silly tigla, let me get you some food. Ponacowa forgot to feed you before he left for the day, huh?"

As Jember fed their tigla, he reflected on the momentous past cycle.

I couldn't believe I'd done it, he thought. *Everyone said it wasn't possible. But using a combination of magic and science, I discovered a new dimension of unlimited, clean energy. I thought I'd finally solved our energy problems.* His bitter laugh floated across the empty room.

Cannibalizing parts from various gadgets, he slowly assembled the pieces he needed. *My team and I built a magical machine that opened a tiny portal so we could syphon energy from that other dimension. Suddenly we had unlimited power and I was hailed as the pre-eminent Sci-mage of my generation. What a difference it made!*

Frowning, he thought, how he'd hated all the recognition, the celebrations, the feasts. All of it. *All I really wanted to do was get back to my lab, my team, my explorations. I even had to stop work on my new storage device at a critical juncture. All because of that discovery. Now I wish I'd never even started that damned project.*

My team and I had to take even more time off to travel around the planet installing the portal device everywhere. While it was nice to travel with my mates Ezarra and Ponacowa, I still had to endure all the celebrations and spend time working to connect each portal to the existing energy grid. I wasted an entire cycle.

He paused, sitting heavily on the stool before his workbench. As the enormity of his situation landed squarely on his shoulders, he leaned forward and covered his face with his hands.

Once we returned home, everything fell apart.

After generations of peace, random violence broke out all over the planet. Quarrels over the smallest slights. Petty jealousies and rivalries we used to resolve peacefully suddenly ended in duels or worse. Jember straightened, then sighed, reaching absentmindedly for a tool he needed to disassemble a mechanism. When his hand found Perti's head instead, he looked down. The tigla cocked his head at him, clearly expecting a head scratch.

"Ignoring you, am I?" Jember said with a chuckle, momentarily easing his tension. Reaching down, he briefly scratched the tigla's head before reaching under the beast for the tool he still needed.

Hunching over his workbench, Jember paused. *I've seen what these Sheitan can do. I should warn Ezarra in case I don't survive. If anything happens to me, she'll continue this fight. Someone has to stop the Sheitan or our race is doomed.*

"Computer, take a message for Ezarra."

"Recording message for Ezarra. Begin message."

Jember winced as the computer's voice reverberated across the lab. It was the only sound he'd heard beside the tigla's complaints since he'd returned from the Sheitan gathering.

He swallowed, trying to clear the lump in his throat before he began, "Ezarra, my love, I may not survive this night, but I must tell you what I've discovered about my energy portals.

"After the violence began, you were the one who figured out the pattern." He smiled. Her gift of seeing patterns was only one of the things he loved about his Tesham mate.

He sighed heavily. Thankfully both Ezarra and Ponacowa are away from the city. *They're safe, for now anyway.*

"The pattern of violence followed the same route we took when we set up the energy portals, only delayed by a few weeks. Finally knowing where to look, I spent several weeks going over every detail of my machine, trying to figure out how it was connected to the unrest."

He picked up another piece of machinery from his workbench, turning it around and around in his hands. "I thought maybe this new limitless energy source had a psychological effect on our population. I also checked to see if the machine itself might be affecting us." Looking down at his hand, he shook his head. *Stop worrying, just finish the machine. Time is not on my side. If I don't hurry, I'll lose this opportunity.*

"It was only when I checked the energy itself that I made some interesting discoveries. First I found that more energy was coming through the portal than was going into the power grid. When I couldn't account for the lost energy, I assigned a drone to watch the portal itself.

"The next day, when I went over the drone's recording, it showed balls of energy detaching themselves from the incoming stream. I watched as one of the energy balls floated aimlessly for a while before it darted off to follow a passing workman. I watched as it leeched off the man's aura. It was feeding on his life force!

"My love, I wish that had been the worst part, but it wasn't."

Tears sprang to his eyes at the memory. He coughed, trying to clear his throat.

"Recording paused."

Damn machine, I just coughed, I didn't tell you to stop recording.

"Resume recording," he growled.

"When the energy ball had syphoned off half the man's aura, it quivered, then seemed to be pulled into his body. But it wasn't exactly the workman anymore. His aura had changed. His new aura matched the pattern of the energy ball. There was no trace of his original aura."

Jember picked up several pieces from the pile on his workbench and started adding them to the half-finished device in front of him.

"The drone's recording followed the changed man until he encountered a social gathering of some kind. He joined the group, then appeared to start a brawl for no reason. But the drone's sensors picked up what really happened. The altered person absorbed part of the aura of anyone he hit. When one of the combatants was mortally wounded, the altered person reached down, touched the dying individual, and syphoned off his remaining aura until nothing was left.

"I knew now that the energy ball was no mindless energy parasite, but an intelligent being who'd come through my portal and could potentially destroy our people."

Jember cursed as his hand tensed, breaking the fragile component he was holding. Dropping off of his stool, he prowled the lab looking for a replacement part.

"I tried to show the recording to my assistants, but they couldn't see the energy, only the actions. From that, I deduced there must be something unique about Tesham physiology that allowed me to see the invaders energy." Jember made a sour face. "Unfortunately, that means I can't prove the existence of the invaders to the authorities.

"After analyzing my readings, I fashioned a weapon that I believed could destroy the invaders. There was only one problem. Since the invaders completely consumed the life force of the original person, I feared killing the invader would kill the host body as well. If it didn't kill the body outright, it would probably leave it in a vegetative state. I realized that to an outside observer, it would look as though I was randomly maiming or killing people. I debated going to the authorities, but I worried that doing so would warn these invaders and allow them to go into hiding."

Finding the replacement part he was looking for, Jember returned to his workbench and resumed work on the device.

"Besides, how do you tell someone that their friends and loved ones have been possessed by aliens? That would only breed mistrust and help the invaders start more fights. That left me with only one option. To save our people, I had to do what must be done, even though others would deem me a cold-blooded killer. Then, once the invaders had been defeated, I could reveal my findings and explain my actions.

"I began my search for the altered people. After killing several of them, it dawned on me that it was a pointless exercise because energy beings were still coming through the portals. That's when I ordered all the portals shut down, effective immediately.

"I wanted to tell you and Ponacowa what I was doing, but I was afraid that you would want to join me. I couldn't risk either of you getting hurt because of my hubris. I created the machines in the first place. I knew at the time that I should have run more experiments, to make sure it was safe, before rushing to tell everyone about my discovery. But I was so caught up in the excitement of solving a problem that had plagued our people for hundreds of cycles that I ignored my better judgement.

"Pause recording."

He slammed down the tool he was using and stared into the shadows cloaking much of his lab, remembering how his people had reacted. The new limitless energy had allowed them to take up their previous wasteful practices. They blamed him for their loss and the return of power rationing. The resulting unrest played right into the hands of the invaders. Unfortunately, the blame fell not just on himself but on all Tesham.

Reining in his anger, he went back to dictating his message for Ezarra.

"Computer, resume recording.

"Last night," Jember continued, "I made a fatal misstep. I followed an invader who led me to a warehouse containing maybe twenty to twenty-five of them. I overheard them call themselves 'Sheitan.'

"I almost ran away. How could I deal with so many at one time? And what if they overran and killed me? Our whole race would be doomed if I were killed before I could stop them.

"I returned to my lab to make better preparations before trying to fight so many of them at once. I'm gathering up everything I need to fight them. I've modified one of the weapons I made to kill the Sheitan into a small bomb that should take out most of the group in one blow."

He put down the completed weapon. It looked like a short rod with buttons and a dial at one end. He only had to arm it and throw it into the crowded warehouse, then he'd be done with all of the Sheitan.

"This is my final warning to you, my beloved. If I am unsuccessful, if they manage to kill me, you must send my findings to the authorities and then take Ponacowa and go into hiding."

Attaching his new device, *the bomb*, he thought, to his belt, Jember changed out the battery packs on the other two weapons he held. *I don't want them to run out of power during the fight.*

"Be well, my loves. I hope that this message is unnecessary and that we all laugh that I even bothered recording it later. But I had to let you know what I've found out, just in case I fail.

"Computer, end recording."

"Recording terminated. Shall I send the message to Ezarra?"

"No, delay sending the message. If I don't cancel it before tomorrow evening, send the message."

Returning to the meeting hall, he used his elemental fire to blast the door open. The Sheitan panicked, running for the far wall.

Excellent, now's my chance. Jember thought. He lobbed his Sheitan-killing bomb into the crush of bodies, managing to take out half of them before they fully registered his presence.

Damn, I had hoped to get most of them with the bomb. There are too many still standing.

Jember brought up both of his weapons, firing at the remaining Sheitan. *I can still do this. There aren't that many left,* he told himself.

But they broke into two groups, one hiding while the other rushed him. He was forced to waste energy fighting on two fronts, keeping one group from overrunning his position while making sure the other didn't escape.

Jember caught a flash of light from his weapon. *Oh no, not now! I can't be low on power already.* He checked. Both batteries were nearly depleted. *I can't stop them! I have to get back to my lab.*

He turned and fled the warehouse.

The Sheitan gave chase. They pursued him relentlessly. Every time he thought he'd lost them, they found him again. He led them all over the city, hoping to lose the mob so he could return to his lab and recharge his now-useless weapons.

I can't keep this up much longer. I'm so exhausted that I can barely stand, let alone cast a spell. I need to rest. I'd hoped to avoid leading them to my lab, but my wounds are slowing me down too much. If I don't head there now, I won't survive at all.

Once safely inside his lab, he activated the external monitors. The horrible truth was laid bare. The Sheitan had been joined by the Xerian authorities.

There's no way to stop the Sheitan now without hurting my own people, he thought in despair.

Flipping the emergency switches, he locked down the building, automatically closing off every means of access to his lab and activating the magical shields.

That's supposed to prevent any contagion from escaping the lab, but it should buy me some time to work.

Shifting gears, Jember began preparations of a different kind.

If I can't stop them from getting into my lab and killing me, I can at least save all of my data.

Retrieving his newest invention from its storage container, he placed it gently into the center of the power circle inlaid in the floor. Staring down at the image he'd worked with so many times over the years, he felt pride at its craftsmanship. The four-spoked gear, which to him represented everything his people, the Tesham, stood for, had come to him in a dream one night. The solid, many-toothed gear was the representation of the scientific side of their heritage, while the voids between the spokes represented the four elements of the magical side of their heritage. The hole at the gear's center represented their spirit, which allowed them to deftly meld their disparate natures. Even though he'd only shared the symbol's meaning with a few of his closest friends and partners, they'd all begun to use it for their rituals.

"Computer, transfer all Project Sheitan data onto the Tesseract Storage Device."

"TSD transfer initiated," came the disembodied voice from the overhead speakers.

He huffed a weary laugh. *It's almost funny that the TSD, my pride and joy before finding the energy dimension, should be my last hope of defeating the Sheitan. This prototype already holds our entire history and yet still has the capacity to store enough energy to power our devices.*

Jember shuddered. It was only a matter of time until the Sheitan breached his defenses. He had seen what they did to those they defeated. His life force would be consumed, gone like it had never existed.

"Transfer complete."

Wait! He stood stock still as a new idea formed in his mind. *That's it! The TSD stores energy* and *data. Why can't it store my energy, the data of my soul?*

Jember raced around the room, gathering components for the complex spell mixing science and magic that was still forming in his head. Soon he had everything he needed to cast his circle, fire up the machines and begin the transfer.

He was placing the components around his circle when he almost tripped over Perti. He smacked his forehead as the tigla reminded him of Ponacowa and Ezarra.

I have to tell them what I'm doing, so they can bring me back.

"Computer. Record new message to Ezarra."

"Recording additional message for Ezarra. Begin message."

He paused for a moment, composing his thoughts before he began.

"Ezarra, Ponacowa, by the time you get this, I will be dead at the hands of an angry mob. Don't believe the lies they will tell about what happened."

He finished the last of his preparations and moved to stand inside the circle with the TSD.

"Please trust in me, my loves. All of my research is on the TSD."

He reached out and tapped a series of buttons to activate the machines.

"Please keep it safe—"

The lab's door buckled, then exploded into the room.

Saying a quiet prayer that Ezarra would understand his message and be able to save him, Jember gave the command.

"Computer, send message and begin the transfer."

The mob surged into the room.

The leader of the mob stepped forward. Jember identified a Sheitan aura surrounding the man. The smile he wore was the coldest thing Jember had ever seen.

"I knew someone had discovered us. However, until you showed up and attacked, I did not know who." Fury written across his face, the Sheitan raised a weapon, fixing it firmly on Jember's chest.

"Any last words?" he sneered.

Jember felt himself growing weaker as his ritual transferred his soul to the storage device. *Just a little longer and I'll be safe.*

"This is far from over," Jember said through clenched teeth. Gathering his will, he shouted a spell.

"Malleh Deiten!"

His lab plunged into darkness, it's internal defenses activating.

Weapon fire burst from all around the room, instantly followed by screams from the mob. A weapon discharged nearby, sending burning pain across Jember's arm.

He fell.

The Sheitan leader's head came into Jember's view over the edge of the dais he'd fallen behind. The man scrambled over the edge, then stood, looking down on Jember.

"Did you think you could stop me, little Tesham? I shall enjoy killing you myself."

Jember felt himself slipping away. *The spell is almost complete.*

The agony of Jember's arm wound was nothing compared to having the last of his soul ripped out of his body and thrust into the waiting TSD. The pain built until he thought he couldn't take it anymore.

The last thing Jember saw was the dazzle of the Sheitan's weapon.

* * *

He woke from the nightmare screaming and drenched in cold sweat. The sheets and clothing clutched at his body, refusing to let him go, keeping him bound to the dream. He looked around the room. It was dark. *This isn't my lab! Where am I?*

Suddenly the room flooded with light.

He blinked his eyes, trying to make sense of the apparition coming toward him.

"Are you okay, sweetie? I heard you cry out. Did you miss me?"

A long-haired creature helped him out of the cage where he lay and into dry clothing. It carried him into the next room where another creature, this one hairy all over, was sitting up, obviously awakened by his screams. The first creature gently eased him onto the soft, padded surface beside the hairy one before climbing in on his other side.

"He's shivering something fierce. Do you think he's sick?" asked the hairy creature.

"I don't think so. I think he just had a bad dream," the long-haired one replied.

He tried to ask them who they were, but all that came out were guttural sounds. He couldn't seem to make his mouth produce words.

"Adam, maybe we should let him sleep with us for the rest of the night."

"Okay, but only tonight. He's got to learn to sleep in his own bed." The hairy creature pulled a heavy material over them all. "Turn out the light, Chelsea, or we'll never get him back to sleep."

The long-haired creature reached over to a side table and the light vanished.

Laying back down, she whispered, "It's okay, Riley, mommy and daddy are here. We'll keep you safe."

* * *

Want to go deeper into the world of The Third War?

Read some fun backstories on Riley, Tessa, Alex and company on our blog:
http://www.thirdwar.net/#!blog/c112v

About Orion

Orion has published short stories, poetry, and some non-fiction pieces, as well as a previous novel. Writing her first novel, a fanfic in the world of Blake's Seven, titled *Thieves in Time*, meant hauling her computer across two counties every weekend in the early nineties while working with her previous co-author. Some of her flash fiction can be seen in Wild Wrods, a collection of prompt-driven, five hundred word short fiction written by the members of the Kickstart Writers Meetup Group in Snohomish, WA. Dreaming of Xeres is the first book written in the world of The Third War. She really enjoys writing online with Kyros.

Orion has been a school teacher, librarian, factory worker, office worker, jewelry maker, glass etcher, gypsy business owner, science fiction convention and SCA vendor, metaphysical bookstore owner, and one summer, a mail carrier for the railroad. Raised on a farm in Indiana, she visited Europe at seventeen and has lived in Illinois, two separate times in California, and Hawaii. Currently, she resides in Everett, WA with her two cats, a piano, and walls lined with books. Her friends have sworn that they'll never help her move again!

About Kyros

Kyros has always been an avid reader and has written short stories since he was in middle school. In addition to writing, he's worked as an EMT, a factory worker, a network engineer, and an electrician in the military. Then in his late 30's, he went back to school to finish his degree. He graduated in 2008 from the University of Washington with a Bachelor's Degree in Technical Communication. Even though Kyros worked in the software industry for a few years writing help documentation, he never gave up on his first love, writing fiction. When his job abruptly ended in early 2013, he decided to try his hand at finally writing the novel that had been banging around in his head for at least twenty years.

Like his co-author, Kyros grew up in small town Indiana in the middle of nowhere. As soon as he could, he left Indiana and headed west. This landed him in the Seattle area where he lived for eighteen years. Shortly after moving there he met his future co-author at a science fiction convention. They became fast friends and for a few years even owned a bookstore together. Eventually work and his heart led him to the San Francisco Bay area where currently he lives with his two husbands, two dogs, and a very opinionated African Grey parrot named Abby.

www.ingramcontent.com/pod-product-compliance
Lightning Source LLC
Chambersburg PA
CBHW072321280626
47159CB00027B/248